An enchanting mystery . . .

From the moment he set foot in Wolfram Castle, Count Kazimir Vasilov knew it held far-reaching secrets. For example, was Melisande Davidovich a pawn of her father, or did she have more knowledge than she was revealing?

Melisande Davidovich . . . even her name was an entrancing combination of her French and Russian sides, the mystic and the stoic. Lovely and golden, charming freckles dotting her smooth skin, a honey-colored lady of infinite attraction . . . her voice was golden and silky, faintly accented with her French birth. She seemed uneasy around him. His immediate fascination with her only heightened, but when he looked into her eyes, he saw revulsion mingled with perturbation.

There was something about her, some connection to himself. What was it? It was a feeling of enchantment. Or could she be the reason the gypsy witch told him to follow the chalice to find the cure for the curse that bedeviled him?

Awaiting the Night

Donna Lea Simpson

BERKLEY SENSATION, NEW YORK

THE BERKLEY PUBLISHING GROUP
Published by the Penguin Group
Penguin Group (USA) Inc.
375 Hudson Street, New York, New York 10014, USA
Penguin Group (Canada), 90 Eglinton Avenue East, Suite 700, Toronto, Ontario M4P 2Y3, Canada
(a division of Pearson Penguin Canada Inc.)
Penguin Books Ltd., 80 Strand, London WC2R 0RL, England
Penguin Group Ireland, 25 St. Stephen's Green, Dublin 2, Ireland (a division of Penguin Books Ltd.)
Penguin Group (Australia), 250 Camberwell Road, Camberwell, Victoria 3124, Australia
(a division of Pearson Australia Group Pty. Ltd.)
Penguin Books India Pvt. Ltd., 11 Community Centre, Panchsheel Park, New Delhi—110 017, India
Penguin Group (NZ), Cnr. Airborne and Rosedale Roads, Albany, Auckland 1310, New Zealand
(a division of Pearson New Zealand Ltd.)
Penguin Books (South Africa) (Pty.) Ltd., 24 Sturdee Avenue, Rosebank, Johannesburg 2196, South Africa

Penguin Books Ltd., Registered Offices: 80 Strand, London WC2R 0RL, England

This is a work of fiction. Names, characters, places, and incidents either are the product of the author's imagination or are used fictitiously, and any resemblance to actual persons, living or dead, business establishments, events, or locales is entirely coincidental. The publisher does not have any control over and does not assume any responsibility for author or third-party websites or their content.

AWAITING THE NIGHT

A Berkley Sensation Book / Published by arrangement with the author

PRINTING HISTORY
Berkley Sensation mass-market edition / November 2006

Copyright © 2006 by Donna Simpson.
Cover art by Phil Heffernan.
Cover design by George Long.
Interior text design by Stacy Irwin

ISBN: 0-425-21285-8

BERKLEY SENSATION®
Berkley Sensation Books are published by The Berkley Publishing Group,
a division of Penguin Group (USA) Inc.,
375 Hudson Street, New York, New York 10014.
BERKLEY SENSATION is a registered trademark of Penguin Group (USA) Inc.
The "B" design is a trademark belonging to Penguin Group (USA) Inc.

PRINTED IN THE UNITED STATES OF AMERICA

10 9 8 7 6 5 4 3 2 1

Prologue

MOONLIGHT PEEKED between the buildings that lined one side of the street in the ancient city of Braunschweig. The sound of the Oker River along the other side softened the harsh clatter of hoofbeats; two men rode to face each other, dismounted, and slowly walked the remaining distance.

The older of the two, standing in the silvery trail of faint moonlight from the crescent, spoke first. "Go on . . . go back. Do not continue on your journey, for the relic's fate is not yours to decide. You must give up your pursuit of it. I know why you want it, but it must never be." Though the man speaking was handsome in a harsh and ascetic way—his movements were graceful, his face gaunt but perfectly shaped—his words, couched in the most formal of Russian diction, were brusque and uncompromising. His hair was silvery in the moonlight and perfectly tidy. One would not have thought he had been in pursuit of the other man for so long, had lost track of him, and had had to double back to meet him here, in this ancient city, for as always, he was impeccably clad and shod.

"You do *not* know why I want it!" The younger man was darker, his shaggy hair almost black, and he was more robust, his torso, arms, and legs thick with muscle. His mien was menacing; a scar traveled from the middle of his left cheek and interrupted the natural line of his lip so he looked perpetually as if he sneered. He stood in the shadows, deliberately choosing darkness over light. He sighed deeply, and his next words were milder, his tone almost conciliatory. "I mean no one harm, and I seek only to do what is right."

"Why should I believe you? If you truly wanted what was best, you would leave the hunt to me."

"I cannot," the darker man said, his tone sharper, his temper clearly restrained only with great effort. "You must know that, Roschkov. I cannot let you have it."

"Nor can I allow you to find it first. It seems we are mired in a dilemma."

They stood, both determined, each sure he knew what was best and would do it. A noise in the distance, shouting, and a "hallo" made them both start and glance around.

"This is not a good place to be having this discussion," Count Kazimir Dimitre Vasilov, the darker of the two men, said. "To be Russian in Germany is not always to be welcome. I would advise you to leave, before something terrible happens to you."

The other Russian's eyebrows rose at the implied threat, if that was what it was. "No place is safe in this uncertain time. My fears go beyond this earthly sphere, Vasilov. You must know what I mean." Count Gavril Sevastjan Roschkov stared into the darkness of the shadows, refusing to be intimidated. He would not concede defeat to the man before him—not until the grave claimed him . . . if it ever did.

"I know what your fears are, and I pity you, but I will not relinquish my claim to the artifact we seek."

"Then I must find it first. I must have the chalice!"

"I don't want to hurt you, Roschkov, but I will if I have to," Vasilov said, hardening his heart against the other man, though he was clearly ill and perhaps even dying.

The other man, the austere lines of his beautiful face pulled into an ugly grimace, whispered, "Vasilov, give up your insolence. Let me make this decision. Have you not hurt me enough in this life? Have you not killed the only one who mattered to me? Leave me this quest, I beg of you."

Vasilov stayed silent, unable, as always, to answer when the past was brought into the conversation. He glared through the dim lamplit night at his adversary. He and Gavril were once friends, but never would be again. Their past history was too complex, too steeped in pain and suffering, and Roschkov was now too dangerous. No animal, and that included man, was as dangerous as when he knew he was trapped and saw a way out. Death, for Roschkov, was the final trap, and the chalice offered a way out.

Roschkov glared back at the brawny man in front of him, though inwardly he was shivering at the danger of the moment. If Vasilov should kill him, there would be no one to stop him in his madness. He pretended to have the best interests of all at heart, but Gavril knew deep in his very soul that he could not let Vasilov win this battle.

The man was dangerous; he had killed before and would again if he felt the need. He must be stopped at all costs, but Gavril would not be able to stop him if their current contretemps developed into a duel in this lonely, friendless place. Braunschweig was an ancient German city, but for two Russians, perhaps not the safest of places. His German was better than tolerable, but he would never be mistaken for a citizen of the country.

And Gavril was no match for Vasilov when it came to sword or fist, even if he had the might of the Lord on his side. Free will given by God was such that if Gavril engaged in this quarrel, he could end up lying on this lonely street with his lifeblood seeping into the gutters and trickling down into the river that burbled below.

No, he must defeat Vasilov with reason and the power of truth and justice. A lonely duel in a dark town, the too easy disposal of a body down the embankment into the river, the sword that glinted at Vasilov's hip; such a place and time was not to Gavril's advantage. In a battle one could not afford to lose, one must choose his battleground and his weapons wisely. Decision made, Gavril whirled on his booted heel, his cape swirling, and walked away, the tension within him wrought to a fine-honed edge as he waited, wondering if the other man would be so base as to attack him from the rear.

But he didn't. Gavril turned as he heard hoofbeats. Vasilov had mounted, and, cape flaring out wildly, he thundered past Gavril through the black night.

"Damn you to hell, Kazimir Vasilov!" Gavril shouted, fist in the air.

A window in one of the timbered buildings opened, and a querulous voice demanded, in guttural German, to know who went there.

Gavril replied in the same dialect, with soothing, conciliatory words, and the window closed, but then another voice was raised in question—a watchman. Gavril Roschkov crept to his horse, careful not to let his booted heels clatter on the cobbled surface. He must follow Vasilov and get to the relic first. He mounted and walked his horse through the shadows thrown by the buildings that lined the ancient river. Gavril would not underestimate his rival. Count Kazimir Vasilov was intelligent, determined, and ruthless. That combination of attributes, if such they could be called, could make him deadly.

Gavril must keep him from getting the ancient chalice even if it costs him his own life, or Vasilov could become invulnerable, and his wicked heart would cause such awful terror as had never been seen. It was not that the relic was evil; in and of itself it was not. Nor was it inherently good. Intent could make it either, for its full potential was not developed yet.

Good or evil—ah, that was the dilemma, wasn't it? Staring at the silvery crescent of the moon as he came out of the shadows, Gavril Roschkov sighed. Such a source of power was the relic they both sought; it all depended upon the person who wielded it—whether it was used in the service of mankind, or to aid the devil. He knew what to do with it, but that meant he had to find it before his opponent. He had to stop Kazimir Vasilov from snatching it first, for that could be a devastating blow.

Gavril raised his alabaster mount to a trot, and then, as he left the town and knew he was safe from the night watch, he began to gallop, following the path he knew Vasilov must have taken. He had no choice but to follow, for the relic beckoned.

Chapter 1

MELISANDE DAVIDOVICH stood in the huge great hall of Wolfram Castle and turned in a complete circle, trying to feel the spirit of the place. From the moment she had entered more than two years before, devastated and frightened, having just witnessed, weeks before, the brutal murder of her mother and grandmother on the hillside near their home in the Artois region of France, she had felt something from this old castle. Cold and formidable it may have appeared to others, but to her it bore the air of strength and protectiveness, its giant wings outspread to shelter her from danger. It held secrets and mystery and a long and violent history, she had heard, but for her it was a refuge from brutality. Her uncle Maximillian, an old friend of the von Wolfram family, had been right to bring her to safety at Wolfram Castle.

But lately it had seemed cold and unfriendly. Why? The warm spirit of it was closed to her; she couldn't catch the comfort it used to hold. Had all ease fled with those who had left? Is that why it had seemed so odd and inhospitable these last weeks? Surely that could not be true, for though she missed her uncle and Count Nikolas von Wolfram—he was master of the castle—she still had friends. Countess Uta, the eldest family member, had drawn her in with gruff but loving amity from the very beginning of her stay, and Christoph and Charlotte, Nikolas's nephew and niece, had become fast friends.

"Whatever are you doing standing in this gloomy, drafty place?" Charlotte von Wolfram, daughter of the late Count Johannes von Wolfram, descended the grand staircase that wound down from the gallery above. She silently padded across the flagstone floor.

Melisande turned and gazed at her younger friend. Though Charlotte was, in truth, just a couple of years younger than she was, Melisande felt older by decades. She had seen things and lived things that no young lady ought to: her mother and grandmother's murder, the Terror that brutalized her country, her horrifying flight from the madness, and her fortunate rescue by her Uncle Maximillian. It was all two years past, but it still haunted her daily. Until recently, though, she had at least felt safe here in the bosom of the kind von Wolfram family.

Germany was her home now, and this castle, nestled in the low-rising hills leading to the Harz Mountains south of Hannover and Braunschweig, was her haven. She couldn't help but feel, though, that one chapter of her life was drawing to a close. She had merely existed for two years, haunted by fear, plagued by nightmares of the awful things she had witnessed. That had ended now; she must rebuild, and life must go on.

Unfortunately, other nightmares recently had crept into her midnight slumber.

She glanced over at Charlotte, who stared at her with an expression of bafflement on her pretty face. "The castle . . . isn't it strange that it feels empty? Don't you find it so?" Melisande's whispered words echoed up to the beamed roof fifty feet above. Pennants fluttered from the gallery that overlooked the hall, and flambeaux, tended by the outdoor workers, lit the interior with the smoky smell of oil and tar. Though it was just early evening and should still be light, spring had crept over the land not with sunshine, but with gloom and soggy, cheerless, wind, rain, and snow, so the great hall was dim and shadowy.

"It's been weeks since they all left. You should be accustomed to this by now, and Meli, you should be happy they're gone!" Charlotte, countess and temporary mistress of the castle, said to her friend. "We are free! Free of Uncle Nikolas's grim looks and Aunt Adele's disapproving sniffs! You never did like Aunt Adele; you can admit it, you know. She frightened you, but she is gone, gone off to Venice!" Charlotte raised her slim arms and whirled, her fashionable dress twirling with her. "We can laugh, we can dance . . . we can even run if we want!" She lightly tripped to the staircase and bounded up a step, then back down to the marble floor.

"Nevertheless," Melisande whispered. She gazed around and rubbed her arms against the chill of the huge hall. Something was wrong, but what? She felt, and had for some time now, like she was being watched. When she went walking outdoors she was always looking over her shoulder and had even caught sight of someone or something behind her, though common sense told her it was just her imagination playing tricks on her. She no longer went out alone but usually invited little Fanny, the only English-speaking servant, with her.

"When I was very young and felt like this," Melisande continued, "my grandmother would say that I was seeing things. I thought she meant imagining things, but . . . now I don't think that's what she meant. She felt things, too, and saw things; she always knew when something bad was going to happen. I remember . . . I remember just before she was murdered, she knew it was going to happen but was helpless. She tried to convince mother and me to join my aunt in Italy, or my uncle Maximillian here in Germany, but mother would not leave her alone, and then . . . and then it was too late."

Charlotte stared at her with wide eyes and a blank, open-mouthed expression. She stammered, but finally said, "Oh, Meli, I am sorry."

Melisande shuddered and shook her head, pushing away the memory of that awful day, the pain, the confusion, the last few moments when her grandmother had cried out that heaven would protect Melisande, even as she and her daughter died. It was like she implored some higher power, and Melisande had felt a protective warmth surround her as she watched in horror, crying, while the two women went down, battered by the throng.

"I cannot think of that!" Melisande said, trying to brush away the dread. She would not let herself become depressed of spirits again when she had just attained some measure of peace. It was absurd to think anything was truly wrong; the awful menace that had haunted the von Wolfram family for so long, Bartol Liebner, was gone. He was dead, his evil, destructive plans to destroy the von Wolfram family thwarted by the strength and intelligence of Nikolas and his new bride,

Charlotte's former tutor, once Elizabeth Stanwycke, now the Countess von Wolfram since her quick marriage to the count. But after the rapid courtship and marriage—sped, it had been whispered to Melisande, by the new countess's pregnancy— the count, his older sister Adele, his future brother-in-law (Melisande's uncle Maximillian), and the new Countess von Wolfram had all left to take the count's other sister, fragile and unstable Gerta von Hoffen, to Italy to recover from her terrible ordeal at the hands of the late Bartol Liebner.

Still, Melisande was frightened. It had been growing for the weeks since the party had left the castle until she could no longer ignore her fear. If she was truthful with herself, it was the dreams with which she had been plagued that haunted her.

"I just miss them," she said with a dismissive shrug, making light of her feelings to Charlotte, not wishing to explain her agitation. "I suppose I felt safe with your uncle and new aunt here. Count von Wolfram was so kind, so very . . . I don't know how to thank him enough for rescuing my father from the hands of the Russians as he did." She glanced anxiously over at Charlotte, who still stared at her, certain that her friend, who had only ever known Wolfram Castle as a home and was secure in the knowledge that her family would always be there to protect her, wouldn't understand how she felt.

Christoph, Charlotte's older brother and master of the house while his uncle was gone, bounded down the steps from the gallery. "What are you both doing standing in this gloomy place?"

It was almost exactly what Charlotte had said, and Melisande smiled. The brother and sister, so alike in their blond good looks, were not generally so synchronous in what they thought and said. While Charlotte was volatile and mercurial of temperament, Christoph was more thoughtful and deeply sensitive.

"Meli is . . . is mooning on about not feeling safe now that Uncle Nik is gone," Charlotte said in a careless tone, pushing a hairpin into her blond braided coil more securely as she hunched one shoulder and stared at the floor.

Count Christoph von Wolfram stilled and turned from his

sister to gaze at Melisande. "What do you mean, you don't feel safe?"

Melisande bit her lip and watched him; the shroud of clouds outside the castle parted, and a shaft of light from the setting sun beamed at an angle through the high windows that lined the front of the castle and soared above them in the great hall. That brilliant beam of sunlight caught on him, and his golden hair glowed like a halo for a moment. The last thing she wanted to do was injure Christoph's brittle feelings; it seemed that he, too, was brooding and uneasy lately. Though the awful time was over, he still hung on to the darkness, refusing to let it go. It had only been a month or so, though, since the end of the horrific reign of terror Bartol Liebner had inflicted on the family; perhaps she was asking too much. Perhaps it would just take more time for him to heal after all he had been through, just as it had taken her this long to begin to recover from the awful things she had seen and experienced.

Melisande said, "I didn't mean I don't feel safe now, Christoph, I just meant . . ." She stopped, unsure of how to go on.

"Just say what you think, Meli," he said, drawing himself up to his full height.

He looked . . . different, Melisande thought. She hadn't noticed until now, but he seemed taller and bulkier. More—what was the word? Resolute, he appeared more resolute. "I didn't mean I don't feel safe," she repeated, "but with Count Nikolas here . . ." She shrugged, at a loss for how to explain. The older count, Christoph's uncle, had an aura of command. Somehow, in his presence, one was sure nothing bad could ever happen. Even though many bad things had, she realized. It made her current worries even stranger, but there it was; she was plagued by uneasiness.

"With my uncle here you felt as if there was a real man in the castle, one who could save you from anything," Christoph said, his tone bitter as he stared at her.

Charlotte's wide blue gaze was still on Melisande. Brother and sister both stared at her, waiting, it seemed, for an answer to an unexpressed question. "I don't know," Melisande said with an impatient shrug. "I'm sorry, I'm just . . ." She couldn't even finish, for how could one explain the uneasiness she was experiencing? It made no sense. She rubbed her arms again, chilled to the bone. "Don't listen to me, I'm just . . . I think I'll go up to see my father."

Count Christoph wheeled on his heel and bolted out the front door, held open by one of the multitude of silent servants.

"I don't understand you, Meli," Charlotte whispered, staring at her, the hushed hiss of her tone echoing to the vaulted ceiling. "It's all over! Awful old Uncle Bartol is dead. And I don't understand why it even affected you at all. *I'm* the one he tried to kidnap, and poor Christoph . . ."

She didn't go on. She didn't need to. Though it had not been openly canvassed, Meli knew some of what had happened. Count Christoph had been drugged and seduced by his own troubled aunt, Countess Gerta von Hoffen, while she was under the control of Bartol Liebner, and he was haunted, Melisande thought, by guilt and self-loathing. She should be trying to help him recover, not adding to his melancholy with unfair comparisons to his invincible Uncle Nikolas, with whom he had a fragile and slowly mending relationship after years of estrangement. But, she thought, with a measure of defiance, she could not help her feelings; they just were, and it was up to her to figure them out. Her mistake had been in saying anything to Charlotte. "I'm sorry. Please don't take it the wrong way." She began her ascent up the staircase toward her father's room. He must be her priority now. Badly beaten in Brandenburg by some Russians who seemed to think he had a stolen art treasure with him, or knew its whereabouts, he was only slowly recovering.

But she stopped three steps up and turned back, staring down at the other young woman. "Charlotte, it has nothing to do with any of you, I think. It's . . . it's me. I'm . . ." She shook her head helplessly, not able to explain. What could she say about the dreams that haunted her? Charlotte would surely think her friend was going mad. Melisande shrugged once more and then turned away and headed up to her father's small chamber, following the path of golden light from the sunset that beamed through the huge glass windows that fronted the castle.

Tiptoeing into his room, Melisande quickly saw that silence was not necessary. Her father was sitting up in bed with a querulous look on his once-handsome face. "Papa!" she exclaimed, crossing to his bedside. "What is wrong?"

"Finally, someone to take notice of me! Poor invalid that I am, I thought I had been forgotten," he exclaimed. Though his accent was Russian, he spoke in perfect English.

As did Melisande. Most of the household members used the language. Count Nikolas had judged it best, since, he said, the servants did not speak, nor did they understand English, and so it cut down on the amount of gossip that leaked from the castle down to the village. Given what they had all been through recently, and how little of that any of them would like to hear gossiped about in Wolfbeck, the village below the castle, Melisande thought the count wise.

"Did you not have supper?" she asked, filling his water glass from a pitcher left by his bedside. The water was very cold, which meant that the maid had been in only moments before.

"Yes," he said, grudgingly. He shifted in his bed and groaned. "I wish that little maid, Fanny, would come back. She is the only one who seems to understand how best to rub my legs so they feel better."

Melisande narrowed her eyes and gazed at her father. When Count Nikolas had rescued him from a jail in Brandenburg, he had certainly been hurt. He was badly bruised from a severe beating, though not a bone was broken. But she knew something of nursing—it was a natural skill for her, one handed down by her grandmother, who excelled at it—and some of her healing concoctions had proven efficacious, as well as the recuperative properties of time and good food and proper bedrest. It had been more than a month; he should be much better than he was, and she could not imagine why he still suffered so. "Fanny will not be coming again." She busied herself with straightening his bedclothes. "You . . . you frightened her."

He reddened, his thin cheeks losing some of their sallow color in favor of feverish spots of red high on his sharp cheekbones. "I did nothing," he said, angrily.

"Papa," she said, patting at his bedcovers and making her voice as soothing as she could. "I did not say you did anything purposely, but . . ." She took a deep breath, avoiding his eyes.

She hadn't wanted to say anything to her father, but he must stop asking after Fanny. "Fanny is very young, you know. The poor girl may have . . . may have misunderstood your sense of humor. She told the count that you propositioned her, and so before he left he ordered that she not be made to wait on you any longer."

"Lying little informer!" he grunted. He pushed down in the bed and turned on his side away from his daughter. "It is a conspiracy," he said over his shoulder. "None of you want me to get better."

"Papa, you know that's not true!" Melisande drew the drapes closed against the dying purple of sunset, but in closing them she saw a flash of movement against the melting blanket of snow and stopped to gaze out. Christoph was out there, heading toward the woods, stamping with long strides near the fringe of coniferous green. Where was he going? She turned her mind away from her conjectures and closed the drapes with a jerk. It was not her place to wonder. Christoph was her friend; he had only ever been kind and considerate to her, even when in the midst of his ordeal. She turned back to her father. "You know that everyone here only has your best interests at heart."

He turned onto his back and stared at her as she lit a lantern with a taper from the fireplace. "I know that *you* do, my daughter. I have failed you often, my pet, but never again; I think I have a way to make things better. I haven't told you about it yet, but I will soon, you must know. You have suffered, and your poor mother . . ." He broke off and looked away.

He had been in jail on some petty thievery charge while her mother and grandmother were murdered, and Melisande tenderly reflected that he had never forgiven himself. He did love her mother, he just was not formed by nature to be a good husband. But it made her uneasy when he spoke of a way he had to make it up to her. He had promised that he was done with his life of crime, and she intended to hold him to his promise. He was never going to steal again, he had promised.

"You didn't fail me, Papa, and you don't have to make up to me for anything. You would have saved Mama and Grandmother if you could, but not even Uncle Maximillian could help. Please don't blame yourself."

He grabbed her hand, tears in his eyes. "It is a miracle that you survived."

She squeezed his hand and released it. "Grandmother prayed, and I escaped. It *was* a miracle."

He sighed and settled himself back on the pillow. "I'm so filled with ennui, my daughter. Are there any good books in the count's library?"

"You know I cannot go into the count's library," she chided. It was barred from anyone's use but Count Nikolas's own, not an unreasonable request, given how open he was with the rest of his household. It was virtually the only room, other than private suites, that was off-limits. "I will fetch anything for you from the ladies' library downstairs, though."

"Bah! Wearisome." He thrashed restlessly. "I want something manly, something interesting. I don't know why the count would bar his family from using his library. What is he hiding? Is he ashamed of something?"

She chose not to address his wild surmises.

"Surely, my pet, you could steal into his library for me and find some books," he said, his tone wheedling.

She didn't answer his suggestion, not seeing the need to reaffirm her negative. "I assure you, it is not all novels and poetry in the ladies' library," Melisande said mildly. "There are travelogues and science books. Art history—surely you would like that, given your interest in art? They are not all in German, you know. Some are in French and even a few in Russian."

"Are there any . . . astronomy books?" he asked, plucking idly at the velvet bedcover.

"I didn't know you were interested in astronomy."

"I am captive in this bed, an invalid. One becomes interested in a great many things when one has time to think."

"I can look for you, Papa," she said, pleased that he was at least trying to put behind him his past conniving ways. "I will find something on that topic, I promise, even if I have to ask the young count, for Christoph may have books on that subject in his own suite; I know he has studied astronomy and has an interest in the topic. Just get some rest, though. You look fatigued."

"Geology, too, pet. I am a scientist at heart, you know."

"I thought you were an artist at heart," Melisande said dryly.

"You wound me," he said, putting one long-fingered hand over his heart. "It hurts me deeply that you would speak to your father that way! I told you I am trying to break free of the old ways, and yet you will not believe me. You, of all people!"

Were those tears in his eyes yet again? Melisande shook her head. "Sleep now; I will bring you books in the morning. Goodnight, Papa."

IT was cold still, though April was well on in its progress. Christoph felt the snow crunch under his feet in the growing dusky gloom, going from wet and slushy to crisp and still frozen as he entered the depths of the forest. What had possessed him to enter the forest that almost surrounded the castle at this time, with day turning into night all around him, he did not know, but he was compelled to run, and he wanted woods around him. He began to trot and then picked up the pace, feeling his heart pound and his lungs heave. It felt good; the woods whipped past his vision, becoming a blur as he was alone inside himself.

Bubbling up within him was a desperate need to be free. He pelted on, somehow never tripping, flying over logs and branches, bounding over the silvery, gurgling stream that just two weeks before had been frozen. Free. His heart pounding, his ears ringing from the thrum of blood, he was aware as he ran of shadows near him, gray figures keeping pace, threading through the dark trunks and green conifers as quickly as he, and yet he was unconcerned. Nothing would hurt him here.

As he ran he felt the peace enter, slipping into his soul, replacing the awful weight of responsibility heaped on his shoulders just before the marriage trip to Italy by his uncle, Count Nikolas von Wolfram. It all was complicated by his need to reassess everything he had ever thought or felt about his uncle. He had hated him for so long, suspecting him of killing his mother and father and uncle Hans von Hoffen. Now he knew the truth; those were lies spawned by the evil intent of Bartol Liebner, who was in truth the murderer, but it was an arduous task, breaking the habit of years.

Perhaps it was good that his Uncle Nikolas was gone for a while, but before he left, Nikolas had taken Christoph aside and told him that it was his job now to look after the ladies.

The ladies. His sister, Charlotte, feckless, a little wild, and occasionally petulant.

And Melisande Davidovich. Sweet, lovely Meli.

His heart pounding, his mouth tasting of blood, he stopped running and leaned against a tree, gasping for breath, the darkness a comforting blanket of anonymity surrounding him. Beautiful, elusive, pure of heart Melisande. Since the moment she had entered the castle two years before, shaken by her recent brush with death while escaping the Terror in France, he had felt a connection to her. Even in his darkest hours, when he thought he was going insane, when he was not sure anymore what was truth and what were lies, nor even was he truly certain of what was real and what was a part of his dreams, Melisande was always there. Her voice, her hand on his, her soft eyes, they all soothed him.

But he had always known he, with his dirty secrets, wasn't good enough to lick the bottoms of her dainty boots, and despite the fact that he thought he might love her, he would never tell her so.

AS Melisande walked through the wintry woods, she came to a clearing, a spot where the forest opened to the sky and the snow lay in an unbroken blanket. But as she was about to move to the center, a wolf bounded from the woodland and then turned and looked at her, its beautiful silvery eyes eerie in their intensity and humanity.

Moonlight bathed the forest in a silvery glow, glinting off the banked, crystallized snow. The wolf's fur was silvery, too, with a ruff of darker fur over its heavy shoulders. She should be cold, she thought, looking around the clearing, for she was only in a nightgown, and her feet were bare. She should be frightened; she was in the company of a wolf! But in fact, she didn't feel much of anything.

Another wolf bounded into the clearing, a darker wolf, and it bared its teeth in a snarl, a low growl emanating from it as it crouched, confronting the silver wolf with a threatening stance. Melisande felt a cry building in her, a wail of fear, but somehow she never let it go. Instead she watched, fascinated by the scene, for the wolves ignored her as they circled each other, snarling and snapping, fur bristling. The moonlight, oddly, touched only one, the silvery wolf, while the darker one slunk in the shadows away from the glow.

Then the primitive dance reached some peak and both wolves lunged at each other, fangs bared, each yelping and snarling with guttural intensity as they leaped into battle. The dark one bowled the silvery one over and was about to go for the jugular.

"Stop!" Melisande hollered, and bolted upright in the darkness of her bedroom.

Heart pounding, mouth dry, forehead damp—the vividness of the dream this time was even more intense. She covered her face with her hands and breathed deeply, in and then out, trying to get control and push back the wave of horror that had overwhelmed her as the wolves entered battle. It had seemed so real, so immediate!

Wolves again. Why was she suddenly dreaming of wolves, every night for the past week or so? There were wolves around the castle; she knew that, for Count Nikolas had warned everyone to stay out of the woods, especially at night, not that she would ever have any reason to enter them, day or night. But she dreamed about the woods often for some reason. Mostly, lately, she met a wolf, and now, two wolves. But at other times she had known she had to go to the forest to meet someone or find something, she just didn't know who or what.

Lying back in her bed, she pulled the blankets up to cover her completely. The next morning she was going to go up to Countess Uta's suite. The countess was the oldest of all the von Wolfram family; she was sister to Count Nikolas's grandfather, if Melisande understood the family background correctly, but to Melisande, she was a friend. There was some connection there that transcended age or station. As eccentric and obstreperous as the woman could on occasion be—she was almost blind and suffered greatly from arthritis and assorted other ailments—she was also wise, her knowledge of the family deep, and she loved to tell stories of ancient times and folklore. It was through Uta's recitation of those stories that Melisande learned German, for she had known very little when she first walked through the door. There was not another soul in the castle to whom Melisande would dare to tell her wolf dreams.

Calm once more and her resolution made, Melisande settled herself to sleep. She never dreamt about the wolves twice in one night, so she was safe now. Tomorrow she would ask Countess Uta what she thought the dreams meant. Likely nothing more than that she was uneasy after recent events.

Tomorrow.

Chapter 2

"SPRING IS truly here," Melisande said to Fanny, as the younger girl helped her in the stillroom, a small room off the conservatory, with a concoction she was preparing to help her father's recovery. "Though you would never know it, the way the snow is holding on." She ground some woodruff, or "maitrank" as it was called in Germany, in a mortar. Though usually used as a stimulant and blood cleanser in a drink consumed in May, it also had other qualities. It would help to bring any more bruises to the surface from the beating her poor father had endured in the jail in Brandenburg. She still didn't understand exactly what had happened, why he was in jail, nor who the Russian was who attacked him, but every time she tried to speak to her father about it, he moaned and got one of his dreadful headaches. He had been through such an awful time, and she must remember not to be too severe on him.

As her mind turned inevitably to the evil done by men, she said to Fanny, "As soon as the weather becomes warm enough, I must get out and destroy Bartol Liebner's flower beds, for aside from the fact that there is a dangerous amount of poppies, I have this sense that his wickedness has tainted the earth where he tended his evil plot."

Fanny, who was planting some herb seeds in clay pots, gazed over at her steadily. "I think we should have a priest to bless the ground. Surely that would help, do you not think so, Miss Davidovich?"

Melisande cast the girl a quick glance. "I told you . . . when we are here working like this you should call me Melisande. It is my name."

"But I am a maidservant, miss, despite your great kindness to me," Fanny objected, turning her gaze downward shyly, toward her work. "And it would not be seemly."

Melisande stared at the girl. There was something so familiar about her. What was it? It was as if she was a part of a memory or dream, and yet she could not catch hold of it. She had long ago decided not to question the poor child about that sense of familiarity, for she might not feel the same way. Fanny was shy and sensitive, not given to sharing confidences; all Melisande knew about her really was that she was the daughter of the English valet of the elder von Wolfram, but that her father and mother were both long gone. "This first brew I am making is for my father. As I told you, herbal remedies are about balancing the humors . . . helping the body find its own center again, a stability in the core. For Papa, he needs to find strength, but also, there are other concerns. I shall put one sprig of the chamomile in, for he has been nervous lately."

Fanny sniffed but didn't say anything, and Melisande was grateful for her forbearance. Her father must have done or said something that the poor girl misunderstood, for he would never make an improper suggestion to Fanny. Sometimes he was his own worst enemy, for people were constantly misunderstanding him and accusing him of dreadful things.

Fanny finished her potting and dusted her hands off. "Will you consider it, miss? Having a priest bless the ground where Herr Liebner had his garden?"

"Hmm . . . I don't know," she said, smiling inwardly at the girl's perseverance. It must be something in the castle's water that made the female residents so stubborn, for Charlotte was just as single-minded, and so was Uta, her old friend. Melisande emptied the mortar full of ground herbs into a linen bag and tied it at the top, setting it aside. "I . . . I don't even know a priest here in Germany."

"But surely . . . I know we are of different faiths, miss, for your background is Roman Catholic, but there *is* a church in the village. Any man of God would do, wouldn't he?"

"*Any* man of God?" Melisande echoed. She was shocked at such a radical statement from Fanny, but then, the girl often evinced a surprising independence, surprising since she had been raised a servant, and from what Melisande had seen,

German servants were even more disciplined and remote than French. Melisande picked from her collection of dried herbs some twigs of sage and some salad burnet. These she stripped from their branches and carefully checked for any discoloration. With the work of her hands so familiar, her mind was free to wander, and thinking of the differences between the French and Germans forced her mind back to her childhood home; she and her mother and grandmother had lived in an old, whitewashed house on a verdant hillside surrounded by vineyards and herb gardens. Their family had once been grand and important and lived in a palatial mansion but had lost much of its land and almost all of its wealth. Melisande had never felt the lack of material possessions, though her mother had. Life had been good, except for how much she yearned for her father.

Though her mother excused her husband's behavior, explaining that he was a rambler and could not be tied to one place, Melisande had always been deeply disturbed by his absence. Why did he not love her enough to stay with them? Her father, in a touching display of his discernment, had brought her a lovely old red amber rosary for her twelfth birthday on one of his rare visits. That single loving gesture gave her hope that he would eventually come and live with them. She wished for it fervently, and even prayed, feeling sure if she just focused all of her prayers on that outcome, she could effect a change and see realized her childhood wish for an intact family. But it never happened.

Faith, though, had taken a severe beating when the Terror claimed her mother and grandmother and might have taken her too, but for intervention and rescue by her mother's half brother, her uncle Comte Maximillian Delacroix. How could a good and loving God permit such awful events, she had wondered. How could good people, such as her mother and grandmother had been, be taken by a mob of their neighbors and beaten to death in front of her eyes? Those were questions for which she still did not have answers.

The von Wolfram family was not especially religious, but it did have a glorious old chapel on the other side of the great hall, an enormous octagonal turret room that matched this wonderful conservatory in shape, though its windows, instead of being clear leaded glass such as these, were stained and threw a brilliant array of colors around it at sunset and sunrise both, since the corner towers soared above the height of even the central section of the old castle. Sunshine, when it shone—rare so far this spring—flooded both tower rooms, refracting and occasionally lighting even the gloomiest corners. She had, when particularly troubled, used the chapel to pray, taking her red amber rosary there and counting out the aves. Though comforting to repeat the old rituals of her youth, she didn't know whether she had prayed with the same intense fervor and deep, unquestioning belief.

Was it prayer that brought her father back to her safely, or was it simply the strength and goodness of Count von Wolfram, a man she admired more than she had ever said aloud? In fact, she had cherished a growing love for him in her heart and for a while had hoped he might choose her to be his wife. But he had ever only treated her with the same kind indulgence he did his niece, Charlotte, and so she had for months understood his love for Elizabeth, now his wife. The inevitability of their love for each other had been apparent to her from the beginning, almost from the first moment that lady had entered the castle, and her hope had died then, perhaps for the best.

"Miss?" Fanny said, touching Melisande's arm.

Startled out of her reverie, she answered, "Yes . . . yes, I'll think about having the land blessed. It would depend greatly on Charlotte and Christoph's wishes, of course, and I wouldn't want to do it until I had it stripped of the poppies. I despise poppies! It took much time and care to wean the poor Countess Gerta from the effects of Bartol Liebner's drugging. Poppies will forever symbolize that awful effect, for me."

Fanny was silent, but without being asked she cut a piece of thread for Melisande and handed it to her, seeming to know exactly what she needed. Melisande tied the burnet and sage leaves together. "Is the water hot yet, Fanny?"

The girl moved to the stove that was kept stoked to heat the conservatory and stillroom and glanced at the kettle that sat atop it. "I think so, miss."

"Bring it here," Melisande said, then dropped the tied leaves into a thick crockery dish. She took the kettle, the handle of which was wrapped with a padded cloth, and poured the boiling water over the leaves, then covered the bowl with a clean cloth. "Now we let those infuse," she said handing the steaming kettle back to Fanny. "That infusion will help poor Countess Uta with her pain. I am going to go up to her soon after I see my father, and I will take the herbal tea with me."

"How did you learn so many things?" Fanny asked, with a wide-eyed admiring look. She took the kettle and set it back on the stove, refilling it with water ladled from a crock under a nearby table.

"I started when I was very young, and my grandmother— my mother's mother—was proficient in the old healing ways." Her voice clogged with tears as it did whenever she thought or talked of her grandmother, but she just cleared her throat and said, "Men of science may say it is all superstition, but I cannot believe it is so. For every ailment known to man, I believe nature provides a remedy."

Fanny, returned from her task, looked askance.

"What is it? Do you not believe it is so?"

The girl cast her eyes down again, but said, finally, "I . . . that sounds a little like heresy, miss . . . I—I don't mean to be impertinent."

"No, Fanny, say what you think. Never feel that you must censor your thoughts or speech where I am concerned. I would have you be honest and forthright in your opinions, for I despise lies and hypocrisy."

"Well . . . I think that God has ways we were not meant to understand. Illness is punishment, sometimes, or it is sent to humble one who shows too much conceit, or sometimes it is the expression of the devil's hold on that person. It is heretical to think that we mortals can divine the true nature of an illness and find a cure for it."

"I used to think that way myself, but now . . ." Melisande fell silent as she tidied the workbench of rough timber, sweeping the herb cuttings into a basin under the table. Was Fanny right? Was she taking too much upon herself in her belief that nature fulfilled most of man's needs? Or was she confusing God and nature, when she should be seeing them as one and the same? It was a struggle, for her faith was an old habit broken down by the events of the last couple of years in her life. And yet her grandmother had been a devout woman, and even the priests in her village went to her for curatives. This self-reliance, though, and belief in the abilities of nature, was it insolence? Was it an affront to God?

A wave of dizziness swept over her, and she swayed.

"Miss!" Fanny exclaimed and took her arm, guiding her to a stone bench in the corner. "Miss, are you all right?"

Melisande could hear her but not see her. Everything was black. A strong scent assaulted her nostrils and her stomach twisted. What was wrong? "I-I cannot see, Fanny, help me!" she cried, reaching out in front of her with scrabbling fingers. But then, just like it had come, the awful blackness was gone and her vision returned. "Fanny, no!" she cried, for the girl had bolted to the door to call for help. "I'm . . . I'm recovered now, it was just passing." She put one hand to her forehead, feeling the heat rise into her cheeks. "I think perhaps I have not eaten yet today, and that was foolish of me."

Fanny came back to her and crouched at her side, clutching Melisande's hands in her own work-roughened ones. "Is that all it is, miss? Are you sure?" Her face was white and her eyes wide with terror.

"I'm sure," Melisande said, with more firmness than she truly felt. She had alarmed the poor girl enough; she would not trouble her now with any further worries. "I'm sorry for frightening you. It is nothing. I will go have some breakfast, and I'm sure it will completely pass."

She stood and walked with Fanny to the door, glancing back once to the bench and wondering at her momentary blindness; it had left her with a lingering headache that throbbed, and her eyes burned. She took a deep breath. "I just need some food," she said, and exited, closing the door firmly behind her.

After eating, she made her way to her father's room with the herbal potion. He was often sleeping, so she tiptoed and entered quietly. "Papa!" she exclaimed, finding him away from his bed standing in the middle of the floor.

"Daughter!" he cried, but then staggered and fell to his knees.

She screamed and raced to his side, kneeling by him. "Oh, Papa, are you all right?"

He moaned. "Thank a merciful Lord you came when you did, for I would have fallen and been alone. No one comes near me; they all shun me but you, my dearest child." Again he moaned. "Help me to the bed. I was trying to walk, for I hate being a burden on you all."

Awkwardly, with the earthenware mug of drink in one hand, she put his arm over her shoulder and tried to help him to his feet, but he was so badly hurt he could not manage it. "I'll have to get one of the footmen to help me. I'm afraid you are too heavy for me alone."

"No! I will . . . I will try harder." With a long groan, he pushed himself up, and with her help staggered to the bed.

She set the potion aside and helped him get under the disarrayed covers; he fell back against the luxurious pillows with a sigh.

"I may never walk again," he said.

"Nonsense, you *will* walk again. It has only been a month, and you will recover completely in time. Look," she said, picking up the crockery mug and cradling it in her hands, "I have brought you a tisane of herbs. It will make you better and will bring to the surface any deeper bruises you have suffered at the hands of those barbaric Russians."

"I . . . I feel the need to pray," he murmured, his voice broken. "I have been so wicked in the past, and I wish to atone. Prayer will guide and strengthen me. Prayer . . . ah, but I have no rosary. Tell me, daughter, do you still have the rosary I gave you for your birthday so many years ago?"

"Yes," she said, pleased that he remembered what was a precious memory to her. She set the tisane aside. "Oh yes, I do. I love it dearly, Papa."

"Please, bring it to me that I might use it to pray for one fraction of your goodness and piety!"

"I am not so good as you think," she said, touched but fearing his view of her was out of keeping with the truth. "I'll bring you the rosary later. First, drink the herbal potion and sleep some more. You will feel better after. We will help you walk again, I know it." She rose, pulled up his covers and kissed his forehead. "I will come back later, I promise."

She left the room in a thoughtful frame of mind, retrieved the second concoction, and ascended to Countess Uta's suite of rooms. The countess's mute servant, Mina, answered her tap at the door and ushered her in to Uta's chair by the window, where the old lady dozed in the rare spring sunshine. Not concerned, Melisande sat down opposite her and waited, letting the sunshine soothe her into a less fretful state of mind.

"*Ach*, little one, I had begun to fear dat you were going to forget your promise to come to me today," Uta said, her tiny blue eyes fixed on Melisande's face. Though almost blind, she had a disconcertingly direct stare.

"You know I could never forget about you," Melisande said. "Though you persist in viewing my visits as charity, in truth, you do me far more good than I do you."

"*Güt* girl, better dan my own niece," Uta said, referring to Charlotte's reluctance to dance attendance upon her ancient great-aunt.

"I brought you an herbal drink for your arthritis," Melisande said, offering her the earthenware tumbler.

"Foul potions," she said, with a grimace. But she drank it readily enough. "Though I do not belief in all dis potions and herbs, your remedies I take." She stretched her fingers and flexed them. "Dey do feel better. You haf the magic, my child."

"No, not magic," Melisande said, shifting uneasily. Mina, in the background was listening intently. She picked up the earthenware mug and took it away, surreptitiously sniffing it when she thought Melisande was not watching.

"It isn't true," Melisande said, in a loud enough voice that Mina could hear it, too. After the recent trouble in the house and Bartol's misuse of herbs to render others hallucinatory and drugged, it was no wonder the maid was faintly suspicious. "There is no magic; it is nature only that gives you back the use of your hands. Herbs *can* be used for great good."

"Harnessing the power of nature, child, is a kind of magic. Do you not think it is so?"

"But do you think God will forgive such interference?"

"Did God not put the wildflowers and herbs on dis earth to use? Do not be foolish, child, for you never haf been before."

"It was just something Fanny said," Melisande mumbled.

"I . . . I fear I am taking too much upon myself. Is it heretical?"

"*Ach!* Is not heretical to use the abilities dat God gave to you. It would be shameful not to."

Melisande didn't answer, and so they talked for a while about the household, and she brought the old woman up to date on Charlotte and Christoph, neither of whom visited her as often as they should. While they spoke, Frau Liebner came in and took her customary seat across from Countess Uta. Frau Katrina Liebner, though related only tenuously by marriage to the von Wolframs, was an honored and valued guest at the castle. She had come back after ten years in England, bringing with her Elizabeth Stanwycke, an English tutor for the bumptious Charlotte, whose manners Count Nikolas wanted to correct before arranging for her a marriage with an English lord. Together Elizabeth and Nikolas had uncovered the wicked plans of Bartol Liebner, Frau Liebner's brother-in-law, to destroy the family, and after solving the long-standing mystery had fallen in love and married. Though Melisande understood the need to remove Countess Gerta from the house and Count Nikolas's determination to protect his frail sister, she regretted that the solution necessitated them all leaving for the arduous trip to Italy.

"I had a letter this morning from Elizabeth," Frau Liebner said, drawing it out of her pocket and peering at it in the light from the window. "They are past the most dangerous part of the journey in one way. With the unsettled situation over the Rhine and the French everywhere, poor Maximillian was concerned. He would be in danger if they were stopped by the revolutionary forces. But it seems that they avoided the French completely, and now, we hear that a treaty is to be signed with those devils—I beg your pardon, Melisande, no slight was meant to your nationality . . ."

"I am only half French, ma'am, and that part is not a revolutionary," she said, happy to hear even indirectly about her uncle's trip. He, she supposed, was too taken up with his new wife, Countess Adele, and taking care of his new sister-in-law, Countess Gerta, to write until he was settled at his sister's villa in Venice.

"Very good," Frau Liebner said, and looked back down to

the letter. "Anyway, clever Nikolas managed to avoid trouble, and they are now waiting to begin the expedition through the mountains at the Brenner Pass. I understand they wait until there are a goodly number to make the trip safer. He does not expect any difficulties. Elizabeth, however, is feeling uneasy, she says, besides the illness that is to be expected in her state and with the roads as they are. She wrote to ask after you, Melisande."

"Me? Why would Countess von Wolfram ask after me?"

Frau Liebner set the crossed papers down on her lap and stared into her face. "I do not know, but she says she has been worrying about you lately. Are you well? Are you happy? She wishes me to answer."

"I . . . am perfectly well, thank you, ma'am," Melisande said faintly.

"Are you certain? You sound hesitant."

"No, not hesitant at all," Melisande answered, not wishing to speak of her dreams with the other woman there. Countess Uta she could say anything to, but she did not know Frau Liebner well enough.

"*Mein* dear," the ancient countess said, putting out one knobby hand and grasping Melisande's in a surprisingly powerful grip. The herbal remedy was certainly working, for just weeks before she had not been able to close her fist at all. "Tell me, for do not think dat I haf not noticed. You haf been . . . troubled. Tell me why. Dis woman," she said, with a nod at Frau Liebner, "is good also for telling dis to, despite her foolish appearance."

Frau Liebner gave her a look and opened her mouth to retort, but then clamped her lips together again and shook her head. "I will not allow you to draw me out, Uta. Melisande, my dear child, if you wish to speak in confidence to this crabby old woman I will think you weak in the head but I will happily leave the room. However, I will not be able to tell Elizabeth anything, and she truly does seem concerned. If there is anything at all, tell me. I will only relate to her so much as you wish me to, I promise."

"I would have you tell her I am perfectly fine, ma'am, for what good could it do, even if there is something, to worry the new countess at this time? And in her state? And just now beginning an arduous journey through the Alps?"

Frau Liebner nodded. "Sensible girl. We will tell her you are happy, but worried only for your father. That will appease her. Now tell us all."

"Yes," Uta said. "Tell us all."

There was a long pause. Silence settled over them, and the beauty of age was that the two elderly women were not impatient for her to begin speaking.

"Something is going to happen," Melisande finally whispered, staring out the window. A few flakes of snow fluttered against the glass; spring was having a hard time asserting its dominion over stubborn winter.

Frau Liebner reached out to Uta and took her hand. "What do you mean, child?" she asked.

After a moment's hesitation, Melisande confessed her dreams, the wolves, and the dreadful feeling she experienced of someone watching her every time she left the castle walls. If she did not tell someone, she feared she would go mad, but telling them did not offer her the relief she sought. At least they did not call her fears foolish, nor did they tell her she was imagining things.

"Wolves. What does dis mean to you?" Countess Uta murmured.

"Nothing!" Melisande sighed in exasperation at herself. "Nothing. The count has oft warned us not to go to the woods after sunset, for wolves are there. I know that. It is all I can imagine as the source of my dreams."

"Do you know to whom dis evil you speak of is directed?" Uta asked, her tiny, almost blind eyes fixed on Melisande's face.

"No!" Melisande cried. She leaped up and paced to the window, and then back to the two friends. She crouched in front of them. "All I know is . . . all I *feel* is . . . something is going to happen—something bad. It approaches, this evil, and day by day grows stronger." She gazed up at the two old women through a veil of tears and clasped her hands in front of her, a gesture of supplication, but to whom? "Something terrible is going to happen, I feel it deep in the marrow of my bones, but that is all I know, and I can't prevent it!"

Chapter 3

CHRISTOPH PAUSED just inside the door to his great-aunt's chamber and watched her, wondering at his revulsion toward her. She was his elder kin, and he should revere her as his uncle Nikolas did, but all he could feel was an antipathy so strong it bordered on disgust. She sat in the stream of weak spring sunshine fingering a fur pelt, her nearly blind gaze turned to the window. She was as wrinkled and sagged in upon herself as a rotting plum, her ancient body betraying her in age, and his youthful frame quivered with fear.

Was that it? Was the sum total of his distaste fear and the hatred of the inevitability of age? He had been summoned, and when it came down to such a command, he could not ignore it, for beneath his distaste was a deep reverence for family and respect for the old woman. But now, at the door, he could not take a step toward whatever it was she had to say to him.

"*Kommen sie, kinder. Kommen sie hier,*" she said, her voice still harsh and strong.

It was the push he needed. He entered, watched by Mina, and made his way to her chair, bowing before her, taking her hand and kissing the soft, wrinkled skin on the back of it. She smiled, but it was more knowing than pleasant, and he shifted uneasily on his feet.

"Sit!" she commanded, still in German, and he plunked himself down in the chair opposite her as she fingered the gray pelt on her lap.

The silence lengthened as Mina went about her work, the cleaning she would not allow any other servant to do in the ancient's room. Uta seemed content to stare in Christoph's direction until finally he shifted uneasily and said, "What is it you wanted of me, aunt?"

"Can I not request the charity of a visit with my nephew?"

"My apologies, honored aunt, for not visiting more often, but my studies . . ."

"Enough," she said, holding up one hand. "I did not ask for excuses. I would force no young man to spend time in my company if he finds it tedious. I thought you would come to me on your own. I thought you would feel the truth and ask me what it meant. But I have had a sign and must wait no longer."

"A sign?"

"Yes, yes, a sign," she said, impatiently. "My little Melisande. She senses the truth, and I cannot delay. You must learn your true inheritance. What I have to say to you now no one else must hear."

"What is it then?" he said, abruptly.

"Do not be impertinent, young man. What do you think this thing is?" she asked, holding up the worn pelt in her hands.

He gazed at it in distaste. "It is the fur of some disgusting creature."

Her hand flashed out, but he caught it before she slapped him. Unexpectedly, she smiled at his insolence.

"You are quick. The spirit is stronger in you than I thought, the spirit of your ancestors. What do you know of them?"

"I beg your pardon?"

"What do you know of your history, Christoph, son of Johannes, son of Jakob?"

He shrugged, at a loss as to what she expected him to say.

"Very well. You know nothing and are an idiot, it seems. However, you have a proud and difficult heritage, one that I . . ." She turned away and glared at the wall, her mouth working. She defeated whatever tormented her and turned her weak eyes back to him. "One that I must pass on before my time here is done. Before I die or descend into idiocy, I need to tell you what you are. You will pass this on to your younger cousin, Jakob, when the time is right."

A lecture on the proud von Wolfram history, it seemed,

was his fate. He began to stand, saying, "Great-aunt, if you please, may we speak of this another day, for I . . ."

"No! Sit." She threw the pelt at him as he sat back down. "You said this was the pelt of a disgusting animal. Not true. It is three hundred years old, that bit of fur, that ragged reminder of the first von Wolfram male to suffer the transformation."

"Transformation?" he asked, fingering the dusty fur. Some crumbled in his fingers and he dusted his breeches off with an impatient gesture and sneezed at the dust.

"You breathe in the soul of your forefathers, my nephew, and it is time you learned the depth of your potential. I have sensed, of late, a shift in you. Tell me this," she said, leaning forward in her chair with difficulty and wheezing. "Tell me," she said, her voice rattling in her chest, "do you find yourself full of the need to go out into the woods? Do you run, my nephew, until the blood pounds through you and leaves a bitter taste on the tongue?"

He gazed at her in surprise and then glanced over at Mina.

"She did not tell me this. No one did. I felt it from you. And my sweetest darling Melisande has felt it too, though I do not think she understands. She dreams of wolves. She dreams of *you*."

"What?" he said, jarred from politeness by the mention of his unknowing beloved.

"She feels you," Uta whispered. "She feels you change. The wolf in you that shares your human spirit is demanding that you acknowledge your animal quality, that you give in and transform, becoming . . . the werewolf."

"That is preposterous," Christoph shouted, rising and tossing the pelt away.

Mina strode across the room, grasped his arm in a hard grip and gestured angrily, but Uta put up one conciliating hand. "Stop! He is shocked, Mina, that is all; release him! I cannot blame him. If I thought I would continue on living, I would not have told him so abruptly, but I feel in my bones . . . he needs to know." To him she said, "Do not dismiss this, my nephew, for there are things in this world you do not yet understand. Your uncle at first resisted, but now, Nikolas is werewolf and uses his power for the good of his family. It is a privilege and it is a burden. That," she said, pointing over at the scrap of fur on the floor, "is the wolf skin kirtle every eldest von Wolfram male for three hundred years has used to transform, and so shall it aid you until you become strong in the ways and do not need it anymore, and then you shall pass it on to your cousin Jakob, to whom you will teach the ways of the wolf. Then you will use it to teach your own son, when the time comes."

"This is absurd," he said, staring down at her, wondering if her wits had finally wandered away from her through the mat of her soft, wooly hair and lace cap.

"You thought the werewolf legend only. But legend is so often based in fact, and so it is with this. You are shocked right now, but think. Have you not felt the wildness in you? Have you not thought you could run until your breath was gone? Have you not felt the need for blood? That is the beauty and the danger, for it can be deadly, the temptation—"

He turned as if to go.

"Hear me out!" she said, urgently.

At her tone, he turned back, the habit of honor for the elderly ingrained in him under his skin. His mind was racing: pondering, reflecting, wondering, but finally dismissing the absurd assertion of his aunt.

"One moment more only," she said, hand outstretched in supplication. "When you run, take with you the pelt of the wolf, feel the wildness within you, desire the transformation, and you will feel the change come upon you. Do not turn back from it! It will be painful, and for a moment, I am told, you will feel as if your skin is being ripped from you with hot pincers. Do not quail, but be steadfast. You must use the change, for dire is the fate of any man with such potential who does not transform. If you do not—"

A loud tapping at the door interrupted her, and Christoph turned as Mina went to the door and opened it to the butler, Steinholz, who bowed low and said briefly that there was a visitor for the count.

"A visitor? Where?" Christoph said, eager to get away from his aunt's chamber.

"The public waiting room, sir," Steinholz said.

"Excuse me, please, honored aunt," he said with a deep bow, "while I attend to our visitor."

Uta was silent, and Christoph strode from the room and down the stairs, grateful for the excuse to depart from such an absurd conversation. Werewolf! What utter nonsense.

The public rooms on the main floor were reached by huge carved wood doors off the great hall, in the dark shadows beneath the gallery. Christoph marched up to the enormous double doors, squared his shoulders and took a deep breath. Whomever this was, and it must be someone grand for Steinholz to bother him with his arrival, he would handle him just as his uncle would, as befit a Count von Wolfram and the master of Wolfram Castle.

THE day was silvery, with the pale gleam of sunshine dancing on the thin crust of ice that rimmed the river coursing through the center of Wolfbeck. Count Kazimir Vasilov slowed his mount to a trot over the wooden bridge and then to a walk through the village, noting the prosperity, appreciating the simplicity of the beamed buildings and the sturdy, sensible garb of the villagers who walked by, eyeing him with unease. He could almost feel himself at home, in the Russian village commanded by his forefathers, but there were differences, discrepancies as subtle as color and smell and light, but there, nevertheless. This was not home.

"You there," he called out to a likely looking peasant, using the appropriate dialect of their language, he hoped, to make himself understood, "what direction would take me to Wolfram Castle?"

But the man just scuttled away, peering backward over his shoulder until he stumbled and fell on a patch of ice in the shadows of the buildings overlooking the street. The same farce played itself out over and over, until Kazimir grew irritable and thought perhaps he would ride out of the village and select a likely road. But he was thirsty and hungry. Though time was pressing, he still needed to eat and drink, and so he paused in front of the largest public house; a groom took his horse, and he entered, ducking his head under the low lintel and striding into the smoky, warm room. He shed his cape and flung it down on a wooden bench.

A scuttling fellow began to approach him but eyed him

uneasily and backed away. What was wrong with these peasants? Did they not want his gold?

Another man, older, but with a look of some wealth, approached him instead and bowed. "Gracious sir, may I bring you beer?"

"If it is good beer, certainly," Kazimir said, eyeing the fellow.

"It is my own, honored sir, and shall be served from the dimpled hands of my lovely young daughter Magda, if that pleases you, sir."

"Very good." He took in a long breath, and the scent of meat roasting made his stomach growl. "I require food, as well."

"Yes sir, indeed sir, prepared by my own wife," he said. "What, if I may be bold, sir, brings you to our village?"

Kazimir sensed some oddness in the man's address, and when he looked toward the doorway, he saw a pretty blonde girl watching him with avid eyes. "You may not be so bold," Kazimir said, staring at him. The fellow bowed and stepped back. "What is your name, my host?"

"I am Wilhelm Brandt, and I am mayor of this village."

"And who is the girl who watches us speak with such interest?"

"That is my daughter, sir. If you wish, you may spend some time with her, for she is a very pleasant girl." He gestured to her to join them.

The girl glided forward and curtseyed. "I am Magda, sir. I do not believe I know your name."

"I am Count Kazimir Vasilov."

"Did I not tell you, honorable sir," Brandt said with a leer, "that the girl is pretty and willing to please?"

Disgusting man! There was no mistaking the message; he would prostitute his daughter if it would bring gold into the household. "I wish for no company, fräulein. Bring me beer and food, that is all I require of you." The girl, with a haughty shake of her curls, stepped back, but as the man was about to turn, Kazimir added, "One more thing, Herr Mayor. When I leave I wish to see Wolfram Castle, of which I have heard much. How would I get there?"

Brandt gazed at him steadily, a peculiar grimace on his face. "Wolfram Castle? You are Russian, sir, yes?" When Kazimir nodded, the man said, with a puzzled grimace, "And what does another Russian wish with Wolfram Castle?"

"Nothing that is any of your business!"

The girl, who had been avidly listening still, curtseyed again and skittered away, through the door and out of sight.

Another Russian, so he was too late. Kazimir sighed, deeply, and after getting the directions he required, dismissed the man abruptly, displeased with his inquisitiveness. How did Gavril get ahead of him? It must have been the half day Kazimir spent finding his way again, after being guided wrong by a fellow who thought he said Wolfsburg and sent him northeast, when his destination was in truth southwest of Braunschweig. So Gavril Roschkov was already up at the castle, and now Kazimir would have to proceed with caution, knowing the minds of those in the castle were already poisoned. But he had one advantage over his opponent: many years before he had spent some time studying at Heidelberg University, and there, though he met and caroused with many fellows, one man had become his friend. They had been similar, so much so that people had remarked on the similarities and had mistaken them for brothers until they had learned the truth, that one was Russian and the other German. Time had separated them, but there was no doubt in his mind that he would be welcome as a visitor in that man's home. Count Nikolas von Wolfram, even fifteen years later, would still welcome him.

SEARCHING in his soul for quietude, Christoph paced across the floor to where a tall, slender man stood by the blazing hearth. One bare month had passed since he had emerged from the fog of drug-induced stupor, and still, sometimes, Christoph imagined the peaceful oblivion of that existence and even, occasionally, wished himself back in time. Emerging had been painful, especially when faced with what he had done, the shameful sexual affair with his aunt that still haunted him, clinging like a foul odor steeped into his being. Every day now he had to learn anew how to conduct himself as, his uncle had commanded, a count, a proud German, and master of Wolfram Castle.

The man turned. He was silver: his hair, his skin, his eyes, and even his voice, when he spoke, had a silky, silvery tone. "Count von Wolfram, I am Count Gavril Roschkov. Your servant." He bowed and then straightened.

Christoph stared at him, fascinated by the man's face. He was all bones, as if carved from some blond wood, like an effigy in a tomb. There was a stillness within him that Christoph instantly envied. The man had spoken perfect German, but Christoph, who was beginning to think his Uncle Nikolas more wise than he had thought before, answered in English, wondering if the Russian would follow. "I am Count Christoph von Wolfram. To what do I owe the honor of this visit, sir?"

The Russian raised one silvery eyebrow, but instantly shifted and answered in impeccable English, "May we . . . be comfortable?"

"Certainly," Christoph said, ashamed of his gaucherie. He led the way to chairs set to the side of the hearth. "May I offer you something to drink? Perhaps brandy?"

"That would be most welcome. It is cold, still, I fear, though spring has crept into the countryside, and spirits may warm me."

Christoph rang for refreshments, and they chatted while waiting, about Germany, the region near Bavaria, and the trouble with the French, as well as the possible solution, a treaty that left them independent. The proposed third partitioning of Poland was not canvassed, Christoph noted, respecting the diplomacy that made the Russian avoid such a delicate subject. Footmen entered with trays, and Christoph waited until they had left the room, at his request. There was something in the Russian gentleman's mien that spoke of a desire for privacy.

"I honor your discretion, Count von Wolfram," Roschkov said. "I assume that discretion is one of the reasons we speak in English and not German?"

Christoph did not answer, merely saying, "What is it of which you wish to speak? I feel certain you did not come to discuss politics."

The Russian tented his fingers before his mouth and eyed Christoph, his thin lips pursed in thought. "I have heard that a certain man of my country, one Mikhail Davidovich, was brought here from Brandenburg by . . . you?"

Christoph paused and thought before answering but could see no point in denying it. Though he knew Melisande's father had been jailed and beaten in Brandenburg, accused of theft, this Russian count posed no threat, not alone as he was. "By my uncle, Count Nikolas von Wolfram, who is now traveling to Venice on his wedding trip."

"Ah. I congratulate you on acquiring a new aunt. Is she German as well?"

"She is English, formerly Miss Elizabeth Stanwycke." The Russian was silent for a long moment, and Christoph added, "She was brought here as my sister's English tutor, but my uncle found her pleasing and married her."

"How . . . plebeian of him."

A swift anger rose in Christoph. "State your business, Roschkov, with Davidovich."

"You are loyal; that is an honorable attribute. I wish to see Davidovich."

"Why? You do not know him." That had been a guess, but he felt sure the Russian would have said if they were acquainted. This was most certainly not one of the Russians of whom he had heard, who had beaten poor Mikhail Davidovich so badly.

Roschkov narrowed his eyes and observed Christoph for a long moment, and then said, "I feel sure I can trust your discretion. I do know him slightly; I am afraid the man is in danger. There is someone who wishes him harm, and I have come to warn him."

"Warn him? You came all the way from Brandenburg to warn Mikhail Davidovich that he is in danger. What is he to you, that you would put yourself out so?"

"We are, as I said, acquaintances, and I would not, when it is in my power to prevent it, see him hurt, or perhaps even murdered."

"Murdered?"

"The man from whom he is in danger has killed before and will kill again."

Chapter 4

"AND I am to accept your word on this?" Christoph said.

"No, just let me see him, talk to him. Let *him* decide."

After thinking about it for a moment, Christoph said, "Only if I am there. He is a guest in my house and you are a stranger."

Roschkov nodded.

Christoph had only been in Davidovich's company for a few hours in the entire month the man had been convalescing. Melisande loved her father, and that was enough for Christoph to welcome the man unreservedly. But else, his own deep feeling was that the fellow was not worthy of the love his daughter liberally bestowed upon him. He was a guest in the castle, though, and as such, Christoph would protect him from any perturbation.

Davidovich was dozing, the state of his bed clothes a testament to the fact that his sleep was anything but peaceful. Christoph had decided against bringing Melisande into the room with them, or even telling her about the visitor at this point. He had his own questions about her father, and perhaps this mysterious visitor would shed some new ray of light on the man's murky past and present.

"Mikhail Davidovich, you have a visitor, sir," Christoph announced loudly, throwing back the curtains on the weak light of day.

The man gasped and sat up in bed, his pale, drawn face leaving Christoph with the sense that perhaps he had been unfair in his suspicion of the man's physical state.

Count Roschkov approached the bed, his beautiful carven face blank of expression. "Davidovich," he said, still in English. "I am Count Gavril Roschkov. Do you remember me?"

Quivering, the man shook his head slowly, his eyes wide,

with dark shadows rimming them. When he shrank back up against the carved headboard, his face darkened in the shadows. "I do not know you. Who are you? Who has sent you? Why do you torment me? Who sent you?"

Christoph turned toward the Russian. "It seems he does not know you, Count Roschkov. You are, perhaps, mistaken?"

His pale face immobile, one gleaming bead of perspiration slipping down from his high, wide forehead, the count did not answer. He stared steadily at Davidovich. Then he spoke in Russian.

Christoph opened his mouth to speak, to ask him to go back to English, but then Davidovich visibly relaxed, his shoulders sagging as if relieved of a great weight. He replied, and for a few minutes the exchanges were swift and animated. Damn, but he should have spent time learning Russian instead of ancient Greek! "Stop!" he finally said, holding up one hand.

Both other men turned to gaze at him.

"Sir," Christoph said to Davidovich, "Count Roschkov asked before if you knew him, and you indicated that you did not."

Davidovich looked to the Russian count, who nodded, and Melisande's father said, slowly, "I . . . was mistaken. It was the beating, you know," he said, putting one shaking hand to his forehead. "I do know the count. He has been . . . very kind to me."

"So he is not the Russian you fear, the one who beat you?"

"No, I—"

"What is going on here? Who is this, and why is he in my father's room?" Melisande marched into the room and looked from Christoph to the Russian count and back again.

Christoph explained and introduced the other man.

Melisande, the moment she was introduced to the elegant count, the second his hand took hers as he bowed and kissed the air a polite one inch above, experienced a tangle of emotions. The touch of his hand was cool and soft, like brook water in summer. But he was worried, she felt, looking into his silvery eyes. He was deeply concerned about something, some approaching trouble. She looked to her father, who sat up in bed, alert, glancing from her face to the Russian's.

In English she said, "Papa, who is this man?"

"He is a friend, my daughter, a good and kind friend, come to repatriate me. I am taking you back to Russia."

THE castle was large and brooding—not as big as Kazimir's own gracious home in Russia, but with an air of secretive menace. Almost surrounded by dark coniferous forests, the towering castle squatted on the rocky hillside that rose up behind it in stark isolation, drab gray blocks of stone uniting to form an impenetrable medieval fortress, with turrets and battlements, soaring conical peaks, and gleaming leaded glass windows on one turret side, richly colored stained glass on the other. Two timber wings stretched behind the castle, blocky and ugly, more modern in appearance, as if added as afterthoughts, which they no doubt were. A pack of wolflike dogs announced his arrival and rushed at his mount, but with one command he silenced them, and they slunk to a distance, watching him with wary eyes as he dismounted. A groom, surly and dark of mien, came and led his horse away. Kazimir resisted the urge to call out that his mount had better receive perfect care; it would be insulting when he knew, remembering Count Nikolas von Wolfram's behavior, that only the best of care of the animals would be tolerated.

A huge raven sat up on the peak of the porte cochere and croaked out a greeting. Kazimir looked up. "Yes, my friend, I remember you from the village. You follow me, perhaps?" he said out loud, in an ironic tone. "Or do you lead?" He smiled, remembering Nikolas von Wolfram's fabulous family stories, the legends he grew up with from his great-aunt and retold with great élan, about ravens and wolves and the deep, dark forests of his German home, but then Kazimir sobered and strode up through the porte cochere to the huge double doors.

A servant, alerted by the stable staff, perhaps, opened the door and bowed low. Kazimir marched past him into the great hall. In German he said to the footman, "I am come to visit Count Nikolas von Wolfram."

The servant just stared. Was he deaf? Or dull? Another servant, a hunched man with a deformed shoulder, scuttled into the great hall, and the first servant whispered to him urgently. Their whispers echoed up to the gallery above. Gavril had gotten to the household first, that Kazimir already knew, but this suspicious behavior was not tolerable. "I will see Count von Wolfram this second!" he thundered, his ringing tones like a hand clap, echoing back to him.

"I am here," came the words in perfect English, the voice youthful and clear, as a young man strolled down one of the two curved staircases from the gallery floor.

Kazimir gazed at him, puzzled. He switched to English, surprised by the choice of language but willing to go along with the change, saying, "Who are you? You are not Count von Wolfram."

"But I am sir. Who are you?"

"I will not be toyed with. I am looking for Count Nikolas von Wolfram."

The young man, almost as tall as Kazimir but slender and blond, with a fresh complexion and a calm manner, approached him. "My uncle is on his way to Italy on his wedding trip. I am Count Christoph von Wolfram. I'm sorry you have missed him. Are you an acquaintance?"

Kazimir felt the younger man's gaze like a touch; it traveled his face, lingering on the scar that carved his lip into a sneer. It was a blow to learn that Nikolas was not there, for it complicated his quest gravely. The day outside had dulled, and the light that came in the soaring glass windows that fronted the enormous great hall halved, creating obscure shadows in all the corners of the great hall, under the gallery. "I am. We attended university together many years ago."

"He will be sorry that he missed you, sir. If you wish to leave a letter for him, you may use one of our salons to write in before you make your way back down to accommodations in the village."

Carefully, carefully. Knowing Nikolas was not here changed how Kazimir must handle this problem. His quest was far too important, the danger all too real, to alienate those of the household. The chalice was here somewhere, and the blood moon was only eight days distant. "So you are . . . his nephew? I remember a nephew and niece. He spoke of you often." It worked, the fellow's austere expression softened.

"Did he? I remember waiting for him to come home from

university . . . He seemed so old and important to me then, my uncle."

Kazimir had a sudden sense from the young man that things since had not been as good between them, and that the pleasant memory was distant. "Count, though I hoped to find Nikolas here, I came for a reason far more important than just a visit. I know that already you have another Russian visitor, Count Gavril Roschkov."

The younger man's pleasant expression froze. "And you are . . . ? You never have told me your name, sir."

"I am Count Kazimir Vasilov, and I . . ." He heard voices from above and feared he was running out of time as the young man's attention strayed. "Count Gavril is not what he seems," he said, hurriedly, glancing up at the gallery, "and no matter what he has told you, you must not believe him, for he has motives hidden from view. He has come to see Mikhail Davidovich, this I know, but he is a danger to the man, and a danger to others."

He saw on the young count's bleached face anger, and had a sense of having stepped wrong.

"How is he a danger to Mikhail Davidovich?" he asked, his tone taut with strain.

To hold back or reveal all? Or all he was willing to tell at this early junction? There was much that he would never reveal, much that Gavril would be hiding, too, so Kazimir merely said, "That I cannot yet say. For in truth, though I know he is seeking Mikhail Davidovich, I am not sure of his exact motives."

"And I am to believe you, blindly and with no proof?"

He had counted on dominating the younger man, but there was in Christoph von Wolfram's demeanor a building fury. "Has he offered any proof that he is an ally to you and your family? Do you have any evidence negating what I say? You cannot simply believe the first man to arrive, as if—?"

"Stop!" the count commanded, putting up one hand. He turned and stared up at the gallery above, but then looked back at Kazimir. "Count Roschkov claimed acquaintanceship with Davidovich," he said, quietly, hurriedly. "But at first the man did not seem to know him until Roschkov spoke in your native tongue, with which I am unfortunately not familiar. Then, and *only* then, Davidovich, appearing relieved, admitted to knowing the count. What am I to make of that?" The young German frowned and then said, more slowly, "It seemed to me before the count spoke in Russian that Mikhail Davidovich feared Roschkov, and he asked who sent him. What am I to believe? I do not trust Davidovich, and yet the happiness and well-being of someone very dear to me depends upon him. I will not see Melisande hurt."

"Melisande?"

"Melisande Davidovich, his . . . his daughter."

"If you fear that Roschkov will injure Davidovich or this lady, then . . ." How to go on? How to bend the younger man to his will? "Tell me this . . . does Roschkov stay here?"

Slowly, von Wolfram nodded. "I was convinced, against my judgment, to invite him to stay, as Davidovich's friend, you understand."

"Christoph!"

A sweet-toned voice drifted down to them from above, and both men turned to look up. Kazimir felt an unwelcome tug of attraction at the sight of a beautiful young woman gazing at them from the gallery railing. Her hair, bound up simply with blue ribbons, was honey-colored and her figure sweetly round, but her voice in that one word—it had been like an arrow piercing his heart. A shiver of presentiment trilled down his spine. She was more than she appeared, this young woman.

The young German count stared, too, and when Kazimir glanced over at him, he could see how it was. The look of hopeless adoration on the fellow's face was so plain. This was a woman for whom he would die. This was Melisande Davidovich.

"Let me stay," Kazimir urged in an undertone, "if only to protect you all from the pernicious influence of Gavril Roschkov, who despite his soft mien does *not* have your lady friend's best interests at heart, nor does he care one bit for Davidovich's well-being. Do not be misled; he is here for himself only, but his purpose could be lethal to others. Let me stay; introduce me as an old friend of your uncle's, for that I am."

There was a long moment of silence, but then Count Christoph said, "Meli, we have another visitor. This is Count Kazimir Vasilov, an old friend of my uncle Nikolas."

Chapter 5

"THE RELIC is too dangerous for the likes of you to possess," Gavril Roschkov said, his mellow tone not diminishing the intensity nor the meaning behind his words. "I will not allow it!"

"It is not your decision to make," Kazimir Vasilov retorted.

"Leave it to me to find, I say! I plead with you, do not follow this path. It will destroy you."

"No, it will give me all that I want, all that I need, and I intend to leave this place with it in my possession. You are the one who risks destruction; you don't know, Gavril, the terrible consequences you will bring down upon yourself! In truth, the chalice is neither yours nor mine, but my intentions are honorable, yours are ruinous. You must abandon . . ."

Both Russians looked up from their fervent conversation as they became aware that Melisande had entered the room. Though both had spoken Russian, she understood them, having set herself the task of learning the language as a way of ingratiating herself with her father when she was but a girl. She had never lived in Russia, nor had she even been there. She had an antipathy for it; it figured in her father's tales as a cruel winterland of harsh beauty and frozen hearts. His announcement that Count Roschkov was going to repatriate him, and that she must go back with him, had stung her deeply.

"Please, gentlemen," she said, in English, "feel free to continue your conversation."

They exchanged glances, and she decided in that moment not to reveal her ability to understand their language. Count Kazimir Vasilov came forward and bowed before her. "We were not formally introduced earlier, when you spoke to Count Christoph from the gallery. I am . . ."

"Count Kazimir Vasilov," she said, softly, puzzled by the heavy pulse in her throat and the heat that flushed her, traveling over her breasts and across her skin as he straightened and gazed steadily down at her. At first glance the Russian was similar to Nikolas von Wolfram, and to that she had to attribute the warmth that flooded her face. He was big, broadshouldered, and dark, like Nikolas, but an ugly white scar slashed his upper lip and up into his left cheek, carving it into a sneer, and it destroyed his good looks. She was repulsed and attracted, both emotions warring within her breast. She looked away from his steady assessment.

Count Gavril came forward, and she met his silvery gaze, relaxing just from the relief of his coolness. "You speak English. I noticed that before," he said.

"It is the command of Count Nikolas von Wolfram that every one of the family members speak English—or French—within the walls of Wolfram Castle. The last years have been difficult ones for the family, and the less the serving staff has to gossip of the better."

"Do you not speak Russian then?"

Melisande turned slowly and gazed at Count Kazimir, who had posed the question. There was an inquiry beyond the obvious there. He wanted to know if she had understood their words as she came in. They were quarreling about some object, variously called between them the "relic," and the "chalice," and though she didn't understand of what they were speaking, it was clear that there was a connection and a conflict between them that they were not revealing. She must speak to Christoph of this, for she would not have him, nor her father, duped. "No," she said, "I do not speak Russian." *Though I understand it perfectly,* she thought.

"When you return to your homeland, you must learn," Count Roschkov said, silkily, ambling toward her.

"My homeland?" She turned to gaze at him. "My homeland is France, for I have never in my life been to Russia."

"Ah, but your father will take you home, and you will finally know the other part of you. Your mother's death was a tragedy, but at least your father is devoting himself to your well-being."

"What do you know of my father, sir? He has never spoken

of you, but now claims you as an old friend. All I know of
Russians is that a Russian—or more than one, for he is not
clear on that subject—beat him when he was in Brandenburg.
They apparently accused him of thievery and brutally assaulted him, having bribed the Germans for access to him.
Though he told them that he did not have the treasure they
claimed he stole, still, they were unrelenting."

"They?" Gavril Roschkov asked quickly, puzzlement on
his face. "Did he say there was more than one?"

"And has he always told the truth, Miss Davidovich?" That
was the darker Russian, Count Kazimir Vasilov.

"Who are you to judge him?" Count Roschkov said, turning on Vasilov, each word an icicle dropped on stone.

"I make no judgment. I simply ask a question."

"It is an impertinent question," Melisande said, though
doubt of her father's veracity was beginning to plague her. He
was trying to mend his ways, he had told her, but the consti-
tution of a habitual liar was such, she believed, that it took fortitude to resist the urge. Did he have that inner strength of
character? He was hiding something, but what it was she
could not say, and whether it was important or merely shameful, she could not even guess. And yet she would never expose
him to the scorn of strangers. "But else, it is not to his own re-
lation I trust in speaking of this Russian who beat my father,
but to one whose word I hold above all others."

"And that would be . . . ?"

Count Kazimir Vasilov was not going to leave this point, it
seemed. He stood before her, one thick brow raised. She
stared steadily into eyes that held secret depths. She would not
be intimidated . . . not with so much at stake. "Count Nikolas
von Wolfram told me. It is he who rescued my father from the
animal—or animals—who nearly killed him," she said, her
voice quavering in anger. "Count Nikolas told me that the
Germans in charge of the prison were bribed to look the other
way, allowing a Russian or Russians to question and . . . and
beat my poor father. It was only because of Count Nikolas's
status and connections that my papa was freed!"

"Ah, so it was indeed my old schoolmate who aided your
father," Count Vasilov said, easily, moving by degrees closer
and closer and circling behind her. "I attended Heidelberg

University with Nikolas, you know. Or perhaps you do not know, for the young count has had little time to speak of anything, what with the eventful day he has had so far."

The fever of his nearness was burning her up the closer he got, and she felt the urge to loosen her closefitting sleeves and bodice; one droplet of perspiration trickled down between her breasts. "That must have been many years ago," she said, "that you and Count von Wolfram were schoolmates."

"Yes, it was many years ago now. He was my elder by two years. I was a reasonably good student, not first-rate but not terrible. Nikolas . . . he was good at everything, and . . ." His voice trailed off.

He was close, so close she could touch him if she reached out one hand, and he had paused just behind her. His breathing, deep and even, was quickening, and waves of heat radiated from him. She turned to see why he had stopped speaking; he was gazing at her, an expression of puzzlement on his face, his shaggy brows drawn down low over dark brown eyes. She gazed at his lips, the white gash of scar interrupting the ruddy perfection of a full bottom lip and thinner upper. The thudding of her own heart was loud in her ears.

"Miss Davidovich!"

The cool silvery tone of Count Roschkov's exquisite voice broke through the suffocating heat and brought her back to the public room, the fire blazing in the hearth, and the two men, so different, but both there with some related mission. She took one step away, and Count Vasilov, his expression still uncertain, moved away, too, and turned his back on them both.

"Miss Davidovich," Count Roschkov said. "I am concerned that your view of our homeland has been forever tainted by your father's bad experience."

"Do you mean being beaten nearly to death by his compatriots?"

Count Vasilov glanced over his shoulder at her and narrowed his eyes but looked away again without comment.

Count Roschkov strolled toward her and took her hand in his own, covering it with his other. His skin was cool and smooth and quenched the fire within her. "No . . . no. Though I understand your ire concerning that grave abuse, I mean how he was mistreated in the country of our birth . . . how he was misjudged and driven to a life not befitting his gentility. I think those circumstances have caused you to judge our mother country too harshly. There is much beauty there, and much kindness beneath the austerity."

She looked up at him with gratitude. "Perhaps that is true." She sighed a deep, shaky sound of relief. "However, my father is in no condition to travel right now, so I would ask—"

"No, no, do not concern yourself, Miss Davidovich. I am perfectly content to remain here at your service until such a time as both you and your father feel he is fit to make the trek to our homeland. I am in no hurry. No hurry at all."

Surely he was a little too vehement? They had agreed in principle that they would go back to Russia; she had trespassed on the good graces of the von Wolfram family for long enough, and she felt that she *must* take this offer of repatriation, now that she had her father. They would find some way to live. And yet the count did not seem in any hurry, as if he did not mind so much lingering in Wolfram Castle.

"Meli, I—" Charlotte rushed into the room, then made a comical little stop, and put one hand over her mouth. "Oh, I'm so sorry. I hope I interrupted nothing?"

Melisande bit back a smile. Charlotte's curiosity about their two visitors no doubt made her find an excuse to disrupt the conversation. At twenty, she was determined never to leave her home, resisting every effort of her uncle to find for her a husband, and yet naturally she was interested in men, so the Russians' arrival could not go unheralded.

"Count Roschkov, Count Vasilov, this is my friend, Countess Charlotte von Wolfram. She is Count Christoph's younger sister."

"I would have known it even if I had not been told. She has the same features, the same delicacy of expression and freshness of complexion," Count Gavril Roschkov said, stepping forward and taking her hand, bowing low over it. "Only more fully realized in the feminine way."

Charlotte's expressive face bleached, and then her cheeks reddened as she gazed over at surly Count Kazimir Vasilov, who merely nodded a greeting. Her chin went up. "And you, sir? Do you have no appreciation for my beauty?"

He simply stared at her. Melisande felt her friend's morti-

fication and experienced a swift surge of anger at the churlish
Russian; surely he could forgive the gaucherie of a young
woman and offer her some sop to her vanity? "I think, Charlotte, that Count Vasilov does not flatter, even when a lady is
deserving of compliments."

"No, I never flatter, for those are just empty words. Countess Charlotte, you are a very pretty girl. I must say, though,
that Miss Davidovich has true beauty." He bowed, stiffly.

Melisande felt her young friend's mortification, and would
have responded angrily, so perhaps it was fortunate that
Christoph entered just then, with Frau Liebner on his arm. For
the next hour they all talked in stilted sentences, and
Melisande took the opportunity of the elder dame's determined conversational style to sit back and watch. What were
the two Russians doing there? That it had something to do
with her father, she was certain, but what? Her dread fear was
that it still had to do with the item he had been accused of
stealing. Why did they persist in believing he had stolen whatever it was? Had he not been searched time and again while in
captivity?

Was one or both of them involved in his abuse in Brandenburg? If she could slip away she would question him, but now
was not the time. She would visit her father in the evening,
after dinner, and make him tell her what was going on. It almost seemed that her father had chosen one side against another, for Count Vasilov and Count Roschkov were clearly
adversaries in the hunt for this chalice of which they had been
speaking. But how could they possibly think he still had it, if
he ever had?

TWILIGHT limned the forest with slashes of golden light,
the sky a fading bruise-purple backdrop. Only desperation
could draw Magda Brandt toward the blackness of the coniferous woods on such a night, when snow still lingered and the
air smelled of it, warning of a coming snowfall that could arrive suddenly and last for hours. She pulled her cloak more
tightly around her and shifted the wrapped burden in her arms.
Good black bread and blood sausage, cheese wrapped in cloth
and a bottle of dark beer: that should be enough for now.

She had much of which to speak, and that was what pulled her to her destination. In her father's inn, the dark Russian's arrival, need for guidance to Wolfram Castle, and even his name had fulfilled part of the prophecy she had been told and affirmed that she had chosen the right path to remove herself from a position that had become, lately, unbearable. A few flakes of snow came down as darkness crept over the land, but visions of her future kept her warm with a golden hazy glow. By July she would be resident in a summer palace on the shores of a great inland sea—she had learned the name but could no longer remember it—where she would consort with Russian royalty. Then, as autumn tarried, she would move majestically to a winter palace and attend balls draped in furs and jewels on the arm of a Russian prince, who, restored to his rightful position and filled with gratitude for her part in that restoration, would present her to court as his princess.

When she thought of that veiled future ballroom, she could envision her own clothes, she could see the jewels, but the rest stretched out in a magnificent blur, her mind unable to fill in all the details of a life of which she had little comprehension. That lack of clarity frustrated her and spurred her onward. Someday soon she would see and know more of that life than anyone in Wolfbeck could comprehend. A great lady. She would be a great lady in Russia and leave behind the shame and degradation of this life.

And to think that in one sense she had her father's disgusting habit of offering her as whore to every visiting man of apparent wealth for her opportunity. She smiled in secret delight as she sped through the forest. When her Russian prince had come to Wolfbeck and had been offered her company, he had agreed, but in the tiny chamber off the tap room he had made her understand, in his halting German, that he would never use her so poorly. Instead, he pressed gold into her palm and talked to her for a while. Then he said if she wished to leave this awful village, he could make sure she did. All she had to do was a few favors, and he would see her crowned in jewels in a far-off fairyland of frozen rivers and a glorious, glittering royal court. Well, perhaps he had not expressed it quite thus, but whatever he could not say in German, she had easily supplied from her imagination.

Magda stumbled over a log in the darkness of the forest but doggedly righted herself, fearing that the dampness she felt spreading through her bodice was some of the beer from the earthenware bottle. The stopper must have worked loose. It was cold, so very cold. Her breath came in frosty puffs, and she felt lightheaded, but she could not stop. Her new friend needed food, and she would provide it. She would do whatever she needed to earn her place in his heart and his life. Gratitude would bond them. He would be grateful for her part in recovering that which had been so foully stolen from him, and she would be grateful for him taking her away from her home, a place of unutterable shame and misery.

It was her only hope, and she clung to it fervently. All she needed to do was everything she was told, and life could begin. Nagging doubts she swept away. Her other problem would have a solution once she got away from home. Then and only then she would worry about her other dilemma.

There, finally, was the hut. Was that a faint light she saw? She swallowed back her instinctive fear and steeled her courage. This was not easy—even in his great kindness, her friend was fearsome—but it was necessary. Her only alternative to this God-given way out of her predicament was disgrace and isolation, and perhaps even death. She took a deep breath and pushed open the hut door.

IT was absurd. There was really no other word for it, and he could not even contemplate it without feeling ridiculous. And yet, Christoph sat on the edge of his bed fingering the dusty fur pelt that he had found when he returned to his room after dinner. Who had placed it there? The last thing he remembered about it was flinging it onto the floor after his great-aunt's preposterous account of his supposed affliction, if one wanted to call it that, or his gift, of werewolfism.

And yet, Uta had known things she should not have known, about his feelings of late, his need to run in the woods, his hunger, his sense that his blood was boiling, bubbling through his veins like pitch. He had thought of it as a release, his running, of all the pent-up energy and madness left from the awful events of the last year or so, and yet the relief was only ever temporary.

Shame drenched him, riddled him. He could not even contemplate what he had done without disgusting himself. Drugged or not, surely no decent human being would have behaved so, allowing a seduction between aunt and nephew? If he had been a whole and decent man, it could never have happened; he would not have succumbed so easily. His uncle wouldn't have.

His uncle. Nikolas von Wolfram. Werewolf? According to Uta, he was a werewolf, from a long line of werewolves.

Pah! Christoph tossed the fur into the corner and flung himself down on the bed, but in seconds he leaped back up, retrieved it, and made his decision. As sure as he was that it was a preposterous story made up to frighten little children into staying out of the woods at night, still, somewhere within himself he would wonder until he had dismissed the idiocy as folk tales and fairy dust by testing the ludicrous tale. However Uta had managed to have the pelt delivered to him, this was no doubt what she had intended he should do, for some unfathomable reason of her own, and so he would do it and then be able to fling it down at her feet and tell her to stop spreading such idiotic tales, and especially to more impressionable minds like his sister's.

He strode downstairs and out to the frozen sward of grass that swept from the castle down to the woods on the northern side. He entered, using a path he knew well from his youth and upward, and began to trot over the snow-covered forest floor, feeling the need to remove himself from the castle anyway. Melisande—his own sweet, lovely, untouchable Melisande—had been agitated and distracted since the arrival of the damnable Russians, and now there was talk of her leaving with her father to go back to his homeland in the company of the regal Count Gavril Roschkov.

And he could say nothing to criticize the plan, because even his own reason told him it was eminently logical and supremely sound. Russia was Mikhail Davidovich's homeland, and the protection of a count of such apparent eminence as Roschkov would give them the new start they needed. His own argument, that she could stay in Wolfram Castle forever, was nonsensical. There was no future for her in a place where she could never find a husband. She deserved to sparkle in the Russian royal court and bedazzle some man of wealth and significance, who would lay his fortune at her dainty feet.

His pace picked up, and impotent fury swept through him. He could not even fight for her, could not ask her to marry him, for he was not worthy even of her tiniest grain of compassion. Anger ground into his gut; he clutched the pelt in his fist and shouted out loud his ire. Louder and louder he yelled, until even to his own ears it began to sound like howling. He ran, his breath coming in gasps, but then smoothing out until breathing in and out became food for his body, his lungs swelling to capacity and then deflating, becoming more capacious with every stride. Again the silent gray shadows of wolves flitted through the forest just beyond him as he howled aloud. His mind emptied until there was just the running.

When the agony hit his gut, he was unprepared and stumbled, falling to the ground and doubling over, feeling the wrenching deep within him, as if his body was trying to tear into two. Fear writhed through him as he rolled on the snowy ground, the crunch of every crystal of ice like a drum beat in his ears. His nose was assaulted with smells; snow smelled clean and faintly earthy, with a tang of some chemical odor when it melted on his fur. Thousands of other scents assailed him: animals, small ones, their hearts beating quickly in fear, and larger ones, their hearts pounding as they chased the delicious tiny ones, relishing the scraps of meat tucked around brittle bones that snapped between powerful jaws. Wave after wave of pain hit him, but through it all his gaze became sharper, the night air clear like day, and yet color all off, odd . . . shadow and light and movement more important than reds and blues and yellows. He rolled on the ground and howled, and the answering cry from the wolf pack in the forest was a language, telling him of game to be chased, family to be fed, ties to reaffirm, life to be lived that night in the depths of the forest.

And he king of them all, a creature to be feared and revered, watched and obeyed, and ultimately respected. The pain receded, and he got to his four feet . . . four! He shook off the clinging scraps of garments and stood. Where to hunt?

Where were the smells best? He lifted his nose to the air and sniffed deeply, alive to every fragrance, the tang of pine, the scat of other animals telling a long tale of their skittering movements through the underbrush, and the richness of earth from where he had writhed, grinding through the snow to the dead leaves and dirt underneath. Stretching, forepaws before him and sinews powerful beneath a coat of thick silvery gray fur, he felt a fierce joy, the sense that he was finally one with something, that life now made sense in a way it had never made sense to him before.

Of course. It was so very simple. Life was to be lived; hunting, killing, eating, sleeping, feeding family . . . that was all that mattered ultimately. Bonds were forged with those necessary activities, beginning always with the hunt.

And yet he knew he did not need to hunt; his belly was still full with the dinner he had eaten just an hour before. So for now he would run. He ran, and it was glorious, feet pounding in rhythm, claws digging into the ground and pushing off to carry him over rocks and felled trees. Everything was new, including how it looked to be running so close to the ground, the perspective so different, so true. This was how the forest was meant to be viewed.

But exhaustion soon overwhelmed him and fear beset him; what if he could not change back? He knew nothing . . . didn't even know how to accomplish it. He had dismissed his ancient aunt's words and had not listened; it was disgraceful to disrespect her as he had, his wolfish mind knew. How did one make it back into the human form he loathed at this moment, but knew he needed to resume?

He stopped running and in the shadows of a tree, stood, panting. The moon was rising, a glistening crescent that sent waves of heady joy through him. He threw his head back and howled, then listened to the answering song from the pack. One with it all, he felt on the edge of discovery. And yet the fear still lingered. He knew nothing about himself; it was as if he had been reborn. Damnation, but he needed to go back. Reason was a struggle in this form, but he felt sure that resuming his human form was going to be just as painful as becoming a wolf, though it was something he instinctively knew he needed to do, and soon.

Melisande, what would she think to see him like this? Melisande, her sweet face radiant, her silk-soft hair. Ah, there was the change coming, the connection to his human form reasserting itself with the peal of her name in his heart. The pain roiled in his gut, and yet the thought of Melisande helped him remember why he must become human again and connected him to the man named Christoph. He did not trust the Russians and would not let Melisande out of his sight until he was sure Count Gavril Roschkov had her best interests at heart; that was all that mattered. Then he would decide what to do with his own life. He collapsed to the forest floor, the snow dashing into his eyes. Gasping, rolling, writhing, he felt his skin split like an overripe fruit and howled in pain.

Melisande. He focused on the vision of her lightly freckled face, and the blue of her eyes finally came into clarity, the gold of her hair—he could see color again! Beyond the clearing, glowing eyes watched him; it was the wolves of the forest, curious about his transformation. But he was not afraid of them, not even in his vulnerable form—terribly vulnerable he realized since he was without clothing. Apparently he needed to remove his clothes and leave them where he could find them between transitions, an embarrassing oversight he would not allow to occur a second time. The wolves would never harm him, for he was their superior, and they respected the connection he had with a world they did not understand.

But then they scattered, and Christoph, human again but naked and cold, heard a rustling. He crept to a tree, crouching behind the trunk.

Magda Brandt hurried past, on her way toward the village. Where had she been? What could possibly bring her into the forest on such a night, on any night? She heard something and stopped, crying out with alarm, then she ran faster. Christoph staggered to his feet, intent on following her but—He looked down at his naked body glistening wet from the melting snow in the pale beam of faint moonlight. He was in no shape. He would just have to find out tomorrow. He would go down to the village and question her, for he had a sense that something was very wrong, for her to be deep in the forest after dark. He crept back up to the castle, and with difficulty made his way to the scullery door and skulked in and up the stairs, feeling

lucky that he had encountered no one in his late-night peram-
bulations.

Finally in his room, grateful that he had, at this point, no
personal valet to oversee his comings and goings, he dropped
into bed weary to the bone and slept the first deep sleep since
he had recovered from the drugging of his uncle Bartol.

Chapter 6

COUNT KAZIMIR Vasilov turned in a circle, eyes wide open but unseeing in the darkness of the midnight great hall, trying to feel Wolfram Castle and all its secrets. He had known from the moment he saw it that it held puzzles, enigmas, dilemmas deeper and more far-reaching than just those surrounding the people who inhabited it.

Some mysteries were clear enough to identify. Where was the chalice Mikhail Davidovich had stolen from the church in Constanta, Romania? How had he hidden it while imprisoned in Brandenburg? For Kazimir was sure he had it still, despite the man's apparent intransigence even as he was beaten. And why did Gavril Roschkov, sworn in enmity to Kazimir, seek it? Did he truly wish to use it, as Kazimir suspected, or were his intentions more admirable? Was Melisande Davidovich a pawn of her father, or did she have more knowledge than she was revealing?

Melisande Davidovich. Even her name was an entrancing combination of the French and Russian sides of her, the mystic and the stoic. Lovely and golden, charming freckles dotting her smooth skin, a honey-colored lady of infinite attraction. Her voice, speaking English as was the way in Wolfram Castle, was golden and silky, faintly accented with her French birth. She had seemed uneasy around him; it had come to him in waves, that trembling awareness, a perfume of alarm that puzzled and yet attracted him. His immediate fascination with her only heightened, but when he looked into her eyes he saw revulsion mingled with perturbation.

There was something about her, some connection to himself. What was it? It was what he had sensed as he stood before the castle, a feeling that the enchantment he had long ago endured would find an echo within the walls of this formidable fortress. Or could she be the reason the gypsy witch told him to follow the chalice to find the cure to the curse that bedeviled him?

He didn't know and could not allow himself to lose concentration on his purpose, so he stood, emptying his mind of all the detritus of a long day and closed his eyes, spreading his arms wide. Deep in his mind's eye he saw the castle spread out before him like a web, passages and hallways and people scuttling to and fro, and at the center of it was a woman. He stilled his heart rate, pulling in a long breath and holding it, then releasing it slowly, in a long, controlled sigh that echoed to the upper reaches of the great hall, beyond the gallery. That was where the enigma lay . . . an old woman was at the heart of it, an old woman who knew things that no one else knew.

Would she tell him anything, or was her information reserved for others?

He opened his eyes and began a slow ascent to the upper floors of the house, down silent corridors and passages, past doors where he could almost feel the inmates sleeping, some peaceful, some restless. Pausing, he put his hand to one door and felt a wave of longing. Ah, Melisande Davidovich. Her sweetness called to him even now. He could feel her beyond the door, innocent of artifice, perhaps, but beguiling in her provocative purity. How easy it would be to lose himself to such a lovely heart and mind, for such a dark character as his own sought tempering, the ameliorating quality of virtue. But he had a purpose that was more important than the surge of sexual awareness that even now tingled in his body, the robust evidence of his manhood stirring with cravings not experienced for some time, since he had dedicated himself to another objective.

Besides, he thought, stroking the thick wood door with one finger, despite the pleasure being with her would bring him, he was certainly beyond the redemption offered by the sacrifice of a good woman. He was tainted, damaged by the hex that damned him forever to live half a life. Forever, or until he found the cure.

That thought was the spur he needed to move on; he pulled himself away from her door by sheer will and found stairs at the end of the corridor. His objective was higher. Something about this castle puzzled him, but he couldn't put a name to it. It held its own mystery, but he could not decide yet if that was his to discover, or whether it was immaterial to his purpose. Another floor up, he walked silently down the hall, narrower than the one below, and began to feel he was close. Here was his goal. On this uppermost floor he would find an answer to some of his questions.

A door called to him, and he put his hand on the handle, pushing down and letting the door swing open. The room was dark and silent, but the lone inmate was not sleeping, even in this, the middle of the darkest hour of night.

"You I haf been awaiting," she said. "Enter, and shut the door."

"HELP! Help me!"

Melisande fought her way out of the deadly embrace, the hot animal breath fogging her frightened mind, and finally in the dark sat straight upwards, panicked, great heaving breaths wrenching her slight frame. She put one hand over her breast, feeling her heart pound so hard it seemed it would shatter the confines of its cage. The darkness enclosed her, but it was blankets only that had her tangled and confined, and she pushed them aside, flinging her legs over the side of the bed and padding over to the window, throwing open the curtains and hopping up to sit on the thick ledge created by the stone walls of the ancient castle.

"Wolves again," she said, into the darkness, encircling her knees with her arms. This time the wolves had been fighting over her until both had leapt on her and battled each other over her body, their thick writhing bodies bruising her with their combat, sharp teeth flashing above her, bloody foam flecking her skin from their snapping, snarling quarrel.

The waxing moon emerged from behind the dark woods beyond the castle, and in the gleaming, narrow path of light she saw at first just a movement, and then more forms. Emerging from the shadows were wolves, and Melisande started back in fright, but then, knowing she was safe up in her room in the impregnable castle, she watched, her breath bated, her limbs trembling, her heart pounding.

Two separated themselves from the pack and moved toward the castle, seeking, it seemed, the dull gleam of platinum light. They trotted toward the castle across the long green grass, up the knoll until they were about ten rods distant and then stood, staring up at the castle, directly at her window, it seemed to her.

"What do you want?" she whispered, hands on the cold glass. After long minutes of staring up at her, the two turned and headed back to the forest, casting one long, lingering look back before reentering the dark shadows.

Wolves.

This was ridiculous! She leaped down from her perch. She was not going to sleep again, and knowing her father's habits, decided a midnight visit would do them both good. She had questions for him and would stand no evasions this time, unlike her evening visit to him when he claimed exhaustion yet again to forestall serious conversation.

The castle was dark and still around her, her flickering candle throwing just a pale wavering shimmer before her, but his room was close, and she crept to the door, opening it and peeking in. If he was sleeping, she thought, she would leave him be. "Papa?" she whispered.

He sat up in bed. "Daughter! What are you doing up at such an hour?"

"I couldn't sleep, Papa. I had a terrible dream. I have been dreaming of wolves lately . . . such awful dreams."

"Come here," he said, patting his twisted covers.

She crossed the room and sat up on the edge of the bed, wondering what it would have been like to have had him near as a child, in the home her mother shared with her grandmother. He had lived a peripatetic life, and so from her earliest childhood he was vaguely remembered from brief visits between long absences, occasioned sometimes, she now knew, by stays in jail for petty theft. Even though her family's history made it one of the most important families of the area, despite having lost its money and its manor, she had been jealous of the other humbler children in her village, those who had fathers who came home every night from their work in the fields, or the bakery, or in town as bankers or vintners or cloth merchants.

But when he did come to stay for a while, what magic he would weave! He would tell tales of his travels, wondrous stories of the Orient, and the Levant, of open bazaars and veiled ladies, harems and seraglios and desert sands. He spoke of strange creatures with humped backs and others with long necks. The other children she knew called him a liar for his stories, but they all still gathered around and listened, open mouthed, while he beguiled them by producing a coin from thin air. He would give it to one, saying, solemnly, that they must use it to purchase candy, or it would disappear again. Then, after creating a cloud of pretty smoke and producing from it a single flower, he would finish his story with a chuckle and a wise nod, saying that enough was enough. There were things, he said, best left to the imagination, and things children did not need to know about.

Gazing down at him in his invalid state, she hesitantly said, "I missed you so, Papa, when you left that last time, before Mama and Grandmother died. Where did you go? And why did you stay away so long?"

"My little one, my daughter," he said, gazing up at her, his eyes pale in the golden light of the single candle.

He put out his hand, and she took it. His face, once alive with laughter, now held only sadness, and there were lines she had never noticed, pouches of skin sagging down, making his jowls soft.

"I was a terrible father to you," he whispered, his voice trembling. "Never did I do what I ought to have. If I had, your mama might still be alive. I should have taken her away. Taken you both to my home, back to Russia."

Russia. That is the one place of which he had never told his magical tales when she was a child. "Why have you never spoken of your parents? Are they still alive? What happened to them? Do you . . . do you have brothers and sisters?"

He shrugged and looked away. "No, my parents are not alive. They died many, many years ago when I was still a lad," he said, softly. "I had a brother, but he was taken. I don't know if he lives or not."

"Is that from when you know Count Gavril Roschkov?"

Her father's face bleached a little, and his eyes widened. "No . . . no."

"Then how? How do you know him?"

He put one hand to his brow. "I'm so tired, Melisande, my darling. Can we please . . . I should get some sleep."

"Papa! We need to talk. This thing that you were accused of having stolen . . . what is it? Did you—" She shook her head. She couldn't ask. And yet, she must. Until now she had treated her father as if she were still the child he left behind. But now she was a woman, and she needed to know some of the truth about him and his life. "Did you steal this thing, what the Russians accused you of stealing? And what was it?"

Tears filled his eyes, and his expression changed, becoming beseeching. "How can you ask such questions of me? I am your father."

But she pressed on. "The two Russians, who are they? Why are they here, if not for this item you are said to have stolen? Is one of them the Russian you fear? Is it . . . is it Count Vasilov?"

"I cannot speak of it! Please . . . do not ask me."

"Papa, I—"

"I feel faint, " he said, putting one long-fingered hand to his brow. He turned his face away into the shadows. "Melisande," he said, faintly. "We spoke before about the rosary. I feel a need of it . . . do you have it?"

"Yes, of course, but—"

"Could you bring it to me in the morning?"

"Certainly, Papa, but please . . . who is this Count Gavril Roschkov? And why is he taking such an interest in us? And why do you trust him to take us back to Russia?"

"Please my darling daughter, right now I feel I need rest. Sleep. I am weak still . . . so weak."

How convenient that he should feel weak just when she began to press for answers. "But—"

"No! Just know this," he said, blindly reaching for her hand and grasping it, giving it one squeeze and then releasing. "Everything I am doing now, I do for your good. I am on the cusp of some great things, child, but it is delicate, so delicate. You ought to be rich. You ought to have wealthy men lay themselves and their fortune at your feet. All this I will give to you."

Was he going to conjure a wealthy husband for her out of the air? She bit back a harsh retort about his tall tales and stories and got to her feet.

"But the rosary . . . please, Melisande," he said, his voice muffled and his face still in the shadows, "my darling daughter, bring it to me. "

"Perhaps. I suppose I will bring it on the morrow. Goodnight, Papa. I expect that you will be well enough to get out of bed soon. *Very* soon." She picked up the candle and made her way to the door. "And I expect," she said, gazing back at the shadowed hump in the bed, "that you will have answers for me, too. I will not wait forever."

She exited and flounced down the hall toward her own room—the sitting room between their bedchambers was locked off for her use only, and so not a through way—but then a noise on the staircase from the fourth floor of the castle made her stop. Who was out this time of night? She flattened herself against a wall and blew out her candle, irrationally afraid. Who could it be?

A bulky shadow slid ahead of its creator down the staircase. The flame in the sconce that lit the stairs wavered with the motion of the form passing and threw the big shadow eerily across the wall, but even as the figure descended, emerging from the staircase, Melisande could not make out who it was. Then the man—for such a large figure could only belong to a man—paused.

Melisande held her breath, her back pressed to the wall, her fingers trembling around the warm but extinguished candle. This was idiotic, completely and utterly absurd, and yet she could not move, could not allow herself to just step forward and demand to know who was there.

"Miss Davidovich," a deep voice commanded. "Come out of the shadows, for there is, truly, nothing of which to be alarmed."

"Count Vasilov," she said, forcing herself to step away from the wall, trying to regain her dignity after such a foolish interlude. "What are you doing wandering the halls so late at night? Have you . . . lost your way?"

He was close, and he moved closer, his bulk a blot before the weak light of the lamp, his features in shadow. "Yes, I fear that I have lost my way," he said.

But she was not sure it was truly an answer to her question.

"You had a candle," he said. "Why did you extinguish it?"

"I . . ." It seemed so silly now. "I was afraid," she said, trying to make out his eyes in the darkness of the hall. Foolishly, she felt if she could just see his eyes, she would rest easier. "I was afraid when I heard footsteps, for I wasn't sure who would be about at such an hour. I was . . . was visiting my father."

He reached out one big hand, and she thought for a moment he was going to seize hold of her, but instead he took the candle from her hand and went to the wall sconce, removing the glass—it must have been scorching hot, but he touched it as if it were as cool as ice—relit her candle and returned it to her, with a deep bow. Now she could see his eyes, the pupils large and as black as obsidian, but the irises a warm brown flecked with amber.

"You should return to your bedchamber, Miss Davidovich," he said, indicating her room with a nod.

"You know which is mine?" she asked, surprised.

His lips twitched. "Oh, yes, I think there is more than one man in this household who knows exactly where you lay your head to sleep. I am one of them."

She felt a chill down her back, but it was not fear. "What . . . what does that mean, sir?"

"Good night, Miss Davidovich," he said, and turned away.

"Why . . . what were you . . ." She had many questions for him, but he was already gone, presumably toward the guest chamber assigned to him by Christoph. Though, surely he was not going in the right direction for that. Secretive man . . . infuriating man! What was he doing at the castle? He was an old school friend of Nikolas, but that did not explain why he stayed, nor did it explain why Christoph allowed it.

Who was Count Kazimir Vasilov? And two Russian counts arriving within hours of each other . . . that could not be mere coincidence, so what did they both want, and why could they not just be open about it? She would demand answers on the morrow, for there were too many secrets, and if there was one thing this family did not need, it was more secrets.

Chapter 7

"WOLFSBANE . . . I need to find wolfsbane," Melisande muttered, staring at the wall of forest in front of her, trembling inside and yet determined in her course of action.

"I beg your pardon, miss?" Fanny calmly stood by, waiting, hands folded in front of her. Her steady gaze was on Melisande's face, but her own expression gave away nothing.

"I . . . I need a certain herb from the forest, as I said, and . . ." Melisande quivered inside. How could she explain that she was driven to do something about the dreadful dreams that plagued her nightly? It had come to her in the early morning hours, as she stared up at the ceiling sleepless after a long night, what she remembered from the previous year, deep within the heart of the forest near a stream. Wolfsbane . . . aconite. She had gathered seeds at the end of the summer to grow the wild herb as another aid to ward off Uta's terrible arthritis, but it would take three years, at least, before the plants would come to fruition. To quicken the process, she needed to gather the roots to plant near the castle. *That* would repel the wolves that plagued her. They were becoming more daring in their forays, if her vision of the night before was any proof. When even the scent of Nikolas's wolf dogs was not enough to deter them, they were getting too bold.

And she was frightened. Their invasions into her dreams, the sense she carried with her during the day of their nightmarish battle for her mind . . . what did it mean? She could weep with frustration, for no matter how much she pondered and prayed, she still did not understand this obsession that clouded her mind and pounded in her heart. Wolves.

The uneasy feeling was growing again as she neared the forest, that sense of being watched, spied upon. Ridiculous.

She was allowing herself to become fragile and precious about her feelings, and she would not let what Uta had said about her—after speaking about her feeling that something bad was about to happen, the old woman had pronounced that she was a seer, a visionary, but Melisande would not give countenance to that—to infect her with some sense of self-importance. She was just Melisande, as she always had been, and her only gift was that she listened well, was sympathetic to people's ills and had some ability to make them feel better with the bounty of nature.

Gathering her courage about her like a cloak, she said to Fanny, who still watched her quietly, "Let us go into the forest. Wolves are not about by day . . . that is the truth, for Count Nikolas told me it was so." Raising the hem of her cloak and stepping past the line of underbrush into the forest, Melisande led the way, basket over her arm. Fanny carried the cutters and a ball of twine in a smaller basket.

She knew the way and would not get lost. Yet that was not the genesis of her fear; with every step the sense of being watched grew stronger, and she had to grit her teeth not to stop every few paces and glance around. It was just a feeling, she reminded herself. Just a feeling, and only because she expected the feeling to occur now. She must talk herself out of it.

"Miss Davidovich?"

"Yes, Fanny?"

Melisande stepped over a mossy fallen tree and paused, looking back at Fanny, who lifted her cloak and gown and stepped carefully over the log. The girl was white-faced, and her lips were pursed.

"I . . . I have this feeling that we're being . . . watched."

Melisande swallowed hard and looked around. The day was bright but frigid, and snow still lay within the protected bounds of the forest. "We're almost to the stream," Melisande said, not willing to address Fanny's specific complaint. It was too familiar to her and worrisome in its similarity to her own feeling.

"All right, miss, please, let us just go on and do what we must."

Melisande examined her face, and satisfied that the girl was still controlled and calm, they continued, her ears alert for every sound. She heard a rustling nearby but tried to ignore it. A small animal, likely, just emerging from its winter hibernation. Or a bird disturbed by their presence.

And then she heard another sound, a tap-tap-tapping. What was that? She tried to listen even as they made their way along a rudimentary path that led through the woods. Something fell in front of her from a tree, and she cried out and jumped back, but it was just a clump of snow, melting off the higher reaches of the trees from the strengthening spring sunshine. The two young women progressed more quickly as the tap-tap-tapping stopped, wordless in their haste.

"We're almost there," Melisande said, her breath coming in quick gasps from their hurried progress.

And then the blood-chilling sound of a howl stopped her cold.

"What was that?" Fanny said, grabbing hold of Melisande's arm.

The howl came again, and it had an eerie human quality that chilled Melisande's blood. "I don't know. It doesn't sound . . . it doesn't sound like any wolf I've ever heard, and yet what else can it be?"

The two clung together, and Melisande realized that silence had fallen—complete silence. No birdsong, even. Was that a movement deep in the forest? Or was she seeing things?

"I will not be chased from the forest by phantoms," Melisande said loudly. "I will not!"

She marched on, a firm grip on her basket and Fanny's arm, until finally she heard the trickle of water, the melting having reached the brook that fed the Wolfbeck River, and the place where she had seen the wolfsbane the previous year. But how to identify the exact spot beneath the mantle of snow that still clung to the bank of the stream?

"I don't remember—" she began, but stopped as the eerie howl echoed through the woods again.

Fanny whimpered, her blue eyes wide and her bonnet askew as she whipped around toward the sound.

"Fanny, calm yourself," Melisande urged.

"We should have asked one of the men to accompany us," Fanny said. "Perhaps the gardener or one of his helpers."

"No! I will not explain my mission to anyone," Melisande

said, but could not further defend her actions. How could she say that among some of the serving staff, she was character- ized as a witch for her healing potions? A benign witch to be sure, and one to whom they turned when the toothache trou- bled them, but a witch nonetheless. Though she didn't believe in magic herself, she had been unsuccessful in dispelling the rumors surrounding her.

"I know," Fanny said, giving her an understanding look and squeezing her arm. "I know what the staff is saying. Let us just get what you need, Miss Melisande, and get out of these awful woods."

A half hour of scrabbling through the snow led Melisande to some roots that she was almost certain were what she needed, and she used the small trowel she had brought to dig them up. Fanny was the perfect helper, unquestioning, quick, and intelligent. "The plants," Melisande explained, "will grow so much more quickly from roots. But we must be very care- ful, and I must be sure that Count Nikolas's wolf dogs do not ingest any part of them, for it could be deadly to them." At Melisande's command, they both wore gloves to handle the plant and stripped them off once they were done and the roots were securely wrapped in rags. They began back and had gone just a short ways when Melisande realized they had taken a wrong track and were heading in the opposite direc- tion.

"I think we're going the wrong way . . . Let me look," Melisande said, and gazed up at the sky, judging from the po- sition of the sun and turning, accordingly toward the castle.

"What is that?" Fanny asked pointing behind her.

Melisande turned. In the distance was the faint hint of smoke coming from a spot in the woods. "I . . . I don't know," she said, her words catching in her throat, "but I don't think we ought to investigate. I think we ought to go . . . and . . . and quickly. I will tell the game master about the smoke we saw. It is likely nothing . . . nothing at all."

She dragged Fanny away and hustled them both through the woods back to the castle grounds, not looking back. Never had she felt as strongly that she was being watched, and never had she felt as strongly that the watcher was a malevolent force, someone—or something—she did not want to meet.

* * *

"GO you and follow that girl, find out what she does, find out why."

Magda deciphered the Russian's painfully broken German and took it to mean she was to follow Melisande, whom she had spotted as she was coming to the little hut in the woods. "I do not understand why," Magda grumbled, but did as she was bid anyway, trudging away from the shack, leaving the stew she had brought to heat in a pot on the tiny fire in the crude hearth.

The gentleman was more peculiar than she had at first thought, she realized, difficult to please, just like all men, but odd and capricious, too. He talked to himself sometimes, in his jumbled foreign tongue, and often appeared to be listening to voices that she could not hear. She caught up to and followed Melisande and Fanny back toward the castle, hanging back but keeping Melisande Davidovich's blue cape in sight. What were they doing in the forest? And what was it that the two girls had? Melisande, especially, was holding something bundled in the basket she clutched to her, and the gentleman wanted to know what it was, even more so after he had learned who she was. Though her first name seemed to mean nothing, when he heard her last name from Magda, his dark eyes had glowed, and an odd light of fanaticism had burned, and he had commanded, in his halting and broken German, that she follow the girls and discover what they had. He had seen her in the woods before, he said, and had watched as she gathered dried berries from some bushes at the edge of the forest, but now that he knew who she was, he told Magda that she may hold the key to that which had been stolen from him, for it was her father who was the thief.

She did as she was bid without question. There was something in the man's eyes that said he should not be crossed. Every day revealed some new oddity in his behavior. He now answered her owl hoot, the signal that she was approaching, with a weird wolf howl. Perhaps it was being Russian that made him so strange, but it didn't really matter. What mattered was that he must be who he said he was for he had gold and jewels; he had shown her the precious things he carried in a leather pouch close to his body. There was about him, too,

an air of command that could only come from his background
as a Russian prince. Once they were wed and back in his
proper strata of society, once he could assume his princely
robes, he would no doubt seem quite normal.

As she tripped through the woods, an awful thought occurred to her. Perhaps all Russians were just like him, with
long fingernails and hair, tattered clothes, and enjoyed
howling like wolves. What kind of court would that be, she
thought. But no, it was just his lack of a proper valet and the
comforts he was accustomed to that caused him to look as
he did and live so. She had seen another Russian, the one
who had come to her father's inn, and he had appeared normally clothed, if rather scruffy and frightening, with a sinister and threatening air.

Being robbed of his proper place in the Russian court had
changed the man she served, but being restored to that position would allow him to live like a prince again, and then . . .
then she would live as his princess, with furs and jewels, rubies perhaps, and sapphires. Wouldn't Charlotte von Wolfram
be jealous! Then she would not hold her nose so high in the
air. Magda would, perhaps, even invite Charlotte to stay with
her at the summer palace.

They would attend balls, Magda thought, her pace slowing
as she wandered along a broken path, and she would introduce
Charlotte everywhere as her German friend, her best friend
from childhood, she would say, with some truth. Once, long
ago, they had played together occasionally, when her mother
had worked up at the castle. But that had ended, and now
Charlotte would barely deign to speak to her when she came
down to shop in the village. As a Russian princess though . . .
then Charlotte would have to defer to her and acknowledge
Magda's superiority.

Now, where had Melisande gone? Magda looked around,
her blurred and dreamy vision clearing. She had lost sight of
her quarry . . . *damn* her foolish daydreams. She would just
make up what had likely happened when she told the gentleman the tale. Or . . . *or* she could go to the castle and try to
discover what they had in the basket. That must have been
where they were headed, after all. Magda cast one glance
back into the forest. The Russian gentleman would be so

pleased with her, would he not, especially if she discovered something of value? Perhaps he would even reward her with one of the jeweled pieces he kept concealed on his person.

Her mind made up, she trudged on to the light beyond the fringe of forest.

Chapter 8

"THOUGH IT is still far too early to plant the garden, I can start these roots in a pot," Melisande said, as she and Fanny entered the castle, discarded their capes with a bowing footman and headed toward the conservatory. "Then, when the garden is prepared, they will have already begun to grow."

"I'm not sure I understand, miss, what this plant will do?"

"Aconite is a powerful herb that can be used in an ointment to aid arthritis, which is the ailment poor Countess Uta suffers. My grandmother suffered so, and I am well aware of all the remedies."

"But last autumn you said you feared this plant. This is the one with the hooded appearance, is it not?"

"Ladies," Count Gavril Roschkov said as he entered the great hall by way of the huge carved oak doors under the gallery. "Where have you been on this blustery April day?" He rubbed his long-fingered hands together and smiled gently, his gaunt face pale. "It is far too cold for such delicate blossoms to be exposed to the raw spring air."

Melisande was saved from having to reply to Fanny's uncomfortably precise memory by the count's fortuitous entrance, but just as she was opening her mouth to speak, a loud rapping filled the great hall, and Steinholz, the butler, rushed to the door. This was not a common occurrence. Melisande looked toward the huge doors expectantly.

"Magda!" she exclaimed.

The mayor's daughter, dressed warmly in sturdy boots and a thick gray cloak that was rimmed along the bottom with snow, entered. Her pretty face was set in a determined expression. "Hello, Miss Davidovich," she said, with a quick curtsey.

"Did you . . . walk all the way up here?" Melisande asked in German, shifting her basket of wolfsbane roots to her other arm. She turned to Fanny and handed her the basket, murmuring to the maid to take it to the conservatory and she would be along in a few moments.

Magda's gaze followed Fanny, but then she said, "Yes, I walked up from the village. My father had need of the cart today. Deliveries, you know."

"It is terribly cold to walk so far, Magda."

"Oh, I don't care about a little cold." Her eyes had an odd avid look, and she examined every inch of the great hall, her glance darting everywhere, but finally settling on Melisande.

"Still, you should have waited to visit until your father was able to spare the cart." Melisande turned to Count Gavril Roschkov and made the introductions, adding, "Fräulein Brandt's father, as well as being the mayor of Wolfbeck, is the local brewer and hosteler."

"What is going on here?" Christoph, with Kazimir Vasilov, descended from the upstairs, both dressed more casually than proper and each with a sword in his hand. Steinholz, the butler, who had disappeared upstairs the moment he allowed Magda to enter, stood on a step just above them with a worried expression on his round face as he panted and grasped the baluster, trying to catch his breath.

Magda, her face white, curtseyed, but appeared to have run out of things to say. Melisande frowned and examined her, then turned to Christoph. "Magda has come for a visit, so perhaps I ought to call Charlotte and we will take tea together." The etiquette of the moment was tricky. Melisande was still, in a sense, a guest in the castle, and felt a little odd suggesting it, especially since Magda Brandt had never visited the castle before in such a manner. As the daughter of the mayor, Magda was of the foremost family in the village, but the villagers and those of the castle rarely interacted.

Christoph descended the rest of the way, and his puzzled glance took in Melisande and Magda, and the refined Count Roschkov. "Magda, what are you—"

"I just came to speak to Miss Melisande," she blurted out, and came toward her. "We could go wherever you were about to go . . . after . . . after Fanny," Magda said to Melisande.

"All right," Melisande said. It was the best solution. Far better than a stilted conversation between Charlotte and Magda would have been. Charlotte, very aware of her elevated position in the small world of Wolfbeck society, treated Magda with open disdain at best, aloof coldness at worst. Strictly speaking, her behavior was correct, but it was poorly done all the same. No young lady of breeding should act so contemptuously of anyone, even someone so far below her status. Melisande led Magda away, toward the conservatory, where Fanny had gone with the basket of wolfsbane. She glanced back once before exiting the great hall to find Count Kazimir Vasilov's steady gaze on her. She turned away, the memory of their meeting the previous night bringing heat to her cheeks and a flush to her whole body.

"What is it you wished to speak of?" she asked Magda, as they entered the conservatory.

Fanny was by the potting bench finishing the work she had set herself earlier, of labeling the pots in her careful script, using the Latinate names with which Melisande had provided her. The basket awaited Melisande, the root still wrapped.

Magda followed, wordless, watching her eagerly. What was wrong with her? She had been odd lately, the last couple of times Melisande had made her way down to the village. At first it had seemed that the girl was depressed of spirits, but lately it had reversed, and Magda appeared to be excited about something, like she had a secret too big to hold onto for long. Perhaps she would reveal it now. Melisande led the way to the potting bench and the covered basket. There was no reason in the world not to do what she needed to do; the wolfsbane was just a root like any other.

"Of what did you wish to speak, Magda?" she repeated, as she donned gloves and pulled the wrapped root out of the basket.

"I . . ." The young woman cast a sly glance at Fanny and then made a moue of distaste. "It is . . . personal, Miss Melisande." She cast a look of disdain at Fanny. "I do not speak in front of serving staff."

Melisande bit back a hasty reply. Magda, as daughter of the town mayor, was very conscious of her own place in society, perhaps a little too conscious, just as Charlotte was of her elevated position. These girls! If they had any idea of what lay outside the insular confines of their tiny village, they would know how unimportant they were in the great wide world. Melisande remembered a little of French society, having been an observant child from a young age. Those whose good opinion was worth courting were often the most polite, even to those far beneath their own position in society.

Fanny curtseyed and said, in English, "I would be happy to go attend to the needs of the elder ladies, Miss Davidovich, if I am in the way here."

Replying in the same language, Melisande said, "Don't be silly, Fanny; you know you are never in the way. But Magda does seem to have something on her mind. Perhaps go, as you say, and offer your services to Frau Liebner and Countess Uta."

Magda narrowed her eyes at the unfamiliar words in a language for which she had no use. English, she had oft told Melisande, sounded slippery, like a fish one tries to hold but it wriggles from one's grasp. Fanny exited, with just a murmured word of leave-taking.

"Now, Magda, what is it?" Melisande was not feeling too charitable at the moment and was weary of indulging everyone's precious sense of self importance. But the German girl now seemed in no hurry to talk. She stared at the basket and bit her lip.

"What is it?" Melisande asked, sharply, pausing in her work.

Magda started. "I . . . I . . ."

Melisande, impatient, began to unwrap the knobby root from its protective layer of blue cloth. Magda watched, eyes wide open, staring. What was wrong with her? When Melisande pulled out the dirt-encrusted root, Magda fell back with an exclamation of surprise, sitting on a stool. Pulling out a large clay pot from under the potting bench, Melisande frowned as she went about her task and said, "Magda, I'm sorry, but I have little time for guessing games. Did you truly have something serious of which to speak?"

"What is that?" Magda asked, pointing one long finger at the root.

"It is . . . aconite," Melisande said, preferring to give the less common scientific name.

"Oh. What does it do?"

"It's an herb; it will grow and provide a remedy for Countess Uta's awful problems with her hands and other joints."

"Oh." She appeared disappointed. "Where did you get it?"

"In the woods. Is that all?" Melisande asked, finally reaching the end of her patience.

"Yes. I must go now; Mama will need help in the tap room." Magda jumped up and fled the room.

Melisande watched her go, so astonished she could not even give voice to her surprise. What was that about? One more mystery among many. She had had enough of mysteries, though. As she troweled some earth into the pot, she determined that she was going to discover what was behind those mysteries in the household that directly concerned her. Unfortunately, that seemed to be most of them.

"YOU are really very good," Kazimir Vasilov said to young Count Christoph von Wolfram, his voice echoing in the marble-floored exercise room. He put one hand over his heart as he caught his breath. They had been at it all afternoon, and it was more exercise than he was accustomed to. "Far better than you indicated when I offered you a practice duel."

"My uncle would have me believe I am lazy and undisciplined. He wished me to join the army, but I refused. I fear I have been nothing but a source of dissatisfaction to him," Christoph said, laying aside the sword with which he had been fencing. He had barely broken out in a sweat despite the vigorous nature of their duel.

Kazimir handed his weapon to a waiting footman, who bowed and took it and Christoph's to be cleaned properly by the cutler, who in this household doubled as the swordmaster, sharpening and cleaning the blades. The amenities of the castle were very civilized, far more than Kazimir was now used to, having lived a nomadic life for the past several years, and it was comfortable to have good servants. Perhaps he would take advantage and bring his personal appearance to a more elegant state once more, as the supercilious butler had indicated he might want to do before dinner in a polite family. It was not that he wished to make a better impression on the lovely Miss Melisande Davidovich, he thought, pushing aside that notion, but since the elder Count von Wolfram had seen that there would always be trained gentlemen's gentlemen available for family members, he could avail himself of their services to see to his shaggy hair. Kazimir eyed Count Christoph. "If he disparaged your ability, then Nikolas is a worse judge than I remember him to be."

"What was he like, my uncle, when he was younger?"

Grabbing a cloth from another waiting footman, Kazimir wiped his damp brow. "He was a man all of us younger fellows respected. Nikolas von Wolfram was a natural leader, and though he could have belonged to any set, he gathered about him some of us who were at loose ends and therefore in danger of becoming dissolute wastrels." It was unfortunate that Kazimir did not stay under his influence longer, or his life may have taken a very different turn, he thought.

"Ah, yes, my uncle, always the very picture of perfection," Christoph said.

There was a bitter edge in the young man's tone. Though he was cultivating the count's friendship as a way to get closer to Mikhail Davidovich, there was something appealing in the lad. Perhaps it was a remembered sense of inferiority with which Kazimir had struggled at the same age. "He has not become smug, has he? That would be too bad."

"No, he is not smug. Smugness would be an imperfection, and my uncle has not one single blot on his character. That would be human." Christoph dabbed at the faint line of perspiration on his upper lip and then tossed his own cloth back to a waiting footman. "I'm sorry; that was very cross sounding, and a personal observation only. May I offer you refreshments in my uncle's library, Count Vasilov?"

"Certainly. But I feel we are to be friends. Can we not just pass over the formality of address? I am Kazimir to those who accept my friendship."

"And I am Christoph," the younger man said, holding his hand out. They shook. "That would be good, sir. I will therefore meet you in the library in half an hour or so."

It was more than that before Christoph sent word to the

Russian that he awaited him, but in truth, he was uneasy about invading his uncle's retreat. And yet as the master of the castle, he certainly had the right, if anyone did. The Russian count was ushered in by a footman, and Christoph greeted him, indicating a seat in one of the chairs near the fire. There was something about Kazimir Vasilov that intrigued him, and he was intent on discovering what it was. Also, there was clearly more to the Russian's visit than he was even saying. He, Count Gavril Roschkov, and Mikhail Davidovich were entwined in some deep mystery, and it was time Christoph discovered what it was.

The two men spoke for some time, but then Christoph made a decision to dig for the information that was not being offered willingly. "I have allowed you to stay here, sir, for you said that Count Gavril had a sinister purpose in befriending Davidovich. Since then, however, I have seen no proof of your assertion, nor any evidence that Roschkov is dangerous." Christoph felt a growing confidence in what he was doing. It seemed that since transforming, everything was sharper, his sight, his sense of smell, and his belief in his own ability to do what was necessary for his family and friends. "What is going on between you?"

The man accepted more brandy, offered by a footman presumably unable to understand of what they spoke, since they both used English, as dictated by Christoph's absent uncle.

"I have known Count Gavril Roschkov a long time, Christoph."

"Yes. So what brings you both here in search of Mikhail Davidovich?"

Kazimir Vasilov stared at him. "You seem . . . different from the first moment I met you. Why is that?"

Different. Was it so apparent? He needed to speak to his aunt, Countess Uta; he needed to figure out how much of him was wolf, how much man, and how to balance the two halves so it would not be obvious to those who knew him that he had experienced such an overwhelming change. "I have not altered in such a brief time, you are just seeing a different side of me, perhaps. Please do not evade the question. Why do both you and Count Roschkov seek Mikhail Davidovich?"

The man still stared at Christoph, his dark eyes holding

puzzlement. "In truth, I am not certain why Gavril seeks Davidovich. But as I told you, I fear that he has no good end in mind."

"Why do you think so?"

"Gavril Roschkov has never been the same since the death of someone whom he loved more than any other, his sister. His actions since then have often puzzled me."

"And what does that have to do with Mikhail Davidovich?" Christoph asked sharply.

"I don't know."

"Then how are you connected with him?"

"His beloved sister and my elder brother, both now dead, were man and wife."

Just then another footman came to the door, bowed low, and announced that the ladies were gathered and dinner was served in the dining room.

Chapter 9

DINNER THE night before, in Melisande's opinion, had been unbearably awkward. Count Kazimir and Christoph had entered together, and Count Gavril appeared disturbed by that. Conversation was disjointed at best, absent at worst. Charlotte vainly tried to preside at the dinner table as her Aunt Adele would have, directing a smooth flowing conversation, but became irritable when both Russians appeared to vie for Melisande's attention. She then lapsed into brooding silence that could not be broken by any amount of cajoling on Melisande's part. Though they were all to sit in the drawing room after, and Christoph pointedly asked Melisande if she would play the piano for their guests—he earned a dark look from his sister for not including her in the request, for she loved to sing and enjoyed showing off her voice—Melisande pled a headache after the long day and went directly to bed. She just could not deal with Count Vasilov's steady gaze, Charlotte's moody behavior, and Christoph's brooding watchfulness. For once she had no nightmares of wolves, just an agonizing dream of her grandmother that left her weeping into her pillow and feeling a lingering sadness through her morning chores in the stillroom.

Now she was going to do her duty, and usually her pleasure, by going to sit with Countess Uta after lunch. Melisande could feel Uta's bleary gaze on her as she came in and sat by the old woman, a book in hand. She had intended to read to the countess, but had a feeling that would not be what was needed or wanted. The old woman had been acting very mysterious the last couple of days. She asked many questions about the two Russians and about her father's involvement with them but seemed especially interested in Count Kazimir Vasilov. Melisande had no reason to think the questions would stop.

She was right.

"I haf never liked Russians," Uta said.

"It is wrong to dislike someone based solely on their country of origin," Melisande said, taking her seat and clutching the book to her chest.

"Pah! Do not say to me such words, girl. I will dislike dem if I care to. What think you?"

"I . . . I don't quite know what I think."

"You do! Dis one I haf heard of, the big, dark one with the scar, he has got you interested, yes?"

Melisande shifted uneasily, remembering the feel of Count Vasilov's warm breath on her neck and the sense of her heart thudding, as if it would leap from her breast, at his nearness. She supposed that was what she was trying to avoid by not being in his company too much, the devastating attraction she felt toward him. Was it really attraction, though, or something else? Fear, perhaps? But why? She would rather talk of anything else, and so introduced the first subject that occurred to her. "Countess, wolves only hunt at night, is that not so?"

The old woman shrugged but did not question the rapid change of subject. "So it has been thought, but dey are also in woods during daylight, I haf heard. So . . . dey are perhaps out in both day and night. Why do you ask such a thing?"

"Yesterday I was in the woods with Fanny getting another herb I hope will help with your joint pain, and we were startled by something. I didn't know what it was, but then we heard this odd howling. It didn't quite sound like an animal . . . but what else could it be but a wolf?"

Uta was silent for a long minute. "Dis I cannot say."

"They frighten me so," Melisande mused. "I don't know why. It is just that . . . those dreams . . . the wolves . . . and then hearing the howling in the forest in the middle of the day . . ." She glanced over at her old friend; she appeared so weary, more so than was normal. "Are you feeling unwell? Should I call Mina?"

"No!" Uta put up one wrinkled hand, then reached out blindly with the other. Melisande responded by putting her own in the woman's grasp. "My own girl, listen to me good. I haf felt for some time your . . . your . . . how does one say the word in dis dreadful language . . . ripening, perhaps."

Melisande felt the heat rise to her face. Despite her affection for Countess Uta, the old woman's bawdy notions and speech occasionally embarrassed her. She tried to pull her hands from the countess's grasp.

"No! Do not pull from me! *Stille, liebchen.* You need husband soon, and I thought perhaps Christoph was the one for you." She frowned and muttered under her breath. "I was misled, I think, by my own wish to keep you here. Not good to think of my own desires, but nefer mind dat. But dis Russian, dis Count Vasilov . . . what think you of him?"

Successfully regaining her own hand, Melisande sat up straight and clutched the book even more tightly to her breast. "You have not met Count Vasilov. He is hard to understand at times. His motives are . . . unclear. I think perhaps that Count Gavril Roschkov is more . . . he is gentler, and more polite. The other gentleman stares so, and . . ." She didn't know what else to say.

"Ah, so the big one, he frightens you. Dis is not reason to dismiss him. Only maidenly fears. Is natural. Oder one, I haf heard from the little girl, Fanny, is thin, pale, sickly. Do not wed sickly man or he will gif you only sickly children. Or no children."

Impatient in the face of such nonsense, Melisande said, to change the subject yet again, "Do you wish me to go on with the story I began reading to you? The one Frau Liebner gave me?"

Petulant, Uta turned her face away and glared with her almost blind gaze toward the window. "No. If you will not listen to me, go away."

"I didn't mean—I'm sorry, countess. Please, don't be angry." She took in a deep breath. "But . . . but you cannot interfere in my life. I will not allow it." The other woman was silent. "Countess," she said, more gently, "Uta, you don't understand. There is much there that I cannot fathom. The two Russians . . . there is something between them, some antagonism, and yet some connection. I can feel the link, and yet they are at daggers drawn all of the time. They say things in each other's presence, and there is some hint of . . . of struggle. They came here looking for something, and it has to do with my father, but no one will tell me what it is. I cannot think of trivial things such as lovers and marriage when this is happening."

Frau Liebner entered the room and approached. She glanced from Melisande to Uta and back. "Is she being captious this morning, you poor girl?"

"Of course not, ma'am. But I fear . . . I fear I have tired her. I will go now, if you are come to sit and talk with her." Melisande rose and curtseyed to the two ladies, but Countess Uta merely gave her a frosty nod.

In a thoughtful mood, she went to find Charlotte, but she and Fanny were deep in some discussion. Not wishing to interfere, and feeling somehow that she was not wanted, by Charlotte, at least, she left them alone. She had to get away from the castle. It was spring, and finally the snow was gone from the lane. She had no wish to explain to anyone, but she simply had to get away from the castle for a few hours. The chemist in the village had some of the things she needed to distill her potions—pure alcohol, glycerine for the salves—and so to the village she would go.

Alone by choice, taking not even Fanny with her, Melisande set out in a small pony cart kept specifically for the ladies of the castle. The day was brilliant if still cold, but well wrapped in a cloak and scarves, she set the old pony trotting and made her way to Wolfbeck over the sparkling river in quick time.

The ostler of the tavern nodded and smiled when she left her cart with him, and finally feeling free to breathe and calm down, she set about her business, visiting the chemist, buying a length of ribbon for Fanny from the milliner, and then just walking the steep street, the timbered houses and shops crowding over the walkway in quaint fashion. She was enjoying the respite from the tensions of the castle.

And yet even here, in the safety of the village, she felt that sense of being watched and several times looked over her shoulder, only to find nothing. Surely she had had enough turmoil in her life that she did not need any more. Wolfram Castle had been a place of refuge for her, though it was all an illusion, she now knew. The peace she had found there was purchased with other people's suffering, in particular poor

Christoph. She could not imagine why Countess Uta should think her a fit match for him. In status it was perhaps not unheard of, but she felt nothing for him but a sisterly interest. For a moment she wondered if Uta's plans were prompted by some indication of interest from Christoph, but she discarded the notion. Christoph had been kind to her, but surely she would feel if there was any interest from him beyond that.

With the end of the family's turmoil and the blooming hope of some normalcy in the castle, the uncertainty of her own life had come back to her. Her life was destined to be difficult, the gift of her father's sins, perhaps. He was up to something, but would not confess what, nor would he tell her what frightened him. Though he resolutely refused to see Count Vasilov, saying he had nothing to speak to him about, he never gave her any reason for his behavior. He was determined upon some course of action, that she was certain. She didn't know how she knew, she just did.

As she moved back toward the tavern to reluctantly reclaim her pony cart—she could not put off returning to the castle any longer—she saw a familiar figure slumped against a wall. Magda Brandt! Melisande quickened her pace. "Magda," she said, coming to the young woman and putting her arm around her shoulders. "What is wrong, you poor girl?" she said to her in German. "What is it?"

Magda looked up, and her pale face, framed by disorderly blonde locks, was tear stained. "Miss Melisande . . . oooh!" She clutched her hands. "I just had a bad turn . . . not . . . not feeling well."

"Let me help you home," Melisande said, and guided the girl toward the tavern and up the stairs that led above it to the Brandt's comfortable, though not lavish, home.

Magda's ineffectual mother rushed forward and crooned over her only child, guiding her to the fireside seat, a bench of rushes. While the woman made something to drink, Melisande sat down at her friend's side. She pushed back the blonde curls and cradled Magda's cheek in her palm. "What's wrong? Is it a physical ailment or—"

"Just . . . just a bad turn." The girl clutched her stomach.

Frau Brandt brought her daughter a soothing drink. Melisande could smell the green herbs steeped and identified the stomach-soothing qualities of mint and chamomile. She nodded in approval at the older woman, who faded away to her tidy kitchen area just a few feet away from the fire. "Perhaps you ought to lie down for a while, or—"

"No. Father will need me in the tap room."

There was silence for a moment. "Perhaps I should go," Melisande said, moving to stand.

"No! Please stay. Talk to me!" Magda clutched her hands and dragged her down to sit by her side.

"All right," Melisande said, not unwilling to be delayed from going back to the castle.

They spoke for a few minutes about inconsequentials, but then Magda fell silent, darting glances toward the kitchen area, clearly waiting for her mother to leave the room, which the woman finally did, going down to prepare the meal for those who frequented the tavern for dinner.

Melisande waited. Magda had something on her mind, that much was clear, but she did not begin immediately. Instead, she said, "So, you have company at the castle."

"Yes."

"Russians, I have heard."

"Yes, of course . . . have you forgotten? Magda, you saw them both when you came up to the castle."

The girl's blue eyes widened. "I know. Yes . . . I saw them both. So handsome the one is, despite the terrible scar. Do you not think so?"

Melisande felt the heat flush her face and knew her cheeks were turning cherry-blossom pink as she thought of Count Vasilov, his powerful presence saturating the castle so that now there was no corner to which she could go without thinking of him. "He is, certainly, but a man is not to be measured by his appearance, Magda. More important is his heart and his mind."

"Oh, yes . . . yes of course," Magda, agreed, nodding. "How is your father doing?"

"He still is not walking," Melisande said, frowning into the fire. "I don't know what else to do. I have tried every herbal potion I know of to heal him, but still my father cannot walk. I am so afraid he never will."

"Where does your father stay? In one of the guest chambers?"

"No, he has the bedchamber just beyond mine that my uncle used to have before he married Countess Adele and left for Venice. Why?"

"Oh . . . no reason. You were speaking of an herb for your father. Is that what you were bringing back to the castle from the woods?"

"No, that was . . ." She stopped and glanced over at Magda, who was watching her intently. She had almost named wolfsbane, but that was something she did not wish to divulge to anyone, her foolish dreams and growing fear of wolves. "You asked that when we spoke. Do you not remember what I said then? It was merely the root of aconite, an herb that aids in the treatment of Countess Uta's joint pain. Fanny and I have planted it, for it will grow more quickly from the root than from the seeds I collected last autumn."

"Does your father ever talk about . . . about his trouble in Brandenburg?"

"Magda! Why would he? It was terrible, being falsely accused of theft."

"But is your father not a thief? And could he not have brought something back to the castle? Have you seen anything? Has he shown you what he stole? Where did he put it? Is it still in the castle?"

Melisande felt the torrent of questions like a blow to the stomach; breathless, she stood abruptly and started toward the door. "It . . . it seems that you are feeling better, now, and I must get back to the castle."

Magda jumped to her feet and followed. "Miss Melisande, please, did I say something to anger you?"

Melisande looked back into familiar blue eyes. On her face the girl had plastered an expression of penance, but in those eyes was something else, some hidden meaning. When she went back to the castle, Melisande resolved, she was going to ask her father once again what the Russians wanted, even while she tried to figure out why Magda was asking such pointed questions, and why the girl was interested. "Not at all, Magda," she answered, stiffly. "I hope you are feeling better."

She started out the door but looked back once more. Magda was staring at her with a gaze in which some powerful emotion burned. It almost looked like resolve.

Chapter 10

THE EVENING candles burned in the formal drawing room after dinner, and they were all gathered, Melisande, Charlotte, Christoph, and the two Russian counts. This time there was no escaping for Melisande, and with her resolve hardened to try to get to the bottom of the mystery that swirled around her, she was happy enough for the chance to be in all of their company. Christoph had brought out his violin, and Melisande played the piano as Charlotte sang a plaintive Italian love song.

Though Countess Charlotte's voice was sweet, Kazimir watched only Melisande. The hunger he had begun to feel for her in the night was growing, shattering his will, breaking down his resistance, humbling him with an awareness of how much he would sacrifice for one night in her arms. He did not doubt that he would resist, but it was tempting to see how far he could break her own will, for she felt it too, and the hunger that gnawed in his gut raised his awareness of every beat of her heart and every quickening of her pulse.

Only one other time in his life had he been so enchanted, and it had led to disaster. What was it about him that he craved his own destruction? Or this time, was he seeking salvation?

He watched Melisande from a distance, how her fingers flew over the piano keys, how her body bent and swayed with the flow of the music. Her hair, dressed high and away from her heart-shaped face, glowed, the coils gleaming like the best honey from the comb, lustrous and sweet. His treacherous body ached and throbbed, arousal a mere heartbeat away in her presence.

He looked away and encountered Gavril's steady, resentful gaze on him. So it always would be, and perhaps, having done the man a grave wrong, it was just. And yet he could not let old regrets soften his wariness. Gavril had his own motives for being in the castle, and his objective was the same. Mikhail Davidovich's stolen treasure was dangerous, and whoever got to it first would wield its mighty power. Kazimir could not let Gavril have it, and he could not allow Davidovich to keep it.

Melisande, honey-sweet Melisande, was the key to it all. He hadn't decided how much she knew about her father's plans, but since he did not have access to the father, the daughter must be his tool. The old woman had told him in the night that she believed Melisande had powers. Why the elderly countess trusted him with such information he did not know; she seemed to think he was the fulfillment of some kind of predestined design. Maybe there was something in that, for the gypsy witch in Constanta had told him that to have the curse on him lifted, he needed to follow the chalice, and that had brought him here, to Wolfram Castle. Countess Uta knew what he was, so perhaps her revelation to him that she suspected that Melisande had powers was why he had been sent on this quest. Follow the chalice and find his deliverance.

So . . . could Melisande be his salvation? He shook his head. Somehow he could not see himself finding relief at the end of this journey. In the beginning he had just wanted to make sure no one else suffered from the dreadful effects of a curse such as the one he toiled under. Now he was convinced that fate was using him as a pawn in some terrible end game. While he could not believe he was the instrument of God, he would not allow himself to be the tool of Satan, and so every step must be carefully considered.

It was all too simple, in truth; he was there because Mikhail Davidovich was a thief, and Gavril Roschkov was a dangerously ill man who feared the yawning blackness of the grave. Kazimir's task was to stop a horror that would swallow more innocent people in its cavernous maw. It was simply the end of a long road, this place and this situation, a road that began with the awful tragedy that mired Gavril and him in distrust and bitterness. If he found a solution to his personal hell it would be a sweet reward, but he did not expect it.

On an impulse, he stood and drifted toward the musical

group, circling behind the piano and coming close. Melisande was aware of him. He could see the pulse beat in her throat, and her fingers trembled. He got closer still, breathing her in. Christoph, a talented and impassioned violinist, had his eyes closed as he threaded expertly through the song. Charlotte, her youthful face glowing with the love of performing, was in character as the broken-hearted Italian girl she was portraying within the love song.

But Melisande—her neck so elegant, her skin like pearl— made him greedy, and he could almost picture his thick fingers threaded through her golden hair as he lowered his face to lick her skin. It would taste like honey, and he would find satiety at last, forgetting everything but her bosom and her arms and her lovely rosy lips, the skin tender and fragrant and delicious, food for the gods. Hunger burned in his gut.

She looked up at him, her eyes full of alarm, and lost her fingering, the song faltering to a halt. Gavril stood and approached the group, as Christoph, pulled out of his trance by Melisande's faltering, stared down at her. Charlotte merely looked petulant, her rosebud mouth twisted in an ugly grimace.

"Why did you stop, Meli?" she asked.

"What is wrong, Meli?" Christoph asked her.

What *was* wrong? Melisande stared up into Count Kazimir's dark eyes. The intense force of the man was unlike anything she had ever felt in her life; she had experienced his gaze as a touch, and when that sensation had moved over her breast and across her arms, she had begun to shiver all over. It had been too real, as if he caressed her skin, naked to his touch and his view. And . . . she had liked it. The sensation was entrancing, blissful, and for one moment she had forgotten where she was and what she was doing, and so had stopped.

Charlotte pouted. "I was just about to do the high part, Meli! How could you stop just there? Now we will have to begin all over again."

Christoph, glancing from Melisande to Count Kazimir, put down his violin. "No, I think perhaps Meli is tired, Charlotte."

Count Gavril added his voice to the discussion. "I think Count Vasilov alarmed her." He said, his cultured tone holding a tone of resentment. "He was looming, and that cannot have been comfortable."

"No!" Melisande said, standing. "No, n-not at all. I think I would just prefer to talk. Let us go and sit." She guided them all to the half-circle of settees and chairs by the fireside. "You two gentlemen know each other from some time ago, is that correct?"

"Count Vasilov's brother and Count Roschkov's sister were married," Christoph interjected.

Melisande glanced at her friend in surprise. He nodded and smiled, encouragingly. "Is that true?" she asked, gathering both men in her questioning gaze.

"It is," Count Roschkov said.

"What . . . happened?"

"Both died tragically," Vasilov said, staring at the other Russian.

Melisande glanced back and forth between the two. "Together? Was . . . was it an accident?" she asked, feeling like she was treading on thin ice, gingerly stepping around awful black holes.

"It is rude to ask personal questions, Meli," Charlotte interjected, yawning. "I'm sure the gentlemen do not wish to speak of such sad matters."

"Charlotte, stay out of the conversation if it bores you," Christoph said.

"Do not tell me what to do," she snapped. "And do not try to play that you are Uncle Nikolas."

Count Gavril smiled, with a sadness in his eyes that Melisande found heartbreaking.

"Just so did my sister and I used to quarrel when we were young," he said, gently. "There was about the same number of years between us, too, four or five."

Melisande caught Count Kazimir's steady gaze on the other Russian. "So you were . . . family, you and Count Vasilov?"

"Until she made an unfortunate choice that killed her," Count Gavril said, his mild gaze becoming more intense and his voice tight with suppressed emotion.

"I don't understand," Melisande said, but neither of the Russians responded with an explanation. This was getting tedious. Christoph was watching the interaction with a tense expression on his pale face, but Charlotte was bored, yawning behind her hand. "Count Gavril," Melisande said, "what did you mean, she made an unfortunate choice that killed her?"

"He means," Count Kazimir said, "that Franziska—"

"I mean that Franziska was betrayed by someone she may have thought she could trust. Is that not so, Kazimir?" Gavril's silver eyes sparked with emotion, the first Melisande had ever truly seen there.

"Betrayed? That is a strong word, Gavril."

"And one I do not use unwisely. My poor sister suffered for her choices, and suffered unfairly."

"Now is not the time nor the place to discuss our falling out."

"Falling out?" Gavril said, rising. "Is that what you call it?" With more energy than he had ever displayed, he crossed swiftly to Kazimir and slapped his face, the sound ringing out in the quiet drawing room. He turned then, with military precision and bowed to the others. "I beg your pardon, but I find I cannot be in the same room with this man with civility and so I will remove myself. I am very sorry. Count Christoph, Countess Charlotte, Miss Davidovich, excuse me." He glided across the floor, swung the door open and left the room.

Melisande turned to Count Kazimir, who had not responded to the insulting gesture, though he would have been within his rights to demand satisfaction. His scarred face looked wooden. "What did that mean, sir?" she asked.

He gazed at her without expression. "It means that we see a tragic episode very differently, Miss Melisande."

Their eyes locked, and she searched him, trying to see beyond the hard façade. "And how is that? Why do you see it so differently?"

"I'm not sure, but though we both suffered a loss, he of his sister and I of my brother, it did not affect us equally. My brother died after his wife, and in a sense, it was . . ." His hooded eyes seemed thoughtful as he paused, but then he finished, saying, softly, "It was a release of a sort for my brother. A blessed release."

"Because . . . he had lost his wife?" Christoph guessed.

"You might say that," Count Kazimir responded.

But Melisande thought there was more. He was closed to her, like a locked jewel case, with no indication of the contents, whether refuse or riches. "Why does Count Gavril say you betrayed his sister?" she whispered.

Kazimir merely shook his head. "It is not my tale to tell. But I will say this: I think the tragedy has changed him from the noble man he once was into a bitter and dangerous fellow." He looked toward Christoph. "I have told you this, and I stand by my words."

"Why don't you just tell us what is going on?" Melisande cried. She leaped to her feet. "What is it? Why are you both here?"

He gazed at her steadily. "Why don't you ask your father?" he asked quietly. He stood and bowed. "I think I have trespassed long enough on your good graces, ladies, Count Christoph." He swiveled on one heel and left the room.

"What rubbish," Charlotte said, flinging herself from the chair. "It is all melodramatic nonsense, like the silly puppet shows that amuses children. You will see," she said. "There will be nothing at all behind it, just like that puppet show." She flounced from the room with just a "goodnight" called out to both of them.

"What is wrong with her lately?" Melisande asked Christoph.

But he didn't answer. He was gazing steadily at her. "Melisande," he said, taking her hand. "Could we talk for a moment?"

"Please, Christoph," she said, tears coming to her eyes. "I can't think of anything right now. It is all so confusing. Papa is hiding something, and I don't know what it is. And Count Kazimir and Count Gavril . . . what are they really here for? I have to find out. Goodnight, Christoph." She hastened from the room, unable to bear another minute of talk. Her father had a lot of explaining to do. There was something behind all of this, and he must know at least some of it, for he was involved, perhaps innocently. When she entered his room, he was reading by candlelight one of the books she had found in the ladies' library, a weighty tome on astronomy.

He glanced up. "Ah, Melisande, so you deign to visit your

troublesome old papa." He sighed and set the book aside, closed with a paper to mark his place.

"Papa," she said, refusing to be drawn by his complaints, "the time has come for you to tell me the truth. I feel certain that the Russians are here because they think you have something . . . something you stole." She had long pondered the situation, and it was the only thing that made any sense at all, but even then, she could not understand the need for such utter secrecy. "What is it?"

He turned his face away.

"And if they think you have it, why can they not just be honest about it? Papa, listen to me!" she said, leaning over the bed. "What is it that is so important they both want it but will not speak openly about it?"

Her father grabbed her wrist. "Shht! Be quiet." He glanced beyond her to the door, which stood ajar. "Have either of them said aught to you?"

"No!" She paused, remembering Count Kazimir's earnest expression as he told her to ask her father. "Not . . . not really. That is why you must tell me," she said, trying and failing to get her wrist from his surprisingly strong grasp. His face was white in the candlelight, and beads of sweat formed on his high-domed forehead, from which his lank hair was tossed back.

"Tell me, daughter, why have you not yet brought to me the rosary I gave you? I told you I wanted it. I need . . . I need to pray."

Melisande finally pulled her arm from his grasp and rubbed her wrist. She watched her father's eyes. He was terrified, though he struggled to overcome his fear. Who frightened him . . . Count Kazimir Vasilov or Count Gavril Roschkov? Though he had claimed Count Gavril as his friend, he still did not wish to be alone in the room with him, it seemed, for always he demanded that she be present when the man was visiting.

But he would not see Count Kazimir at all, and in fact trembled at the very name. An awful thought struck her in that moment, and she wondered that she had not thought for it before. Was Count Kazimir the Russian who had beaten him so severely in the jail in Brandenburg? The question trembled on her tongue, but she turned her face away. Knowing it was true would be more awful than not knowing at this moment. Why, she was not sure; what did she feel for the man? How had he become important to her after only casual contact, moments of sensation, brief seconds of powerful emotion? There was something dark within him that frightened her and yet drew her like a magnet. His sheer vitality, the intensity of his physical presence, made her blood pump and her heart race.

She could not afford to feel anything for him, though, not now, and perhaps not ever, and so she put away all thought of him. Instead, she turned back to her father and said, "Please, Papa, just tell me. What is it? What do they want from you?" She briefly thought of his plea for her rosary, but that could not be it. He had given her the rosary ten years before, and this trouble was recent, of that she was certain. "What is it, Papa?" she whispered.

He shook his head. "Melisande," he said, his tone casual. "I heard the servants speaking outside my door. One of them said to the other that there was a poacher in the woods . . . that someone had seen smoke. Is that true?"

She stared at him. "Please . . . don't try to change the subject. What do the Russian counts want—"

"But is it true?"

"That there may be someone in the woods? Well, I suppose. I saw smoke. I have heard things. I thought it was my imagination. What does it matter?"

He shook his head but didn't answer. "My darling," he said, with real tears standing in his eyes. "I have been a terrible father to you. No matter what happens, always know that I loved your mother, and I would give anything if I could trade places with her in the grave."

"Easy words for you to say," she said, examining his sallow, gaunt face in the candlelight, "but—"

"No! Not so easy for someone as selfish as I have always been. But know this . . . whatever I do from now on will be done to better your life."

"Even going to Russia? Papa, I'm frightened. Russia sounds like such a harsh place."

"Yes, and it can be, but when one has the protection of

someone powerful, one need never fear." His eyes widened. "Power is everything!"

He was speaking of Count Gavril. So he trusted him that far. She sat on the edge of the bed. "Please, just tell me everything. I feel there is some story here that you are not relating."

"That may be true, but what I do now, I do for your good."

A trill of fear rippled down her back. "What is going on? Why won't you *tell* me?"

He sighed and looked away. His expression, when he looked back at her, was resigned. "My dear, all will be well soon, I promise you this, and then I will be able to tell you everything. Now go on to bed."

She stood and regarded him steadily. She now had no doubt about one thing; her father had stolen something, something that he felt had enough value that it was somehow going to provide for her future. She was equally certain that he was determined not to tell her what it was until he had brought to fruition some plan.

"So you will not tell me what is going on?" she said, one last time.

"Going on?" He shrugged and made a face. "There is nothing to tell. Nothing at all."

She sighed—nothing to tell. Well, she could not force him to confide in her. "Goodnight, Papa. I'll leave you to your book. When do you want to try walking again?"

He twisted his face in a grimace. "I will walk soon, I promise, Melisande. Go. Run along."

She headed toward the door.

"But . . . bring me the rosary tomorrow . . . please, Melisande," he begged.

She paused, hand on the doorjamb. His request made her uneasy, and she didn't quite know why, but she did know that she would not be bringing him the rosary. "Goodnight."

She left him resuming his reading, but once in the hall, she could not just tamely go to her room and sleep. She felt jittery, as if every nerve in her body was singing with tension. The castle was almost silent, with just the occasional doors closing as servants finished their work and went to their well-deserved beds. Perhaps, she thought, holding her candle high, she would go down to the conservatory and check on her newly potted wolfsbane. Was it an excuse to avoid having to seek sleep? Perhaps. Sleep did not hold for her the rest it should, while wolves invaded her dreams.

She slipped along the hall to the gallery and then descended the wide grand stairs that wound down to the great hall. The candle flame flickered as a breeze raised the short hairs at the base of her neck. Another door somewhere closed, and she felt a riffle of fear, but stoutly told herself she was being ridiculous . . . until, that is, her candle flame puffed out.

She stopped at the base of the stairs and thought, as darkness enclosed her, what to do. Go back up? She could feel her way, likely, up to the gallery where the faint glow of a lamp beckoned. Or she could call for a servant. There would be someone somewhere still attending to the last nightly rituals. But she would feel so foolish, and she never liked to make the servants run for her. She was a guest and never forgot that, no matter how kind they were.

But the fire in the dining room would be banked for the night, no doubt, kept going to light others from the next day. She knew her way so well and knew where the tapers were. She could get one and light the candle and go on with her task. Determined upon that course of action, she moved to her right, to the overhanging gallery where the darkness was deepest. Just ten feet and she would find the door to the dining room, and then to the huge hearth where the banked fire would draw her with its heat.

Someone—or something—moved. She felt a current of air and stopped. "Who's there?" she asked, her voice quivering faintly. She steadied herself. "Who is it? Stop creeping around, whoever you are, and come out this instant!"

A bulky, dark presence approached, and she was engulfed in strong arms; lips sought hers. She struggled and beat a hard-muscled shoulder, but then she felt a rush of warmth, and a deep welling of safety, security, freedom from fear.

His lips moved down to her neck, and she threw her head back, surrendering for the moment to the overwhelming sense of suffocating need, but then her sense returned. "Stop! Count Kazimir," she cried softly, knowing whose lips caressed her, "please stop!"

He did so instantly, and released her. But he didn't say a word.

"Why did you do that?" she whispered, touching the damp spot on her flaming cheek where his kiss had left its mark. She had felt the unique shape of his lips, twisted from the scar that marred his face. She blindly put out one hand and touched his cheek; he turned his face in to her palm and kissed it.

"You wished me to," he then said, his deep, harshly accented voice a thrilling murmur in the velvet darkness.

"How ridiculous!" she said, drawing back her hand. "I did not."

"You may say so now, but I felt it earlier as you played the piano. As I watched, you felt me . . . I know it. A man knows these things, you see."

"How ridiculous," she cried, breathless at the truth of his words, remembering the caress of his gaze over her skin.

There was silence for a brief moment, then he said, "Where were you going?"

"To . . . to the conservatory to check on my plants, but my candle went out, and I was going to the dining room where the banked fire—" She stopped abruptly. She did not need to explain to him. It was disconcerting, this darkness, making her babble just to fill the void. If she could just see his eyes . . . but no. Something occurred to her. "What are *you* doing down here?"

"Please, let me guide you where you need to go. My vision in the dark is extraordinary."

"Can you . . . can you see me?" she asked, reaching out again and encountering his chest. She hastily drew her hand back.

"Oh, yes, Miss Davidovich, I can see you. You glow, as all fair beings do."

She drew in her breath sharply at the sadness and hunger in his deep voice. "Why did you really kiss me, count?"

He was silent for a moment, his breathing raspy. "The truth? I have wished to from the first moment I saw you, standing above me in the great hall, gazing down from the gallery." His murmuring voice echoed up to the vaulted ceiling and came back as a sigh.

"Really?" she whispered.

For an answer, he took her in his arms again and molded her body to his, then sought her lips, kissing her deeply with a sweet lingering touch. Intoxicating and delicious, his mouth tasting of brandy, she surrendered again, allowing her own tongue to touch his and trace the shape of his lips. She let the fog drift over her as she felt her feet barely touching the floor, her body bent to his ardor. But as his kisses trailed lower, she pulled back and staggered away from him.

"No! No, count, you must not do that again. I was foolish to allow it, for if we were seen . . ." She straightened her dress. It must have been the dark, for she would never have allowed such a transgression on her person in the light of day. Darkness was dangerous, for it induced a forgetfulness that tempted her into actions she would later regret, she had no doubt. But as a first example of what it felt like to be in a man's arms, it was treacherous food for thought, and she knew sleepless hours would be spent analyzing it until she could rob it of its power over her senses. "I think we should both go to bed . . . uh, to our rooms. I hope you have found yourself comfortable, sir, and that young Friedrich," she said, naming the boy who was training as a valet, "is seeing to both your and Count Roschkov's needs. I notice you have allowed him to trim your hair, a much-needed improvement."

A rusty sound, like a hinge that needed oiling, erupted in the dark. Count Kazimir was chuckling, and she smiled. It did not seem to her that he easily laughed or even smiled, and she had begun to wonder if the Russian temperament was even more gloomy than the German.

"What makes you laugh, sir?"

"You are such a little hostess; even in the dark after being thoroughly kissed, you can think of my comfort and valet needs, and notice my haircut!" He laughed out loud.

She bridled. "Pardon me for thinking of your needs. I will not do so again."

He sobered immediately. "My needs are far more complex than a valet," he growled, pulling her back into his arms.

But she pushed him away and returned to the comparative light of the great hall, where the moon had risen and glowed faintly through the high-arched windows that soared four stories in the front of the castle. "We should both go to our rooms, count."

"Certainly, Miss Davidovich." He had followed and took her arm, escorting her up to the gallery, where he took the candle from her and lit it from a sconce. He then bowed. "I will go to my room, and you may go to yours." He straightened, and with a faint, teasing smile, added, "Unless I have an invitation to *your* room."

She should slap him, but the smile on his face, the way it pulled the terrible scar, caught her attention, fascinating her. Reaching up, she touched it and he flinched. "No! Oh, no, do not recoil from me," she murmured, cupping her hand around his chin and thumbing the scar. She raised herself up on tiptoe and kissed the spot. "I do not know how you got it, sir, but though it makes you look decidedly wicked, it does not—" She was going to say detract from his good looks, but she stopped herself, feeling the blush rise through her. How had she come so far in such a short time?

"Goodnight," she whispered and headed up the stairs quickly, and so to her own room, where she closed the door behind her and leaned against it.

He had never answered her question, she realized, when she asked what he was doing so late at night prowling the castle. Nor had she asked the thousand other questions she should have. Instead she had been misled by hypnotic kisses that left her confused and uncertain. And yet even with that knowledge, if she was in his arms again, she knew all sensible thought would flee. For some reason his physical presence blotted out common sense. With a rueful shake of her head, she thought she must conquer that odd affliction, for it would never do to allow such trespasses from a man she wasn't even sure she should trust.

Left behind in the gallery with the faint light of the moon shining, Kazimir felt his heart rate slowly return to normal, though he could still feel the tender touch of her thumb against his hideous scar. Accosting Miss Melisande Davidovich in the dark, kissing her, engaging her in teasing conversation, kissing her again, had all been done with a purpose, to deflect her attention from what he was doing prowling the castle at a late and unsuitable hour, for she would have run into him if she had kept walking, and how frightened she would have been then! He would not hide from himself the truth; he could have simply said something to her, could have distracted her with conversation, but ah . . . kissing her! It had been a sweet departure from restraint. There was more in his attraction to her than the beauty of her face and form, but he feared pondering it, worried about the effect it would have on him.

The deflection of her attention had worked, but the toll on him had been heavy. It would have been easier to go on, easier to remember his objective, if he had not touched her. In truth, he had not told her a single thing that was a lie, for from the very moment of seeing her above him in the gallery, like an angelic presence in the heavens, he had felt the pull to touch her, to taste her, to consume her.

Other men would feel the same toward her, no doubt, and in fact young Christoph was drowning in love for her; Kazimir had already determined it was so. His rigid will had made him determine it would be best if he did not ever touch her, but now . . . now he would always know that in her arms lay blissful forgetfulness.

He could not afford that as he was working against time, his enemy. Grimly, instead of going up to his own room, he headed back downstairs and to his task, unraveling the secret life of the castle, for within that secret, the enigma he could feel at the heart of the vast structure, he felt sure lay the answer to at least some of his questions.

The riddle of Miss Melisande Davidovich, and whether she could lift his awful curse, must wait for another day.

Chapter 11

CHRISTOPH HAD not slept well; the fascination between Count Vasilov and Melisande and the scene he had witnessed in the drawing room the night before troubled him. Why had Melisande stopped in the middle of the piece of music she was playing? She never had done so before, and the look that was shared between her and the Russian was unforgettable. It haunted him still. He had tried speaking to her, but she brushed him away as if he were an insignificant gnat.

There were other things troubling him as well. He took the stairs up to Uta's room two at a time, hoping she was alone, and he was relieved to find her so. He moved swiftly across the room to the chair opposite her and sat, waiting for her to awaken from her slumber. She spent most of her time in the chair, finding it more comfortable, she claimed, than her bed.

She looked terribly gray, he noticed for the first time. Though he had never had much time nor use for his great-aunt, he had come, in the last week, to realize how much at the heart of the castle's life she was. No one living could remember a time before she was there, in that suite of rooms, holding all of the family's tales close to her heart and relating them to anyone who would listen. But she seemed to be shrinking in on herself, wizening day by day, fading to nothing, gradually.

She awoke, her tiny, bleary eyes opening. She saw him, but did she recognize him?

"Christoph! It is good that you come to me now," she said in German, her voice weak. "I feel sure I have not much time left."

"What do you mean?" he asked, panicked. When she

reached out, he took her hand, though normally he would shrink from such contact.

"Do you think I am eternal? I am old and tired. It is time, almost, to rest. But I have worried that you did not have enough knowledge, and I am glad you have come back. Tell me, have you . . . ah, but I can feel it in you," she said, squeezing his hand with what little strength was left in her. She sighed and smiled. "You have tried the wolfskin."

"Yes," he said, eagerly. "I have. It's true, I am as you said. I am a wolf!"

"Not a wolf, a werewolf, and you must remember the difference. *Never* must you allow the animal part of you to overwhelm the human side. That will be your struggle, for the animal side of you will tempt you with ease."

He frowned down at their linked hands. He could feel her life ebbing, like the tide pulling away from shore, and wished he could infuse her with some of his own growing strength. His forearms looked thicker, and one look in the mirror in the last couple of days had showed him that even his neck had cords of muscle standing out that had not been there before his transformation. "Why do I feel as if every muscle and every sinew in my body is straining, thickening, like cord braided into stout rope?" he whispered. The change in his own familiar body was unnerving, and yet there was a thrill of raw power running through him.

"That is the transformation! For the men with the potential, it gives health and strength and great recuperative powers. And your senses will be heightened."

His senses . . . yes, that was true. Now when he was near Melisande he could smell her skin, could almost taste her in the air. He trembled and thought of the few times he had been out since the first time. The transformation had become easier, though the pain and shock had not worn off. Perhaps it never would. "The first time, I was afraid I would not be able to transform back. It was only when I thought of . . . of those here in the castle that I was able."

She nodded slowly. "That is the danger, for I have heard tales . . . stories of those who never came back and who roam the forests, ever hungry, dimly remembering that once they were men."

He shivered. "It . . . intoxicates you, Uta, it fills you with this sense that life is far more simple than we humans make it, that it comes down to hunting and eating and providing for our families. That is all there is."

"You must fight such feelings, Christoph," she whispered. "For it is the devil that tempts you so. To be a werewolf is a terrible thing, for it is to walk the line between human and animal, one foot in both worlds, never truly belonging to either."

"But *why*, then? *Why* did you tell me, give me the ability to change? I could have lived my whole life not knowing, and then I would have just been who I was, Christoph, not this man-beast, with this decision to make every time I choose to transform." He could feel the split within him, like a cleft in rock, and wondered if he would ever feel whole again, one being, either animal or man. And yet the change was beginning to strengthen the part of him that was damaged by his drugging and his disgraceful sexual affair with his Aunt Gerta.

"It was more dangerous to leave you in ignorance. I had no choice, Christoph, and so you will have no choice but to tell Jakob when he becomes a man. To leave you without the knowledge of your other side would be to condemn you to a fate far worse than death, for a man with the capacity who does not choose to use it becomes the 'unchanged.' A werewolf can remain 'unchanged' his whole life if he chooses, but it creates a dreadful tension in him, for it is a denial of his true self. Eventually he will become thin and frail, he will age quickly, and so will fade, the human side unsupported by the animal side, until finally he diminishes into a wraith. There is no safe haven of the grave for a wraith. It is a living death, and he is doomed to walk the earth gray and ghostly forever, with no connection to anything or anyone."

That grim fate did sound far worse than death, and finally he understood Uta's urgency to impart the truth before she faded from life herself. She saw it as her task, and now it would be his, when she was gone. "Are the women of our family never to know the truth, never to be able to transform?"

"Women of our family have a different task, or ability, and their choice is, in a way, far more difficult and dangerous. "

Her voice had become fainter, and she finally stopped, exhaustion claiming her. Her chin sank down on her bosom, and

Christoph sat for a few minutes, petrified with fear, wondering if he had killed her with his need to know, but she snuffled peacefully for a few minutes and then awoke.

"Listen to me, Christoph," she said, grasping for his hand.

He gave it to her again and felt no disgust or distaste in doing so. Between them now there was no rift, for he accepted the burden she was even now letting go of, the burden of family knowledge and the need to pass it on.

"You must make the right choices always," she whispered. "It is a danger, for you, straying from righteousness, for a werewolf who chooses evil over good becomes dangerous even to himself. Walking down that path will eventually lead you away from the human side of you until you become something worse, even, than an animal. At least a wolf kills only to feed itself and its family. A werewolf who has lost his way back to being human kills for joy and power until he becomes thirsty just at the thought of blood. That is where the awful legends have come, of werewolves eating children and consuming blood. Those are the dangerous ones, and though they are no more terrible than the awful humans who walk among us—bloodlusty humans like Bartol Liebner was—having chosen evil, their terrible power makes them even more dangerous."

A knock sounded at the door, and then Melisande came in the room, book in hand. She smiled when she saw Christoph there. His heart pounded at the sight of her, so unexpectedly. What would she think if she knew he was a werewolf? Would she be intrigued or disgusted? It was tempting to find out, to see if he could fascinate her with his newfound strength.

"How nice!" she said, in English. "You make a striking picture, the two of you in the sunlight from the window, Christoph so fair and handsome, the sun glinting off his golden hair, and you Countess Uta, so wise and solemn, with the light on your white hair."

"A portrait of two fools, one young and one old," Uta growled.

Christoph rose and offered his seat to Melisande, but she hesitated.

"I would not like to interrupt," she said.

"No, please, we have done talking for the moment, for I

fear I have tired my aunt," he said. He crossed the room in two steps, took her hand and guided her to the chair. "I know this is a time she would be loath to miss, with such a fair lady to talk to and read to her." Her slim hand was warm in his, and he felt a surge of love swell his heart. He only just stopped himself from bringing it to his lips. It was too soon for that, but perhaps . . . perhaps he was not so unworthy. He could offer her much, after all. He was a German count, and a von Wolfram, and a werewolf. He was powerful, and she had just called him handsome. Perhaps he could become worthy enough to win her after all.

ANOTHER day in the castle had wound to a conclusion, the long hours spent by Kazimir first in riding—getting out on his mount and exploring the countryside was a blessed relief for his weary mind—but then in trying to unravel the puzzle of how to ensure success in his quest when he was among people who had no reason to trust him, and every reason, perhaps, to *not* trust him.

The night before had been a complete failure. Kazimir had returned to his search after meeting Melisande, but he was shaken, intoxicated by the encounter and reeling from the sense that he had no control over his response to her. He had gone back to his task of exploration, but his confused impressions and embattled senses left him fit for nothing but bed. Tonight would be different, for after dinner he had deliberately stayed away when the family group had gathered and had chosen instead to pace in his room until he heard the sounds of the household retiring for the evening.

It had not been easy, not after taking his meal with them all and watching Count Gavril Roschkov weave his silvery enchantment around Melisande. The man was filling her with stories of Russia, a Russia he had clearly created in his own mind and heart, a Russia of golden sunlight and simple, honest, handsome peasants, beautiful landscapes, exciting cities. The young woman was being swayed, entranced, and her uneasiness of Kazimir's poorly-hidden lust for her led her to avoid him. It was infuriating, but with Gavril's persuasiveness and access to her father, it was likely that he would eventually turn her against Kazimir. Just today Gavril had spoken hope-fully of her first foray to her father's native land; he openly spoke of his intention to take Mikhail Davidovich back and clear his reputation with the power of his own excellent name.

But Gavril would no more leave now than Kazimir would. He sought the same thing, and if his method was different— he clearly hoped to convince Davidovich that the chalice would be safer in his hands than wherever it was this mo-ment—his eventual aim was suspect. It was revenge he was after, revenge against Kazimir, but in taking his vengeance, what other horror would he mete out?

It was imperative that Kazimir find the chalice first. Where was it?

Night had long ago fallen as Kazimir crept from his room and down the stairs, standing in the gallery overlooking the great hall simply feeling the pulse of the household around him. He drew inside of himself, closed his eyes, bowed his head, and listened. At first when he had arrived, he could sense Countess Uta in her lair, her life force the center of the castle, but in the last few days she had withdrawn, as if she was weakening. Now, though, without her overriding pres-ence clouding his mind, he could sense the life of the castle it-self. Someone—or something—was awake, still, and moving about. Servants perhaps.

But no . . . servants were not furtive. Servants knew they had every right to go about their business, and did so as rap-idly as possible, aching for the reward of sleep after an ex-hausting day. This was someone who did not wish to be noticed, who had no right to be where he was or doing what he did.

Kazimir had explored the layout of the castle, which was fairly simple, laid out in a U formation, with the vast great hall, the conservatory and the chapel at the base of the U, but still he had a feeling the castle was hiding something. Some-thing that this person knew.

The darkness was no impediment, and he silently climbed the stairs again and walked the halls, feeling the occupants as they slept, or restlessly paced, in the case of Christoph von Wolfram. Kazimir steeled himself as he descended the stairs in the newer section and passed Melisande's door—her room was directly beneath Christoph's—not to pause and feel her presence. It weakened him, and he could not afford that when he was so close to discovery.

Someone was somewhere he ought not to be; it might be Gavril, for he had good reason to hide his true purpose from the castle's occupants. But no . . . Gavril's method was not the search. He was too weak to pace the halls and stairs, searching for the chalice that *must* be hidden somewhere. His method was the insidious seduction of Mikhail and Melisande, the soft weaving of words at which he was so skillful. Kazimir could not expose him without revealing his own less-than-honest self, too, and so both of them remained silent, locked in an uneasy truce of sorts, a truce that would be broken the moment one of them discovered the whereabouts of the relic.

Kazimir's greatest fear was that Gavril already had the other missing piece to the puzzle, and that was what hastened him in his quest. He paced the length of the hallway along one branch, but it was to discover as he went that he was moving away from the other soul who slipped through the castle. Who was it?

He turned back and returned down to the gallery and knew that he was going the right way now, even though he still could not see anyone, nor truly hear anything. Someone was nearby, but where?

And then below, in the great hall, he saw movement. Someone was keeping close to the walls, but heading toward the front door. The moon had just begun its nightly passage, and so the great hall was still almost pitch dark as Kazimir moved down the stairs. There! With his near-perfect sight he spotted the figure who slipped along in the darkest of shadows. Then the man paused and turned, his face catching a glimmer of the light of the rising moon.

It was Mikhail Davidovich! Kazimir reeled back in surprise. Far from being an invalid still, Davidovich moved very well on his own.

Chapter 12

KAZIMIR'S QUICKLY drawn-in breath alerted the thief, and the man whirled, peering through the dimness and seeing enough to frighten him. He stumbled away, back into the dark shadows underneath the gallery, and disappeared. But he was no match for Kazimir, surely! And there was nowhere for him to go.

Rapidly moving down the rest of the steps, Kazimir dashed to the spot where Davidovich had disappeared, but the man was gone. How was that possible? Kazimir opened the only set of doors near the spot to find the doorway led to the large, formal reception room, and he darted in, but the cavernous space was empty and cold. The man was gone. Kazimir could feel the vast, frigid emptiness of the room. As impossible as it was, he had vanished.

Striding across the space, his long step bringing him to the far reaches of the room quickly, Kazimir felt along the wall. There was only one possible explanation for someone who did not believe in magical disappearances. And when he found the crack, he knew he was right. With pressure, he found a way to slide the panel back, and there, yawning before him, was a secret passage, narrow and dark. He slipped in and was confronted by stone steps that he could dimly see rose to the next floor and twisted, disappearing around a corner.

It was true. This ancient place was threaded with secret passages. That was the secret that lay at the heart of this place, the enigma he had dimly felt even before he knew the truth.

But what to do now? Confront the thief in his lair? Demand of him the chalice?

With so much reason to remain silent, Kazimir had no confidence that even fear or intimidation would make Davidovich speak. Even threats of bodily harm would just make him turn to Gavril or Christoph. And with Christoph having no reason to trust Kazimir, and every incentive to protect the woman he loved and her father, Kazimir would find himself staring up at the castle from the outside with no opportunity to find the chalice before Gavril.

He had to play a different game than his instincts would persuade him was right. He had to use stealth. So far Davidovich did not know he had discovered the secret of the passages. Perhaps Kazimir could follow the lying thief, who still claimed invalidism to his own daughter, and so find the hiding place of the unholy and powerful relic, the Blood Amber Chalice.

But now, his patience stretched beyond his ability to bear it. He had another objective. Silently, he threaded his way back out through the reception room, to the great hall and toward the kitchen through the doors under the gallery. Ever since the curse was first laid on him, he had been plagued by the need to release the awful tension inherent in the duality of his nature. He slipped out into the crisp, clean, night air and ran across the grassy lawn down to the dark edge of the forest. He slipped past the forest edge and into the fragrant depths of a coniferous grove.

He stopped and took in a deep breath, letting it out slowly. Feeling the eager energy build within him, he slipped out of his clothes and began to run, racing along the pine-strewn forest floor, leaping logs and boulders. When the transformation hit in mid-stride, he howled as the savage joy ripped into him, the elation of running as one with the woodland creatures. The first time it had been agony, but now the change happened almost painlessly. Loping swiftly, four paws pounding the earth in rhythm and feeling other gray creatures slip through the forest just out of sight, he let the worries of the man named Kazimir slip away until he was just a wolf—a big, black wolf.

THE smell was here, on this log; bending down, nose to the damp deadwood, the part of Christoph that was human dimly felt alarm, while the part that was animal felt only a sense of urgency to find this other who invaded his realm and force him out. This was not the scent of another wolf, this was the scent of another *werewolf*, and the sense of alarm won out. Christoph loped back to where he had shed his human attire and transformed, wearily dressed, and headed back to the castle. Somewhere nearby, either in the castle or in the village, was a man who was as he was, a wolf at times. Was it right that he felt angry and alarmed? Was it his task to flush out the other and drive him away, or must he coexist with this interloper? He knew so little still. Every time he transformed, he thought of more questions to ask Uta. He would go to her immediately and ask what to do about the other werewolf and how to identify him in his manly form.

Morning sun was rising in the eastern sky, glinting merrily off the icy crystals that had formed on the long weeds at the edge of the forest. He wearily trudged home across the sward to the castle and into the front doors. The butler, impeccably dressed even at this early hour, bowed as he entered and made his way towards the stairs that led up to the gallery floor, but the sound of weeping made him stop.

Charlotte was groping her way blindly down the steps, holding on to the polished baluster. "Where have you been?" she cried out, when she saw him. "Where were you? I looked and looked, but you weren't anywhere, and—"

"Charlotte," he said, alarmed, striding the few remaining feet to the stairs and intercepting his sister as she stumbled to a halt at the bottom. He put out a hand to steady her and said, "What is it? What has happened?"

His sister fell into his arms, weeping.

"What? Charlotte, control yourself! Tell me what is wrong."

From above, over the gallery railing, came the exhausted voice of Frau Liebner, and she said as she gazed down at them, "It is my dear Countess Uta. She will not awaken. She lives, but she is in some unconscious state and I fear . . . I fear that the end is near."

The day went on in a blur. He had visited the countess's suite to find her where she so rarely had been, in her bed, under the covers, with her faithful Mina at her side. But there was nothing to do. She was 89, he discovered from Frau Liebner, who talked about her when he visited, relating how when she first came to visit the castle many years before, the countess was hale and hearty, a woman who insisted, against all advice, on climbing the stark conifer-shrouded hills beyond the castle, and who consorted with the ravens who wheeled and soared above, their harsh cries answered by the Countess Uta von Wolfram.

As was his duty, he wrote to his uncle, now likely on his way through the Alps by way of the Brenner Pass, but there was no guarantee Nikolas would receive it in time if he wanted to come back for Uta's sake. In passing, Christoph mentioned the arrival of the two Russians, stated their separate claims to his hospitality without elaborating on his suspicions and concerns, and sealed the letter with his personal seal.

The household was quiet. Melisande was taken up with her herbal remedies and with tending to the various concerns of Charlotte, Frau Liebner, and of course, Uta. The two Russian counts he had found arguing in their native tongue, but they had fallen silent upon his arrival in the room and had made only desultory conversation in English after that.

Finally worn out from concern for Uta, angry at the tension that saturated the castle, furious at the mystery that surrounded Melisande's father and the two Russians, Christoph went to the stable, took his mount, and with no real idea of what he was doing or why, he headed to the village. The simplest mystery plaguing him, he realized, was what Magda Brandt was doing in the forest in the night the first time he had transformed into a werewolf. He had been distracted from that mystery, but now it seemed like something to focus on that was simpler to solve than how his heart ached for Melisande and how jealous he felt every time one of the Russians spoke to her, or how sad he was at Uta's condition, and his fear that he would never speak to her again.

The day glittered with spring sunshine, and his heart lifted a little. If this was the end for Uta, then he was happy he had taken the time to know her better. She had always been there in the castle, but he had feared her when he was a lad and found her distasteful as he grew. Now he held her in his heart with a prayer, for she had loved her family and had worn herself out to give him the last advice he needed to be wise with his terrifying power. Now, knowing her better, he could revere her properly and mourn her sincerely, when her time came to pass into the other realm. That was a gift, and if this sadness was the result, then he would simply let it be in his heart, knowing it was a good thing and not to be rejected.

Handing his horse off to the ostler, he mounted the steps up to Magda and her parents' home above the tavern. Frau Brandt was not there, nor was Herr Brandt; there was just the little maid of all work in the home, besides Magda, but when he told the maid to fetch her mistress, the girl came back with a frightened look and said Fräulein Magda would not see him.

"What do you mean, she will not see me?" he thundered, and the girl, little more than a child, hid behind a chair and would not come out, though she muttered in broken phrases that the young mistress was ill and was seeing no one.

At that moment, Herr Brandt came clattering heavily up the stairs and stared at Christoph. "So," he said, with an unpleasant look. "What my ostler said is true. You have come to seek out my daughter."

Christoph remained silent, wondering at the tone of insinuation in the man's voice and the expression of defiant familiarity.

"If I were you, good sir, I would leave the girl alone."

"Is she truly not well?" Christoph asked, concerned for his childhood friend and surprised to find himself so.

Brandt shrugged. "Girlish fancies . . . women oft think themselves ill. Whenever something does not suit them, they claim to be ill. You know what women are like, count?"

Christoph saw a movement beyond the curtain that backed the room and for a moment, caught a glimpse of Magda, who stared, her face white, her eyes huge, before she again disappeared.

"If you like the girl, though," Brandt said, glancing toward the curtain. "I will send her up to the castle for you." He chuckled, a filthy look of knowing familiarity accompanying the gurgling sound. "She should be up there anyway."

"What do you mean by that?" Christoph demanded, but the man would not answer and only shrugged again when pressed. He was forced to leave unsatisfied or break the man's head open for insolence, which was what he really wanted to do. But restraint was vital, he had come to realize, with his growing strength. If Uta had taught him anything, it was that with his new power came a heavy weight of responsibility, and he would not let her down.

With nowhere else to go and nothing else to do, he rode out into the country to think. He had once thought his life complicated, but his werewolfism, his growing love and desire for Melisande, her approaching departure, and the interference of the two Russian counts was even more tortuous. What was he to do when there was no one of whom to ask advice?

MAGDA, bundled in a cloak but still shivering, feeling miserable and yet compelled to go out by her only hope for the future, hustled through the forest along a familiar path as she reflected on Count Christoph's appearance in her own home earlier.

What had it meant? He had never come to her home before, even though when they were all children she used to accompany her mother up to the castle when more hands were needed for some celebration or feast, at Christmas or Easter, and she had played with Charlotte and Christoph, whom she had at one time adored for his kindness to her. He had even given her one of his toys once, a carving of a wolf, and she had cherished it for a long time until her father had taken it from her and smashed it with a hammer. That all seemed so long ago, and in fact it was when his father and mother were still alive, before the awful tragedies had begun.

But why now? It alarmed her awfully; she should have taken the opportunity to talk to him, to try to get some information from his perspective of the Russian gentlemen and Melisande's father, but she had just been ill and was still feeling as if she would vomit again any moment. It was not something she wanted to do in front of Count Christoph von Wolfram. For the first time in a long time she had been glad for her father's interference, though his lewd suggestions to the count had been unbearably offensive.

There was the hut just ahead, nestled among the trees, cold and deserted looking as it must remain. She hooted softly and heard the answering eerie howl of the Russian gentleman. He spoke of wolves often and said he wished to emulate them, for they were proud and noble beasts. For her own part, she thought that a mad idea. Who would want to be like a beast in the forest if one was a Russian prince?

She pushed through the doorway into the dim interior, lit only by the open window, a heavy canvas cloth that usually covered it pulled back to give light. In the corner, huddled in a blanket, was the prince. Or at least he said he was a prince. She *had* to keep believing in him, for he was her only hope for a future away from Wolfbeck and her miserable existence, which would soon be much worse if she did not get out. She moved forward, her offering held out before her.

"Bread, sir, and cheese this time. Good cheese."

"Is that all? What about wine?" he said in his inadequate German. He was forced to keep his commands to her simple, as his grasp of her language was pitiable, but better than her complete unfamiliarity with any other language but her own.

"No, but I have brought you more of my father's beer, the finest—"

"Slow!"

"Beer, my prince." She handed him the earthenware bottle and retreated. He smelled terrible, but then he had little ability to wash as a poor wanderer, he said, until he was restored to his rightful throne with the aid of the stolen piece that proved his birthright. Then he would bathe in fragrant lavender water, and she would bathe in milk to whiten her skin, as all the great ladies did.

He grimaced at the simple brew offered to him but pulled out the stopper and drank it down greedily enough. Slowly, and with many pauses to let him understand, she told him about Count Christoph von Wolfram's visit to her home. And had she spoken to him, he asked, his dark eyes glowing like coals in the dim reaches of the hut.

"No," she answered. "I . . . I was not well, and—"

"Not well? You had a chance to find out things and did not?"

Shaking, she admitted that she had hidden away, but that her father had driven the young count to leave anyway. The Russian prince rose, and Magda cowered against the doorframe. He was tall, she realized anew; huddled in his ragged clothes in the corner he seemed smaller, frail almost, he was so gaunt, but he was very tall, taller even than Christoph, who was a fair height for a man.

"I begin to think, girl," he said, in a gruff accent, "that you are truly not helping me, that you make promises and yet are going to betray me when the moment is nigh for me to attain my rightful position and return in glory to my homeland."

"No, I would never . . . sir, you must believe I am faithful—"

"You had *better* be faithful, for if you are a lying whore," he roared, coming closer, towering over her with his dirty, claw-like hands outstretched, "I will kill you," he said, making a motion like wringing the neck of a chicken. "And then I will leave you for the wolves of the forest to rip to pieces." He threw back his head and howled aloud, wailing.

Whimpering, she scuttled out of the door, her stomach twisting in agony. She babbled that she must return and help her mother, and dashed down the path, pausing only to heave and retch, her mouth filling with awful bile.

"Get me the red cup!" he cried, coming to the doorway, holding his hand up over his eyes at the sight of the day's brilliant light. "I must have the red cup, and before the eclipse of the moon! The blood moon is coming!"

Chapter 13

THE CASTLE was nighttime quiet once again, after a long day in which the pervading sadness of the ancient countess's state had made all within reticent and sober. But Kazimir was prowling yet again, intent on discovering the route Mikhail Davidovich used to creep through the walls and downstairs. Where was he going when he did so, and why? Did it have anything to do with where he had the Blood Amber Chalice hidden?

He made his way over to the wall in the dining room, the one sure egress to the secret passages, and slid the panel back, but just then he heard a commotion. Hastily, he pulled the panel back into place and raced out to the great hall, where a terrible noise floated down to him, a crash and an outcry, and then the sound of many feet pounding down the hallway above.

A figure scuttled down the stairs and past him, a young woman, who headed directly for the front door. She shot the huge bolt back with a great effort and ran out into the night.

"What's going on?" Kazimir shouted. Above in the gallery, Count Gavril and Charlotte von Wolfram approached the railing. Confusion reigned, with more shouting and babbled questions.

"What are you doing down there, Kazimir?" Gavril said. "Is this your responsibility? Did you set the girl to this task?"

"What are you talking about?"

"That was Magda Brandt. Are you trying to say you did not let her in to steal the chalice away?"

"What? No, I . . ."

"Papa! Papa!" Melisande screamed somewhere above.

Kazimir raced up the steps toward the room he knew was

Mikhail Davidovich's. There he found the door to Davidovich's room wide open; the man was on the floor but seemed fine, and Melisande was crouched at his side.

"What happened?"

"Magda Brandt was here . . . I don't know how she got in or what she wanted," Melisande cried. "She was in my father's room! Where did she go?"

"Out," he said abruptly, trying to ignore the look of fear on Davidovich's pale face. "I will go out and find her."

"Why was she here? I don't understand."

"Nor do I." Kazimir exited, bolting back to the gallery, where he was confronted by Gavril, who grasped his arm.

"Stay out of this, Vasilov," he said, his gaunt face as pale as pewter in the moonlight that streamed through the windows.

"This is my business as much as it is yours, Roschkov," Kazimir said, pulling his arm from the man's feeble grip.

"God help you if this is a part of your plot," Gavril said. "I will not let you use the chalice, nor will I . . ."

"I do not have time to listen to your ravings. It is you who are the dangerous one and you who have been seeking the chalice ever since my poor mad brother told you the old legend of its power," Kazimir said. He left Gavril behind and raced past a frightened Charlotte von Wolfram, wide-eyed and lovely in her night rail, clutching young Fanny's arm. Down the steps he bolted and toward the front door, where Magda had exited, leaving the door wide open as a bleary-eyed butler in a gray robe stood staring at it, blinking and gaping.

"I will see what is amiss, Steinholz," Kazimir said, in German, to placate the fellow.

He bounded out through the porte cochere to the moonlit lawn. There in the dew he saw a trail left by the frightened girl. She had headed for the woods, not down the lane. Why the woods? *Never mind,* he thought, *mine is but to follow and figure it all out later.*

Senses quivering, alive to every sound, even the pounding of his own heart, Kazimir loped to the edge of the forest and paused only a moment before pushing past the brushy border and plunging down a crude path. It was tempting to transform, but there were things a werewolf could not do, and that was to seize hold of a human and question them. This was one task which required a man, not an animal. Pausing every few yards to be sure of his trail, he followed, but when he got to a silvery stream and a clearing, he stopped. Which way? He lost her trail here and could not figure out why. She must have either crossed the stream or ran down it. Those were the only two possibilities that would account for her trail going cold like this. And yet the water was freezing; what guilty secret was she concealing that she would do something so hideously unpleasant as wading through frigid water? "Damnation," he cried out loud. If he was wolf he could likely catch her scent! He was considering his options when he heard another being crashing through the forest and, prompted by some instinct, he hid behind a thick stand of brush near a clearing.

A wolf bounded into the opening and stopped, nose in the air. It was beautiful and silver, youthful, with thick fur and boundless energy. It sniffed the ground near the stream and then stopped, looking around with a weird preternatural awareness, as if it could sense his presence. The very oddness of the scene struck Kazimir, and so when the wolf, at a more leisurely pace, trotted back into the woods, he followed. Where was it going?

He did his best to keep pace but had to stop every few minutes and reassess where the beast was headed. When its path turned, finally, and the woods began to look familiar, Kazimir had an awful thought that was soon confirmed.

There, near a pile of clothes at the edge of the woods, the wolf had stopped and, head bowed, began to whimper, then fell to the ground where it writhed and groaned, then stretched and lengthened, finally transforming in the silvery moonlight into a naked human figure clutching a wolfskin pelt.

Count Christoph von Wolfram rose, shook himself, and dressed, then wearily, his head bowed in exhaustion, headed out of the woods up toward his home, Wolfram Castle.

Christoph von Wolfram . . . a werewolf! Kazimir should have known. He had sensed it in the woods but had never imagined it was the young count he was feeling the presence of. Perplexed by the various threads of this tangled mystery, Kazimir had no choice but to return to the castle.

The household roiled with turmoil until dawn, when finally some of its inhabitants rested. Kazimir had sent word through the little maid, Fanny, to Melisande Davidovich that he had not found Magda Brandt, but made no mention yet of Christoph von Wolfram and his secret. He wanted to see the young man himself first, but he was sleeping, a footman told him when Kazimir inquired, and had ordered that he not be disturbed.

And so, after fruitless hours of waiting, Kazimir slept for a few hours himself, but awoke, still wearing the same clothes he had the night before, with the perturbed sense that all was not well. Things were coming to a head, and he needed to figure out where the damned chalice was. He wanted no one else to get it but himself, and that before the eclipse of the moon, which was fast approaching.

He roamed the castle anxiously pondering his dilemma. Every choice he could possibly make was fraught with problems. The blood moon, or lunar eclipse as it was more commonly called, was just days away. When it occurred, the wicked power of the chalice would be at its height. Gavril Vasilov intended to take the chalice, use it to transform into the most foul of supernatural beings, and then would destroy him as vengeance. As much as he did not want to lose his own life, Kazimir feared what the wrath of a devious, intelligent man like Gavril would lead him to do once he had the physical power to wreak havoc. It was too chilling a fate to even consider.

Christoph von Wolfram descended to the village after learning of the event of the previous night. But his news was grim when he returned.

Kazimir watched the young count's face as he related the news to his sister and Count Gavril in the drawing room. Magda Brandt was nowhere to be found. Had Christoph von Wolfram surrendered to the dark forces, Kazimir wondered, pondering what he had witnessed in the night? Was that the explanation behind Magda Brandt's disappearance? He knew from experience the pull toward purely animal acts of self-preservation. If Magda caught Christoph in the act of transforming, or if he feared she had, would he have attacked her and killed her? "So she is just gone?" he asked, breaking the shocked silence that followed Count Christoph's news of Magda's disappearance.

"So her father says. No one has seen her since yesterday. The worst is feared. Wolves . . . wolves have long been thought to be a problem in the woods. Her father speculates that with the girl's propensity for wandering, she had been caught out late and had been attacked." He frowned. "What was she doing in the castle? What did she want? Do either of you know?" He cast his icy blue gaze from Gavril to Kazimir and back again.

Kazimir looked over at Gavril. Their gaze held.

"Well, Kazimir, do you know anything? Anything at all?" Gavril said.

Breaking the intensity of their locked gaze, Kazimir examined Christoph's pale face. Was his the mien of a killer? Had he let the lure of destruction take him over in his wolf state? He couldn't believe that. There was a purity to the young man, a nobility just as there had been in Nikolas von Wolfram.

"I know nothing of Magda Brandt's disappearance," he said. "Nor do I know what she wanted with Mikhail Davidovich. But I wish to find out, Gavril, and I think you know why. Why don't you explain to Count Christoph your real purpose here? If you do that, I will, too."

Gavril was silent. As Christoph von Wolfram demanded to know what Kazimir meant, he simply turned and walked away. Perhaps the young man deserved to know what was going on in his own home, but the explanation would be long and tedious, and Kazimir had no heart for it. There was too much else to do. First, he wanted to know if Mikhail Davidovich had any explanation for why Magda Brandt was in his room. It made no sense to him, unless she was his confederate in some way.

With that end in mind, he went in search of Melisande. Miss Davidovich, the weary butler told Kazimir, was in the family chapel.

The chapel. He well knew where it was. Even from the outside one could tell its location by the gorgeous, ancient stained-glass windows that soared the height of one of the octagonal turret portions on the front corner of the castle. The other side was plain glass only and was the conservatory, using the brilliant light that refracted within to foster the growth of the family's considerable flower and herb gardens. The old portion of the castle was enormous, towering above the newer timber sections, and the turrets soared even higher. Therefore, even though the chapel was on the west side, sunrise and sunset both set the stained-glass windows aflame, the jewel colors glowing in the half light of daybreak and dusk.

Diffidently, knowing deeply how little right he had to be in this or any other house of God—if he was superstitious or God-fearing he would have expected to be cut down by a bolt of lightning as he passed the threshold—he entered the chapel and quietly closed the arched oak doors behind him. Candles added another quality of light to the slanting sunlight that sparkled through the colored glass and left gold and green and red trails across the plain gray stone walls of the opposite side.

On her knees, head bowed before the cloth-covered altar, she was the very picture of piety. If he had any decency, any pity, he would leave her alone in her prayer. But some things could not wait, and this place was quiet and deserted, perfect for a private talk. Hardening his heart against an unexpected flash of doubt, he made his way down the short central aisle— the chapel had only a few oak closed pews—until he could hear the murmur of her whispered prayers and the click of her prayer beads as she told the aves, pausing at the paternosters and the Gloria Patris, but then he stopped, uncertain how to interrupt her, or whether to interrupt her or not.

She stopped, and head still bowed said, "I am almost finished, Count Vasilov. Please wait until I have said all I need to say."

He did not need to answer. If she sensed his identity so easily, she would know of his acquiescence. He took a seat near her and waited.

She spoke her prayers in French and wept softly when she whispered Countess Uta's name, then uttered another prayer for Magda Brandt's safety. She crossed herself and then was done but did not move.

He watched her, feeling the tendrils of anxious care curl toward his heart; he struggled to harden himself, rejecting such soft and weak emotion as concern. She was lovely, and he felt budding passion for her, but he could not care for her beyond that. He did what he did in his life to try to compensate, merely because he had long ago learned that to stray too far from a certain path was to invite madness within him. But it did not mean there was room for gentleness, nor for sentiment.

"What was Magda Brandt doing in your father's room in the middle of the night?" His voice rang out and echoed in the cavernous upper reaches of the vaulted ceiling.

She turned, her face pale and her golden hair, partially covered by a patterned shawl, glowing in the faint light from the candles. "He says he doesn't know."

"Do you believe him?"

She shook her head, reluctantly, and looked away, clutching her prayer beads to her chest. "No. He knows, but he will not tell me." She stared back at him. "And I think you know, too. And even Count Roschkov. It is all tied in together, why you and Count Roschkov are here, what my father is hiding from me."

He moved to kneel beside her, knowing he must keep her from asking too many questions, determined to find out what he needed to know without divulging anything. "Miss Melisande, I—" He broke off as he stared down at the rosary she clutched to her breast. The beads glowed red in the golden light of the chapel, the decades told with silver carved rosette beads. There could not be two rosaries like that in the world; it was the Blood Amber Rosary, stolen from the church of Saint Demetrius in Constanta, Romania. He swallowed and controlled his breathing, quelling the teeming questions that invaded his brain. One question only was important. "What a lovely rosary," he said, then cleared his throat, determined not to alarm her. "Where did you get such a beautiful old piece?"

She gazed down at it fondly and smiled, gently, thumbing the rare red amber beads. "Isn't it lovely? It's so precious to me."

"But . . . where did you get it?" Every sense was heightened, the feel of the stone floor, the chill of the chapel, the warmth of the faint touch of sunlight that glowed through the stained glass.

"It was a very special gift given to me ten years ago. I was just twelve and . . ."

"But who gave it to you?"

She frowned and stared up at him. "My father." She stared back down at it. "It is the only gift he ever gave me during one of his rare visits to my mother and me."

Her father, Mikhail Davidovich, master thief. Ten years before, the Blood Amber Rosary had disappeared from the church at Constanta while on display for a high holy day; since then its companion piece, the Blood Amber Chalice had been guarded, kept under lock and key, not used even for the feast day of Saint Demetrius. But then, this last winter, the church fathers had decided that the chalice *must* be used in a ceremony marking the three hundredth anniversary of the Slaughter of St. Demetrius, and it had disappeared. It was as if, the church fathers said, the thief knew exactly how to find it, how to get it, and knew the church intimately.

Mikhail Davidovich had been in Constanta, had been tracked to Brandenburg, and that was where Kazimir had found him. A little bribery in the right places with the officials of the jail where Davidovich had been placed as a result of some petty theft of food had gotten him an hour alone with the man. It had been in vain, as the fellow, seeming frightened, had refused to admit possession of the chalice no matter what Kazimir did or said. And then, with the power of his connections, Nikolas von Wolfram had freed Davidovich and spirited him away to safety, though Kazimir had not known for a while that it was his old friend Nikolas, having just heard, mistakenly, that the thief's savior was "some fellow from Braunschweig."

But all along Davidovich had known exactly where the Blood Amber Rosary, the companion to the chalice and almost as deadly, was kept—in the hands of his innocent daughter. Did he know what he had? He *had* to know, and he *must* have intended to use it himself. Kazimir really didn't know how many people knew of the legendary powers the chalice promised. He had heard the story from his long-dead brother, Urvan, who was obsessed with anything that he thought would bring him freedom from the demons that plagued his mind, but it was possible that many knew what the chalice and rosary offered.

So Davidovich must be added to the list of those who

wished to use the unholy pair. Now it was a race to see who could find the chalice, join it with this, the Blood Amber Rosary, and wait for the eclipse, the blood moon. Or destroy them both, keeping from the world a force of such unutterable evil it might not survive.

He was tempted to snatch the rosary from her . . . just take it that moment and smash it into shattered bits of red amber, but to do so would be to show his hand. So far only *he* knew the rosary was in this castle . . . he and Melisande's father. He could not afford to be hasty in this, because no one knew for sure if the chalice or the rosary separately held power, so he intended to be careful, find the other piece, and then do what he must.

But this answered one question for him. He had long been sensing from Melisande Davidovich some kind of unique force, a deep power, but now he thought it must be the rosary he was sensing all along. It glowed with strength and with the ancient curse attached to it. She was not the source of his attraction, then, he hoped. She was not the enchantress; it was surely the rosary only that exerted power over him. But he would resist the pull of the pair, gather them together, and destroy them. Then, as the gypsy witch had promised, he would be free of the curse that kept him a werewolf.

"I'm so afraid for Uta," she said, gazing up at him, her eyes filling with tears. "I came here to pray for her. She has been so good to me."

"She is old," he said, "and perhaps has reached the time in her life when she is ready for death."

"But I keep thinking if I could just have a few more minutes of her time, I could tell her what she has meant to me, how she reminds me of my beloved grandmother who was taken from me."

He touched her cheek and thumbed away one tear, feeling it soak into him. It should burn, like holy water, one such as he, for he had no right to be hearing her confidences in this sacred place. But he was hypnotized by the bluebell intensity of her gaze. "How did she die?"

She told him briefly about how the people of her village, seduced by the promises from the Revolutionary Council that they would be able to keep any wealth that they seized, and infiltrated by outsiders who roused their suspicions of her grandmother's innocent doctoring, calling it witchcraft, finally came to take the house. "Grandmother knew what they were there for. She had been fearing it for some time, had even spoken of it, and tried to make mother and me leave, but we would not go. She would not let them in. She said they had no right to be there, and she would not answer to them, but to a higher power. She meant God, but I'm afraid they took that to mean she would summon the devil, and . . . they attacked." She lowered her head and was silent for a long minute. When she spoke again there was a quiet determination in her voice. "We all ran, then, to the hills, but it was too late. I watched my mother die. I watched my grandmother die! I will not watch Uta die, not without telling her how much I c-care."

"Do you not think she knows?" he said, hating even as he said it the platitudes all people muttered to those who mourned. He cupped her cheek with his hand.

His touch was gentle, and she found herself turning her face into his hand. Strange how the one man in the world she should be wary of was the one with whom she felt safest. He was strong, but restrained. He was passionate, obviously, and yet kept those passions ruthlessly contained most of the time. There was something about him, though she did not know what it was. "I knew something bad was going to happen," she murmured, moving to take a seat in one of the pews, the hushed atmosphere of the ancient chapel leading her to make confessions even to this mysterious man.

He sat beside her and took her hand, winding his own fingers around the red rosary beads he had commented on just moments before. Their hands were bound together as if in the sacred bonds of a wedding ceremony. "What do you mean? How did you know?"

She shivered, and he put one arm around her. She hesitated a moment, but then decided to borrow strength from whence she could. He had plenty to spare. She leaned into his warmth and said, "I've been dreaming . . . strange dreams. Dreams about wolves. They were getting worse and worse until I dreamt of the wolves attacking each other and fighting, blood everywhere . . . so much blood!" She drew in a ragged breath. "Even today, when I tried to sleep . . ."

His breath came in raspy gasps. "Wolves . . . you dreamt of wolves? Are you ever . . . ever hurt in these dreams?"

"No. No, not exactly. I am a witness to the bloodshed mostly. The wolves . . . at first there was just one, a big dark one with burning eyes. And then more came, until finally there are four, quarrelling and fighting. Uta told me it was a portent, and that I had . . ." She trailed off and shook her head.

"Had . . . ?"

"Had vision. The 'sight,' as the old women of my village said my grandmother had. But I don't believe that. They were just dreams."

"And yet you say you felt something bad was about to happen."

"Yes, ever since my father was brought here. But could that not be just a sense from other things, from . . . from secrets he is keeping from me?" She gazed up at him earnestly.

He was silent for a long moment, and then said, "I would say that you should listen to your heart. Do you think that Countess Uta's illness was the bad occurrence you feared?"

"No," she said searching her heart and mind. "I think there is something else, something I have not yet discovered. Why was Magda in my papa's room? Where is she now? If Uta could just speak to me . . . I feel the need of her wisdom, for she seemed to know something about me that I did not even know myself."

"She is far lapsed into the state of unconsciousness," he said gently, squeezing her fingers.

"But I could help her," she said, gazing up at him through a veil of tears. "I know of an herb . . . Even at this time of year the new shoots will be beginning and there would be enough. I think that I could bring her back to consciousness. It is possible. It is something I learned from my grandmother, a power not to be used lightly, but in this case there is an extreme need."

"Yes?" he said, seeming to know there was more.

"However . . . it is in the depths of the forest where it grows, and I'm frightened. Fanny and I were followed by something—or someone—the last time we were in the woods, and I have not been back since. I'm so ashamed! I should be braver, for Uta's sake. I feel sure she would not let fear stop her." She stared at him and then said slowly, "But you . . . I would feel safe with you," she whispered, her voice a breathy murmur shuddering and echoing in the vast upper reaches of the chapel tower.

She gazed up into his dark, shadowed eyes. Why did she trust him? She knew he was hiding something, but so was Count Gavril . . . so was her own father. She would get to the bottom of the mystery, but first she had a more important task. "Will you help me? For Uta's sake? Will you go with me?"

Chapter 14

"OF COURSE I will go with you . . . for your own sake,"
Kazimir said. "You could ask almost anything of me, you
know, and I would do it." The more she trusted him the better,
he thought, and to gain her trust he needed to be her cham-
pion. It suited his purpose as well as it suited hers. "However,
the woods are vast. Are you sure you know exactly where to
find this herb?"

"Yes, I know where it grows. I don't go too far into the
woods; I have ventured only so far as the stream that feeds the
Wolfbeck river. I'm afraid I would get lost if I went farther.
There's too much forest for anyone to investigate, in truth, for
the von Wolfram land and the forest that covers much of it go
on for miles and miles. But last summer I charted where every
herb I use in the forest grows, for some must be left in place.
They will not thrive in the cultivated gardens of the castle and
need the rich soil of the forest floor for sustenance. So it is
with the mushrooms and other fungi I sometimes need for
medicines."

"How did you learn so much?" he said, rising and taking
her hand in his, pulling her up from the pew seat.

As he guided her back to the great hall, she told him more
of her grandmother, a healer in her French village, and how
she learned at her knee, becoming far more proficient at the
healing arts than her mother, who had no natural affinity for
it. They parted ways as she retrieved her cloak, and then they
met again in the hall, under the watchful glare of Steinholz.

They exited through the porte cochere, over the crushed
stone drive, and across the green sward that led to the vast
forest that almost surrounded the castle. He should dig for
whatever information he could discover about her father's

travels and his past as a thief. But instead, as he glanced sideways, feeling her leaning on his arm as they approached the woods across the damp grass as the golden dart of the lowering sun penetrated the budding trees, he found himself curious about her.

"You must miss your home."

"Home. What a precious word. I do miss so much of home."

They approached the brushy edge of the woods, and he helped her past it to a path he knew well. "Tell me about it."

She spoke of her youth when her mother spent some time in Paris, a society woman of some importance, and then their retreat to her grandmother's smaller country abode in the Artois region near Lille when the family's money was lost and the first rumblings of the revolutionary terror were beginning.

"Our home overlooked a valley where the vineyards stretched for miles. We greeted the sun every morning, my mother, my grandmother, and I, with gladness, for always there was something to do, lessons to learn, the herb garden to work."

Her expression was pensive, and he knew she must be thinking of the tale she had related in the chapel. "You must despise the people of your country, the common folk, for what has occurred, the disgusting demolishing of all that was fine and sweet and rare, for—"

"No!" she said, holding up her free hand. "I despise what they did to my mother and grandmother, but . . . but if you listen to my Uncle Maximillian, though I was too young at the time to truly understand what was occurring, he warned the king and his court . . . told them of the disaffection of the people, of how desperate they were making them with their foolish ways and greed. You cannot drive people into a hole and expect that they will not defend themselves, teeth bared, as a badger will, viciously. Men who cannot feed their children will take desperate measures; I fault those who forced them to such terrible conclusions."

"You forgive them so easily?" He gazed down into her eyes and helped her over a fallen log.

"No, oh no, not the individuals who had trusted my grandmother for so many years, and then turned on her when it was politic to do so, to gain our home by killing those to whom it belonged. But the awful turmoil my country is suffering . . ." She sighed and shook her head, not finishing her thought. "Well, it is my country no longer."

"You do not think you will ever return home, to France?"

She glanced over her shoulder to the faint light of the edge of the forest. "My life has taken another path, but I have found kind people who have given me a home, and I cannot regret meeting Uta and Christoph and Charlotte and . . . and Count Nikolas."

He felt a pang of something terribly close to jealousy when he heard the sadness in her voice. She had had hopes in that direction, he thought, suddenly, hopes that Count Nikolas would in time ask her to be his wife. And knowing how handsome the count was and how kind he had been to her, how could he be surprised? His greatest surprise was that her tenderness for him had not found in his breast an answering passion. What kind of man could know Melisande Davidovich and not surrender to her sweetness? What kind of man could see her every day and not notice how kind she was, how sweet her tone of voice, how lovely she could be in a pensive mood, or . . . he cleared his throat, forcing his mind away from such fruitless contemplation. "Are we almost to the spot?"

She paused, got her bearing, and said, "Almost." She looked up at him. "Thank you, sir, for this. I would never have ventured here without some aid."

Stiffening his resolve, he decided to change the subject. "I cannot help but notice that Count Roschkov has inveigled you and your father into a position of trusting him."

She frowned, holding up the bottom of her blue cape as she picked her way through a tangle of underbrush near a clearing. "I do not understand you, sir. He has been kind to me, certainly, and he has made promises that he will help us to settle in my father's former home village, but I cannot think there has been trickery or deceit involved."

"And is there nothing beyond that . . . that *kindness*? Has he not insinuated himself into your good graces?"

"I fail to understand you."

He bit back the dislike he felt for Roschkov and made his words deliberately milder than his feelings would dictate. "He has offered you and your father a home, has he not?" He glanced sideways and watched her cheeks pink more than the exertion and cool air would have dictated.

She sighed and was silent for a long minute. "If you know of anything to Count Roschkov's detriment—anything other than your own clear distaste for the man, that is—I would ask you to speak plainly, sir, and not equivocate. In truth, I am growing impatient with you. It is clear that you both have motives for being in the castle that have to do with something my father stole, something you both want. Why should I trust either of you?"

"Has he never told you why he is at Wolfram Castle?"

"He would have me believe it is concern for a fellow Russian," she said, with an acerbic edge in her normally mild tone. "He is not being any more forthcoming with information than you or my father."

"And yet," he said, softly, "You trusted me to bring you out here alone."

She stopped, looked up into his eyes and took in a long, shaky breath. "If none of you will tell me what is going on, then you leave me no choice but to guess and go with my sense of what is right and wrong. I have allowed Count Gavril to think that my father and I will return to Russia with him at some point in the indefinite future. I have told you I trust you. I do not think either of you have any cause to hurt *me*."

She dropped his arm and led him on, climbing through a thicket, finally, to come to a very small clearing, just barely a spot where some movement was possible. She stopped and glanced around. The forest was tight around them, gray trunks of barren trees and dark pines thickly crowding them. The forest floor was dry, the leaf mold and pine needles providing a blanket over the sodden earth.

"We are here," she said. "This is the place, and we have had enough melting temperatures during the day and rain, too, overnight, so the snow has melted. That is good. I pray the first buds have started from the ground." She began a slow circuit of the small clearing, her keen eyes scanning the ground. Occasionally she brushed away dead, wet leaves.

He watched for a few minutes, staying at the edge of the sylvan grove, puzzling out her character. Every time he thought he had a grasp on it, like a drifting mist she showed another form, displayed another depth, and slipped away. Should he tell her everything? Enlist her aid in the search for the chalice? Oddly, it was the first time that thought had occurred to him. Initially that was because he had suspected that she was her father's confederate, but now . . . perhaps when they returned to the castle they could talk and figure out what was going on and where her father had hidden the chalice. He would tell her what her rosary really was, as difficult as that would be when he could see how she cherished the piece.

He stayed back and just let her search. He didn't know an herb from a fungus and would likely just stomp on the very budding plant she needed if he tried to help. He felt a prickle at the base of his skull; something was wrong. He had the sense that they were being watched, and he never ignored those feelings.

Melisande seemed to feel something too, for she straightened from her search and looked around, finally concentrating on one spot. "Magda!" she cried. "Magda, come back!"

"Where?" he cried.

"There!" She pointed.

He followed her gaze and saw the girl, standing about twenty feet away, almost camouflaged in her gray cloak by the gray trunks of winter-bare trees. She looked healthy and well, but frightened.

"Magda!" Melisande cried again and started toward her, but the girl turned and fled. "Count Vasilov, please, go after her! I cannot run in these dratted skirts and this cloak. Go!"

"No! I can't leave you alone in the woods!"

"Go *now*, find her, make sure she is all right! Please, I beg of you. I will be fine alone for just a few minutes."

He paused only a moment, but saw the desperation in her eyes. He felt it too. If he could find Magda, bring her back to the castle . . . He glanced around and memorized the spot where they were. "Stay here, then, and I will come back for you," he said. "No matter what, *stay here!*" He ran after Magda, but the girl had a head start on him now.

Where would she have gone? He pelted through the forest in the direction she had disappeared but could not see her. He was almost ready to give up when he saw her again, just out of reach, looking at him, her eyes wide and frightened. "Fräulein Brandt! Wait! I mean you no harm," he shouted, switching to German, remembering that she had no other language. But she turned and fled again, and he followed; her path twisted and turned and doubled back on itself. One moment he would see a glimmer of light and knew he was near the edge, perhaps even toward the castle, but then she would double back on herself and take him deeper into the forest. Very much deeper.

It almost seemed like . . . he stopped dead.

Melisande! He took his bearing and swiftly began to head back to where he thought he had left the young woman, but it took precious minutes to figure out how to get there, after so many wrong turns and misleading paths. He finally found the way and, gasping for air, dashed into the small clearing.

She was gone. Wildly he looked around, hoping she was just searching the edge of the woods for her precious herb, or that he had mistaken the clearing for another, but no . . . her basket lay splintered on the ground, her head scarf adorned a bush, and she was gone. His mind raced as he tried to figure out what was going on. Was Magda Brandt in confederation with someone, then? Someone else who searched for the chalice? She must be, and the most likely culprit was Gavril Roschkov. But why would he steal Melisande away when he was already in the castle and could search for the chalice just as easily as Kazimir? It made no sense, and he was wasting precious minutes trying to figure it out. Darkness was falling, and he had to find Melisande Davidovich. He seized her scarf, held it to his nose for a moment, and then began to search.

Chapter 15

"LET ME go! Release me this instant!" Melisande cried, struggling and trying to regain her footing. Somewhere a wolf howled, and it almost seemed in pity or in answer to her.

The bundle of rags, though—her captor seemed no more than that—was strong, and her cloak and heavy skirts tangled in her feet. She couldn't get away from his powerful grasp, nor could she see him, for all her effort was spent staying on her feet and stumbling after him. The light was dying, fading into purplish shadows, but as she staggered and stumbled, a confusion of fearful thoughts darted through her mind.

Who was this? What did he want of her? Where was he taking her? Where was Count Vasilov?

"Count Vasilov!" she screamed, hoping he was nearby. "Help! Help me!"

Pain shot through her skull and the world went black.

When she awoke, it was to darkness; at first she thought a long time had passed, but then she saw that a faint hint of purple twilight was still visible through a crack in whatever awful, odorous shack she was in, so she could not have been unconscious for more than a few minutes. Her head ached—he had hit her hard enough to make her faint—as did the muscles of her shoulders and arms from being dragged so far and struggling so hard. She gagged, her stomach roiling, at the awful smell of this place, and she bit her lip hard to keep from crying out or weeping. A trickle of blood in her mouth was a welcome reminder that she needed to keep her wits about her.

Taking a deep breath, fighting the gagging reflex, she struggled to sit up, untangling her booted feet from her heavy cloak. There was some faint source of warmth in the hut, and she looked toward it, making out the huddled shape of her ragged captor.

"What do you want?" she asked, in German. No answer. She repeated the question in French and English to no avail, and so tried Russian, her rusty, terrible accent—her Russian had been learned from books and practiced with her father only recently—creaking like an unused gate, but he moved finally. He turned from the fire, and she could feel his gaze on her, though she could not see him.

The door scraped on the dirt floor, and Melisande tried to get up, but the creature lifted a club and shook it in a menacing manner, so she fell back. Someone was coming in. Was it Count Vasilov . . . Kazimir? She couldn't see, and whoever it was moved over to the huddled form of her captor, and they murmured together.

"Who is it? What do you want of me?"

"Miss Melisande, please do not move and do not try to get away, or it will go worse for you."

"Magda?" Melisande cried at the familiar voice. "Magda, are you all right?" she cried in German. "Are you—" She stopped talking as her mind grasped what Magda had just said to her. "You are in league with this devil!"

"No, no," Magda said soothingly, as she moved closer to Melisande. But at a grunt from the man, she stopped a distance away. "He is no devil," she said, reaching out one hand in a pleading gesture. "He only needs you for a little while, and then he will let you go."

"I do not understand! Who is this . . . this . . ."

"He is a prince," Magda said, eagerly, twisting her hands together over and over. "A Russian prince, and he is going to take me with him once he has what he needs to prove his stolen birthright, and we will go back to Russia and live in his summer palace on the . . . some sea, I cannot remember the name. And I will be a princess!"

The man had gotten up from his spot by the tiny fire and moved toward where Melisande huddled in the corner.

"Perhaps . . ." Magda began, hesitated, and then rushed back into speech. "You have always been kind to me. Perhaps you may come and be my companion."

The man loomed over her now, and in the dim light she

could see his face. It was dirty and gaunt, with a long beard and long hair framing it, but the eyes . . . his eyes looked familiar, as if she had seen them very close to her, dark and compelling, but with a flat look of madness. Where had she seen eyes like his? Somewhere . . . and recently, too.

She could not think of it for long, could not wonder, when fear overwhelmed her. What was to become of her now?

"Oh, Magda," Melisande whispered. "What have you done?"

DARKNESS closed in, and still Kazimir could not find where Melisande had gone. Someone had taken her, of that he was certain, but who? And why?

Finally he knew he could look no more. His vision was excellent in the darkness, but with the moon not set to rise for a time, and with needing just that little bit of light to aid his vision, Kazimir knew he was endangering Melisande just by stumbling around in the darkness. He could feel her sometimes, could sense her, caught a whiff of her provocative natural scent, and yet when he turned and followed, it drifted away like smoke on wind and disappeared. He feared his desperation was leading him astray.

He should transform and seek her. As a wolf his senses were many times more sensitive, and he could cover more ground more swiftly. But what if he found her? As a wolf he was limited as to what he could do to help her. And it was just barely possible that she had somehow escaped whomever had seized her, and if she had, she would have headed back to the castle as the nearest haven of safety. He must go there, if only to alert her friends to her disappearance.

Shame was like a bitter taste in his mouth, for she had trusted him, and he had let her down. He should never have left her side in the woods, but if he had it to do over again, with her looking at him and begging him to go find Magda, he feared he would do the same thing. A trap had been laid using Magda as the bait; he was sure of that now, even though he could not imagine who had laid the trap, nor why, nor could he think of any way he could have foreseen such an occurrence.

But he very much feared the trap had to do with the rosary and chalice. None of it made any sense to him, though. Who would take her out in the woods? What was going on?

He tromped through the forest and found his way out, trudging up to the castle in the dark purple of night. Steinholz looked askance at him as he came in, weary and covered in twigs and dirt from his desperate search through underbrush and groves.

"Is Miss Davidovich here?" Kazimir asked. "Has she come back?"

Steinholz shook his head.

"Are you sure?"

"Yes, Count Vasilov," the butler said. "I have not seen her since she left the castle in your company."

Accusation was heavy in the man's voice. "Where is Count von Wolfram?" Kazimir demanded.

"In the reception room, sir, next to the dining room."

Kazimir raced to the reception room, next to the dining room. He threw open the doors. There, by the fire, was the company gathered to await dinner: Christoph, Countess Charlotte, and Gavril. He ignored the others and strode to Christoph, facing the young man with a grim sense that this was not going to be easy, especially knowing how much the young man adored Melisande.

"Melisande Davidovich has been taken captive."

For a few minutes it was impossible to make them understand him, for it seemed, on the face of it, an absurd statement, that he had accompanied Melisande on an expedition to the forest to find an herb, but finally Christoph sent for Fanny and asked her about Melisande's whereabouts. The girl, tearful, said she did not know, had not seen her for hours, and could not say. She had been in the conservatory doing some tasks Melisande had asked of her. The girl went searching, led by a shocked Charlotte, but Melisande, of course, as Kazimir had known, was nowhere, not even in her own room.

"Where is she?" Charlotte cried, as she returned. "What can have happened? We must find her."

Kazimir turned and faced the suspicious glare of Christoph and Gavril.

"What have you done?" Gavril said, his pale face ghostly in the flickering firelight.

"Steinholz can tell you . . . He saw us leave together," Kazimir said, aware of the seconds slipping away, desperation stealing into him. "She asked me to accompany her . . ."

"Why would she ask you to go with her?" Count Christoph, his pale face dressed with two high spots of red on his cheeks, demanded of Kazimir.

Kazimir explained again about Melisande's intention to find the herb that would restore Countess Uta to consciousness.

"But why you?" Christoph asked. "If she felt the need of protection, why not me?"

"Perhaps I was simply there at the moment when she needed someone. I do not know."

Gavril paced over to Kazimir and stared into his eyes for a long moment. "What have you done with her, Vasilov?" he said, his voice hoarse with rage. "What did you do to her out there in the forest, what—"

"I swear, Gavril," Kazimir said, "I swear that I have done nothing to harm her."

Christoph said, "We must search, immediately."

"But first we have to tell her father that she is missing," Charlotte cried. Tears welled up in her blue eyes; one over-flowed and trickled down her cheek and she wiped it away, hastily. Fanny sobbed, and Charlotte put one arm over her shoulders.

"Of course . . . her father!" Christoph said, clutching his blond hair in both hands.

"I will accompany you to tell Mikhail," Gavril said. They exited together, and with the reception room door open to the great hall, their footsteps echoed as they mounted the stairs.

"What were you *really* doing out in the forest with Melisande?" Countess Charlotte asked of Kazimir. She and the maid clutched each other tightly and she glared at Kazimir.

"Yes," said Fanny, emboldened, perhaps, by her mistress's closeness. "Why would she go into the forest with you? I do not understand."

Kazimir stared at the two girls, both blonde, pink-cheeked

and with large blue eyes, and shook his head. "What I have said is the truth. She was concerned for Countess Uta and determined to get the herbs to bring her back to consciousness. She wished someone to go with her. She said she had been having nightmares and was afraid to go into the forest without someone to protect her." He paused, swallowed hard, and said, his lip twisting in fury directed only at himself, "I failed miserably."

They heard shouts, and Kazimir raced out to the great hall, trailed by the two young ladies. Christoph bounded to the gallery railing, followed at a distance by Gavril, who was even paler than usual and clutched the balustrade, leaning heavily as if he had suffered a great shock.

Christoph bolted down the stairs to Kazimir and took his shirtfront in his long-fingered hands. "What is going on? What have you done?"

Kazimir shook him off and shoved him away, dangerously close to the head of the stairs that led down to the great hall. "What is wrong? What do you mean?"

Gavril, panting and weak, had finally made it to them. He leaned heavily on the carved oak finial and gasped, "Mikhail Davidovich is gone. He is nowhere to be found, and no one has seen him for hours!"

Chapter 16

MELISANDE FOUGHT back tears. The madman and Magda murmured together in the corner near the crude hearth while she shivered and retched, fear roiling in her gut. None of it made a bit of sense to her. What did he want from her?

Her mouth was dry as dust, and she could not even swallow; all she tasted was the foul odor of the hut. Her captor kept throwing bundles of dried leaves on the fire, and smoke and cinder filled the air. Where, she wondered, was Kazimir? She had the sense that she couldn't have been taken that far from where she had started out, but in all her forays into the forest, she had never come upon a hut such as the one she was in, so it must be beyond the usual paths. She looked up, aware of the dark blot that was her captor. He loomed over her again.

He muttered some words in Russian, but she couldn't understand him. His wording was indistinct, and his words tumbled together. She shook her head and he raised a fist, menacingly.

"No, don't hurt her," Magda screamed and darted over. "What do you want?" she asked the man.

In halting German he muttered to her.

"Miss Melisande," Magda said, her eyes wide and frightened, clasping and unclasping her hands before her, "he wants you to tell us where the cup is. He needs it. If you give it to him, he will leave you alone."

"Magda, how can you consort with this fellow? How can you? How could you help him capture me like some rabbit in a trap?"

"Please," Magda said, tears welling in her blue eyes, shadowed in the dim light afforded by a crude lamp she had lit and now held high. "Just tell him where the cup is, and I promise you—"

"How could you betray me?"

The man pushed past Magda and began to roughly handle Melisande, pulling at her clothes and turning her around. She lashed out and fought him, scratching, biting, trying to get a purchase on his ragged cloak so she could push him away, but he was strong, and ferocious in his determination. What did he want? Still, she struggled and felt something come loose; her rosary tore away from her waist.

He pushed her away, and in the dim lamplight, he held it up. With a guttural cry of triumph, he shook the beads and then turned and glared at her. This time she understood him, though he still spoke a harshly accented, oddly inflected German. "You have the Blood Amber Rosary. And yet you would have me believe you do not know the significance of this? You have the cup, too. I know it from my bones." He pulled a dull silver pistol from a fold in his cloak and pointed it at her. "If you do not tell me where it is, I will kill you."

"No!" Magda cried. She darted to stand between Melisande and her captor. "Please . . . Miss Melisande has done nothing wrong against you! If she says she does not know where the cup is, I believe her."

"Liar!" he shouted, but then secreted the pistol back under his cloak, turned and went to the other side of the hut to sit by the hearth.

"Please, Miss Melisande," Magda said, looking over her shoulder and then bending near to her erstwhile friend. "I would give up this cup the prince says you have, for once he has it I know he will leave this place and leave you all alone. I cannot say more, but you must give it up to him! More depends on it than you even know."

"I don't know what cup he is talking about!" she cried.

And yet . . . she stopped for just a moment and thought. Was this cup the relic of which Count Gavril and Count Kazimir spoke, the chalice? It seemed that her father had indeed stolen something, and that was what they all were after, Melisande thought, Gavril Roschkov, Kazimir Vasilov, and this . . . this beast. "What is so important about

this mysterious cup?" she asked, trying to calm herself, trying to think beyond her terror.

"It is what the prince needs to prove his birthright."

"Then why did he take my rosary? What has that to do
with this?"

"I don't know," Magda admitted, with tears in her blue
eyes. "I don't understand."

A bruise shadowed the young woman's cheek, and her lip
was cut and a little swollen, Melisande noticed for the first
time. Her white blonde hair, usually clean and tidy, was un-
kempt. There was blood in her ear. Melisande quivered; did
that animal beat her? Surely she would not still be helping
him if that were so. More likely her wounds had just come
from her forays into the forest. Melisande hardened her heart,
mindful of her own pain and suffering. "Magda, why are you
helping him?"

"He is going to take me away from here, and I will be his
princess."

"What nonsense! I thought better of you than that. You
have sold your soul to the devil for earthly gain," Melisande
whispered. "What could possibly be worth going to hell?"

Magda's expression hardened. "What do you know of my
life and my soul?" she questioned, the words spat out like
foul-tasting fodder. "For that matter, what do you truly know
of hell? I have been in hell my whole life. Hell adorned with
crystal and diamonds will be better than hell serving peasants
in a beerhall and fending off their groping hands." She turned
away.

How simple it was for Miss Melisande Davidovich to
make such judgments, Magda thought. She was an honored
guest at Wolfram Castle. She had a safe home for her life, if
she so chose, and any fool could see that Christoph would
marry her the moment he found the courage to ask. She would
be a countess, then, and have everything she could ever desire.

Magda turned and gazed at the prince muttering over the
rosary he had snatched, and then at Melisande, huddled in
misery. This wasn't what she had anticipated as her task,
though . . . not what she pictured doing for the Russian gentleman. It was supposed to be just errands, and she had imagined providing him with food, telling him whatever she found

out, taking care of his needs in any way she could. Perhaps even lying with him when necessary, as disgusting as that would be in his present filth. Magda stared at Melisande, a trickle of blood from the blow to her head visible even in the poor light from the fire in the hearth. She wished she could explain further to Melisande why she was helping the man, but it would do no good. The prince beckoned and in his broken German, issued his next orders.

Gladly she left the hut and stumbled through the dark, lifting her skirts to make her progress more swift. The half-circle moon rose, and the glimmer of light helped her find her way. Once she found a familiar path, she ran until her breath came in ragged gasps, ran to try to escape from her sense of terrible guilt and responsibility.

She reached the edge of the woods and paused to catch her breath, gazing up at Wolfram Castle, so forbidding in the pale stream of moonlight from the waxing moon. Some of the tasks the prince had commanded her to perform had been exciting. Her foray into the castle to deliver a message to Davidovich, the thief, had been amusing enough, though with a few frightening moments.

There was a gleam of light in the great hall flickering through the high arched windows; she must go up there and give them the message. She tried to remember the thrill of what she was doing, and the prize at the end, but the vision of Melisande huddled in misery in the dirty hut in the forest came back to her time and time again. Melisande had from the moment she arrived been the kindest of all the inhabitants of Wolfram Castle to her, and this was poor repayment. But if the father and daughter would just give up to the prince what was rightfully his, then all would be well. She had been assured that no harm would come to anyone. Trusting that was becoming more difficult, given her own recent experience, she thought, touching the still-painful bruise. But it seemed to her that the only way past this experience was to see it through to the very end.

She should never have expected the prince to be any different than other men, but backing out of this scheme was impossible now. She was too deeply involved and had nowhere else to go if it all ended badly. She had to trust in the prince.

She clamped down on her lip and then yelped in pain. The cut was swollen still, and she had to wait a moment for the pain to subside; it throbbed and was hot to the touch. Her life just *had* to get better, she thought, with a desperate lurch of fear. For if it didn't, it would surely go in the opposite direction, and very quickly. She estimated she had only a few months before things became very much worse.

Stepping out of the woods, she straightened, tugging her cloak down and tidying her hair as best she could. This was not going to be easy, for now she would be revealing to all at the castle her own involvement in recent catastrophic events. She trudged across the lawn.

If this went poorly, the blame, she decided, as she approached the awful and frightening Wolfram Castle, which loomed over the landscape like a dark raven perched on a hillside, with dark wings outspread, rested squarely upon the slender shoulders of Countess Charlotte von Wolfram. If that lady had not been so disdainful in recent years, then Magda would not have felt so compelled to turn away from those at the castle in this, her hour of great need. If she had any reason to think she could have turned to those at the castle for help, the Russian's offer would not have tempted her to this difficult and treacherous path.

She stood quivering before the door, but finally raised the huge wolf's head knocker and let it fall, the sound resounding like a thunder clap. Steinholz, the haughty butler, opened the door and stared at her, his dark, bloodshot eyes wide.

Christoph, who was dressed for the outdoors, strode into the great hall and caught sight of her, dwarfed by the enormous double doors. "Magda! What are you doing here?"

"I . . . I have come to deliver a message," she said, unsuccessfully attempting to keep her voice from quavering.

The dark Russian count Magda had seen in the village in her own father's tap room before he came to the castle, and then in the castle the day she had dared to visit, raced down the grand sweeping stairs. He, too, was dressed to go outside.

"What is she doing here?" he asked, in German, knowing she spoke only her native tongue and wanting her to understand him. "Command her to tell us, Christoph, where Melisande is."

Christoph ignored him and said, "Magda, what is your message. Is it to do with Melisande? We were just going out to look for her, but . . ."

"Melisande is safe," Magda gasped, eager to say her piece and get it over with. "She will not be harmed if . . ." She paused, trembling.

Christoph strode forward and took her arm in a hard grip, his cloaks swirling around his booted legs, "If what? What is going on? How are you involved in this?"

The other man joined him. "This is the girl who led me away from Melisande, who tricked me into abandoning her. You," he said to her. "Who are you? What do you know?"

"Stay out of this, Count Vasilov," Christoph said, not taking his eyes from Magda.

It was much more difficult than she had anticipated, the habits of a lifetime reasserting herself. Christoph was her liege, lord of Wolfram Castle in Count Nikolas von Wolfram's absence, and no matter what, he had at one time been kind to her. Charlotte raced out from one of the halls beyond the great hall.

"Magda," she gasped, coming to an abrupt halt. Her chin went up. "You look as if you have been out whoring again."

Magda touched her lip, and the pit of anger in her belly reasserted its dominance. Trembling with anger, she turned to Christoph, ignoring the countess. "Melisande Davidovich is safe." She let a swell of triumph trickle into her. "And so is her father."

"Where are they?" Christoph demanded, his blue eyes blazing with wrath. He shook her. "Where?"

"A secret place," she said, twisting out of his grasp and stepping backward. "You could never find it alone. Unless the Blood Amber Chalice is turned over immediately to me, they will both die . . . s-slow, horrible deaths." Horrified anew by the words she had been told to repeat, she bit back fear.

The dark Russian stepped forward and said, his voice harsh with anger, "Who has done this? Whom do you serve, girl?"

"I serve a prince, a Russian, like you, sir. Only he is a prince." She summoned her courage. "The Blood Amber Chalice is his only proof that he is who he says he is, and he needs it to take back to Russia and defeat those who deny him his heritage and his position in court. The prince hired Mikhail Davidovich to steal it from the thieves who took it from his highness, but then he would not turn it over. He . . . he demanded more money. The prince commands you to turn it over, and all will be well; Davidovich and Miss Melisande will be released safely."

She let out a long sigh, the breath she had been unconsciously holding. The message she had memorized had been delivered. Now they would give up the cup, she would take it back, the prince would release the two captives and would take her away from Wolfbeck and her troubles.

Then everything would work out. She would be free.

Chapter 17

"THAT IS outrageous!" Count Gavril Roschkov said, strolling into the great hall from the dining room. "Only a dull-witted peasant would believe such a parcel of nonsense wrapped in idiocy. A deposed prince? A mistakenly misplaced inheritance? A thief running errands for a prince? What nonsense!"

"Nonsense," echoed Countess Charlotte, her breath catching on the word.

"It is true!" Magda cried.

Gavril watched her. She was not stupid; she was clever, but perhaps naïve. He paced toward her, watching her eyes, holding them with his own gaze. He focused all of his energy on her, willing himself, though terribly weary, to stay standing. "How was Mikhail stolen away from here?"

"I left him a message," the girl said, a sly look on her pale, pretty face . . . pretty but for the cut and swollen lip and the bruise on her cheek.

Kazimir and Christoph, miraculously, remained silent, as did the usually obstreperous Countess Charlotte, who was clearly horrified, tears welling up in her eyes as she watched the other girl.

"When you stole into the castle," Gavril said, gentling his voice, holding her gaze as he walked toward her.

"Yes . . . yes! The prince told me what to say and do. Davidovich understood and came to the prince in the heart of the forest." She stood straighter and preened. "I waited and guided him myself. I know the forest well and took the thief to the prince."

"Where is Davidovich now?"

Her gaze fell as he stood before her. "I . . . I do not know, for the prince took him away somewhere. They . . . argued. I think Davidovich was trying to tell him he had destroyed the cup but . . ." She shrugged. "The prince did not believe him."

Gavril bit back his impatience at her repetition of the word 'prince' when indicating the animal who had kidnapped the father and daughter. He must humor her. "What message did you leave for Davidovich that he would place himself in such danger from this . . . prince?"

She looked up at him and blinked. "It was . . . it was in some mysterious hand. I do not know . . ."

"You do not read."

"Yes, I do read!" she said, bridling. "I read the . . . the Bible."

"In German."

"Of course."

"But the written message was not in German."

"No. I could not make out a single word of it."

Gavril nodded. The girl's story was true so far as it went, when one stripped the fairy tale elements from it. The captor was likely Russian, and perhaps he was the one who had induced Davidovich to steal the chalice from the church in Constanta. Glancing over at Kazimir, who had stepped back into shadow, perhaps understanding that his presence unnerved the girl, Gavril wondered anew at his motive for taking Melisande Davidovich into the forest. They had only his word for it that there was some herb-gathering mission. And yet the butler had confirmed that Melisande had gone willingly.

Possibilities swirled in his mind. Had Kazimir tricked her? Did he know that Mikhail was missing, and had he promised to take her to her father? But that made no sense. He didn't have the chalice, or he would not be standing in the great hall with them questioning Magda Brandt. *None* of it made sense. Had Davidovich truly destroyed the cup? No, he wouldn't have, for it would take extraordinary will to do such a thing.

Weariness tugged at him. Being in Kazimir Vasilov's company after all these years was grueling; Gavril struggled every day to keep true to his course and not revile the man publicly, thus perhaps losing the chance to be the sword of justice. He could not give in to his loathing, nor could he let it sap every last drop of energy he had. He must stay focused on the task, to make Kazimir atone with his life for what he had done. Then he could rest. Gavril took a deep breath, glanced around at the others who stared at him, waiting, and said, "This . . . cup we are supposed to hand over to free Davidovich, do you know what it looks like?" He wanted to see what her supposed prince had told her.

"It is red," she said eagerly, staring into his eyes. "It is red and carved of a stone that is not really a stone, the prince says."

"A stone that is not really a stone? What does that mean?" Christoph asked.

Gavril held up one hand to calm the young man, who was becoming agitated. "Who is this prince?" he said, silkily. "I am Russian; I know all of the princes of our great nation. Tell me his name. If he is so wronged, I wish to help him, to serve him in his quest for justice."

Her eyes widened. She clearly was not ready for such a question and such an offer. "I . . . I don't know."

"You did all of this, and yet you do not even know his name?"

"Of course he told me his name!" she cried, stung by his tone. "His name is . . . Urvan Sergei Vasilov."

"No!" That was Kazimir, and he strode forward.

Magda shrank behind Gavril, and Christoph grabbed the count by his arm and pulled him back.

All began speaking at once until finally Kazimir roared, "Enough!" He yanked his arm from Christoph's grip and roughly pulled Magda out from behind Gavril. She stood, quivering, before him. "What did you say his name was?"

She shook her head, mute in the face of his anger.

"Magda, answer him," Christoph ordered, his pale face bleached of all color, even to his bloodless lips.

"Urvan Sergei Vasilov," she repeated, stumbling over the unfamiliar syllables.

"My brother?" Kazimir whispered.

"Your brother?" cried Charlotte and Christoph together.

Magda, eyes wide with terror, fell back from them all, but Steinholz, who had shooed all of the serving staff away, bolted the door, sure of only one thing, that they did not want Magda to escape them yet.

Switching to English and with one long look at Gavril, Kazimir said, "Yes, my brother, or at least someone calling himself by that name. But . . . this item that the man seeks . . ."

"The Blood Amber Chalice," Gavril said, his voice hoarse with emotion. "Name it, Vasilov, for you have been seeking it long enough."

"As have you, Gavril! This cup . . . my brother, Count Urvan Vasilov was indeed obsessed with it, but first he was looking for the companion piece, a piece that was stolen many years ago from the church in Constanta."

How much should he tell them? He did not trust Gavril, for it was clear the man was fading away, and the cup and rosary would give him back everything he was losing and more. Once he used its power, not even Kazimir would be able to stop him from doing whatever he wished.

"Tell them the rest, Vasilov," Gavril said, having recovered his composure. "Tell them why this . . . this *prince* cannot be your brother, though he claims the name."

"What is this all about?" Christoph asked impatiently. "I feel as if I have invited a pit of vipers into my home, for you are all telling lies and holding things back."

"And so was Davidovich," Gavril said.

"I don't care!" Christoph roared, his voice echoing up into the vast black reaches of the great hall's vaulted ceiling. "All I care about is that Melisande is somewhere in the woods with a madman, and I say we get my dogs and go now to tear this . . . this Urvan limb from limb before he hurts her."

"I will be brief," Kazimir said. "And then we must truly decide upon a course of action." He took a deep breath. "Urvan, my brother, is dead . . . or was reported to be by witnesses. But he *was* avidly seeking the chalice." Kazimir turned and gazed at Magda Brandt, who now cowered, her blue eyes wide, tears trailing past the bruise on her cheek. "Fräulein Brandt," he said in German, as gently as he could. "Would you describe your prince?"

Magda gave a halting description, and Kazimir listened and then shook his head. "I don't know. Tell me, does he wear any jewelry on his person?"

She nodded and touched her cut lip. "He . . . he wears a large ring with a red stone on his right hand."

"The middle finger?" Kazimir asked. When the girl nodded, he said, "And does it have a diamond on either side of the red stone?"

She nodded slowly, staring at him. "And . . . he carries a bag of jewels. I saw them." A greedy light gleamed in her eyes. "One is an emerald the size of a pigeon's egg!"

"The Vasilov emerald!" It *was* Urvan; he had taken the emerald away among other gems when he left their home. Kazimir felt as if the very breath was sucked from his body.

"But he is dead," Gavril said, his gaunt face gray. "He has been dead for years!"

"His suicide was a ruse, a fraud." Kazimir passed one hand over his face. "This changes everything."

"How is it possible?" Gavril shivered, the frigid air of the great hall taking its toll finally. He bowed his head and muttered a prayer.

Charlotte, who clutched her brother's arm, cried, "What is all of this? What does it mean? I don't understand. Please, how are we to get Melisande back?"

"We must go now, take dogs, force Magda to show us where they are in the forest and get Melisande and Mikhail back!" Christoph said, his voice hoarse with tension.

Kazimir shouted, "No!" He looked over at Gavril. "It is time to speak of this. But Christoph," he said, turning to the younger man, "we cannot do as you suggest, for to do so would seal their fates. If this is Urvan, and indeed I think it must be, despite my long-held belief that he is dead, then he is cunning and careful. Even more so than I ever thought possible. He will not have Mikhail and . . . and his daughter in the same place. To go now would be to doom one of them, at least, to death. And dogs . . . men? Think, Christoph, think! The noise such a crowd would make would alert him, and who can say what he would do? Kill her? Do you want that? Even if we managed to save Melisande by some miracle, would she thank you for her father's death?"

Gavril reluctantly nodded. "We must be circumspect. But also, since this girl has come to us, who is to say they will be in the same place they were? Urvan will not trust her and will have moved them. This will require great care, not belligerence. It is time to speak of this, Kazimir. As little as we trust each other, there are other lives at stake now."

"Speak of this?" Christoph cried, and Charlotte began to weep against his shoulder. "There is no time for chatter!"

"We must *take* time," Gavril said. "The animal will not hurt Miss Melisande, not as long as he is wanting the chalice. You have no idea of the danger this presents. We *must* talk!"

WHAT did he want with her rosary? Melisande wondered. Her captor sat in the corner crooning over it, telling the beads, repairing the string where he had broken it. Magda had disappeared, and the man appeared to be waiting for her, for occasionally he looked up, listening to a noise outside the hut.

"Why don't you tell me what you want?" Melisande said in her rudimentary Russian. "If I know what you want, I could help you get it."

The man looked up, his dark, fierce eyes wide. He stumbled over to her and shook the rosary in her face. "I have been brought here by this!"

Melisande shrank back. The man was filthy and foul, his odor thick as that of rotting food. His fisted hand, clutching the glowing beads of her rosary, was grimy and his fingernails long and chipped, with dirt encrusted under them. "I don't understand," she said, trying to keep the quiver out of her voice, determined to not let him know how frightened she was. "How could my rosary bring you here?"

The man leaned toward her and dangled the rosary in her face, snatching it away when she reached out for it. "Your father gave you this," he said, then laughed.

"How did you know?"

"He is a thief. He stole it. I saw him, ten years ago in the church of Saint Demetrius in Constanta!"

Melisande fought back the tears. "No! No, it cannot be. He . . . he told me he bought it in a street bazaar . . . he described the vendor, an old man who was selling it to put his daughter through school, he—" She stopped and bowed her head. Lies . . . it was all lies, a pretty story to fool her into accepting the stolen artifact.

The Russian collapsed in a heap on the dirt floor of the hut and held the rosary up to the thin stream of faint, silvery light that peeked through the curtain that covered the glassless window opening. "He stole it; I saw him do it as I watched, for I had been trying to think how to get them. I followed him, but what a clever thief he was! He slipped away and disappeared, and I lost his trail."

"Why . . . why did you want them? What do they mean?" Melisande whispered. She glanced toward the door, wondering if she could get free of the ropes that bound her and escape if she kept him occupied. It was still night, dark but moonlit, for the moon had waxed almost full now. Could she find her way back to the castle? Or could she hide until dawn? Surely Kazimir, Christoph, and the others would be looking for her by now.

"What do they mean? Oh, they have power. So much power, but only when united with their companion, the Blood Amber Chalice. And we need the moon . . . the blood moon. Soon it comes, and then . . ." He held the beads up and shook them, laughing, a creaky, rusty sound. "And then I will have all that was stolen from me. They were not always red, you know, these beads," he said, his voice calming, lilting through the soft, slurred syllables of his native tongue.

Melisande listened, hearing a more cultured note in his tone. She stayed silent, trying to work on the knots that bound her.

"Once, they were golden. This is amber, the gift of centuries past, ancient resin from long dead trees, and holy. This is why it is used to make rosaries and other sacred things. The chalice."

Melisande listened to the man's tale; he halted many times, stumbling through parts of it, recovering, and then telling more. She had to concentrate, for Russian was a relatively new language for her, though it seemed natural to hear it, the longer she listened.

Once, many centuries before, he said, there was a young man in Romania named Demetrius. He was of a well-to-do family, but without the gentling influence of a mother—she had died giving him life—he became wild, spending all of his time with the gypsies in their camp, dancing, laughing, singing. When he was sixteen, his father remarried, and his stepmother felt ashamed that her stepson spent so much time with the ragged gypsies and so convinced his father that the boy needed an education. So they sent him to the monks. Older than the other students, and wild, Demetrius found it difficult to settle down to the rigorous and scholarly ways of the monks, but he was very bright and became interested, soon, applying himself and becoming a scholar.

Melisande listened intently, finding in the man's voice a tonic for her fear. She was so tired; she stopped wrestling with the knots, for they were too tight, and she was weakening. She huddled in her cloak and calmed herself. She must save her strength and look for a way to escape. The man *must* sleep at some point.

He went on with his story.

Demetrius had been at the monastery for three years and had decided to take orders, but then word came to him through a friend from his younger, wild days, that his father, at the urging of his wife, who now had two young children to worry about, was going to send his army into the hills and drive out the gypsies, who had always been allowed to roam freely, as long as they did not prey on the prince's sheep. Demetrius left the monastery and returned home to remonstrate with his father, but the man would not be moved. He was concerned for his young family and wished to please his beautiful wife, and so would do as she wished.

And so Demetrius, asking for two days, bore the gifts he had brought with him for his old friends, a golden amber goblet and rosary, into the hills. He wished to warn them and try to help them find some place else to go. But the army, led by an impatient man who had always hated the gypsies, moved into the hills right away instead of waiting the two days for which Demetrius had bargained.

The gypsy men put up resistance, but Demetrius, rather than fight, fled into the hills with some of the old people and young mothers and children. He had promised the gypsy king to save them. But the army followed; fearing anyone alive would tell the story of how far they had exceeded their order, which truly was just to drive the gypsies off the land, they slaughtered the old men and women, and even the mothers holding their babies to their breasts.

Demetrius, trying to protect one old woman, flung himself in front of her, and a soldier pierced him to the heart. As he died, his blood flowing freely over the chalice and rosary he had been holding as he prayed for the band, the gypsy woman whose life he had died to save shrieked a curse; the generations of Demetrius's murderers would suffer until a man of his father's blood would rise up and atone for the blood of the innocents.

Demetrius's father and even his stepmother were horrified by what had happened, and not only because of their son's sacrifice, also because of the death of the gypsy innocents. When Demetrius's father went to the scene to pray for forgiveness, he found the chalice and rosary driven into the bloody mud of the scene and rescued them, but they were no longer golden. They were blood red. He founded a church on the site, and the chalice and rosary were relics cherished on the feast of Saint Demetrius every year.

There was silence in the dim cabin as Melisande digested the heartrending story of the slaughter of the gypsies. Who would have imagined she could be so moved when her own life was in mortal jeopardy? To think that she had held the rosary all those years, never knowing what she had. "But," she said, rousing herself, "why then do you want these items, if they are indeed Saint Demetrius's relics? They must be sacred and revered, not fought over and stolen back and forth like some child's toy."

"Why? *Why*?" He caressed the crimson beads and held them up. "Because of what happened many years after, when the beads and chalice left the church to be protected by a great nobleman, a descendent of Saint Demetrius's father. That is the reason I sought these beads for so long. When I found your father again, I knew it was meant to be. They are seeking me out, for I am the one who will use them when the moon turns to blood. I paid him to steal the Blood Amber Chalice."

"I don't understand . . ." Melisande began to say, still lost as to why the pieces were so important to the madman, but the lunatic was rising.

He stood, shaking the rosary. "He betrayed me! I knew he would, and my plan depended upon it. I followed him to Brandenburg, and yet let him slip away," he said, waggling his fingers, "knowing he had the chalice, knowing he was going to retrieve the rosary. I followed him here, to this wretched place. But the foolish man . . . he still did not understand my determination and held back the relic. Now he will give me the chalice or suffer. Unless I get it before the blood moon, I will kill both of you."

Seeing the madness in his dark eyes, Melisande had no cause to doubt him.

Chapter 18

KAZIMIR KNEW Gavril's eyes were upon him, but he was not going to tell the entire story. Time was wasting. The moon was calling to him to go and find Melisande, but he resisted the urge to slip away. Being a wolf had its benefits, but rescuing Melisande from the lunatic that was his brother was a task for a man, not a beast. Transformation, he decided, would be saved until it was most efficacious.

Charlotte, after whispering to Christoph, who shrugged impatiently, spoke up. "I think we ought to move to the reception room where the fire is," she said, with a glance at Count Gavril, who shivered and huddled in on himself.

But the count straightened and with a bow and ghostly smile for Charlotte said, "I think we may stay in the great hall. I will not collapse, and a few moments more of discussion only will it take before we decide how best to rescue Miss Melisande and her unfortunate father. Speak, Vasilov, if you are willing to tell the truth."

Kazimir, holding on to his temper even in the face of the other man's goading, kept his story brief, merely saying that the chalice and rosary were treasured in a Romanian church for centuries. "But a sect grew up over the centuries that believed the chalice held some power, and I am afraid my brother believed in it. And so . . . I fear he hired Melisande's father to steal the chalice for him from the church at Constanta in Romania. Why the man didn't then hand it over to Urvan, I have no idea. I did not even know my brother was alive. I knew Mikhail had stolen the chalice, and I heard a vague story in Brandenburg about another Russian," he said, with a glance at Gavril, "but I was misled as to the other Russian's identity. I will not lie; my brother's involvement in this makes it much worse than if it was just some . . . some befuddled fool. Urvan is dangerous. Terribly dangerous."

Gavril was watching him, and Kazimir turned, gazed at him steadily, but did not say a word. The distrust between them must rest for now.

"I cannot believe that Mikhail has managed to conceal this . . . this miraculous chalice on his person or in this castle," Christoph said. "He was rescued by my uncle from a jail cell in Brandenburg! Where would he keep such an item? It is all nonsense. I still say we go into the forest with the help of Magda and rescue Melisande and her father." He turned to the young woman and in German said, "Magda, you will help me, will you not?" He put his hand on her shoulder. "Please? Help me to rescue poor Melisande from this evil man?"

Magda gazed up into his blue eyes, the mirror of her own, and felt a wellspring of hope. It was wrong that Melisande Davidovich, who had only ever been kind to her, should be in such a terrible situation. She herself well knew that the prince could be unkind at times. If this should end badly, she would be to blame, even though she hadn't known what was to come when she made the agreement with the prince. How could she bear it if Melisande were hurt? As much trouble as she was in, she thought, tears welling in her eyes at the kind pressure of Christoph's hand on her shoulder, it could yet be worse. Perhaps . . . perhaps she should throw herself on Christoph's mercy and trust him to help her.

"We cannot trust her," Charlotte cried, stepping forward and gesturing toward Magda. "She led Mikhail Davidovich to danger and helped the demon capture Melisande. She will trick you all!"

Magda watched the young countess's eyes and saw the fury and distrust there. What had she ever done that the countess should be so unkind to her? For a year or more now the girl, once long ago her friend, had been hurtful and harsh toward her when they met. She should not be so. She should be more sympathetic. Anger built, fueled by resentment at injustices she had suffered.

The beautiful silvery man spoke in another language . . . English, Magda thought. *English.* She listened hard. She had begun to learn a very little English, and she caught some small part of what he said. Magda had betrayed Melisande Davidovich, the man said, and was not trustworthy. She thought that might be what he was saying; Charlotte was nodding and agreeing with him, her blue eyes eager. Whoever the devil in the woods was, the Russian count went on, they could not trust Magda to help them when she was in league with such a dangerous man.

Magda stepped away from Christoph's hand, her resolution hardening. These people in the castle, what did they know? Always with the easy life, while she struggled and waited on dirty pawing men in the tap room and dealt with her father . . . with Wilhelm Brandt . . . no, no one would help her when this was all done, no matter what. And no one would believe the truth. She had known that from the minute she had learned all about her past. When this was over, all they would remember was that she had led to the father and daughter's capture.

"There is only one way you will get Miss Melisande and her father back," Magda said, hardening her heart, determined to do what she must for herself. Anything to get her away from Wolfbeck so she could deal with the coming hardship in her life with some degree of comfort. "You *must* give up the cup, the red cup. If you do not, then either Davidovich or . . . or Miss Melisande will die." Her heart ached as she said the awful words, but she had been pushed past endurance. It was their fault, not hers.

The big, dark, scarred Russian looked at her as if she were something one would find under a rock in the river, and replied in German, "We do not know that the cup is here, or even that there is a cup. Perhaps Davidovich never did steal it, or perhaps he lost it along the way, or perhaps he truly did destroy it. Did Urvan tell you where it would be? Did Davidovich reveal where he had hidden it?"

Trembling at his tone, she said, "It is hidden in the castle somewhere, but . . . but where, Davidovich has not said."

Kazimir watched her, heard her stumble over her words, saw the fear in her eyes. She was not doing this because she was innately evil, he decided. She was driven to it somehow. The girl felt she had no choice but go along with Urvan in his madness. Could he use that? Could he manipulate her to lead him to Melisande?

"If the cup is here at all," he said rapidly in English to the others, "Davidovich will not tell Urvan, for if he has held back so long, he no doubt fears that to give up that one piece of information now will be his death. With what else does he have to bargain?"

"I still think there must be a way that we can go and rout out this madman," Christoph said.

Magda watched him with mistrust, the conversation, in a language she did not understand, making her visibly uneasy. It was a dilemma; if they confined her, they gave up her help in finding Melisande. If she managed to escape them, Kazimir thought, she might even know the secret of the castle, the hidden passages, and find a way out, even with the door bolted. They needed her willing help.

"If you do that," Kazimir said to Christoph, watching the girl, "if you hunt him out in the forest, even if you find him, even if you manage to corner him, Urvan will kill before he dies. If you wish to risk Miss Melisande's life, then go ahead. The two—father and daughter—will not be held in the same place. You will doom one, perhaps both."

He had one piece of information that he did not wish to share with anyone. No one else, as far as he knew, knew of the Blood Amber Rosary. Nor would they learn of it from him. The blood moon was almost upon them, and he did not trust Gavril Roschkov.

And Roschkov did not trust him. He could see it in his pale, weary eyes.

"Count Christoph . . . may I speak to you—alone?" Gavril Roschkov studiously avoided Kazimir's intent stare and took the young count off to the dark shadows under the gallery.

"What is it, Count Roschkov?" Christoph said, impatiently, glancing back at the others who still stood in the big open area of the great hall.

"I need to know your position on Count Vasilov." Gavril's steady gaze demanded all of Christoph's attention.

He stared at him for a long moment. "Perhaps you will explain to me, sir, what is between you? And what is it about this damnable cup that is so important?"

"That, I'm afraid, would take far too long to explain, and is it important now? More important is the fact that you cannot and *must* not trust Count Vasilov."

"He says the same of you. I know there is some bad blood there, but it is nothing to me. Why should I believe one of you over the other?"

"Do not forget," Gavril Roschkov said, his silvery eyes glowing oddly in the dark shadows of the overhanging gallery, "that Mikhail Davidovich permits me into his room and not Vasilov. Does that not say that in matters of his and his daughter's safety, I am more to be trusted? But beyond that . . . Vasilov is the reason your young friend, Miss Davidovich, is in the hands of that monster! How can you even question?"

Christoph glanced over at Count Vasilov, who was speaking to Magda while the girl gazed at him with fear. There was much to what Count Roschkov said; they only had Vasilov's word for it that Melisande went with him willingly, and that she disappeared while he was engaged in looking for Magda.

"What if Vasilov is in league with his brother?" Roschkov murmured, commanding Christoph's attention again. "What if this is all calculated to get the cup, and Miss Melisande, once she is no longer of use, will die? As well as her poor father?"

His mind was racing. If only he could get away and run as a wolf . . . if only he could look for Melisande himself. He had a feeling that he could find her from her scent if he could just escape and go on his own to search for her. It was tempting. But what if he was wrong? What if his skills were not yet developed? Melisande's life hung precariously in the balance, and there was between her and death the thin line of his own intelligence.

"Christoph!"

Charlotte's imperious tone cut into Christoph's consciousness, as did the sound of a commotion. "Not now, Charlotte!" he barked, putting up one hand. "Count Roschkov, I must know all! Tell me this minute more about this ridiculous chalice, its supposed properties and—"

"Christoph!"

"*Not now!* Tell me, Count Roschkov! Perhaps then I will believe you."

Count Roschkov sighed, and said, "The cup is much as Vasilov said . . . It is supposed to have magical powers due to an old legend that has grown up around it."

"Christoph!"

"Charlotte, not now!" Christoph cried, waving at her to be quiet. "Leave me be. I am speaking of important things."

But Charlotte raced to his side and pulled his sleeve. "No, *now!* He is gone. Count Vasilov is gone! He and Magda were whispering together. I left the great hall for just a moment, but when I returned they were both gone! They have disappeared together! What shall we do?"

"Gone? What? They have gone? Why did you not tell me?"

"I tried to," she said, with a sharp tone. "But you would not listen to me."

Christoph raced from the shadows of the overhanging gallery into the vast openness of the great hall, then to the huge double doors that fronted the castle, where the butler cowered, his dark eyes wide. To the door Christoph ran, flung it open, and gazed out on the darkness only to see . . . no one. "Steinholz, which way did they go?"

The butler, eyes wide with fear at the mistake he had made in allowing the imperious Russian past him, shrugged and shook his head.

"Why did you allow him to leave?"

Steinholz, trembling from head to toe, stuttered, "He told me to open the door, count. I did not know the Russian gentleman was to be kept here. I . . . You all spoke other languages . . . I did not understand . . . he said they were going to rescue Miss Davidovich! He said you had all agreed to send him and Fräulein Brandt."

Christoph raced outside into the dark, just past the shelter of the porte cochere. The silvery trail of the almost full moon, now far traveled in its night's journey, gave only the faintest light over the landscape, but enough to see that Count Kazimir and Magda were long gone. He needed to follow them.

"We must go after them," Roschkov said from behind, still within the great hall. "We cannot allow them to reach Urvan Vasilov, if that is their objective. Count Kazimir Vasilov is a filthy murderer who should have been hung. He killed my beloved sister."

"What?" Christoph whirled and stared into the castle at the pale, slim Russian, his figure dwarfed by the huge maw of the open doors. "What are you talking about?"

Giving an inarticulate cry of fury, the Russian then forced himself to calm. "I should have broken my silence on this subject long ago!" Roschkov said, one hand trembling as it touched his forehead. "Now . . . oh, what have I done? Now Kazimir and Urvan . . . they must be working together on this to get the chalice! And if he has gone with Magda . . . perhaps he even now knows how to find it, or has hope of convincing Mikhail—"

"What are you talking about?" Christoph repeated, striding back into the castle and up to the count, shaking him by the shoulder. "What do you mean, Count Kazimir is a murderer?"

Roschkov turned and stared at Christoph. "I had sworn myself to silence on this, once there was no hope of retribution through the law. I have pledged myself to revenge, even if it is my last act walking the earth. Urvan Vasilov, Kazimir's brother, was married to my beloved younger sister Franziska. But Kazimir lusted after her in his evil heart and made advances." His open gaze shuttered. "Something happened. He killed her. I don't know why . . . All I know is I got a letter from her just days before she died . . . She *begged* me to come to get her, as she . . . she feared them both. I was on my way, but when I got there, it was to find Kazimir had murdered her. Urvan had disappeared, leaving only a note begging for forgiveness for hurting her; jealousy had overcome him. But he did not kill her. Kazimir did. Urvan said that since his brother had killed his beloved, he could no longer live." He stopped, a look of confusion on his silvery-pale face.

"Yes?" Christoph cried impatiently. "Yes?"

He shook his head, but continued. "The authorities would take no action, saying they had no proof that Kazimir Vasilov murdered poor dear Franziska. The letter was not enough, they said, since Urvan was gone and could not be questioned; witnesses said he committed suicide, jumping from a bridge in another town."

"But that is not true, for Urvan still lives!" That was Charlotte.

"Yes. I do not understand." He clutched his silvery hair in anguish and confusion. "They must be working in league with each other, for both must be devils!"

Christoph shouted at Steinholz to get his cloak and then turned to stare at the Russian, his thoughts tumbling and rattling like die in a cup. "None of this makes any sense at all. If your story is true, if Kazimir made improper advances and then killed your sister, even if Urvan survived attempting suicide, would they not be mortal enemies? Why would they have come together?"

Gavril was silent, just shaking his head, his face twisted in bewilderment.

Christoph bitterly regretted allowing the two Russians to stay at the castle. He didn't trust either of them and didn't care one bit about any cup or chalice, whatever it was. All he cared about was Melisande.

But how was he going to rescue her? How was he to know what was right to do without endangering her life any further?

Chapter 19

MELISANDE HAD slept a little on her uncomfortable pallet of rags and straw but was awoken by voices. Blearily, she peered through the dimness; it was still night, an endless night of horror and confusion. Who else was in the hut? One voice was her captor's, certainly, but there was another voice, more guttural, and whoever owned it was shouting.

Shouting.

She squinted, but the light was awful, the flickering, smoldering fire in the crude hearth just barely making visible the outlines of a broken chair and rough table. She could make out only her captor. He stood, silhouetted by the feeble firelight.

His tone reasonable, he said in beautiful, clear Russian, "Perhaps the girl truly knows nothing. It is possible that her father does not confide in her."

Melisande strained her eyesight but could make out no other figure.

"She is a liar and a thief," growled the other voice, the tone thick with contempt and hatred. "Just like her father. And we must beat the truth out of her, even if it kills her in the doing."

Melisande whimpered and shrunk back, feeling the unfamiliar weight of some binding on her ankles. She felt in the dark and found clasped to her a thick length of chain that was locked onto her ankle. So in her slumber she had been restrained! Who was it who desired her death? She had seen no one so far except her captor and Magda.

"But we have the rosary, at least," her kidnapper said, his tone pacifying.

He rose and turned, staring at Melisande, and his expression changed, his dirty face twisting and his eyes glinting with malevolence. "But now we need the cup," said the other voice, from his mouth, "and then we will own the power."

Horror trilled through Melisande as the guttural, angry voice emanated from the same man who a moment before had sounded reasonable and almost sane. He was arguing with himself! He pointed one long finger at her and said in the same, hoarse voice, "She will surrender the cup or die."

Then his face changed, the expression almost bewildered, and he cried out, holding his head in both of his hands, "Then will you be satisfied? Then will you cease this torment?"

Shivering in fear, Melisande kept herself resolutely still, afraid that any movement on her part would draw his attention away from his internal demons and to her. He shrank down and crept away to the hearth, throwing another tied bundle of dried leaves onto the fire. It hissed and smoked, and a pungent aroma filled the tiny space. He muttered, "Yes, then we will be satisfied." He rocked back and forth on his heels, clicking the rosary beads together under his shabby cloak and crooning over them. "We will have the beads and the cup, and the blood moon will come, and we will transform. Power will be ours, and we will be satisfied."

MAGDA Brandt had not spoken since they left the castle. He had hauled her rather roughly at first, anxious to make haste before their leaving was noted. But now they sped through the forest, faint moonlight silvering it with a hint of misty light, her surefootedness coming from an intimate knowledge of the way. It was some distance, and she took a circuitous route; no wonder no one had yet found them, nor stumbled upon the hiding place. She knew of paths that were virtually invisible unless one knew just what to look for, and would stop occasionally, get her bearings, look for some landmark, then continue leading the way. The moonlight was dying, and night would soon be over. He prayed that he had time to use what was left of it to transform and overcome Urvan.

Urvan . . . he was alive; the fearful wonder of that was something Kazimir could not yet quite grasp. But it was true. Urvan was alive and still obsessed with the magical power of the Blood Amber Chalice and Blood Amber Rosary.

Finally, after they climbed through a thick tangle of dead vines, Magda halted. "This is it," she said, her voice trembling. She pointed to a crude hut that squatted crookedly between two pines. A thin ribbon of smoke drifted from a hole in the roof and was wafted away by a puff of air before it could rise even enough to be noticeable from ten feet into the forest. Even in daylight, this would not be easy to find.

"Who is with Urvan, Melisande or Mikhail?"

But she shook her head, mutely, refusing as she had from the beginning to name which captive was inside, or perhaps whether both were contained therein.

"All he wants is the cup," she said, her voice quivering.

It was the same thing—the only thing—she would say to him. It was the only reason she had led him here, because he had promised to give Urvan the cup if he could just be sure Melisande still lived. He had been surprised she had agreed to guide him, for he knew he frightened her, but she had eagerly accepted his offer and slipped away with him.

"If you give it to him," she said, clasping her hands in front of her, "he will release them both."

Kazimir took in a deep breath and let it out slowly. Urvan. What had become of him? Many years ago, the voices had almost taken him over, but he was still struggling for his sanity. Now he must be completely gone; Kazimir supposed he would soon know. All those years ago when the report came that Urvan was dead, it had been a relief. Though no body was ever recovered, there was no way he could have survived, the folks who saw his jump said. Apparently they were wrong. Kazimir took in a deep breath and approached the door.

"Sir?"

He looked back and saw Magda standing there, wringing her hands together in apprehension.

"He is not a prince, then?" she asked.

"No . . . he is a count, like me."

Her eyes lit with an odd light for a moment, but then she shook her head and whispered, "And he was never going to take me away from Wolfbeck, was he?"

"I don't imagine so."

"What, then, is the cup for, if not to prove he is a prince?"

"You do not want to know the power of the cup."

"Tell me!"

"No," Kazimir muttered to her, his fury boiling over but still concerned that his voice not carry. "Have you not done enough damage? Have you not endangered a lady whose hem you are not fit to touch? If she is harmed, I will see that you are sent to prison for your part in this awful affair."

He turned back and quietly crept through the hut's doorway, sidling past the crude door, which leaned at an angle in the opening. He knew he could kill Urvan. He could transform in the blink of an eye, leap on him and tear his throat out. But he also knew that it was not necessarily the answer to this predicament. Overpowering Urvan would not save both captives. Killing him might doom one or both. He needed to assess the situation and decide how best to handle his brother's madness, and the thorny issue of the chalice and the rosary and the impending blood moon. Young Christoph had thought it a simple matter, but it was complicated and fraught with difficulties.

The moment he was inside, he knew Melisande was there; her scent, filling his nostrils, was the only freshness the hut owned. Another smoky smell overlaid every other, the bitter odor of green leaves burning. At first, as he crept in, all he could detect was the faint light of the smoky fire in the crude hearth on the far wall. But then he made out a figure crouched on its haunches, poking at the fire with a stick. The creature turned, and it was Urvan . . . or at least he supposed it must be his brother.

He was crouched and twisted, bent as if the earth's pull was drawing him downward to hell. His hair was long, as it always had been, but now it was matted and threaded with gray, and his lined, sagging face was covered in smoke and dirt. He appeared little better than a feral creature. Once he had been tall and regal, a giant among men. Once he had gazed at his younger brother and announced his marriage to the most beautiful lady in all the land, Franziska Ivanne Roschkov. He had spoken of the children they would have and the sweetness she would bring him, the repose he would find in her arms. But the voices had already begun long before, and he imagined conspiracies everywhere, plots to take away his land among the peasants, and he even accused Kazimir and

Franziska of plotting against him. He was seized by a mono-mania, a desperate search for the legendary chalice and rosary, with their promise of dark power and hideous transformation.

When the paranoia took over, that was when the real trouble began, and when Kazimir made the mistakes that led to this awful conclusion.

Urvan saw him. "You have come, my brother," he said.

Kazimir stilled. Whatever he had thought would happen, it was not that Urvan would welcome him so calmly. It was almost as if he was expected. "I have," he said, carefully. He glanced around, but the light inside was faint. It was choked with a filthy haze of smoke, and Kazimir felt his throat constricting. He coughed.

Urvan chuckled. "Can you not breathe?"

Kazimir desperately wanted to find Melisande and take her from this awful place, but he had to deal with Urvan first. He started toward him, but his brother drew a long, wicked pistol from under his filthy robe. Instead of pointing it at Kazimir though, he pointed it toward a dim corner of the hut.

There was a clank, and peering through the dimness, Kazimir could make out a figure; as his sight adjusted, he saw it was Melisande.

"Let her go, Urvan!" he growled, clenching his teeth against the fury that threatened to make him forget his purpose. The air was thick, and he felt a wave of dizziness wash over him.

The creature that was once his brother began to shake, but it was a moment before a rusty laugh erupted. With his free hand, Urvan searched under his ragged cloak and pulled something out. He shook it in the air; it was the rosary.

"You!" he screeched. "*You* plotted against me and persecuted me. *You* took what was rightfully mine and perverted it to your own vile use. *You* took the power that should have been given to me."

Kazimir's mind sped through the possibilities as Urvan stared, shaking the rattling rosary in the air. Magda had crept in and stood behind Kazimir near the door. Urvan did not have the chalice yet. If the rosary was gone forever, though it would not make the damnable spell impossible, it would weaken it, perhaps.

"I took nothing from you, brother," he said, trying to stall, trying to figure out the best way to handle this terrible situation. Should he transform now and subdue Urvan? But he had already decided that would not free both captives; he must trust his own ingenuity and make up his plan as he went along.

He glanced over at Melisande, who was watching with horror on her face. Every tender moment they had shared sped through his mind, and he reflected that those moments were gone forever. He had always known how it would end, and so he should not regret what could never have been, but he did. With her he had found a kind of peace he had never known, and had discovered hope . . . hope that in the powers she seemed to possess he might find a cure for his own cursed enchantment. He had begun to think that was what the gypsy seer had meant when he told him to follow the chalice and find his salvation. But that hope was an illusion, he feared. Once she saw him as a beast, she would never look at him without revulsion.

Resolutely turning his mind away from those weakening thoughts, he kept his eye on the beads, which Urvan now turned and rubbed in his free hand. Urvan was the best shot with a gun that Kazimir had ever seen. While he had eventually been able to best him in swordplay and fist fighting, Urvan was a marksman of military precision and training. Kazimir had little to fear from a bullet, unless it was aimed with incredible accuracy, but Melisande . . . he could not risk her being shot.

"Urvan," he said, thinking to try reason. "Give up this quest. Perhaps Mikhail is telling the truth. Perhaps he does not have the chalice."

"Do not think to pacify me," Urvan muttered. He stopped for a moment and clutched his head, the rosary beads appearing like drops of blood against his high domed forehead. "I know," he muttered. "I *know*! *No*," he shouted, "I will not let them trick me!"

It was the damned voices again, Kazimir thought. He lunged forward in that moment to grab the rosary away from

Urvan, but his brother was swifter than would have seemed possible and snatched the beads back, holding them behind him. "I will kill the girl!" he said, turning his pistol again on Melisande, who whimpered in the corner, her chains clattering as she skittered up against a pile of moldering rags. "Do not do that again or I promise I will kill her and her lying, cheating thief of a father, too."

Melisande cried out in that moment, "Father? He has my father?"

"Hush, Melisande . . ." Kazimir began, but Urvan was growing more agitated.

"Davidovich does have the chalice, I know it!" Urvan roared. "Why do you think I followed him here from Brandenburg? He stole it, I know he did, for I hired him to do so." He quieted his voice, and a sly light entered his mad eyes. "And then . . ." He cackled, rubbing his long-fingered hands together. "I was clever . . . so clever! I let him slip away from Constanta with it, as I knew he would. The temptation was too great. The chalice was his, and he knew where the rosary was. I *knew* he would lead me directly to the rosary, for I *knew* that he was the one who stole the beads so many years ago, before . . . before *you*, my brother, betrayed me."

"What do you mean, Urvan, about the rosary?" Kazimir needed to keep him talking. Fatigue was overcoming him, and his eyesight was growing bleary. He fought to stay upright. What was wrong with him? He had to figure out how to defeat him in such a way as would rescue both Melisande and Mikhail. But how? His mind was growing foggy and confused. He coughed on the choking smoke.

Urvan said, "I knew he had the rosary, for I saw with my own eyes at Constanta, many years before. I saw Davidovich steal it right from under the holy men's long noses!" He laughed, a high-pitched squeal of sound. "I tried to follow him then, but ah, such a clever one, Mikhail Davidovich was. He disappeared and slipped away, and . . . I could not find him. Not for many years." He frowned and looked down. "Lost years. Then I wed Franziska, for she could offer me some of what I wanted. Not all, but some. But she . . . you *both* betrayed me, and then she had to go away." He looked up again, his dark eyes wide. "Then I figured it out . . . how to be free, how to pursue the unholy pair and gain what had been denied me! I prayed they would hang you as her murderer," he growled, his mouth twisted in a hate-filled grimace. He took in a deep breath. "Then at long last I found Davidovich and I knew. I was meant to match the blood amber pieces and gain the power. And even more sure was I when the thief agreed to steal for me the missing piece."

His dark eyes widened even more, the black pupils standing out like marble against the bloodshot whites. "It is a sign, you see, that I am the one," he said, shaking one finger in admonishment. "The signs . . . that Davidovich stole the rosary ten years ago, that I saw him, that I found him again, near the church, and that he agreed to steal the chalice. And then . . . he led me directly here, where the rosary came to me, like a lover in the night . . . all signs." He paused. "Tell me, brother Kazimir, did the gypsy in the market in Constanta find you?" He chuckled and laid one finger on his bearded chin. "Let me see . . . did she tell you that you could be cured? Did she tell you it was your destiny to stop me, and that you would find relief from your curse in such a way?"

Through the haze, feeling every nerve in his body twitch, Kazimir tried to understand him. "The witch . . . the gypsy witch in Constanta? The witch in the marketplace who knew all about me, about Franziska's curse, about my transformation . . ."

"Yes, yes . . . I saw you there, seeking the chalice. You fool. You sought to destroy it, but it is too powerful for that. I crossed the witch's palm with gold, and she told you to follow the chalice, did she not? She said, *'follow the chalice and you will be free.'*"

Kazimir nodded, his stomach heaving. His sight was getting bleary.

Urvan stood tall, almost as straight as his former regal self, and said, "I arranged it all. I told her what to say. I am the One, the One who is to become master of all wolves, the werewolf that will kill and feed and hold mastery over every soul . . . even yours, my simpleton brother. I will go home, then, and those peasants, the ones who conspired against me . . . I will transform in front of their eyes, and all of them will die, and their babies I will feed upon, relishing the tender flesh like the most delicious swine flesh."

Melisande cried out in horror. She understood every word of the madman's elegant Russian, for he had drawn up and resembled perhaps what he once was, a Russian nobleman. A mad Russian nobleman. His words echoed in the filthy hut, dancing through her brain like evil pixies. Witches and werewolves and rituals . . . he was insane, but there was an awful sincerity about his words. Kazimir—as unbelievable as it all was, they were apparently brothers—seemed to believe him, even when he spoke of becoming a werewolf, lord of all the others.

And he had her father held somewhere no one else could find. The relief she had at first felt upon seeing Kazimir enter the hut had fled. He was deeply entwined in all of this, so deeply involved she now saw all of his former kindness to her as mere softening, an attempt on his part to get her to divulge whatever she might know about her father's nefarious activities. And the rosary . . . he had been interested in it, had asked her questions, interested beyond mere pleasantry, she now saw. It was all a part of this terrible whole, this thick stew of madness, thievery, legend and magic.

Kazimir looked ill; his hands were twitching, and he appeared fevered. Melisande tried to understand what was happening, but all she could think about was her father. Where was he? How could she get out of this nightmare and find him?

Her captor sunk back into his raving madness, slunk over toward her, and waved the pistol. "If neither you nor your father will tell me where the Blood Amber Chalice is, I will ensure that you both suffer a torturous death. You cannot deny me my rights and live. First, he will die before your eyes for making a deal with me and then going back on his word, stealing the chalice and then having the effrontery to think he can use it himself!"

"He would not try to use it," she cried out, horrified at the very thought. "Where is my father? Please don't hurt him."

"He is hidden . . . concealed so well no one will ever find him. He is weak, now, and sick." He chuckled. "Just like my brother." He turned and gazed at Kazimir, who was sunk down on one knee. "Look at him! He thought himself invulnerable, but I know more than he. Even one as strong as he can be defeated." Urvan turned back to her and paced close, bending over her, his eyes burning with dark hunger. The hand holding the pistol was dropped to his side as he leaned over her. "But your poor papa!" he said, with mocking sympathy. "He must give me what I want . . . One of you *must* heed my words! The cold is weakening Mikhail Davidovich, and the dampness. He coughs and is fevered. If he doesn't tell me soon, he may die, even. Someone must tell me! Where is the chalice?"

Kazimir staggered up behind his brother, carrying a rock from the floor of the crude hut. Magda was watching with horror, and Melisande thought, if Kazimir should hit the man, and he should die, what would become of her father?

"No! Do not hit him!" Melisande screamed.

Urvan whirled and struck Kazimir's hand, and the rock flew out of it to the floor. The two men grappled together, wrestling, grunting, and scuffling in the dimness of the hut. Both tumbled to the floor and rolled.

Magda screamed and wailed, while Melisande just tried to keep out of the way. The pistol, waving in the air one minute, disappeared from sight and then went off, the loud report echoing as the dust settled and the two men stilled.

Chapter 20

ONE OF the men rolled away from the huddle and rose.

It was Urvan. Was Kazimir dead? Despite his deception, despite her doubt of his intentions, she prayed he still lived.

The Russian kicked at his brother, and Magda, sobbing, was told to get a rope. If Kazimir lived, he was unconscious. With Magda helping, Urvan, surprisingly nimble, secured his brother's legs and arms in thick coils of rope.

"How can you help him, Magda?" Melisande cried, watching. "How can you? He's mad, can you not see that?"

Tears streaming down her face, making trails in the dust that coated her cheeks, Magda glanced over at the Russian, doubt and fear clouding her expression. "He . . . he has promised to take me away from here."

"Is your home so awful that you would do this monster's bidding to get away?"

With bitterness twisting her mouth and tragic knowledge in her tear-filled eyes, she gazed at Melisande's face as she tied the last knot in the ropes that bound Kazimir and said, in a low trembling tone, "Do not speak of my home. What do you or any of you in your fine castle know about my life? Yes, my home is so awful that even a whisper of hope that he will take me away is worth it. If I don't leave . . ." She shook her head. "I *must* leave. With him or alone, I must leave before . . . before too long."

Melisande didn't know how to respond. What could she say? Magda had always appeared happy, spirited, sure of herself. Was there more in the girl's life than anyone knew? Was there a desperation underlying her spirit? Urvan rolled Kazimir's dead weight over onto the dirty pallet of rags by Melisande.

"Hear me!" He pointed at her, his long dirty fingernail jagged and broken. "Dawn is breaking. Your father will have one last opportunity to tell me where the chalice is. He has hidden it at the castle. If I do not get an answer, then you will suffer for it."

He stooped down close to her, and she stared up directly into eyes that were shot with blood in the yellowed whites. Reaching out, he took one long strand of her honey-colored hair and let it slip through his dirty fingers, his ragged nails scraping the tender flesh of her neck and the ruby ring he wore on his hand glinting dully in the pale dawn light that was just beginning to filter in the one window. "So pretty! Who would believe that such a fool as Davidovich would breed such a pretty little thing as you."

She twisted away from his touch and hid her face in Kazimir's cloak, breathing in deeply his scent of male muskiness and fresh air. Even the scent of the dirt ground into the heavy cloak was preferable to the stale puffs of air from Urvan's fetid breath. Kazimir moved and groaned.

"Melisande," he murmured.

"Kazimir! You are alive!"

As Urvan went to mutter to Magda, Kazimir twisted until his face was close to Melisande's. She gazed into his dark brown eyes, then examined the blood that trickled down from a wound on his head.

"I'm sorry," she whispered. She worked one hand free and stopped a trickle that threatened to go into his eye. "But if you had killed him . . . I could not let you jeopardize my father's life. If Urvan dies, and my father has no one to find him, he will die as well. I know this in my soul."

Quietly, his voice deep with emotion and pain, he said, "You did what you thought best." He sagged and barely shook his head. "What is wrong with me? I feel . . . weak. I am burning up with fever. And I'm so thirsty."

Urvan, with one long, last look at the two of them, left, muttering and growling in his thwarted fury.

"I don't understand any of this," Melisande said, glancing over at Magda, who stirred up the fire and put a pot of water over it, then lifted the cloth that covered the window, allowing some of the smoke to escape. "What is it all about? What is this curse you spoke of? And this chalice my father is supposed to have stolen . . . what does it all mean?"

Kazimir struggled to roll over onto his back and sighed. "The Blood Amber Chalice. He stole it from the church of Saint Demetrius in Constanta, a town in Romania. What my demented brother apparently knew that I did not until I arrived here was that Davidovich knew so much of the church and agreed to perform the thievery because ten years ago he stole the Blood Amber Rosary."

"*My* rosary. Why is it called the Blood Amber Rosary?"

"Once, long ago, it was just plain amber, a gold color, but then tragedy struck, and both pieces turned the color of blood."

"He told me the old story, the history, but it sounds more like superstition to me than truth. But what is this legend attached to it? Why does your brother want it so? What does he think it will do? I understood only little of what he spoke, but he talked of becoming a werewolf. How ridiculous. And revolting!"

Kazimir wished his hands were free. Her lovely face was twisted in anguish, and he would have touched her soft cheek, brushed back her wild locks, if he could have. The depth of his tender feelings surprised and frightened him, for what use were those sensations to him? He turned his mind away from fruitless longing to the awful scene just minutes ago. Panic seized him as he tried to figure out what had gone wrong. He had known he had only a brief time left before dawn robbed him of his ability to transform. From long experience, he knew that he could be a wolf in daylight, but only if he transformed while night still held dominance, and so he had tried. And tried. Nothing had happened. And so panicked, fearing his ebbing strength would leave him helpless, he had seized a rock and tried to use it. If his strength had been normal, even Urvan's sudden awareness of his plan would not have stopped him.

But he was weak. And unable to transform. He had no heart to explain the curse upon him, and could not bear her inevitable revulsion when she discovered the truth about him. There were other worries at that moment more pressing.

"Please," Magda said. She had approached them, and both

turned as best they could to see her. "Please, forgive me," she said, tears coursing down her face. "When I first began, I didn't know I would have to do anything more for him than just fetch him food and help him stay alive out here in this hut. You must believe me. I . . . I didn't know what the chains were for, I swear it! Now I must do what he wishes. He is a dangerous man, and I . . ." She hung her head and fell to her knees.

"Help us escape now," Melisande murmured, urgently, "and we will help you get away from Wolfbeck. I promise you this. Whatever is wrong Magda, we can resolve it. I'll make sure you have what you need."

"I need a husband," she cried, hoarsely, beating the dirt floor of the hut with an open hand. "I need money and a place to live. I need to escape from Wolfbeck." She stood, calmer, and shook her head. "You cannot give me what I need. There is nothing for it but to continue, to finish what I have begun. We will find this chalice, release you both, and he will take me away from here, as he promised. I *must* believe that!" She turned away and went back to the fire, sitting on a low, crude stool and poking at the embers.

Kazimir watched her for a moment. He had thought himself so clever, but it appeared Urvan had told Magda to lead him there. This was all part of his devious plan. But now what? It was imperative that Kazimir make sure the chalice was not used for its sinister purpose. Once unleashed, the awful beast would be invincible.

But now he had another concern. He would die rather than see Melisande Davidovich suffer for a single moment. She had every right and reason to distrust him, but against all hope, he murmured, "Do you trust me?"

"Should I?"

He thought about that before answering. Should she trust him? What had he done to earn it? Despite knowing there could never be anything for them, he hoped to save her from future horror and would do whatever was necessary to free her. "Yes, you should. I will never willfully do anything to harm you, I swear on my life."

"Tell me all, then. Tell me what is between you and your brother. Tell me what you did that he is so furious at you for."

He slumped down, trying to loosen the ropes at his wrist. Urvan was still strong, stronger than he perhaps had imagined, and the knots were tight and secure. Or was it just that he was weak? He felt depleted, as if every drop of blood had been drained from him. "There is no time for discussion of the past now. We must decide what to do when Urvan comes back."

"Roll over," she whispered, "and let me try to loosen your hands from these ropes."

He did so and felt her nimble fingers tugging at the thick knots.

Feverishly she worked at the knot. "We must escape," she whispered. "I'm so afraid."

Kazimir tried to look over his shoulder but could only see the faint glimmer of Melisande's glorious hair as she bent her head, trying to see the ropes to unknot them. "I know. I should have confided in you, but . . . for a time I thought you were part of your father's plan to use the . . . the chalice and rosary."

"*Use* them? Do you really think he would have, if I can pretend I believe in this bizarre legend for the moment?"

"The legend, as bizarre as it sounds, is true. There is magic in this world, Melisande, more than we acknowledge. You know your father better than I. Though he stole the chalice at Urvan's request, I think when he realized that he already had access to the companion piece, the Blood Amber Rosary—and likely realized that was why Urvan had approached him—he either decided to keep the chalice and use its power, or he was afraid to give it to Urvan. I don't know which is true. He pretended his invalidism, though, that I know, staying in bed to fool us all into thinking him helpless and yet using the secret passages in the castle to navigate. With what purpose?"

"No. No, I do not believe that my father would want such foul power as seems promised by this ludicrous legend," Melisande said firmly. "I can't get these knots untied!" she murmured and sagged down, weak and exhausted.

He wished he could touch her. He wished he could kiss her once more. Most of all he wished he could see her free of this terrible situation. He coughed, his throat clogged with dust.

Magda approached, offering a ladle of water. "The prince

said I may give you water," she said, her tone diffident once again.

Kazimir took a long, cool drink. The water had an odd, earthy taste but wasn't unpleasant. It cooled his fever, at least, and soothed his parched throat.

After a while, the crude door rattled and was pushed aside, daylight streaming into the hut as Urvan entered. His face twisted with an expression of awful glee, he rubbed his hands together and approached his two captives. "Oh, Miss Melisande, your father is a delightful man, a most interesting man," Urvan said in Russian. "I know much more than I did before I left this place."

"He told you where he has the chalice," Kazimir said.

"I was not speaking to you, traitor! I was speaking to the sorceress."

"Sorceress?" Melisande whispered.

Kazimir stared at her. She understood Russian! So even she was keeping secrets. How much of this could have been avoided if every one of them had just told the truth? All of it; together they could have defeated Urvan if they had just found a way past the deceit that locked them all in their separate paths, he and Gavril and Mikhail.

"Yes, yes, your father told me your secret, witch! Though he still claims he does not have the chalice—I know he does—he did deign to threaten me!" He rubbed his hands together, then bent over and checked the knots binding Kazimir's hands. Grunting with anger, he motioned for Magda to join him, and they tightened the ropes, then added another couple of knots. Magda then scuttled back to her fireplace and continued to prepare some food.

"My father threatened you? How?" Melisande's voice betrayed her bewilderment.

Kazimir wondered about this development. A sorceress? What was Mikhail thinking, to say such a thing?

"Yes, he threatened me, the fool. Magda has told me about your potions before—your roots and plants, your concoctions and brews—but she did not know what they meant. But I know. Your fool of a father said if I hurt him, you, being a powerful sorceress, would surely slay me." The demonic chuckle that emanated from Urvan rattled around the hut like a dried pea in a gourd. He rubbed his hands together again and, almost dancing on one foot in his restlessness, said, "He does not know I have you captive! Is that not rich? He thinks you can save him, and I did not enlighten the poor fool. Oh, I have been so clever! Never has there been a one such as I . . . destined to strike fear in every heart. My plans are all progressing, and everything I do furthers my aim. I was clever enough to foil a witch."

"Oh no," Melisande murmured. Her stomach twisted in agony, and she almost retched in her fear. Why would her father say such a ludicrous thing? Not knowing she was held captive, he thought to play on the Russian's superstitious nature, but it had, perhaps, sealed both of their fates.

"Urvan, only consider!" Kazimir said. "If she was a powerful sorceress, would chains be able to hold her? Would she be lying now in this wretched hut? Would she not free herself, at least?"

The hut went black to Melisande's sight, and she heard Kazimir speak to his brother as if from a distance, and then not at all. She was wrenched back in time two years. She could almost hear the raucous babble of the frenzied mob that attacked her mother and grandmother. She saw her grandmother's face, twisted in pain but still with an expression of determination.

As the mob closed around them, and Melisande was almost swallowed up, too, her grandmother had lifted her arms to the heavens and called out, "Protect the daughter of my daughter; shelter her in your arms and take her away from this grave peril!" She had said some more in what sounded like Latin, and Melisande had felt a sudden warmth, as of a blanket enveloping her, and from that moment it was as if she was invisible. She was shouldered away from the mob, and though she could see what was happening, she could do nothing to help her mother or grandmother, for the crowd closed in on them. The shrieks of the two beloved women as they were cruelly murdered still haunted her memory. Even the servants of the household were slaughtered that day, but she, Melisande, was left unharmed. And alone.

A witch . . . her grandmother had oft been called that, though no one in the village rejected her healing potions.

Could she have been a sorceress? And were Melisande's own healing abilities from some other source than just learning and trial? The blackness surrounded her, and she felt herself drift away, consciousness almost gone, but she was snapped back, and her vision cleared suddenly. Determination flooded her being.

This was a dangerous moment; she felt it in the marrow of her bones. He must not suspect she was truly a witch, if indeed she was, or it could mean her death. After all, having powers had not protected her grandmother. Urvan was pacing in the tiny hut, stirring up a cloud of dirt as he muttered and raged, his own voice mingling with the other fearful voice that tormented him with superstition and mistrust. She sneezed, and he turned to stare at her.

"If your contract with the devil, as his handmaiden, is sealed, witch, and you have pledged fidelity to him, then you will have given yourself to him as a brand upon your bargain, a stamp upon your covenant."

Puzzled, she just stared at him, not knowing what to think.

"Don't be a fool, Urvan," Kazimir growled. "The girl is an innocent. Anyone with eyes can see that."

Urvan's eyes widened. In the gruff voice of his other self, he said, "Then proof we shall have. Even you, brother of Urvan, are in league with the devil to defeat us! He fears us, the devil, for Satan reigns only as long as no one challenges him. She is merely biding her time, and when our attention is lulled, then she will murder us."

"Urvan!" Kazimir barked. "Don't be a fool! You know the truth. No one is in league with the devil, and Melisande is not a witch! You must believe that."

"Proof I will have," Urvan muttered, his voice more normal, though his eyes were still wide and his whole body trembled. "And there is only one proof, if what you say is true."

Chapter 21

"DO NOT tell me what I must believe!"

"She is not a witch, Urvan! And she doesn't need to prove anything," Kazimir said.

"But she does." Tears welled in his dark, tormented eyes as he stared down at his brother. "She does, or the voices . . . they will not quiet." He put one shaking hand up to his head. "They *must* be appeased, the demons inside, or . . ."

"If she was this witch, this powerful sorceress, then she would have freed herself. Surely you can see that, Urvan," Kazimir said.

"*She* told me of the girl's potions," Urvan said, pointing at Magda and speaking in his barbarous German.

"No! Oh, no, please sir," Magda said, arrested in the act of stirring a pot of stew over the fire. "I only said Miss Melisande was a great healer and grew herbs—"

"Stop! She has bewitched you all," Urvan said, his dark eyes wide, his movements agitated and restless. "So fair a face . . ." he muttered, staring at her. He crossed himself and ducked his head, turning to stare at his brother. "Do not meet her eyes . . . she will bewitch you. So fair a face, one would think her an innocent." Urvan, his left eye twitching from his anxiety, held out the red rosary. "We think her the handmaiden of hell. If she has not made a covenant with Satan, then the proof is easily given."

"What proof?" Kazimir growled.

"She is unmarried. You say she is an innocent. Then an innocent's blood she must shed, blood red as the stolen beads she wore."

There was silence for a long minute in the hut.

"I don't understand. What do you mean?" Kazimir said.

"The proving I will put in your more than capable hands, brother," Urvan said, with a wicked leer. "Show me her virgin blood, and I will believe you and let her live."

"What does he mean?" Melisande cried, her voice trembling.

"No, Urvan, no!" Damn, but he wished Melisande had not stopped him from striking Urvan down with the rock! He could have found Mikhail no matter where he was hidden, of that he was confident, though it may have taken time. But Melisande didn't know that, nor did she have any reason to believe he could rescue her father from wherever he was concealed. The result was this terrible predicament, for he understood his brother too well. He struggled against the knotted ropes that confined his wrists, but his muscles trembled with weariness. "Urvan, please," Kazimir pleaded, grinding his teeth in fury at his helplessness. "Just think what you are saying."

"It is the only proof I will accept."

"What does he mean?" Melisande repeated.

Kazimir said, as gently as he could, not able to meet her eyes, "He means that the blood resulting from your loss of virginity is the only proof he will accept that you have not sealed a bargain with the devil."

"Loss of . . . oh. Oh!"

"Ah, she understands us now!" Urvan said, rubbing his hands together, clacking the rosary beads between them. He leaned over her and touched her hair. "If my brother refuses to do the deed, then there are other ways your virginity can be tested," he said, with an evil chuckle. His expression changed, twisting oddly, and he said, his voice more hollow, "We shall see the blood or you will die." He clutched his head, and a bewildered expression again crossed his face. "What? What did he say?" He turned away, hunching his shoulder, and began to argue with himself, the guttural voice and his own more melodic tone quarreling, each in turn, the words becoming garbled and the phrases nonsensical.

It was a horrible sight, and Kazimir's blood chilled at how much worse the delusions had become in the years his brother had apparently spent as a solitary wanderer. He was irrevocably gone, and there was only one way this all could end. His limbs quivering with fatigue, Kazimir struggled to sit up. One last try. "Urvan, listen to me. The voices you hear, they're not real. Listen to mine; I have never wanted to hurt you. I'm sorry for what Franziska and I did—"

"Not another word, traitor," Urvan said, turning toward them. "Do this deed or die. Both of you. My little brother . . . do your limbs not feel heavy? Do you not feel weak all over? Are you not fevered, and thirsty and tired?"

Kazimir, the strain of kneeling too much, sagged back down on the floor and coughed, his mouth so dry he could not answer.

Urvan's mouth twisted into a grimace. He chuckled. "Give him some more water," he commanded Magda, and she scuttled forward, offered a ladle of water, and Kazimir drank greedily the odd-flavored water. "Now," Urvan continued. "No more delays. Do it or she dies first, in front of you."

"Melisande," Kazimir whispered urgently in English. "Please, trust me. I . . . I don't know what is wrong with me. I'm powerless and can't defeat him so weakened, but I have an idea. We shall do this without harming you." Aloud and in Russian he said to Urvan, "You must vow to set her free if the test proves her an innocent!"

"Strike me no bargains. I make *no* promises! But I warrant you, her life depends upon this test."

"My brother understands no English," Kazimir whispered to her in that language, "and so I will just say this; I have a plan, a trick. Just go along with me, and cry out when I say." In the dim light he saw her nod, her face bleached pale with fear and two spots of red high on her cheeks. This deception had to work, and he had to find a way to free her, for she was reaching the end of her tolerance; he could tell that by the terror in her blue eyes.

Urvan, with the gun still trained on his brother, commanded Magda in his crude German to free Kazimir from the ropes at his wrist. "I will kill her if you make any move to leave this hut," he growled, "or do not perform the deed. This I vow."

Kazimir, his hands free now, though his leg was still tethered by a thick knotted coil, pushed the stray strands of hair away from Melisande's face and remembered kissing her in the night, his urge to touch her and caress her seeming a terrible prelude to this moment now. "Are you ready?" he asked, softly, trying to communicate in the dim light and with the expression on her face that she need not fear him.

She simply nodded, and he was not reassured, for she did not truly trust him, he thought. He could sense the uncertainty in her but could not blame her. He tugged at her skirts, hearing in the back of his consciousness Magda Brandt wailing and sobbing, her sorrow coming too late to be any good to Melisande. At first Melisande fought him, hitting his hand in reflex, and he murmured, "Please, Melisande, trust me. But this must appear real, and for that I must . . . lift your skirts."

She trembled at Kazimir's command but nodded quickly, gazing steadily into his eyes as if she was reading his soul. He pulled her skirts up and moved closer on the lumpy pallet of rags. Urvan still had the gun trained on them, and Kazimir felt his fury build at the insidious demon in his brother's brain that tortured him and made him perform such vile deeds.

He pulled her close and made motions as of undoing his own clothing and pulling her skirts up, tamping down the fury that bubbled and roiled within him, keeping his focus on saving Melisande from this awful accusation. Urvan had always spoken of witches, his fascination with the supernatural leading him down a dangerous and meandering path to this awful conclusion.

As he muddled around, Kazimir found the sharp edge of a pottery shard he had noticed moments earlier and secreted it near him, then he reached up under Melisande's skirts and ripped at her chemise. She cried out, just as he had hoped she would if shocked by his actions.

Urvan grunted in satisfaction, while Magda loudly cried. Kazimir had parted her legs, holding her knee firmly to conceal him; Melisande was under him now, and he was deeply ashamed that she had been brought to this despicable pass. If only he wasn't so weak, or if he had been able to transform and overcome Urvan, he could have avoided this awful scene.

"Please forgive me," he said loudly in Russian, and pinched her hard.

She cried out in pain and shock; he found the pottery shard and cut his arm under his rolled back sleeve, then made some movements while she sobbed. As much as he was disgusted with himself, the deception would work, and he must be satisfied with that. He moved away from her after pulling her skirts down, catching her gaze as she calmed and pulling up the piece of her chemise soaked in his own blood.

"There," he said, flinging it wearily at Urvan. "There is your proof. Now let her go!"

Magda had rushed over as Urvan grabbed the hank of blood-soaked cloth and began to tend to Melisande, who tried to push her away.

"Go, Magda, leave me be!" she cried.

Urvan lifted the bloody cloth to the light and was nodding in satisfaction, but then Magda, her voice puzzled, said, "But Miss Melisande, *you* have shed no blood . . . what . . . ?"

Urvan, hearing her, stormed over to them, raising a cloud of dust in the dirty hut, and pulled her dress up, seeing the white glow of the pristine chemise, the edge torn and a piece missing, but no blood anywhere under her skirts. He roared in anger and grasped the edge of his brother's cloak, ripping it away to reveal the blood streaming from the wound in Kazimir's arm.

"You dare try to trick me, witch!" he shouted at Melisande. His arm trembling, he pointed the gun and cocked the hammer.

"No!" Magda screamed, throwing herself across Melisande. "No, please, no! Don't hurt her."

Urvan strode forward and kicked her viciously, and she doubled over, rolling away sobbing, holding her stomach. Kazimir bellowed at his brother, "Stop!" as he bolted to the end of his tether. "What have you become, Urvan, an animal?"

A strange calmness overtook Urvan as he backed away from his furious brother, still holding the gun out before him, but now with a steadier hand. Without taking his eyes off the two of them, and ignoring Magda, who wept as she crawled to the corner of the hut near the doorway, he grabbed a disintegrating broom from the hearth and moved back toward them. "I will do what needs to be done myself, then," he said, with the broomstick in his hand.

•　•　•

CHRISTOPH, weary and feeling oddly depleted, limped back to the castle. Nothing. He had found nothing! He had resolutely rejected every offer made to accompany him to search for Melisande because he knew he could cover more ground and was more likely to be able to find her as a wolf, but what good did it do? He had been out for hours, but then dawn had forced his transformation back to a man. It had been sudden and almost involuntary. Unprepared, though he had acknowledged within his wolf mind that he must go back and tell the others he had been unsuccessful, it had hit him in mid-stride, and he had had to limp back, naked and freezing, to where he had left his clothes.

He crossed the dew-silvered grass up to the castle, and Charlotte burst from the huge doors and raced to him.

"Christoph! We thought you were lost, or that something had happened. Frau Liebner came down . . . She didn't know anything had happened, because she has been sitting up with Uta this whole time, but now she wants to see you. Are you all right? What is wrong?"

"Shut up, Charlotte. I didn't find a damn thing. Not a thing. I don't understand it."

"Why didn't you take anyone with you?"

He leaned on his sister and longed to tell her everything; she had helped him through ordeals before. But now was not the time nor place to tell her he was a werewolf. How could he, with her world in such turmoil?

As they walked up the slope, he went back in his mind to the woods. Why could he not find Melisande? At first he had known he would be successful. He had sensed her, could smell her in the air. But then as he got deeper into the woods, he lost the scent and something repelled him; before he knew it, he had gone in circles.

It was as if he lost time, for he would be searching, nose to the ground, on the trail, and then he smelled a bitter scent and would find himself somewhere else. It happened time and time again. Every time he thought he caught her trail, he was misled; it was like a mist over his senses, clouding him, making him lose his way.

They entered the castle together and went directly to the

dining room. Frau Liebner, her face gray, was sitting with Count Gavril.

"Why would you not let anyone accompany you?" Count Gavril said, as Charlotte helped him sit. "Poor lad, you look as gray as I do."

"Leave him alone," Frau Liebner said, gazing steadily at him. "I understand why he needed to do this alone."

Christoph met her kind, weary gaze. He should have realized, as close as she was to Uta, she would know what he was. If only Uta could help him. More now than ever, he needed her.

"Food . . . he needs to eat," Frau Liebner said. "And he needs the rest of you to not badger him."

"I will eat," he said, "and then go out again, this time with some of the men."

Frau Liebner nodded. Count Gavril gazed at him thoughtfully and said, "Perhaps that will do."

MELISANDE watched Urvan, and it became dreadfully evident to her what he intended. "No," she whispered, scuttling back as best she could against the wood wall behind her. "No, please, I beg of you . . ."

"Then tell him to do it," Urvan said, waving the gun at Kazimir. "Tell him to take your maidenhead and prove to me you are not a witch. The blood moon is coming . . . A witch's power increases tenfold in the blood moon, but I will kill you before that. Do it! Tell him to prove to me you are not a sorceress! Otherwise I will kill you and burn your body."

Melisande shuddered, then looked over at Kazimir, who was straining against the knotted tether that anchored him, trying to get free, his face red, cords of muscle standing out on his neck. Drops of perspiration trickled down his forehead, and he was feverish, the illness that had overcome him worsening now. And yet the rope was secure; he could not get away, could not rescue her from his brother, who stayed just beyond his grasp.

So this decision was hers. Magda had gone dreadfully still. There was no doubt in Melisande's mind that this madman intended to kill her if she did not prove through her own blood that she was untouched.

"You must do as he commands," she said to Kazimir, without looking at him.

Through his teeth he ground out, "I will *never* dishonor you in such a way. I may be many things, and I may be ashamed of what I have done in my life, but one thing I have never done is take an unwilling woman."

"And so you will not this time," she said. She shivered in fear as Urvan stroked the thick rough wood of the broom handle. She could see in the gleam of his eyes that he would not be loath to do the deed. She turned to Kazimir and gazed steadily at him, remembering his gentle kiss and the connection they had established in the chapel before coming out to the woods. She would never forget this time, no matter what happened, but it would be a time of horror and disgrace and the death of her soul, or merely of discomfort and fear; it depended upon which brother took the next step. "Please do not make me beg you to do this," she said, a sob welling up in her voice. "I am not one of those to whom my maidenhood . . . or any part of me . . . is more important than my life. After this, I will still have my life to live and will forget the cost, I promise you."

She saw in his expression some measure of reassurance at her words.

But he said, "I don't know if I *can* do this. My whole life I have tainted all that I have touched, but you . . ." His voice dropped to a whisper, and he hung his head. "You are pure and good and perfect."

She thought of the welter of feelings that had coursed through her in those moments when he had touched her, the longings, the fears, the tangled jumble of sensations and her own dread that she was inflicting him with remembered longings she suffered while infatuated with Count Nikolas, and her jealousy of his wife, Countess Elizabeth. "Not perfect," she whispered. "Look at me! I am far from perfect." She searched his eyes, seeing shame and self-loathing in their shadowed depths.

"No, Melisande," he said, urgently, "I will find a way out

of this, I swear. I will kill him, and I will find your father, I promise you."

Urvan, becoming restive in the face of their conversation conducted in English, began to shudder, and the foul beast that seemed to live within him erupted, his face twitching into a grimace. "Witch! Witch!" he shrieked and began to advance on her, gun shaking, broomstick threatening.

"No! Urvan!" Kazimir threw himself between Melisande and Urvan just as the gun went off; he yelped in pain and was thrown back on the straw and rag pallet. He rolled to stillness as Magda began screaming, a shrill sound that filled the hut.

"Kazimir!" Melisande cried.

The hut was filled with sound, roiling with action. Urvan was shrieking and hopping up and down, shakily trying to reload the gun. Magda screamed still, and Melisande felt madness well up in her as she tried to reach Kazimir.

"Heaven protect him," she cried out, reverting to French. "Please protect him from harm!" She leaned over him, pushing him onto his back, trying to brush his hair back from his eyes. "Kazimir!" she wept, fearing that he had given his life to save hers. "Protect this man," she cried aloud, "and reward his courage!"

Magda wailed more loudly, screaming and pulling her hair.

Kazimir breathed in suddenly, then groaned and sat up, holding his shoulder. "Shut up, Magda," he hollered and groaned again. In the silence that fell, he gasped, "I am shot. I am weakening. What is happening?"

He sagged back down, and Melisande hovered as close as she could to him, as close as her chains would allow, for he had rolled away from her somewhat in his agony. Her chains clanked and scraped as she moved, and Urvan watched her even as he feverishly reloaded the pistol, grunting and muttering the whole time. The guttural voice commanded, the weak voice pleaded; the quarrel between his more rational side and the demon that lived within continued, but increasingly it was the devil who won the arguments.

"Kazimir, " she whispered, hoarsely, dirt clogging her throat and rimming her tear-filled eyes, "are you all right?"

"I will live, I promise," he said, faintly. He spat and coughed, the dust in the clouded interior of the hut just now beginning to settle and filming everything. "I can't breathe. I feel as if someone is sitting on my chest. What is wrong with me? And the wound . . . it burns like fire . . . I . . ."

"You have driven your brother further into madness. Please . . . do what you must!" she begged. "If you still can, please do it! Or he'll kill us both!"

Kazimir struggled to sit up and gazed at her with a look of terrible humility and pain. His scar stood out against even the pallor of his skin, and where his dark beard was coming in, but two feverish spots burned on his cheeks, and sweat poured from his forehead. "How can I do this? How can I do this to you?" He bowed his head.

"I would rather live despoiled than die a virgin!"

He nodded. He still hung his head for a moment and then looked up again. "But let us see what he next does. I fear . . . I fear that if I lose too much blood . . . if I keep weakening . . ."

"What?"

"When the time comes to take us away from here, I will be too weak."

"We can't worry about that now!" she muttered to him under her breath.

"The next bullet from this gun will be for her," Urvan said, done with his reloading and rising, broomstick in one hand, pistol in the other. The red amber rosary hung at his waist from his belt, and the crimson beads glowed as if from some faint inner light. "I will not risk letting a witch live."

"Urvan, think . . . remember our youth, remember how close we were," Kazimir pleaded. "Remember. Trust me . . . I want to help you."

"That Urvan is dead now." His face remained expressionless, but he motioned toward Melisande with the barrel of the pistol and waved the broom. "The moments of her life are trickling away. A few more only remain, unless I have proof that she is not a sorceress, as her father says she is." A ghost of his old self appeared in his expression. "I don't want to kill her, but if I must, first I will seek the proof I require. Or I will kill her, and then you, then go and kill Davidovich too, the traitor. It will be over, but I will have my revenge and die happy."

"Revenge. Now I understand." Kazimir sighed deeply and bowed his head.

Melisande saw his lips move, as if in a prayer. Long minutes passed. Then he looked up at his elder brother, a glint of hatred in his eyes. "I will do this, but I swear that if you do not set her free after this terrible deed is done, then I will find a way to kill you, even if I lose my life in the doing."

He rolled over, stifling a guttural groan from the wound.

Melisande wept at his pained outburst. "Is the bullet . . ."

"I think it went through," he muttered. "The pain is like fire and I weaken; I don't believe I will die, but I may. I have never felt like this, as if every second drains away some of my life. What I must do now is quiet the demons in his head, and I hope lull him into a state of acceptance. If I can." He stared at her in the dimness. "I must ask . . . you are . . . you are a virgin, are you not?"

"Of course!"

"In any case, not every virgin has a substantial discharge of blood after the first time. We must hope, as awful as it sounds, that you are one who does."

"I'm so afraid," she whispered, staring into his dark eyes. "But not," she hastened to add, "so afraid as I would be if this was left up to your terrible brother."

"I will do what I can to lessen the horror," he said, gazing at her and pushing the soft flaxen hair away from her eyes.

"What . . . what must I do?"

"Make yourself as comfortable as you can, and pull your skirts up."

"Do it!" Urvan shrieked.

"Shut up!" Kazimir yelled back, ending on a sob of pain and slumping down. "If you will have me do this, I will be as gentle as I can. This woman has done nothing to merit the despicable behavior of the Vasilov brothers."

"Now what?" Melisande said, biting her lip to keep from whimpering in fear, as she adjusted her skirts.

"Now I must . . . uh, must make myself ready."

"What do you mean?"

His pale face reddening with blotches of dark color, the white scar across his cheek and lip standing out vividly against the color, he did not answer but struggled to undo the fall of his breeches. She saw a flash of pale skin and looked away quickly, lying back on her cloak, but she felt him move around.

"Melisande," he whispered after a few moments.

"Yes?"

"I am ready now. This will be easier, though, if there is any way I can make you more comfortable in what I must do."

"How?"

Oh lord, how to explain to such a sweet innocent? "I could . . . touch you. It might make your body ready to receive me."

She shook her head. "No! No. Nothing could make this easier, and even if it did, then perhaps it will not have the desired effect, the . . . the blood."

"It should make no difference to that. It will just make it easier initially . . ."

"Do it now!" Urvan screamed, and Melisande heard the gun click, the hammer being cocked again.

"Please," she said, "just do what he asks." She quivered as he came closer and rolled on top of her, spreading her legs with his knee. He was heavy, and she felt warm flesh between her bare legs. She shuddered, tears rolling down from her closed eyes. She felt his lips on her neck.

"I am sorry . . . so sorry."

"Why do you apologize for doing that which will save my life?" she whispered, her voice trembling. "If my finger was poisoned and the only means to save my life was to remove it, would you not do so? And would I not count the cost small?"

"All right, my brave girl. You are correct, of course."

He reached down between them, and she felt his fingers between her legs and was shocked to the core as he touched her, diving in to the nest of curls at the juncture of her thighs and spreading her. She felt then his shaft, hard and yet warm and fleshy. He bore down with the weight of his body, and she felt the tip of it enter her. Fear coursed through her, and she tightened involuntarily, moaning with fear.

"Shhh," he said. "Melisande, please . . . try to relax your muscles, or it will be harder for you *and* for me. Think of something else . . . Let your mind go to some better place."

She did her best and felt him push; pain stung her. She bit

down on her lip, refusing to cry out, refusing to show how it hurt.

"Sweet girl, I will need to push harder. It will hurt even worse, but cry out. Let it go! There will be some easing of pain, perhaps, if you do."

"I will not scream from pain; I will *not* give him the satisfaction."

"You must," Kazimir said, forcing himself further into her narrow, resistant passage, "for only if you cry out will he believe you have been breached. Let not your courage lead you astray."

"Foul animal," she muttered, and felt him flinch. "Not you! Your brother."

"I know," he said, pushing harder.

"Mhmm! Oh!" His member was thicker than she had thought it would be, or perhaps her ability to receive him was less than she had imagined. "Is it done?" she asked with a whimper.

"No. God help me, no. Cry out again."

He pushed more, and she felt it piercing her, the pain growing in intensity and the pressure of his filling her almost unbearable. She thrashed and cried out, and her moan lingered in the air, counterpointed by Magda's wretched wailing. "Shut up, Magda," Melisande cried. "How can you cry, when it is I who am suffering because of you?"

Urvan stalked over and kicked Magda until she was silent; Melisande felt horribly ashamed and vowed to not cry out against the young woman again, no matter what.

"I am yours," Kazimir murmured in her ear. "With this deed I become your bond slave, your protector, your husband should you desire one, your servant if you do not," he said, pushing in more until she thought she would scream. "I am yours to command forever."

Kazimir felt her body relax as he spoke, and felt the resistance of her maidenhead; he was at the threshold. It was his now, to breach and take from her her innocence. What should have been an obscene moment, he supposed, now became something more for him, and he whispered again that he was hers forever, feeling it enter his heart as more than a promise, deeper than a vow. He was hers now, not only in duty, but in heart and soul. His care for her plumbed the depths of him, reaching part of his heart he had thought dead and frozen for all time.

It was not what he wanted, and he knew that what he had feared had come to pass. He admired her courage, he loved her fortitude, and he was grateful for this strange moment. Grateful and terrified. He loved her completely and utterly, not for what he was taking, but what she had unwittingly given him . . . her trust. He pushed through and broke the last shred of her virginity, feeling the blood course around him, warm and wet. Strength flooded his body; the source was her courage and will to survive.

"We are done," she whispered, and then cried out loudly.

They stilled, two bodies entangled. Thick and still hard, he pierced her, and there was a bond between them that she knew would never be severed; as much as she had not sought it, it comforted her. If Urvan had done his terrible deed, damaging her with the wicked broom handle as he had intended, she would have been torn and devastated. Though there was no pleasure in this act, and even as Kazimir withdrew she knew that he had not done what men did for pleasure, there was now a bond between them.

Kazimir rolled back, and blood flowed.

Urvan approached and moaned, seeing the stream of blood that stained her white petticoats and knit stockings. "Not a witch," he muttered, and sank down to the dirt floor. "Not a witch."

It was over.

Urvan commanded Magda to help Melisande, and the young woman did, her head hung and her eyes averted from her former friend's.

"Magda," Melisande whispered. "Magda, I'm sorry. I did not mean to be so harsh."

"You had every right to say such things and worse. I have done the unforgivable." The young woman was wretched looking; her blonde hair hung in her bleached face, and she was bruised from Urvan's harsh treatment. She tied some bloody rags into a bundle and tossed them into the fire, where the dampness hissed and sighed.

"I am so sore," Melisande murmured. "But I don't know if that's natural or if . . . if I have been somehow . . . wounded."

"It's natural to feel pain," Magda said, hunching by her. "You will begin to feel better, but it will still hurt some. The next time you do this, it will still hurt, but you will become accustomed to it, and then it will be as if nothing is happening."

"You . . . you've experienced this?" Melisande said, sitting up, her chains clanking. She glanced over at Kazimir, but he was turned away, presumably giving her some privacy, what little was possible in the tiny space.

"Yes. Oh, yes, many times."

"You have a lover?"

"I would never say that," Magda said, her lips twisted in bitterness.

"Was it . . . was it against your will?"

"Occasionally."

"M-more than once?"

Magda sighed. "The first time it was against my will. Then I decided to . . . to preserve myself, to do what must be done. But still . . ." She hung her head. "The filthy deed has been against my will more often than not."

Melisande was heartsick. And she had thought herself a friend to Magda! How could she not see that the girl had been suffering? Even now she was rubbing her stomach, and . . . "Magda, are you . . . ?"

The girl nodded, hand on her gently rounded belly, and tears coursed down her smudged and dirty face, over her cut lip.

"I'm sorry," Melisande said, taking her in her arms. "I'm so sorry."

Chapter 22

GAVRIL SAT in an upholstered chair by the fire in the dining room, head bowed, as twilight finally approached, the perfectly trained and uncurious servants going about their rituals as stolid as automaton figures in a clockwork toy, drawing drapes, lighting sconce lamps, candles, and flambeaux in the great hall. What could he have done differently that would have prevented this poor family being drawn into his turmoil? That was what he had been pondering through the long day, as Count Christoph, an admirable young man, had gone forth time and again with servants and his wolf dogs to search the woods, looking for the lost father and daughter. The reports Gavril received were that time and again, the wolf dogs became confused and went in circles, whimpering and becoming listless, leading the men back to where they began.

He was not needed, not wanted, Gavril knew, and again he pondered the decisions in his life that had left him too weak to be of any use. He glanced down at his hand; one blue vein that crossed the back, rising and falling over the bones and tendons like a ribbon, pulsed with faint life. And yet he was not dying, exactly, he was just fading.

Frau Liebner and Countess Charlotte entered and glanced around the room. "Where is my brother?" the young countess asked, her pale, weary face drained of its prettiness by her worrisome day. With the energy of youth, she had paced and fretted all day and bemoaned the fact that she was a woman and so not welcome as one of the searchers. "I thought we had agreed to meet here for some dinner?"

Gavril stood and bowed. "He has not been here, ladies, though they are laying the table for dinner even now." Servants were just finishing with the cutlery and linen and silently disappeared out the other door at the far end of the large room.

Frau Liebner, with one hand on Charlotte's shoulder, said, "Now, you must allow Christoph to do what he does without question. He may have . . . gone out to search again."

"At night? If he didn't find them in the day, he is never going to find them at night," the younger woman said bitterly. "They are dead! Dead! And I have been so mean to Melisande lately!" She covered her face and wept.

Frau Liebner cast a helpless look at Gavril, and he helped guide her to a chair at the end of the table and made her sit down.

"You could not be mean to Melisande," Count Gavril said, patting her shoulder. "I have never seen two young ladies so close."

She shook her head but calmed some and patted away the tears on her cheeks. "I have been; I've been a spiteful, jealous, hateful cat." Jumping up, she said, "I'm going to see whether Steinholz has seen Christoph." She swiftly moved to the door and out to the great hall.

"Do you think they live, sir? Melisande and her father?" Frau Liebner asked, her gaze still on the door through which Charlotte had gone.

"I pray they do."

She turned and looked at him for a long minute and seemed about to say something but then shook her head. "There is much that goes on in this household that I do not understand, and much more that I do. When this is over, I think it is time to dispel some old secrets and let this family live with the truth, like sunshine. Perhaps, sir, you and Count Kazimir should consider the same resolution. Uta, before she fell into unconsciousness, told me much that she felt and knew. She did not know everything, but she knew that the two of you are bonded in enmity, and if you do not mend your ways, you will be the death of innocent people who have done nothing to deserve that fate."

With that, she turned and walked out of the room, leaving Gavril to ponder again the many missteps he had taken in his life.

*   *   *

NIGHT had finally fallen, and the moon was beginning to rise. The day's searching had been excruciating for Christoph, confined to human form, longing to leap through the brush and over logs as speedily as the dogs. But now he was free. The woods beckoned, and he glanced back up at the castle, looming dark over the landscape. His one regret was he could not talk to his sister about this new life of his, but it was not time. He could not burden her with that kind of information when he did not have time to thoroughly discuss it with her, calm her fears, and support her shock.

Now was a time for action, not for contemplation, and he turned his attention to the forest, the dark line of trees that bounded the formal lawns of Wolfram Castle, encroaching on it like a black wall. Frau Liebner, after consulting with Uta's silent servant, Mina, had come to the conclusion that he and the dogs both were being misled by either spell magic or some herbal deterrent, but that meant that whomever was guilty of this whole awful episode was aware of the presence of were-wolves. How was that possible? However it was so, armed now with knowledge and awareness that would help him re-sist the confusion of his senses, he should be able to overcome it, according to family lore. Now he must go, transform into his bestial self, find the hiding place, and kill Kazimir and his brother Urvan, thereby setting Melisande and her father free. That was the one point upon which he and Frau Liebner dis-agreed. She was of the conviction that Count Kazimir was not the enemy. Uta had trusted him, the woman said, and that was enough to convince her that the Russian was on the side of the angels, as she put it.

But Count Gavril was convinced that Kazimir and his brother Urvan were working together. It was the only theory that made sense, the man said, and Christoph, bewildered by the various tales, thought he must believe him, for his convic-tion was adamant.

With the wolfskin kirtle concealed under his cloak, he slipped into the forest. There he shed his clothes, shivering until he was done and could run, swiftly feeling the transfor-mation come over him, the agony passing more quickly this time and the glorious free feeling that followed more than making up for the discomfort.

The world was so different from this view, he thought as he loped through the forest; he was king, the most powerful beast, and he felt a swelling of pride and then a wave of fury and lust to taste the two Russians' blood beneath his fangs. This was *his* forest, and Melisande was *his* female. He would fight to the death for her if need be, but he had no doubt that faced with him in his present form, the two men would flee or die.

He rather hoped they faced him to fight, for he relished the thought of tasting their blood. There was no indecision now, no hesitation. A wolf knew only one dictate, and that was to kill or be killed when confronted with a deadly enemy.

He caught the scent trail that Melisande had left and howled with joy, the tang of her sweet scent exciting him. Even with the wolf dogs and men searching all day, still he could catch her fading scent underlying it all. He picked up speed as the darkness thickened around him, becoming accustomed to the weird way his sight had altered with his transformation. Everything had taken on tonal qualities of light and dark, rather than any real color, but so many other things had become equally as important as sight, foremost among them scent.

He stopped dead and lifted his nose to the air. Blood! The scent was at the same moment troubling and enthralling, and the tangle of sensations gave him pause, for there were two distinct threads to the blood scent. When the mist of confusion began to descend like a curtain, the repellent odor teasing his nostrils, he paused and focused all of his attention on his task and Melisande and the new scent of blood. He bounded onward and came to a leaning hut that huddled between two pines. Melisande was in there, he knew it. But how could he get in with no hands to work the door?

A faint scraping sound assailed his sensitive ears, and he crouched in the underbrush watching, waiting, his nose twitching.

Melisande! She crept out of the doorway, holding her skirts in one hand and slipping out of the hut. But there, slinking right behind her, was the foul count, Kazimir Vasilov!

Christoph leaped out of his hiding place, howling, and in two great bounds, he was on the count, snapping and snarling,

trying to get at his neck. How he wished he had both the abilities of his animal self and his human voice at the same time!
Then he would be able to call to Melisande to run, back to the
castle, flee, but then he heard her voice screaming and felt her
slim hands beating his neck as he tried to wrestle Vasilov to
the ground.

Vasilov broke free and staggered sideways as Christoph
drew back in puzzlement at Melisande's defense of one of her
kidnappers; he saw her trying to help the Russian to his feet,
tugging him to follow her, fretting about the blood on his
shoulder.

The count shouted out in English, "I am taking Miss
Melisande back to the castle. I am not her kidnapper . . . I
truly am helping her escape."

Christoph, through the confusion, heard a woman's scream
from inside the hut and the roar of a man's voice in what
sounded like thick Russian. As Vasilov and Melisande ran for
a dense section of the forest, a hunched man in ragged clothes
boiled out of the hut, staggering and clutching his head. He
put one hand on the hut wall to steady himself and waved a
wicked-looking pistol. He shouted hoarsely in Russian and
started to follow in the direction the other two had taken.

Christoph crouched, uncertain, staring at the man who
could only be Urvan Vasilov and finally decided to kill him,
sure, at least, that *this* man was a villain and a threat. He
leaped at him, but with a cry, the man loosed his weapon, and
Christoph felt a searing pain slice through him. He yelped, the
force of the bullet throwing him back, down onto the ground.
The man was hoarsely shouting, still, and pelted back into the
hut, perhaps to reload his deadly weapon.

Whimpering, weakening, Christoph crawled into the forest
and limped away. He dragged himself to a grove of bushes
and collapsed in a huddled heap.

"PLEASE don't tell the others what . . . what we did,"
Melisande murmured as she and Kazimir approached the castle by way of the long, moonlight-silvered front lawn.

"To aid in that, let us take a . . . slightly different way into
the castle," Kazimir said, panting, fighting off the fatigue that

still clouded his mind despite his slowly returning strength. His mind was only half on helping Melisande into the castle, and with the other half he worried about the young count, the slim werewolf who had leaped on him, thinking, no doubt, that he was following Melisande with no good motive. If only he could go back and help him, but even the young count would want him to take care of Melisande first; that was the only thing Kazimir was sure about. Christoph cared more for Melisande's safety than for his own.

"What do you mean, a different way into the castle?"

Kazimir led her along the side of the building, slinking in the shadows to avoid the stable hands, who were shutting up the great stable doors for the night; he felt along the stone foundation near a spot he had discovered on one of his searches and found the wooden door along the foundation. "Here," he said, feeling around and finding the secret latch he had known would be there. He pulled the door open, guided her through it and hoped he remembered his way.

"What is this?" Melisande said, gasping, gazing around at the unfamiliar passage. Two years she had lived in this place but had never once known about this secret corridor.

Kazimir took her hand and with his free one felt along the wall until they came to a steep and narrow stone stairway. "This castle," he said, "is threaded with these passages."

"I never knew," she whispered. "But . . . but where are we going?"

"I hope we are going to your room. Or to mine. Either will serve."

Through a bewildering and complex twisting, turning path he found his way; pausing every once in a while to catch his breath, he would stop and seem to sense the secrets the ancient fortress held. Finally, he stopped at one particular wall and put one hand on a part of the back of the thick wood paneling opening. After a long moment, he said, "This is it." He pushed, it slid sideways, and he helped her step through.

"This is my room!" she said, looking around her. "There . . . there is a secret entrance to my room?"

"I will not stay," he said, from the passage. "Unless you want me to."

She looked back at him, hovering in the darkness of the opening, and said, "No. I would rather . . . do this myself."

He nodded, feeling strength begin to seep back into his being now that they were out of the woods. "I will meet you in the great hall, and we will find the others. Then we must decide what to do about your father."

He disappeared, and with trembling hands she stripped off her clothes, bundling them into a knot and hiding the bloody skirts and stockings in her wardrobe and trying to avoid thinking about her ordeal. The long day had been spent in sleep, and in recovery, for she discovered that she could infuse Kazimir with some strength, but it took time. Urvan had disappeared at one point, presumably to take food to her father, then he slept huddled in a corner. Magda, her bruised and battered face wan with exhaustion, had whispered to her that she could not bear to see Melisande suffer any more, and she was determined to help them escape. She had been as good as her word, finding and using an herb Melisande knew of to make Urvan sleep more deeply.

If it had not been for the howling of the wolf outside just as she and Kazimir were creeping out, he would have stayed asleep. As she washed with cold water from the ewer on her bedside table and then dressed, she pondered the strange actions of the wolf. It looked just like one of the wolves in her dreams, slim and beautiful, but ferocious. She shivered. It was her dreams coming true, perhaps, the wolf attacking Kazimir as it had. Why he had shouted out in English that he was not her kidnapper she could not imagine. Thank heaven Urvan's wild shot had wounded it, or it may have followed them.

Finally dressed, she had one thing to do before descending. Uta's room was silent, and Melisande crept in, putting her finger to her lips as Mina, the mute servant, saw her and leaped out of her chair by the window, the chair that poor Uta was usually in. Melisande made her way to her old friend's bed, where Frau Liebner sat in a chair, her head cradled in her arms on the edge of the bed, asleep, it appeared.

Melisande went to Uta and lifted the gnarled hand from the snowy bed linens and felt her pulse. It was slow but even. There had been no change in the old woman's condition since she had last been at this bedside. Though it seemed an eon, it had only been one day.

"Melisande!" Frau Liebner had awoken and started up, her wrinkled face white across the dimness of the canopied bed. "We thought you lost . . . we thought you kidnapped or . . . or dead."

"And so I was—kidnapped, I mean—but I am here now, thanks to Count Vasilov. Has she awoken in all of this time?"

"No," Frau Liebner said, tears in her eyes. "I think it is nearly the end, but when that will come I do not know. She is in God's hands now."

Melisande bowed her head and said a prayer and felt some strange sense of knowledge. She quieted her innermost soul and searched in the darkness beyond consciousness. Uta was there with them, but just at the edge of the room, unable to speak, but present. "Uta, my friend," Melisande whispered, feeling their connection, and using it. "Come back to me. I need you . . . I need your wisdom. Please come back!" She bowed her head again and took Uta's other hand, holding both between her own and sinking deep within herself. She walked, in her semi-conscious mind, to the edge of a forest glade, and there, on a throne of twisted, gnarled wood was Uta; the woman was dressed all in palest green and held a straight branch as a scepter. Her eyes were open, and the film of blindness brought on by age was gone, the vivid blue of her eyes like the winter sky. In the distance, among the trees, stood people, all of them waiting, it appeared, for something . . . or someone. Uta gazed at her steadily, and nodded once.

Melisande sighed and straightened, coming back to her conscious self. She looked over at Frau Liebner and smiled. "Tell me at once when she awakens," she said.

"I don't understand . . . what is going on?"

"She is coming back, but I don't know when, and I don't know for how long she can stay. Tell me immediately." Melisande glanced over at Mina. "And you . . . please, if Frau Liebner is not here when it happens, tell me when she awakens. I need to speak with her." She stood, laid a kiss on Uta's softly wrinkled face, and left the room.

•   •   •

WHEN Melisande entered the drawing room, Charlotte, pale and frightened, saw her first and flew to her side, throwing her arms around her and almost knocking her over in her exuberance. "Meli! Oh, Meli, my dearest friend! How did you . . . where did you come from? Are you safe . . . well?"

"I am," she said, putting her arms around her friend and hugging her, closing her eyes and feeling love for the girl well into her. For the last while, since the Russians had arrived, she had felt a rift between them. Charlotte had seemed different, angry, jealous, and that was not like her at all. Always, even through the awful dark days of the last few months, they had been close, more like sisters than mere friends. Perhaps, though, the rift was how all of the awful time they had been through came out, finally, with Charlotte withdrawing. But now she was so genuinely and touchingly glad to see Melisande that it erased any sense of ill feeling. "I am safe, and I am well, but my papa is still missing."

"And that is what we need to discuss," Kazimir said, strolling to the room.

Gavril, his pale, gaunt face masked in an expression of disbelief, said, his tone hollow, "What is this? Where did the two of you come from? And where, then, is Count von Wolfram? Is he with you? Did he find you, at last?"

"Christoph?" Melisande, still with her arms around Charlotte, glanced from Count Roschkov to Charlotte's face. "What do you mean? Where is he?"

"I am here," Christoph said, calmly, from the doorway.

Charlotte flew to her brother and threw her arms around him, not noticing his wince of pain. "Christoph! Where did you go? I was worried . . . *so* worried for you. You did not leave us a note, you did not tell us anything, you just disappeared!"

"Never mind my story . . . I want to hear from Melisande. And from Count Vasilov. That is most important at this moment."

Melisande told the story, right from the moment she sent Kazimir off to follow Magda in the woods and she was snatched from behind by the foul beast, Urvan Vasilov. "It was terrible," she said, with a shudder, but then she went on to how Kazimir had come in, though she glossed over what happened while they both were imprisoned. She was aware of the strange new connection between them and could see Kazimir glance at her often, his concern for her writ deeply in his dark eyes.

But Melisande's attention was diverted when Charlotte shrieked. "Christoph! Blood! What has happened to you?"

All eyes were on him then, and Melisande could see his dove gray jacket stained by a slowly spreading blotch of vivid red. He merely shook his head, his face pale.

Melisande flew to his side and peeled back the jacket to reveal that his white shirt was red to the waist, and a wound on his shoulder was responsible. "What is this from, and why did you say nothing?" she asked, her voice low and trembling. Without waiting for an answer, she said loudly, "I need water and cloth, and a poultice of . . ." She stopped, took a deep breath, and said, "I will need to do this."

She took control of the situation, and soon she was settled at the hearth with a shame-faced and shirtless Christoph, her deft hands evaluating the wound and binding it with an herbal concoction to promote healing. It occurred to her in that moment that Kazimir, too, had suffered a gun wound but had not said a word of it since he had rejoined them all. He did not even seem, now, to be suffering, though she well knew how weak he had become, how debilitated and gray. Perhaps, she thought, aware of her sense of burgeoning strength, she had been some part of his recovery, for in the daylight hours she had concentrated all of her energy on keeping Kazimir and her father alive. Her papa was still alive, she knew it now. But she set her mind back on Christoph and said, "How did this happen."

"Yes, Christoph, what is this from?" Charlotte, on a low stool nearby, added her voice as Fanny silently aided Melisande.

"It is nothing but an idiotic flesh wound," he said, his teeth gritted, "from my own carelessness. I was loading a pistol to go out to the woods after Meli, and it . . . it accidentally went off."

"I don't believe you," Melisande said, pausing in her work and staring at his pale face. "You are *more* than competent with guns . . . better with guns than ever you have been with a sword. To believe that one accidentally went off . . ."

"Perhaps you should believe the count," Kazimir said, gently and quietly, in her ear.

She cast him a swift, puzzled glance, but he said no more.

Charlotte, though, picked up the refrain. "Yes, Christoph, that is not like you. How did it happen?"

"I suppose," he said, his head hung low, "I was so upset that I was not paying attention." He looked at Count Vasilov for a second.

There seemed, to Melisande, to be some kind of communication, but if that was true, it was quickly over. She finished the bandaging, and he put on the fresh shirt his valet provided. The one awful possibility she had briefly considered was that with all he was suffering silently, he had tried to end his life, but she put away that thought. Christoph was not a coward, nor would he ever abandon his sister like that after all she had been through. It was an unworthy thought, and it shamed her to even consider it.

Seeing her steady gaze, Christoph tried to calm her worry with a smile but feared it had done little good. Nothing had gone how he would have wished. The pain in his shoulder was a minor concern next to the pain in his heart, the pain that had begun when he saw how she and Kazimir had somehow forged a connection in their time together. There was something there, something he couldn't fathom in the glances they exchanged.

"Melisande," he whispered, as the others moved to sit together and discuss what needed to be done to save Mikhail from Urvan, "What are you feeling? I would give anything, even my life, if you would not have had to go through that terrible ordeal."

"I know," she said, putting one gentle hand on his cheek. "I know, my good friend." She looked into his eyes, and in that moment realized what she had been trying desperately to ignore. He had fallen in love with her. "Oh, Christoph," she murmured. "My dearest friend, I wish . . . if I could . . ."

He laid his hand over hers, where it cradled his cheek. He turned his face and kissed her palm, closing his eyes for a long moment. "Don't . . . please, don't say anything," he whispered. "I know you don't care for me that way."

They were silent for a moment together, and then he cleared his throat and said, in a louder voice, "Are you truly all right?"

"Yes, thanks to Kazimir. He saved my life, Christoph." She paused, and when she spoke again, her voice was softer, richer, with a sweetness to the tone that, though present before, was now melting and delicious, like honey. "He's a good man, a strong man, though there is still much I don't know." She took in a deep breath, sighed, and went on, "Now, though, I am frightened for Papa, and . . . and for Magda, for I fear that Urvan is beyond mad."

"I don't understand any of this," Christoph said, his expression grim as he looked toward the grouping of Kazimir, Gavril, and Charlotte. Charlotte glanced toward them with longing but then averted her gaze.

"I have begun to think that there is much in the world—much, even, about myself—that I do not understand." She turned to look at him. "Tell me, Christoph . . . tell me the truth. How did you come by this wound in your shoulder?"

He bowed his head. Though he had never had her, he felt now that she was out of his grasp completely, as lost to him as his youth was now gone, fled with the knowledge of what he truly was. And how could she ever have been his anyhow, now that he had accepted his heritage? Who could love a man who was part animal? "It was purely an accident, Meli."

She nodded and touched his cheek once more. "We must join the others."

"We think," Kazimir said, looking up, as the two of them moved to join the group, "that the logical course of action is to save Magda. I have told them how she helped us by knocking Urvan out and unlocking your chains. I fear that Urvan will kill her for that. I pray only that it has not already been done."

Melisande added her approval to that. "She is now very sorry for what happened, I think, and she *did* help us to escape. And perhaps she knows where my father is."

"That is my hope. There is one more thing," Kazimir said, and he looked directly at Gavril Roschkov. "Gavril, I must tell you this; Urvan has the Blood Amber Rosary. It was here all the time, in Melisande's keeping, though she did not know what it was when Mikhail gave it to her ten years ago. Nor has she ever known since."

"The rosary?" Gavril said, his silvery eyes wide. He shuddered. "And the blood moon is almost upon us. We must keep from Urvan the chalice at all costs, now."

"Yes. If it is in this castle, it's not in any obvious place." All eyes were on him, and he gazed at Christoph, wondering if the young man knew what he was about to reveal. "This castle," Kazimir continued, "is a warren of secret passages threaded throughout the walls and accessed by sliding panels in the woodwork." One look at Christoph's face and he could see that the young man had been completely unaware. Well, now he knew.

"That's ridiculous," Christoph blurted out.

"I have seen them. It's true," Melisande said.

Chapter 23

MAGDA WEPT as Urvan drove her before him through the night like a sheep, hitting her with a stick when she stopped to catch her breath. Her hands were tied before her, and she did not even have a shawl on. The cold pierced her, and in her terrible fear she began to pray, hoping she had not angered the Lord too much to have him listen to her prayers.

"Stop muttering, traitor!" her captor said.

Where once she was free to come and go, she knew that she would never be free again, for her betrayal of his trust had cost her dearly. "Where are we going?" she wailed. A blow from his cudgel struck her so hard she stumbled forward and fell to her knees.

"You deceived me, so now you will share a prison with the other traitor until I determine how to get the chalice. Time is vanishing, and I will have the chalice or you will all die. On your feet!"

She staggered to her feet and moved on through the frigid forest. Finally he stopped beating her and stilled.

"There," he said, pointing to a black, rocky hill barely visible through the trees. He drove her forward again and forced her to her knees. "Crawl," he commanded.

She crawled through a tunnel with no inkling of where she was going. The smell was stale and earthy, and she wept, feeling as if she was descending to her grave, clawing through the wet, frigid earth. She would never come out of this alive. She heard a moan ahead of her, and she crept forward more quickly into the blackness until she could feel the tunnel open into a larger space. She sensed a faint warmth nearby and crawled toward it.

"Herr Davidovich," she whispered.

He groaned and whispered, "Save me, help me." His words ended on a phlegmy cough and moan.

Their captor followed, and with a burning ember he had brought in a tin cup, he lit a candle, the faint light showing an earthy, rocky, moss-walled cavern of about ten feet or so around. Frost dressed the wall in a rime of white, and she could see her breath. Mikhail Davidovich, securely bound, dirty, and ragged and pale, leaned against a rock outcropping.

His bleary eyes opened, and he stared at her. "You!"

"Forgive me . . . please, sir, forgive me!" she cried, utterly broken by the knowledge of what she had done.

"Melisande . . . my daughter, she is well? Do you know anything? Anything at all?" He coughed, his chest rattling with congestion, and shivered. "I fear . . . I fear that that animal tricked me and I endangered my poor Melisande. He tells me now that he has her captive, and she will die if I do not give up the chalice. Tell me the truth, for I no longer know what to believe. Is she well? Or have I killed her with my selfishness?"

As Urvan occupied himself with making a small fire using the dried herbs and some sticks he had brought in a bundle, Magda took a deep, shuddering breath and prepared to tell Mikhail what she could, and reassure him that his daughter was well . . . though she did not think she would tell him all right now. He was weak and ill. He needed to survive this so that he could see her again.

"Please, let me make you more comfortable, first," Magda muttered. "Then I will tell you of Melisande, who is well and back at the castle now."

COUNT Roschkov steadily stared at Kazimir and Melisande, then said, "I would like some proof of these secret passages, if you please. This very room, for example . . . is it accessible?"

Melisande glanced at Charlotte and Christoph, both shocked to silence by this news about the castle they had grown up in. Kazimir was rising, and moving over to the wall, examining the paneling as he went. He went directly to one particular panel and pushed, then slid it sideways. Leaving it open as a chill breeze blew through the room from the dark hole, he turned slowly.

"This is how Mikhail Davidovich concealed the chalice from view, I believe, and how he escaped the castle to meet Urvan after Magda Brandt delivered to him a threat. I do not know what the threat was, but I suspect Urvan may have threatened Melisande, and Mikhail went out, perhaps, to try to bargain for more time. Or more money. He did not take the chalice with him, therefore it is still concealed somewhere in this place," he said, holding up his arms to indicate the entirety of the castle. "Now that Miss Melisande is safely back, I am going to go and confront my brother and free Magda Brandt from his clutches."

Gavril stared at him as Christoph and Charlotte crossed the room and examined the gaping hole leading to the secret passage. "Why do I think you will also be trying to regain possession of the Blood Amber Rosary? And perhaps you have figured some of this puzzle out. Do you think you know where Mikhail Davidovich has hidden the chalice?"

Kazimir was silent.

"What is between the two of you?" Melisande said, her gaze volleying back and forth between the two Russians. "Why are you so buried in enmity? I demand an answer."

Neither man replied, and Melisande gave up in disgust. There were too many other things tugging at her mind, mostly the safety of her father. Why, oh why, did he ever agree to steal the sacred and dangerous chalice for Count Urvan Vasilov? And why, after stealing it, did he not turn it over? His failure to do so plunged him and everyone around him into such danger . . . and all from one man! It was incredible that one person, Urvan Vasilov, could wreak such havoc among them all. She would never know the answers unless her father could be rescued. *When! When* he was rescued. She must believe he would return to her safely.

Charlotte had disappeared into the passage, but Christoph came back out, dusting off his jacket sleeve with a wince at the pain he still felt in his shoulder. "Is it possible that the chalice is hidden somewhere in this maze of passages? Would your father do such a thing?"

Melisande shrugged hopelessly. "I knew nothing about the

passages until Count Kazimir told me of them; how my father found them I do not know, except that unfortunately, his mind was made for intrigue, and so he understands subterfuge and secrets far better than I. He was a magician in my youth, and yet . . . I cannot imagine my father doing any of these things, nor can I figure out where he would hide something he wished to conceal. Are we certain that he even has the chalice . . . that he brought it here to Wolfram Castle?"

Gavril Roschkov nodded, slowly. "He brought it here. That is the one thing of which we can be certain. This place . . . it has magic in it, and a powerful force of its own, though I do not know what the heart of it is."

"I have felt this, too," Count Kazimir murmured. "There is in this place, Wolfram Castle, some power."

Melisande shivered. "I think you are both being overly dramatic. This is just a castle." *And I am just a woman, not some kind of sorceress,* she thought, trying to push away the trembling knowledge in her core that she had beckoned Uta to return. The next hours would tell much, for if what had happened when she was deep within herself was the truth, then Uta was coming back from the distant shores near death. If she did not return, then it was an illusion and she was on the precipice of madness, about to join Count Kazimir's brother.

"Say what you will," Christoph said to the two Russians, "you still are lying to us about something. There are secrets here that I demand to know."

"Ask *him,*" Gavril Roschkov said, with a contemptuous twist to his thin lips and a nod of his head toward the other Russian. "Ask *him* if he is truly what he seems, or if . . ."

"Not now, Roschkov," Kazimir said, a grim look on his dark visage. "We will settle our differences . . . but not now. I have to go and see if I can rescue that poor girl, Magda."

"I will go with you," Christoph said.

Melisande stood. "No, you will *not!* You are in a great deal more pain than you let on, Christoph. Please . . ." She crossed to him and put one hand on his good shoulder. "Please, stay. You will do us no good if you are hurt worse."

He hung his head. "All right. I am little good here, it seems, but even less use going." He turned away.

Charlotte that moment bounded out of the opening, her

dress covered in dust. She sneezed. "Oh, that I had known about these passages when I was a child," she said, clapping her hands together, a cloud of dust drifting from them to the floor. "Christoph, what fun we would have had hiding from our nanny!"

KAZIMIR, after a brief rest and some food, went to try to rescue Magda, saying he wished to use the cover of darkness. He had remarkable recuperative powers, Melisande thought, as she retreated to her father's room, for the gunshot wound could not slow him, and he seemed to have recovered from the dreadful fever he had suffered in the cabin once they left it. She just prayed it was not too late for poor Magda, who had in the end risked so much to help her.

She entered her father's room, the bed now made, but his things left as they were on his side table. She tried to ignore the steady stream of tears that trickled down her cheeks as she sat on the bed and looked through his books and papers, left just the way he had arranged them before he went out to meet the madman who became his kidnapper. All of the years of longing for him, asking her mother why he did not care for her, came back to her. Her grandmother had always been tight-lipped, having little use for the Russian wanderer who had claimed to be an aristocrat as he wooed and wed the young Frenchwoman, Magdalen Delacroix, her mother. But her mother had often spoken of him between his infrequent visits. She had loved him and believed that in his heart, he was a good man who was simply incapable of being what she and their child needed him to be.

Leafing through the book of astronomy, Melisande noted that a chapter on lunar eclipses was interrupted with a page of notes in Russian in her father's lazy scrawl. But there was another sheet, a drawing that seemed to delineate the shape of the castle, with corridors drawn, arrows pointing and secret doorways indicated, between the walls. She set the book aside, flattened the sheet of paper on her lap, and stared at it; now that she knew about the passages, she could see that he had marked the way out from his room. The room *had* been her uncle's until he left with Count Nikolas's party and his new wife, Countess Adele; they had then moved Mikhail there so Melisande would have easy access to him through the connecting sitting room if she so chose, though she had decided to leave the sitting room door locked. There were other secret passages marked, the way to what she thought was the chapel, and a few other corridors. On some of the paths were marked Xs.

What did it mean? Did any of the marks indicate where the chalice was?

She looked up at a tapping on the open door. It was Count Gavril, his lined, weary face with an expression of sorrow on it.

"May I join you, Miss Davidovich?"

From the very first moment of meeting him, she recognized that beneath his calm, unruffled demeanor was a great sadness, and sadness would always find an open heart from her. "Of course, count, please . . . come in and sit down. You look very tired."

"I am always tired."

She hesitated, but then asked, "Why is that, sir? Are you . . . pardon my forwardness, but are you ill?"

"In a manner of speaking. My affliction is hereditary and will end only in my death. This brings me to something of which I wish to speak to you."

She was shocked by the blunt manner he had of referring to his own death, and said, "Sir, please . . . I know something of healing, and if you would let me try . . ."

"No amount of herbal remedies will cure me, my dear, for I persist in adding to my own affliction by not taking the one manner of cure I could."

"That makes no sense. Why would you not make yourself better if you could?"

"I can only say that the cure would make me repugnant to myself. I would rather die."

There was no answer to that, and so she was silent, staring down at the paper, with the curious maze drawn on it.

"What is that?"

"It appears to be a kind of map to the passages, drawn by my father. I suppose this confirms Count Kazimir's assertion that Papa used the secret corridors to move in and out of the house. I just don't understand. What was he up to? And why did he hide all of this from me? He didn't even let me know that he was well enough to walk yet!"

Count Gavril took her hand in his own and stared down at it. "Miss Melisande, your father was, perhaps, grasping beyond what had been given to him in this life because he had a daughter to care for and was trying to better his lot in life for her benefit."

"You think he is dead," she whispered, staring into his gray face.

"I make no such claim. But if he should be . . ."

She pulled her hand away, but he took it back. She turned away though; true, not one of them had seen him alive, but she felt strongly that if he was gone, she would know it. Perhaps she was misled by her own desires, but it was something to cling to.

"Or even if he is alive, I wish merely to reiterate that which has been discussed. I don't believe I will be on this earth much longer, though I hope to complete one task before I go."

"Count, I do not wish to speak . . ."

"No, I know. I understand, truly. But when this is over, then know that you will want for nothing in your life from this moment forward. I will take you—and your father, of course—back to our homeland, and there you will build a new life. I shall endow you with all of my inheritance. You deserve it, and you will stand in the stead of my dear sister, Franziska, who is lost to me forever. I . . . I have no family left, and so everything I own shall be yours."

Melisande was saved from answering when Christoph came to the door.

Melisande had tears in her eyes, Christoph saw, with shock. What was wrong? But the tears were easily explained by their presence in her father's room, and how the poor girl must be feeling. Anger burned in his gut. Everything had been getting better, and then the two Russians descended upon them and upset everything.

"Count Roschkov, I would like to speak with you in private, if you please," he said, hardly recognizing his own voice for the harsh note in it.

"Certainly," the count said, rising and with a last squeeze of Melisande's hand, joining Christoph in the hallway.

"You may not see fit to burden Melisande with the tale of the enmity between you and Count Kazimir, but I believe that as her protector while my uncle is away, I have the right to know, since the poor girl seems to be in the midst of it all."

Count Gavril sank down on a padded bench in the dim hallway and nodded, his silver eyes ghostly, his expression unutterably weary. "Perhaps you have something. I, too, wish Miss Melisande protected from Kazimir Vasilov, for he is a murderer. He killed my beloved sister Franziska."

"What? I don't understand your accusations. He helped her away from the madman's clutches! Tell me what you mean, if you wish me to believe you."

"He killed my poor sister; what else is there to say? How would you feel toward any man who killed your little Charlotte? I should have killed him, but he is stronger than I, my poor sister made sure of that, though she could not know she sealed her own fate in the process," he said, with a shudder. "You cannot imagine the pain of losing an adored sister; my only consolation will be vengeance."

"I don't understand what you are saying . . . how did your sister make Kazimir stronger than you? And what is this accusation that he killed your sister? This is nonsense . . . Why would you live in this house with him if he did such a foul deed?"

"You don't understand," Count Gavril whispered, his silvery eyes full of agony, his gaunt face shadowed in the dim light of the hallway. "He is dangerous. He is terribly dangerous. I had to plan, and be sure, and I needed him to find the chalice, first, though I thought he would have found it by now."

"I am going mad from your accusations and your half-explained stories," Christoph muttered. "Tell me what is going on."

Gavril sighed. "You must understand, with Franziska gone, murdered, I could only piece together what happened that fateful night, the night she died, but there are some certainties. Kazimir Vasilov was in love with my sister, even though she was already married to his elder brother, Urvan.

She wrote me many a fretful letter, asking for advice. Urvan was always moody, difficult, and did not get along with Kazimir, Franziska told me. Kazimir plagued her; he tried to seduce her, and when she rejected him, he took it badly." Gavril stopped, passed one hand over his eyes and sighed.

"I know this is difficult for you, count, but I must understand! You have made a terrible accusation against him, and it is my duty to discover the truth."

"I can only tell you what my sister's last two letters said. I had decided I must go there to find out what was going on. But the morning I was leaving, I received two letters together . . . they had been posted one after the other, two days in a row." He paused and bowed his head.

"What did they say?"

"The first . . . the first said that Kazimir had trapped her alone and tried to . . . tried to force her to submit to him. Urvan, coming upon the scene, misinterpreted and . . . and beat her."

Christoph felt his body go cold. "Kazimir tried to rape her? Did she explain to her husband?"

"No; he would not listen, she told me in the letter." He shook his head sadly. "Imagine my horror as I sat in the confines of my carriage reading such a terrible tale! I wanted to beat against the doors, to tell my driver to go faster. I felt her terror in every line, felt her fear. Kazimir, she wrote me, was fierce, powerful and a warrior. You can see that about him, how strong he is, how brutal. Where do you think he got that scar across his face? It was a fight with a fellow officer, I am told, perhaps another he killed." He shook his head.

"Was that all in the letter?"

"Yes, in the first letter. You can imagine with what trembling fingers I opened the second. She was in a terrible state of fear, she said, for Urvan had become difficult and cruel. He beat her and confined her to her room, jealous and sure that she had become Kazimir's lover, though she was innocent of the charge."

"Poor girl. I would kill any man who treated my sister that way!" Christoph said. He had been pacing, but he stopped before the Russian. "What else did the second letter say?"

Wearily, Gavril bowed his head, and his words were

almost indistinct. "She begged me to come get her, said she could no longer put up with her life as it was. She said . . . she said that to protect herself, she was forced to take Kazimir as her lover and . . . well, use his . . . use his, uh, strength to protect her."

Christoph gazed down at the count's silvery head. There was some evasion there, some half-truth, he felt, but it seemed a straightforward enough narrative. "And so you were already on your way."

"But it was a journey of two and a half days. When I arrived, it was already too late. From what I understand, it came to a head. Urvan discovered his brother and my sister together, and they fought. He said he was going to confine her. Kazimir swore that if he could not have her, then no one would, and murdered Franziska. Urvan was already gone when I arrived at their estate, and he left behind a letter telling me what had occurred, saying that since Kazimir had killed Franziska, he was killing himself out of despairing love for his dead wife."

"But that doesn't make sense. He is very much alive, so his suicide letter cannot be believed. And it appears that he is the one who poses more danger than Count Kazimir," Christoph said, trying to see through what appeared so foggy and obscured.

Gavril trembled and took in a long breath. "That I do not understand," he whispered. "How can it be? Or are we deceived? Is this madman in the woods in truth someone else posing as Urvan?" His expression hardened. "No matter what, I have my own dead sister's word as proof that Kazimir tried to take desperate advantage of her. We cannot trust him, especially not with the eclipse coming and the Blood Amber Chalice unfound."

Setting aside his questions about this mysterious chalice and rosary for a moment, Christoph asked, "How could you not tell us this earlier, if what you say is true?" He burrowed into his own heart and felt, with the wolf within him, that if it was true, surely he would have known it, he would have felt the danger to his sister and to Melisande, his beloved. Oddly, he had felt, with Kazimir, a kind of brotherhood, a kinship of some sort, more so than he had ever felt with this frail man before him. But why would Count Gavril lie to him, and in such a bold-faced manner?

"I do not say he is a danger to any one of you right now, but if he should get the chalice . . ."

"What is all of this nonsense about this chalice and Melisande's rosary? I demand to know the truth of this *now*. What does it—"

He was interrupted by a shouting in the great hall and raced down to the gallery. Kazimir had returned, but without Magda.

"What is it? What did you find, if Magda is gone?" Christoph shouted, as he pelted down the stairs to the great hall.

"The cabin is empty . . . deserted, but . . ." Kazimir said, waving a dirty scrap of paper in the air, "Urvan left a note."

Summoned by the commotion, Melisande, Gavril, and Christoph gathered in the drawing room, and Kazimir read the letter out loud. He already knew the contents but was beginning to feel he had not been open enough with the inhabitants of the castle. This was their problem, too, and it was time to share the puzzle of how to handle it all.

The letter was long and raving, much of it not making any sense, but some of the cryptic references were clear to Kazimir. Urvan, in his madness, had brooded on Franziska's betrayal of him, but what seemed to have stung most was what she had given Kazimir and withheld from him.

"I don't understand much of it," Melisande said, looking around at the others, "except that he has taken Magda with him, to some hiding place where he has my father. What I do not understand is why he says that if anyone approaches, even a wolf, he will kill them? A wolf? I don't understand!" She glanced from one to the other of the men in the room. "Is he speaking of the wolf that attacked as we escaped the hut? How can we be sure a wolf will not wander by the hiding place?"

Kazimir glanced at Christoph, and the young man hung his head. "It is part of his raving, only," he said, meeting her steady, clear gaze. It was difficult now to lie to her, but Christoph's secret was not his to reveal, and his own would keep for another day. When he looked into her eyes, though, he was caught and held, for swimming in their clear blue depths was the knowledge of his own body's invasion of hers. Deeply, down to his core, he had felt what he did, and there was no shame, for what he had been forced to do had created a bond that she now felt too, and as much as he had never intended to follow his wishes, other than a few stolen kisses, her delicious loveliness had stolen into his soul, lightening his darkness with a hint of her radiance. But only a hint; like a glimmer of candlelight seen in a dark forest at a great distance, it could not ultimately shed light on the whole of his gloom.

Nothing would ever do that until he was freed from the enchantment under which he labored. Maybe then . . . perhaps there was hope after all.

"The letter says we must take the chalice to the location he has indicated on his hasty map," Gavril said, "and that the two will be released."

Kazimir met his adversary's gaze and acknowledged the distrust, but he had no time for it. "I do not believe that he will be true to his word. I believe the moment he gets the chalice, the lives of Magda and Mikhail will be forfeit." Melisande gasped and began to cry, but he could not stop, could not address her pain in that moment. "I believe the captives are safe until that moment, though, or as safe as they can be in the freezing cold wherever Urvan has decided to keep them. Time is growing short. The lunar eclipse approaches, and if we have not managed to free them by then, with or without the chalice—"

"The lunar eclipse . . . my father had calculations marked in the book of astronomy that he borrowed." Tears still stained her pink cheeks, but she had choked them back, bravely. "Does that mean . . . what *does* that mean?"

Gavril had, if possible, gone even paler, his skin an ash gray even in the golden light from the fire. "It means that Mikhail was set to use the chalice once he had the rosary, too, and once the eclipse occurred. It means—"

"That Mikhail Davidovich intended to use the chalice and rosary at the height of the blood moon . . . the lunar eclipse," Kazimir finished.

"Use it? What does this mean?" Melisande cried, looking from one man to the other. "Tell me now!"

"Perhaps not, though," Kazimir said, talking as much to himself as anyone else. "Perhaps he had been considering it, but had decided—"

Charlotte, tears streaming down her face, burst into the room and lightly ran across it, grabbing Melisande's hands. "Come quickly! Come now!"

"What? Come where?"

"Uta is awake! She is awake and asking for you!"

Chapter 24

MELISANDE ENTERED the room swiftly and crossed to the bed. Uta, her almost blind eyes bleary, looked up at the sound.

"Melisande," she said, reaching out her crippled hands. In German she said, "You asked it of me, and so I came back."

"How can this be?" Melisande cried, taking Uta's hands in her own.

Frau Liebner, standing beside the bed, wept openly, but, with a deep, shuddering breath, calmed herself and said, "She has been saying that you asked her to come back. I heard you, and you did, you asked her to come back and told me to tell you when. How did you know? How?"

"Enough!" Uta said, her voice creaky. "Water. I need water. And then leave us alone. My time is short."

Mina silently ministered to her mistress and then shooed Frau Liebner from the room, closing the door behind them both. Charlotte, who had followed Melisande upstairs, babbled outside the door to Frau Liebner, but then their voices receded. Melisande sank down on the edge of the bed, still holding the old woman's gnarled hands in hers, trying to impart some of her own strength.

"Stop!" Uta said.

"What?"

"Stop trying to make me live forever," Uta said. "I am tired, and I wish to go. My little brother, sweet Willem, was there, and he had much to tell me, and much to ask. They are curious, those who have gone ahead, for they have no one with whom to communicate. The recently arrived bring news from the world of man. I told him I would come back soon . . . and stay forever."

Melisande's breath caught in her throat. Forever? "Was that who . . . the people in the woods that I saw . . . was that . . ."

"I do not know what you saw," Uta said, with a squeeze of Melisande's hand, "but those who have passed on were there, and we had much of which to speak, but I was not allowed until . . . until I cross over."

"But I don't want you to go," Melisande said, her voice thick with tears. "What shall I do without you?"

"You will go on. Much life ahead of you . . . husband . . . children . . . love."

"I don't think so. I don't think I can marry now."

When Uta wearily commanded her to speak of all that had happened, Melisande gave her a brief version. Her own confusion over all of it made the tale a puzzle, she feared, but the old woman seemed to follow it.

"And so Kazimir Vasilov, he has taken your virginity, but very gently it seems. I am surprised, for he did not seem to me to be a gentle man. But he is a very handsome man, despite the scar, is he not? Has he made a baby in you?"

"No!" Melisande cried, shocked, as she often was, by the old woman's bawdy train of thought. "No, he . . . he did not do all he needed to . . . to make a child."

Uta nodded, her growing weariness evident as her eyes drifted closed repeatedly. "I think you do not know what it takes from a man not to follow his deeply ingrained instincts. That one . . . he has a destiny as yet unfulfilled; it is entwined with yours. Do not believe . . ." She drifted away, all of the tension leaving her body.

"Do not believe what? Whom? Uta!" Melisande clasped the old woman's hands tight.

She gasped and opened her eyes. "Do not . . . believe . . . what people will tell you . . . ask questions."

"What do you mean? Of whom?" But even as Melisande asked, she could feel the old woman drifting away. If she pushed too hard right now, it would be too much for her weakened system, and a collapse would be inevitable. Right now Uta was merely sleeping, but she drifted perilously close to the distant shore again. "Please," Melisande whispered, catching back a sob. "I am being selfish, perhaps, but please do not leave me yet, Uta." A squeeze of her fingers in the old woman's grasp was her only answer.

She stood, new determination flooding her. She was going to find this chalice, take it to the madman, and get her father back. Nothing else mattered.

She marched from the room telling Mina, who hovered outside, to get word to her when Uta awoke again, and stomped back to her room. She changed into clothes suitable for the passages, a pair of thick boots and an ugly gray dress she had never cared for. She bound her hair up in a cloth and went to her father's room.

But the map to the passages was gone. Fury rippled through her, and with her new determination came a sense of her own power. There was something about her that she had never tapped into before, something passed on by her grandmother. She wasn't sure of it yet, but there pulsed through her veins an awareness that she was changed forever. Her loss of virginity freed her in some way; she was a woman, and not afraid of anything. Or anyone.

She flew down the hall from her father's room and across the gallery to the drawing room to find the men—Counts Kazimir, Gavril, and Christoph—huddled together near the fire. "Where is the map?" she demanded, striding over to them.

Christoph started guiltily away from the other two. Melisande looked down, and there, spread out on a small table near the fire, was the map her father had made. She snatched it away from them. "I will take that, thank you very much. I think not one of you will deny that I have a better right to it than any of you."

Kazimir rose to his full height, an impressive and broad-shouldered male next to the slim height of Christoph and the frailty of Count Gavril. "We were consulting only, Miss Melisande. But I think as I am the one who discovered your father's use of the secret passages, I am the one who should investigate."

"I care little what you think . . . what *any* of you think. I have had enough of this nonsense. This all is tied in, in the madman's mind, to the lunar eclipse, which I understand is approaching. When exactly can we expect it?"

Gavril and Kazimir exchanged looks.

"After this night has passed, two nights only are now between us and the blood moon," Count Gavril said.

"Why is the eclipse of the moon called the blood moon?" Melisande asked.

Christoph said, "For a time, our planet's shadow blocks the reflection of the sun . . . the light which makes our moon glow silvery, for the moon has no light of its own, not like the sun. When we interfere . . . rather, when the earth interferes, then the light is obscured and shows darker."

"You will see for yourself," Count Kazimir said. "It is, in legend, a time of great significance, and for the chalice and the rosary, it was the moment when they both turned a deep shade of crimson, the color of rich blood."

"Two nights," Melisande said. "Two nights before Urvan has no more use for my father and will kill him, if we don't find him or the chalice first."

"Wait! Why are we still trying to find the chalice? We cannot give it to this man . . . you both have been saying," Christoph said.

"But they have not said why," Melisande said, narrowing her eyes and gazing at the two. "Except some superstitious nonsense better fitted for a peasant in the field than two aristocrats who should be enlightened beyond the irrational."

"Do you not think that there is more in the world than what you can see, Miss Melisande?" Count Gavril said.

She stopped and could feel her heart pounding as if it would leap out of her breast. Given Uta's recovery and what she said while coming out of it, and given her new feelings of power, how could she deny the possible presence of other mystical powers? "I . . . know there is more than what we can see. But that does not mean I forfeit any rational voice in choosing what I believe in. You have hidden things, both of you, and even now are not telling us all, nor even a fraction of what is beneath all of this."

Christoph nodded. "Given what you have told me, Count Roschkov, do you not think we should be told all?"

"Time grows short," Kazimir said, eyeing Melisande with a thoughtful look. "If you do not care about the prisoners, then we can stop now and discuss everything. If you believe, as I do, that time is short and every moment precious, then I think we should begin to look for the chalice now!"

Melisande nodded. "I do agree," she said, deciding to put everything else aside as she looked for the chalice, the key to freeing her father and Magda. "My father is still alive, I am sure of that, but he is ill, I think. We must find a way to save him, and if the chalice is the key, then we must find it."

Charlotte, who had come in while they were speaking and listened, said, "May I help?"

"Of course," Melisande said. "You will go with me."

All three men looked startled.

"But I thought perhaps . . ." Kazimir and Christoph both said at once and then stopped and stared at each other.

"I would be honored to join you ladies," Count Gavril said, smoothly.

"No. We shall do this on our own." She took the map. "And you gentlemen . . . can search how and when you will. I expect to hear later everyone's progress."

Melisande led Charlotte away. "You and I shall start from my father's room, for in truth, if the chalice is within the walls, then near his room is most likely."

Together they marched across the gallery and to her father's room; Melisande took a deep breath and began to search the room for the access to the secret passages, with Charlotte following and holding the candle.

"Do you think we will find it?"

"If it is here, I don't see why we would not. I have to begin to think like my father, I suppose, though since he is an enigma to me, that is difficult."

"At least you have your father. I know mine only from stories my uncle and aunts tell."

"I know," Melisande said, with a swift look back at her friend. She felt along the portion of the wall indicated on the drawing her father had left. "Here! I can feel a difference here. The wall is cold here." Charlotte held the candle high, and Melisande examined the wall paneling. "Now . . . this should . . ." She pushed the panel, and it slid aside. A cold rush of wind smelling of mold and dust blew in around her. "Oh!"

Charlotte gasped. "How is it possible that I have lived

within these walls my whole life and never knew of these passages?" she asked, leaning past Melisande and peeking into the musty corridor. She shivered. "I . . . I suppose this is how that villain, Bartol Liebner, entered and exited our rooms so easily. I could have . . . I almost . . ."

"I know," Melisande said, acknowledging her friend's past pain and fear. To keep Charlotte from dwelling on the awful episode just a couple of months past when she was drugged and almost died at the hands of the madman, she stiffened her spine and said, "But now we must help my papa and . . . and poor Magda."

"Magda," Charlotte echoed. "Do you truly feel such compassion for her? Despite everything, and how she aided the madman?"

Melisande nodded, unable to speak for the moment, afraid she would blurt out the awful truth of Magda's impending motherhood at the hands of . . . who knew? "Though she was misguided, she had her reasons, and now . . . at least she did her best to free us. I fear she suffers for what she did. Count Kazimir said . . . said there was blood at the doorway of the hut."

They examined the dank walls of the passage for a moment without speaking. Cobwebs festooned the walls, and dust drifted toward their wavering candlelight. Both girls shivered and clung to each other.

"Perhaps we should search other places in the castle first," Charlotte said, her voice weak.

"No. It is here somewhere," Melisande replied. "And I am going to find it. Time is short, the danger is real, and I will not let that madman kill my father."

"And Magda. I fear I have not been very kind to her, Meli. I . . . someone once said she was even prettier than I, and ever since I have held her in dislike. Like . . . like when Count Kazimir said you were far more beautiful than I. I have been so . . . so spoiled and unpleasant lately. I have been a child."

"You can make up for any past unkindness by helping me to free her. The chalice is here, and together, we shall find it." Groping her way, hand out against the cold wall, Melisande began down the passage.

•   •   •

"I don't remember what that wretched map Mikhail made showed," Count Gavril Roschkov said to his companion as they explored the passages from another direction. "We should have made a copy." He stopped and put one hand out, leaning against the wall and trying to catch his breath.

Christoph stopped, held the candle high, and gazed at the pale Russian. "You should have stayed behind, Count Roschkov. You are clearly not well." And he was holding Christoph back, he wanted to add, but that would be cruel, and if he had learned anything in the last months, it was that cruelty, though he was capable of it, was not his true nature.

"I will not get any better, and yet I will not die before my appointed time. So in the interim, I refuse to sit in a chair with a blanket over my knees and do nothing. Let us go on."

"No, wait. I want to know one thing." Christoph held the candle close to the other man's face and examined his ghostly gray countenance. "Tell me, do you truly believe that Count Vasilov murdered your sister?"

"How can I not believe it? If Urvan still lives . . . but that is the crux of this all, is it not? We have only Kazimir Vasilov's word for it that the madman is his brother, Urvan. Miss Melisande is only taking his word for it in her confirmation. Why should we believe him? I know for a fact that Kazimir is dangerous, and I feel deeply that he is a murderer."

"And yet he rescued Meli."

"But how? We do not know under what circumstances."

"Yes, I do; they escaped together, and he did his best to help her through the forest even as the madman—" Christoph stopped, seeing the trap, for he had told no one he was out there as a wolf, and that his injury was from the kidnapper's gun, not his own.

But Gavril, caught up in his own thoughts, did not appear to notice. "If it is Urvan, then his suicide from the bridge—it was very public, and would have been difficult to survive unless there was some subterfuge, I suppose—was intended to allow him to walk away from his life. Why would he do that? Certainly Franziska was dead, and some looked at him as if he was perhaps the murderer, but . . ."

"So you have absolutely no proof for your assertion that Count Vasilov murdered your sister."

"Kazimir Dimitre Vasilov had a reason to kill my poor, dear sister; he was in love with her, but as much as I despise saying it, she was only using him. He surely felt that. And he was driven mad, perhaps, by his . . . by his own power."

"I don't understand you!"

Stubbornly, Gavril said, "All I know is what my sister wrote to me. She was afraid of Kazimir. As far as I know Urvan, despite his jealousy, had *no* reason to kill his wife. Kazimir did," he repeated, his voice thickening, "and he killed her, beating her until her bloodied body was unrecognizable but to me, who loved her most. Think how you would feel if it was your sister, Countess Charlotte! I will *never* forgive the man who murdered my darling little Franziska—never! Kazimir Vasilov is a murdering beast."

Chapter 25

MELISANDE, HAVING made her way ahead of Charlotte in the passage, could not believe what she was hearing. Count Vasilov . . . a murderer? She turned abruptly and ran into Charlotte, who was following with the flickering candle.

"What is going on? Why did you turn?" Charlotte cried out.

"Hello?" came a voice along the passage.

"That is Christoph. Hello!" Charlotte called out. She slipped past Melisande and sped along the passage, candle held high.

But Melisande, reeling from the words she had just heard, backtracked by feeling along the dank wall and found an opening she had noticed from a sliver of light that shone beyond it. She slid the panel aside and stumbled into the room. "Kazimir!" she gasped, as she saw him from behind, by a bed, pulling a shirt on over his head.

He whirled. The pale skin of his chest, darkened by a whorl of black hair across the muscled surface, gleamed in the dying light of twilight from his window. He had just bathed; a steaming basin of water sat near him. Pulling the shirt down over his torso, he solemnly gazed at her as he picked up his jacket from the bed and slipped it on over the loose shirt. "You are exploring the passages," he said. "Have you found anything?"

She shook her head, mutely, gazing at his square face, the dark thick brows like slashes above eyes the brown of chocolate and black hair carelessly swept back from his wide forehead. His solitary nature and hard features made him a difficult man to know. Was he, then, a killer? Was she to believe that his confrontation with his brother was fueled by the murder between them of Urvan's wife?

She hastily pushed the panel closed behind her, then started forward and circled the bed, pulling off the kerchief over her hair. "Tell me!"

"What?" he said, frowning.

"Tell me the truth," she said urgently, searching his dark eyes. "Tell me everything, the terrible truth that is between you and your brother. I have heard one side of the story; tell me now the truth about Franziska."

He flinched and bowed his head.

The silence lengthened. Pellets of snowy rain tapped against the window, and Melisande felt a fearful desperation welling up within her. How could she even care about this when her father and Magda were somewhere, cold and hungry and frightened . . . perhaps ill? Even now she should be crawling through the walls, trying to find the damnable chalice.

And yet the heart of this mystery was Urvan Vasilov and his brother. "*Tell* me."

"There is nothing to tell," he said, looking up at her finally. "Nothing. What is important now is rescuing your father. Then, as I vowed, I will marry you. We shall go back to Russia, and you and your father can live on my estate. I will leave you there in peace."

His cold recitation of his intentions chilled her. "Why would you marry me?" she whispered.

"All of this is my responsibility. If I had done things differently . . . but I didn't. I have made error after error, and now this horror has fallen upon you. I promised in the cabin to take care of you, and I meant it. I am yours. We will marry and I will provide for you. We shall travel back to my home, I will see you welcomed in the village, and then I will leave you alone forever."

Word after word dropped from his mouth like cold pebbles into a frozen stream; they had no meaning to her, though she understood them. Forever. Forever. The vacant emptiness of his eyes smothered her with fear. She had felt the first stirrings of tenderness toward him, but that seemed so long ago now.

This side of him was unpleasant to witness, remote and un-
yielding.

"How self-pitying you sound," she said, responding to
something in his tone that irked her.

"Life has not been kind to me."

Sharp-edged fury bit into her heart. "How dare you say
that?" she cried, throwing her kerchief at him. It fluttered to
the floor and lay at his feet. "How *dare* you?" Her voice trembled, and she took a deep breath to steady it. "I watched my
beloved grandmother and mother beaten to death by a frenzied mob and could do nothing. Even now my poor father is
freezing in the hands of a madman."

"The woman I once thought I loved died horribly, brutally,
and because of me," he said, his fury biting his words into
hard syllables. "I watched as she breathed her last, the blood
streaming from her mouth, death rattling in her breast."

Her heart skipped a beat, and she felt ill. Was he admitting
his guilt? She could not ask, could not probe so painful an affair, even though his words were so imprecise and vague. He
couldn't be a murderer. He just couldn't. Drawing herself up,
summoning all of the dignity of her inner core of strength, she
said, "Ah, then you win, Count Kazimir; with your pitiful
story you win in the stakes of who is most wretched, because
I will not contest it. But I . . . I refuse to remain pitiful, even
if you are willing to wallow in it. I am going to find that most
wretched chalice and free my father and Magda somehow.
Then you, your mad brother, and Count Gavril can all go to
hell in your own tortured manner." She whirled and left the
room.

LATER, with not one of them successful in finding the chalice, they gathered in the drawing room. By lamplight
Melisande examined the crude map her father had created and
tried to work out the numbers, marks, and letters that had been
scrawled around the edges.

"Would your father have taken the chalice outside the castle to hide it, once he was on his feet?" Christoph asked, leaning over the map, too, and trying to imagine what Mikhail had
intended the scratchings to represent.

"I don't think so," Melisande said. "But anything is possible." She was beginning to feel hopeless. What would happen if the eclipse arrived before they found the chalice? "Once I find it," she said, straightening, "I intend to take it directly to where Urvan has demanded and give it to him."

"I beg your pardon, Miss Melisande," Count Gavril said, pouring a cup of tea from the urn on the table, "but I could never allow you to do that. You would be playing into his hands."

"As much as it pains me to agree with him," Count Kazimir said, coming in to the drawing room just then, "I have to say, giving Urvan the chalice with the eclipse approaching would be not only wrong, but suicidal. He has the rosary. The eclipse occurs in just one more night, after this one, and if he has the chalice, too . . ."

"Davidovich bravely held back the chalice, I think, for that very reason," Gavril said. "He finally grasped that to give it to Urvan would be death."

Melisande sat back in her chair and eyed the two men. "What will occur if he has the rosary and the chalice as the eclipse approaches? The truth."

Gavril and Kazimir exchanged looks.

"Tell us!" Melisande said, impatient in the face of their reluctance.

Kazimir sighed deeply and turned to Melisande and Christoph's questioning gaze. "What I am about to say may seem shocking, but it is, sadly, true." He reiterated the story of the chalice and rosary, much of which Melisande knew, but was fresh to Christoph. "The legend we have alluded to so often—the use of the chalice and rosary at the height of the eclipse—will transform Urvan into . . ." He paused, shook his head, but then continued. "Into a werewolf, but one with such extraordinary powers as will overwhelm any opposition."

"How ludicrous!" Melisande cried, glancing from one face to the other. She looked over at Christoph, but he, for some reason, had not joined her in her disbelief and had, indeed, paled, the two ruddy spots usually present on his high cheekbones bleached as white as the snowdrifts.

"What is this about," he demanded, his voice hoarse and his tone abrupt. "What are you talking about?"

"Why do you think *he* came here looking for the chalice?" Gavril said, contemptuously indicating Kazimir with a wave of his bony hand. "He wants to use them to increase his power."

"That is not true. I have no need of more than I already have, believe me, Gavril. Do not lie, and do not try to conceal your own interest in the awful pair. You want it yourself," he said, pointing a finger at Gavril, "to save you from the wasting illness you suffer, for you know if you give yourself over to the legend and become the beast, it will make you invulnerable, impervious even to death."

"Stop!" Christoph shouted. "I will not have this quarrelling in my house. What if Urvan does get the chalice and becomes this . . . this werewolf? What then? He could still be defeated, could he not?"

Melisande stared at Christoph. Did he truly believe this drivel?

"No," both Russians said, simultaneously.

Kazimir continued. "Nothing could defeat him, for what he would become by drinking of the chalice and burning it and the rosary by the red light of the blood moon eclipse is so much beyond a werewolf as . . . as a werewolf is beyond a true wolf. He would be invincible."

Charlotte, with Fanny trailing her, raced into the drawing room. "Uta is awake again!"

Melisande started toward the door.

"No!" Charlotte said, staying Melisande with one hand. "No! She says she will speak to Count Kazimir. I'm sorry, Meli, but it's true; I spoke to her myself. The . . . the scarred one, she called him, and she wishes to speak to him alone."

"Why?" Melisande whispered, turning to look at Kazimir. "Why would she want to see you?"

"I will go immediately," he said, and trudged up the stairs, his heart heavy. Every step reminded him of each step he had made in the past years, missteps, he had to call them. Priding himself on his strength, he had been weak. Thinking himself clever, he had been astoundingly obtuse. Feeling sure of his way, he had become lost.

Without knocking, he entered the old woman's chamber, remembering how he came to her in the night, and what she had said to him. She had known, somehow, why he was there, and that the outcome of his sojourn among them was in serious doubt. Then—and it seemed so long ago now, so much had happened in the interim—she had said his pride and sullen solitariness would lead him into trouble, and she was right. If he had just reached out, if he had been willing to humble himself, perhaps Mikhail would not have stumbled directly into Urvan's trap. And then perhaps he would not have hurt Melisande as he did. He approached the old woman's bedside, and her mute maidservant melted away into the shadows, taking up her post near the door.

"You, I have been awaiting," Countess Uta said, just as she did the first night.

"And I have come at your command," he said, taking her hand and pressing his lips to the back of it. As before, he felt the connection between them, though he was still not sure what it was.

"You have sipped of nectar that is far sweeter than anything you have ever tasted, am I right about that, Kazimir Vasilov?"

He bowed his head, knowing what she meant. She knew. "I have. I wish now to marry her, but she says no. What shall I do to convince her?"

"Melisande is brave and stubborn. She will not marry merely to satisfy some notion of honor. If you intend marriage, you must make her love you."

"I do not ask for love," he barked, attempting to withdraw his hand from her grasp.

But she held fast. "Idiot!" she croaked.

Her eyes, closed before, opened, and though she was clearly almost blind, there was a luminous power in her gaze that transfixed him. Near to the grave she might be, but she still lived far more intensely than most in the household.

"I know you, Kazimir Vasilov. I understand you. Our souls speak, and though I do not understand it, it is so. But listen to me good; you are a fool, and a knave. While my nephew breaks his heart over her and understands truly her value, she is there like a jewel, yours for the taking, if you try. You do not deserve her, but there is something between you, and with every day the tie binds you both more strongly. And yet you

say you do not want her love? Let me tell you, the love of a
woman like Melisande is a prize to be won, not a burden to be
shouldered."

He stilled and felt his pulse, the blood racing through his
veins. "First I must find the chalice and try to save
Melisande's father. Nothing matters but that, for the moment."

"And yet what you do now could turn her from you forever, if you do not take care."

It would be simpler, he thought, simpler if she developed
an aversion to him and refused to marry him. Then, he would
have made the offer and in honor could retire from the field
and leave Christoph to make her love him, if he could. The
young man languished, eating his heart out over her, and he
would make her a good husband.

"No, he would not," Uta said.

"What?"

"I told you our souls speak; you are thinking that perhaps
Christoph would make her a better husband than you. He
would not. As much as I love the boy, he will need to mature
before he could ever satisfy a woman of Melisande's strength.
Right now he loves her for the fortitude he senses in her and
feels that he lacks. But what he will need is a young woman
to whom he can be her strength, otherwise he would always
rely on Melisande and never cultivate his own."

After that long speech, she was gasping, and Mina came
forward, buffeting him on the shoulder as if to say he must
leave now.

"I will do what I think is right, countess."

But she was already gone again, drifted away in a deep
sleep. Her labored breathing calmed. He released her bony,
arthritic hand, and bowed to the grim maidservant, but her attention was reserved only for her mistress, so he left.

The halls were dim, and the house had settled in his absence. Everyone was exhausted to the point of collapse and
needed rest. He retired to his own room but could not lie down
to sleep. When he let his mind rest, he returned again and
again to the sense he had while he took her maidenhood that
he knew love for the first time in his life. He had felt a welter
of emotion clog his brain, confusing him, rattling him down
to his soul. He rejected that sensation; it must not be, and so

he would deny it, even to himself. What had he to do with love? Love was a weakness men submitted to, but there was no room in his life for weakness.

And yet there it was, clouding his thoughts, obscuring every other sensation but the feel of her under him, the touch of her body, and yet more . . . so much more. The mere corporal had little to do with his feelings. He drew in a deep breath. He was bewitched, and yet this did not feel like the first enchantment he had experienced.

He lay back on his bed, trying to find peace, trying to put his mind to the task at hand—finding the chalice, rescuing Mikhail Davidovich and Magda Brandt. No good. Melisande . . . always she was there. He had not spoken to her as he had intended, earlier, and still had news for her . . . or rather a lack of news, in a sense.

Surely it would not hurt to seek her out, he thought, so he paced the corridors, and when he came to her chamber, he touched the door, his fingers laid against the wood surface. She was there, he could feel her, sense her. He scratched at the door, and she called out from within to enter.

She was sitting by her small fire, and when she looked up, her cheeks were wet. His heart throbbed with pain, a sense of her fear ripping through him. Since their experience in the cabin, he had felt the connection Uta spoke of and could deny it no longer. More than just poetic love or tenderness coursed in his veins. They were bound fast to each other; parting from her would rip away a part of his guts.

He crossed the room and knelt at her feet, looking up into her tear-filled eyes. He reached up one hand and cradled her cheek.

"What did Uta want with you?" she murmured.

He remembered how much the old woman meant to Melisande and how it must wound her to not be summoned in the few moments of consciousness she had between lapsing back into sleep. "She . . . spoke to me of you. She knew what was between us . . ."

"I told her. I have never kept anything from her. She is to me like my grandmother was, a confidant, another soul that touches mine."

He nodded. It felt oddly right to be at her feet, in this

attitude of supplication, and it soothed the pain he had felt at his core. He gazed up at her, the glow of the fire sparkling off the tears in her eyes and the strands of honey and gold in her unbound hair. Never had any task been more difficult than breaking down the barriers of his pride and putting into words what he felt.

"Are you . . . all right, after our experience in the cabin at Urvan's despicable hands? Have you suffered since, or do you experience . . . pain?"

He was rewarded by a tremulous smile on her sweet lips.

"I am becoming accustomed to the sense I have, that my body has changed."

"I would have given anything rather than . . ."

"Stop," she said, putting her hand over his mouth, thumbing his scar. "I chose my destiny. I know you would have fought him if you could have, and the end may have been to free us, or it may have meant death. I chose life, and I would do so again. Because of what occurred, Magda's heart was touched, and she helped us escape. I only hope she has not paid with her life for helping us to freedom."

"I went back there again this afternoon, to the hut, to try to find a trail to where he has taken her and where he conceals your father, but there was nothing."

"Will you . . . sit with me for a while? We should be searching for the chalice, but sleep . . . sooner or later we need to rest, and I admit I am exhausted."

But instead of taking a seat in the other chair by her fireplace, he chose to sit by her feet, the filmy skirts of her dress frothing around his knees. They talked, and the fire dimmed to a faint glow. Her voice quieted, finally, and he thought she might be sleeping, but when he looked up, it was to see her regarding him with a steady gaze.

"What is it?" he asked, feeling in her gaze a question.

"You said you thought you loved Franziska. Are you in doubt of that?"

He searched his heart; now with something to compare it against, he understood it better. "I don't believe it was love. In . . . in my life before this," he said, carefully, tiptoeing around the truth of the matter, "I had never experienced that emotion, if the poets are to be believed about its intensity and depth. What I felt for her was the heady rush of passion and desire."

"Oh. Did she love you?"

"No."

"Is that why she rejected you?"

"Rejected me?"

"Yes. Count Gavril told us how you repeatedly pursued her, despite her rejections. He . . . he said it troubled her terribly."

"How would he know any of that?"

"She told him herself in letters to him."

He twisted and gazed steadily up into her lovely eyes. He could not quite believe what she said. "She told him that I pestered her and that she rejected me?"

"Yes, and that you . . . that you attempted to . . ."

He stared up at her, the red of her cheeks glowing. "What? I attempted what?"

"To . . . to rape her."

After a long silence, he said, "I would *never* make love to a woman who was not willing; I think you must know that about me. I have not changed so much from my youth."

Confused, she fell silent.

After a time, he rose. "I should go."

She stood and looked up at him. He stared into her eyes, and what he saw there she did not know, but in the next instant he had reached out, pulled her to him, and he kissed her lips, the initial power of his actions gentling. Swept along by his tender, skillful lovemaking, she indulged her senses, closing her eyes and allowing herself to simply feel.

Reaching up, she threaded her arms around his neck, his hard body against hers warmed her to the core with new sensations, more powerful than she had ever experienced. But the image of her father's face, gaunt and gray, his eyes pitifully imploring, intruded, and she pulled away.

"No," she gasped. "No. I cannot think of anything until my father is safe once more. I need a little sleep, and then I shall be looking again for the chalice."

"Yes," he said, bowing his head. "Of course. I will leave you, Melisande, and see you in the morning."

Chapter 26

BUT RETIRING to his room, taking off his clothes, donning his night attire, none of that meant sleep for Kazimir, not when he was still puzzling over the things Gavril had said to the others about Franziska. Why would he lie like that? After all they had been through, Kazimir had never expected their friendship to last, and it hadn't, but Gavril was an upright and honorable man, scrupulous about the truth, eschewing any kind of deception or trickery. Why would he tell them that Franziska had accused him of attempting rape?

Unless she did. But why? Why would she do that? He had offered her love and solace and a shoulder to lean on when Urvan was making her life a living hell. It just made no sense. It was like believing that the world was round and flat, all at the same time—impossible.

He turned his mind away from the unknowable to that which had come to him as he kissed Melisande. It was as the old woman had said; Melisande Davidovich was worth rubies and more. He loved her with whatever love a man such as he was capable of. But beyond the beauty of her soul and the enchantment he felt in her arms, she possessed something more, a power that held his own in check, something he had never experienced. Always with women he had been careful, for he had felt as if they were fragile and might break if he bent all of his energy and force to them, not physically, but their mind and emotional stability. The darkness of his soul was dangerous to the frail delicacy of womanhood, he had always thought, but Melisande met and challenged him, her vitality forcing his back, her energy burning within like a hot ember. She seared him with her inner strength, and with the something else she possessed.

Magic. She had powers she was perhaps unaware of; he felt it, sensed the enchantment. In the cabin, just the physical contact of their sexual encounter had strengthened him and brought him back from whatever was causing him to become ill; he had known it then and had drawn strength from her, recovering enough to help her out of the hut. And now his desire for her was filling his mind and body, and he paced, like a caged beast. Obsession was a dangerous thing, and he knew himself to be vulnerable to it. He was obsessed with the thought that if he could just love her once, truly make love to her, then it would ease the fearful hold she had on his heart.

Finally his passionate yearning for her was too much; like an itch, it would drive him mad unless he soothed the urge. One look. He would allow himself one look. He crept into the secret passages and found his way to her room by instinct, feeling her warmth, hearing her heart beat in his ears, getting ever stronger as he neared her room. He slid a panel aside, and, closing it behind him, crept up to the bed. There she was, asleep.

One kiss and he would leave her to slumber.

He leaned over her and watched—his eyesight was better in the night than even a cat's—as her sweet lips pursed and puffs of air emitted. Arousal pulsed through his body, and, lightheaded, he closed his eyes and bent over, touching her lips with his. His mind whirled, and as his tongue pushed through her lips, he felt the overwhelming delight he had pushed back when he took her body in the filthy and cold cabin, with Urvan nearby and Magda weeping softly. Then he had rejected the sweetness he had felt even as he did the unthinkable. Now he let it surround him, engulfing him . . . drowning him.

She moaned and moved, and he slipped under the covers, pulling her close, lost to anything but the sensation of her soft skin and his sharp awareness of her own unexpected desire. Returning his kiss, pushing her tongue into *his* mouth, tasting him and sucking his tongue, arching toward his body, as his arousal fit to her curves and burgeoned, hunger ripped through his soul, spiraling into his body like a corkscrew into a cork.

Awake, she moved away for a moment, but then, gazing at

him, searching his eyes, she moaned softly and threw herself back into his arms, surrendering again to the passion that was between them. They rolled together and, lost in the soft darkness, hungrily shared and doubled their yearning. Blissful eons went by, his ache throbbing through him, and yet he was happy in the painful acknowledgment of his unfulfilled hunger.

But then she touched him, her questing hand trembling, she stroked first just his naked thigh under his nightshirt, but then, tentatively, she reached and delicately touched.

"No, Melisande, no. Please . . ."

"Kazimir," she whispered, and his name on her lips was like music, "I don't know what to think . . . what to feel . . . I would like to understand what has happened to me, what I felt in that cabin."

"No! Please, don't remind me . . . don't associate . . ."

"But you saved my life by taking my virginity."

Shame ripped through him, and he rolled away from her in the dark.

"Have I said anything wrong?" she asked.

"I can't explain to you, but if I had been decisive, perhaps if I had been more wary or stronger, made the decision faster, there was one more thing I could have done to extricate you from the peril you suffered, and yet I did not do it."

"Why?"

"I waited too long, and when I finally did try, it was too late . . . I was unable."

"I'm not sure I understand, but if you say you tried . . ."

"But I tried too late!" He groaned and covered his face, remembering the moment when he decided he must transform, finally, and yet could not. If he had only done so before he even entered the cabin, it might have worked. He still could not explain his inability to change, for when he returned to the forest this last time, he had found transformation as simple as always. He sighed. His voice, when next he spoke was smothered. "I was a coward. I am lower than a grub in the earth and not worthy of your sweet understanding."

"Self-pity again. That is your greatest failing." She was silent for a long moment. "What happened, happened. Perhaps it was meant to, for Countess Uta did not seem shocked, nor was she upset. She said . . . she said you had a destiny as yet unfulfilled." She pulled his hands away from his face and stared at him through the velvety darkness. "What did she have to say to you?"

"She told me things I wished not to hear, and she told me things I already knew, though I had not accepted them."

Melisande was silent for a long minute. Wearily, she sighed and said, "Will you hold me, Kazimir?"

He took her back in his arms, and that led to kisses, and that led to more. This time, when she reached out to touch him, he did not stop her, and her small hand closed around him, driving him wild with yearning. "May I . . . may I touch you?" he asked. She had been despoiled and now should be asked for permission to give her back her sense of her own body. He wasn't even sure how he knew that, but it just seemed right to him—honorable.

"I'm afraid," she whispered against his mouth.

"Please, Melisande," he whispered, and kissed her deeply. "Let me show you that the touch of a man can be pleasurable. Let me show you how sweet the feeling can be. Let me give you a better memory."

"Yes," she murmured, stroking him, her single word holding wondrous curiosity and rapture and tenderness.

Her nightgown was bunched up under her, and he let his hand trail up to the soft skin of her rounded thigh. She started when he tickled her but soon parted her legs willingly, and in response to his touch. The ache that had begun was now a throbbing, fierce burning, but he pushed it back out of his mind and concentrated on her, finding the spot to dive into the curls of hair at the juncture of her thighs, and when she gasped, he plunged one finger in to find she was already wet.

Her entire body trembled as she sighed and writhed. It was so long since he had allowed himself the simple pleasure of a woman that he feared he would have forgotten how to give her pleasure, but no . . . he remembered, and soon she was surrendering to his touch so that when he pulled her nightgown down over her breasts with his free hand, her nipples were already pebbled and jutting out, ready to be sampled. As he licked first one and then the other, letting the chill air of her bedchamber peak them even more, he then took one tight bud into his mouth and suckled, drawing much of her breast in and laving it with his tongue. He felt her jerk and tighten, and then she pushed eagerly onto his finger, crying out aloud into the night, incomprehensible syllables of tender delight and sweet elation.

Shivering as the sensation subsided, she crept into his arms, forgetting all about his throbbing erection as he cradled her in his arms, feeling her heart rate begin to subside.

But forgetfulness did not last. Melisande felt the thick length of him butted against her bottom as he cradled her against his chest. Remembering what Uta had said about how much it required of a man not to take what he wanted, she realized that whatever Gavril had said about him trying to rape Franziska was untrue. He could not be one man then and the exact opposite now. She reached down and touched him under her bottom. He was hard, the interesting length and velvet-sheathing-steel feel of his manhood entrancing. She had once taken it inside of her body, but surely there was more than the simple insertion of a male member into a female cavity. Just as when their tongues had dueled . . . who would have known so much passion could come from such an odd activity?

She kissed him, licking his scarred upper lip and feeling him moaning with suppressed desire. Rolling on top of him, her long hair draping over his face, she parted her legs, straddling his waist.

"Let me feel it," she whispered, between luscious kisses.

"What?"

"Let me feel it. Touch me with it, with that," she said, reaching down between them and touching his thick staff, its rigidity making it stand away from his body like a proud soldier, erect and at attention.

He groaned and moved, pushing into her hand. She fit herself to it, but he said, "No . . . it will still hurt, you know."

"But I don't intend to do anything, just feel it."

"Woman, you ask much of me," he muttered, drawing in a long breath. He reached down between them and parted her tender, wet cleft, tickling the nub of her femininity, too, as she settled to feel his throbbing tip.

His teasing touch made her glow with desire, and she sighed as he tickled and teased, then leaned down to kiss him, her body forcing itself down a little onto him.

"We are connected," she said, with wonder, feeling his throbbing as if it joined with her pulse. "Like one."

He took her hips and pulled her down more. It was uncomfortable for a moment, but her body began to adjust, and the fullness was faintly pleasurable, making the nub that he was teasing with his fingers more sensitive.

"Mmm, I . . . I like that," she said, sinking down on him more. It seemed to her that he was bigger than she remembered. Was that possible? She didn't know.

He stopped touching her, and she was about to reprimand him when he pulled her night rail off of her body and tossed it away, then began to touch her breasts, teasing the nipples with his thumbs, and then reaching up and taking one in his mouth, drawing it in. A flood of good feeling trickled through her, and she felt as if she were melting, starting with the molten core of her female part fit over his maleness. His big hands traveled her curves, down to her waist, and back to caress her bottom, cupping it in his hands.

"Yes, yes, please . . . more," she whispered, and then lost track of what she was saying.

He pushed her up, almost off of him, and then pulled her down again, and she felt a wetness. It was from her, she thought, and she worried that it was blood again, but he whispered no, that it was just what was meant to be. Their juices would mingle, and it would help.

Body singing with pleasure, she found he was right, and her juices flowed as he pulled her back down on his stiffness. There was a faint sensation of pain, but then a yearning sense of wanting more filled her, and she pushed down harder. And then she felt a spurt, and then a gush, and he rolled her over on her back and pushed all the way in, his male member pumping, filling her with hot wetness until he collapsed in a heap atop her.

His staff began to soften, but he groaned and said, "No, not yet!" Then he moved, and with the thickness of his shaft and his finger teasing her, he made her forget everything but the sensations that ripped into her and made her buck underneath him, writhing and quaking until she thought she would die from it, and then bliss filled her. She forgot everything for a while, as they stayed wound together in a tangle of bedcovers.

But as she began to shiver with cold, he pulled the blankets up, kissed her, and took her in his arms, holding her close as they fell asleep.

KAZIMIR left her room before dawn, leaving Melisande sleeping. He had memorized much of the "map" Mikhail had made and searched the passages. His greatest fear was that perhaps Gavril had already found the chalice and was simply biding his time until the eclipse was due, when he would make his way into the forest to try to get the rosary from Urvan. No matter what the man said, his presence at the castle was suspicious, and his lies about Franziska even more so.

If he could lie about the past like that, then he could lie about the present. There was much there that Kazimir did not understand and could not chance mistaking. The passages wound up and down, doubling back, confusing him even when he simply tried closing his eyes and sensing the chalice. One thing became clear to him, though: it was in the castle somewhere. But where?

Finally, he gave up for the moment. When he saw the others as he sought out food in the breakfast room, a small, cheerful chamber on the main floor but in the newer wing of the castle, he could see by the exhaustion on Christoph's face and his haunted eyes that the young count had likely spent the night roaming the woods in his transformed state, perhaps looking for Urvan's hiding place. When Melisande came in, she avoided all of their eyes and simply took some food and sat down. With all of the others around, he could not catch her eye, nor speak to her, and so he waited until they divided for the day to search. It seemed that with every new expedition more of the passages were discovered, and the search that had seemed finite and possible now was obscure and confusing. The secret passages wound through parts of the castle no one had thought possible, even up to the turrets on the front and the upper battlements.

"Melisande," he said, softly, as she swiftly made her way down the hall toward the stairs and some unknown destination.

She paused, and turned, slowly. The look in her eyes was not encouraging.

"What is it?" he asked, taken aback.

Rigid and glaring, she said, "I awoke to find myself alone. I did not think you would . . . would creep from my bed like a thief in the night after what we . . . after what . . ."

"Would you have the servants know I spent the night with you?" he asked, drawing himself up.

"If you think what we did was wrong, then no, I would have no one know about it." She lifted her chin. "Nor should we repeat the . . . the experience."

"Perhaps that would be for the best. We should keep to our own rooms until we are married."

"Married?" She stared at him in the gloomy hall, her customary aplomb deserting her. "*Married*? I think that will never happen, sir."

"Let's not be hasty in this difficult time," he said, attempting to soothe her ire. He would have smiled if he was not afraid she would misconstrue that expression as unbecoming levity, but her expression was such as he had seen on only a few feisty women who would not allow any man to ride roughshod over them. It reminded him of what the old countess had said to him about her strength of character, and how it would crush a diffident young man like Christoph.

"I am never hasty, sir. I intend to find that damnable chalice today. Christoph tells me he has searched the woods, too, and even though he knows it better than anyone, he found no sign of my father and Magda."

"Did you not believe my word, that they are nowhere to be found?"

"I'm not sure what to believe," she said, softly. "I am going to search other places than the passages today. We can't afford any more time. The blood moon eclipse is tomorrow night, is that correct?"

"Yes. If we do not find the chalice today, I think we should—"

He was interrupted by an outcry. Both raced down the hall and out to the vast great hall, arriving before anyone else, to find Steinholz, the butler, standing over a woman huddled on the floor. He babbled out that she had been on the doorstep.

One of the stable grooms had found her there, and he, Stein-holz, not knowing what else to do, had dragged her inside.

"Magda!" Melisande cried out, swooping down on her. She sat on the cold stone floor and took Magda in her arms onto her lap. The girl was unconscious, but breathing. Melisande took her face in both of her hands, wincing at the black and purple bruises that shut one eye and adorned her cheekbones like grim flags. Her white blonde hair was matted with blood, and her clothing was torn. She was as cold as death. Melisande held her close and put her forehead to Magda's. "You will recover from this, Magda," she muttered, infusing every bit of strength in her body into the connection between them. "You are strong. You are young. And you *must* recover for the health of your poor unborn child that is so in-nocent of all of this horror."

Magda took in a huge, shuddering breath and moaned. Her eyes fluttered open, and she gazed up at Melisande and began to weep.

"Take her to my room," Melisande commanded the gaping footmen who had arrived after she and Kazimir, as Charlotte and Fanny raced into the great hall.

In the outcry and hubbub that followed, Magda was taken to Melisande's room, and the women—Melisande, Charlotte, and Fanny—allowing no other help but Mina's, an experi-enced nurse, undressed and robed her in a nightgown of Melisande's. Fanny, doing as she was bid, brought the herbal concoction Melisande had brewed for her father's recovery, and Melisande administered it.

Gavril, his gaunt face a ghostly white, hovered outside the door with Kazimir and demanded to know what was going on. Christoph, they both said, had exited alone, trying to follow the young woman's path back into the woods, hoping it would lead them to Urvan and Mikhail somehow.

Melisande told them to go away; she would let them know if she had any news. She finally sent Charlotte and Fanny away, too, for they did not help, and she wanted Magda kept warm and quiet for a few hours so the herbal potion could take effect. Alone she sat, hour by hour, dripping a few spoonfuls of the concoction into Magda's mouth every half hour, as the clock on the mantle struck. It was too quiet, and it gave her

too much time to think. If this was what Magda looked like—
they had to assume, until told otherwise, that Urvan had done
this awful work on poor Magda—she wondered how her father was faring. She should even now be looking for the chalice but could not leave Magda alone while she hovered so
close to death. Outside, the wind was stirring up, and Charlotte had said she thought snow was on the way.

Night crept in, the sky beyond the window purpling.
Melisande ate her dinner at Magda's bedside, worrying for the
girl who had been her friend and wondering if she would
make her way back to them. Melisande had done everything
she could, but beyond that one moment of hysterical weeping,
Magda had remained unconscious.

Exhaustion overwhelmed her, and Melisande felt sleep
begin to steal into her body as she sat hour after hour. At some
point she lost awareness, and then she awoke to find herself in
a chair by the fire. She started and sat up, but a big hand on
her shoulder held her down.

"Hush, Melisande," Kazimir said, his voice a quiet rumble
close by.

"What . . ." She glanced over at the bed.

"The girl will recover, I think, but right now sleep is what
she needs to 'knit the ravell'd sleeve of care.'"

"You read English plays?" she sleepily asked, recognizing
the paraphrase from Macbeth, which her language master had
made her read, though English was never her favorite language. She had struggled with it until she came to Wolfram
Castle and was required by Count Nikolas to master it.

"I have indeed read Shakespeare. Do you think me igno-
rant? I had a very good education, though I was not first in my
class at Heidelberg; Nikolas, ahead of me by two years, was
far superior in learning, always. He was superior in every way,
it seems to me now. He has a studious turn of mind, where I
do not, though I did not disgrace my family. I thought the
scene from Macbeth particularly apt this moment, given that
it speaks of sleep as the 'balm of hurt minds.'"

"Poor Magda," Melisande whispered. "I am not so san-
guine that she will recover. I have done everything I can." Silence fell, and she glanced over at him, his handsome face in
profile, the scarred side turned away. In that aspect, he looked

completely different, like the profile on an ancient Roman coin she had seen once. In one sense it made her uneasy, for she had so become accustomed to his scars that she did not know what to think about this image of perfection.

"Of what do you think?" he asked, not turning toward her.

"What shall we do if the chalice is not found?"

"I have thought of little else this day. Do you trust me?" He turned after he said it and gazed steadily at her.

Did she? She had been angry that he had left her alone after they had made love, but even in her anger she understood why he did it, and in a sense, it was more reason to trust him. He thought of her best interests. He cared. No matter how hard he appeared, he had done nothing to make her distrust him, despite his reticence to discuss his past. "I do," she admitted. "I do trust you."

"Even if we don't find it, I think we are going to need to try to lure my brother out with the promise of the chalice; how is he to know we do not have it? He has only one hostage now, and surely we can use that fact to our advantage. For if he is caught, we can make him tell us where Mikhail is. If he sends Mikhail, then we can save your father. He cannot control the situation. I think once desperation settles in, we can use that anxiety to our advantage."

Hope began to burble like a fresh spring through muddy ground. "Thank you," she said, brokenly, putting out her hand to him. "Thank you for thinking, for trying to help. My own mind has been so muddled and scattered; perhaps your plan will work."

"It has to." He took her hand and knelt at her feet. "Melisande, I pledge to you that I will find a way to save your father and bring him back to you. I swear it." He took her hand and put it over his heart.

She pulled her hand from his grasp and framed his face, thumbing the scar on his lip. Now his face appeared proper to her, now that she could see it in its entirety. She had never asked him how he got the scar, and perhaps she did not want to know. It mattered not. Now was all that mattered between them. She hesitated, but then closed her eyes and kissed his lips.

Chapter 27

IT WAS like opening a sluice gate. He pulled her into his arms and off her chair, pushing her down on the rug in front of the fire and covering her mouth with his, kissing her with an urgency and yearning that swept her away. Her customary restraint battled with the delicious sensation of being carried on a wave of passion.

His mouth moved down to her neck and he held her hands, pinning them above her on the soft rug. "Melisande," he mumbled, as he kissed her over and over. "Kiss me. Give yourself to me."

"Why," she cried out, struggling to free her hands. "Why do you want me?"

"Need," he groaned, "I *need* you." His words became broken and unintelligible as he smothered her with kisses, yanking her dress and petticoats up with one hand and forcing her legs apart. Russian mingled with English, and he muttered her name over and over.

In her whole restrained, careful, fearful life, and more so since the tragedy that took her mother and grandmother, she had feared passion, avoided it, careful never to allow herself to feel it. Even her unrequited feelings for Nikolas were kept secret and separate, and she subdued every urge to show him her emotions. But now, with Kazimir's ardor sweeping over her, she gave in to it. Fevered longing pulsed through her veins, his ardent desire for her an aphrodisiac more powerful than any she could concoct in her stillroom.

They stilled, and time stopped for one long moment as he took her lips, searching her with his tongue, parrying, thrusting, dueling. He pushed against her, and she could feel the power of his desire. Only their breathing echoed in the dark room, harsh and rasping, until a cry tore them apart.

"Melisande!"

Scrabbling out from under Kazimir, Melisande staggered to her feet and raced to the side of the bed, patting her skirts down into place. Magda was sitting up, her purple bruises stark against the pallor of her face.

"I heard you," Magda cried.

Shame colored Melisande's cheek, but then Magda continued, as she clutched her friend's hands between her own.

"I heard you. You spoke to me, told me I must recover for the sake of my unborn child, innocent of any wrongdoing . . . You said I was young and strong, and that I would recover."

"I did." Melisande sat on the edge of the bed, rubbing Magda's cold hands. "I knew you could make it."

"I have to tell you . . . your father . . ."

"Yes?"

Kazimir joined her and hovered nearby, listening.

"He is ill, and Prince Urvan . . . he is worse than he was even before. Is it possible that Satan speaks to him? Is he possessed by demons?"

"The demons are only in his brain, Magda," Kazimir said, gently. "They are not demons of the other world, but merely an illness that has been worsening his whole life."

"I'm afraid he is going to kill Mikhail," Magda said, weeping. Her words were muffled and her pronunciation difficult, because her lip was swollen and split. Even as she spoke, it broke open again, and blood began to well.

"You must hush, Magda," Melisande said. "You are still very ill, and we must take care of you."

"I shall get fresh water," Kazimir said. "And cloths."

Melisande insisted that Magda lie back down, and propped her up with an extra pillow.

"Is she awake?" Fanny said from the door. "Count Kazimir was in the hallway; he said he was going to get fresh water and cloths for Miss Magda."

"She is awake," Melisande replied.

"You must listen to me," Magda said, weeping and clutching Melisande's hands.

Count Gavril entered, and Christoph and Charlotte were

behind him. When Kazimir returned with the necessities, and Mina to help, it was to find the room quite full.

"You must save Mikhail, for he is very ill. He is sometimes unconscious," Magda said.

"Unconscious?" Melisande said, shocked, fear clutching her heart.

"Yes! We were kept in a cave . . . a cold and damp cave with frost on the walls; even a fire did not warm the place. You must save him! He was so very kind to me, and even forgave me for my part in his capture. I have been so wrong! I thought him just a thief, but he has given up thievery and wishes only to care for you, his beloved daughter. But Prince Urvan . . . oh! He is rough and cruel and has dragged the poor man from place to place like an animal. That is when the poor gentleman began to fall unconscious, and now the prince has moved him again, so far into the woods that . . . it is a miracle I found my way out."

Blood streamed freely from her cut lip now, but she would not be silenced. In answer to a question from Count Gavril about the hiding place, she sobbed out that he would have moved his captive again, since she escaped, for he was crafty and determined and had taken weeks to prepare for this time. He had arrived in Wolfbeck some time before, knowing that others would come, knowing he would need to force Mikhail to give up the chalice. But he was becoming more mad, too, and if he did not get the chalice, he would kill Mikhail, he said.

Mikhail had whispered to her a message, before she escaped, Magda said. "He told me to tell his daughter that he put the chalice in the one place in the castle that he knew it would be safe. He was about to tell me more, but . . . but . . ."

Melisande did not need Magda's horror-filled expression to tell her the truth. Her father had then lapsed into unconsciousness and had not regained his wits before Magda made her way out of the underground den.

"Prince Urvan is going to kill him if you do not stop him. I . . . I think the prince let me escape, for he knows I will come to you, and he knows you are his only hope of getting the chalice. He wants it. He says . . . he says he must right a great wrong that was done to him by his brother and his wife. She was a faithless whore, he said, and gave to Kazimir what she should only have given to him, her husband."

All eyes turned to Kazimir.

"Were . . . you and she lovers, then?" Melisande asked, pain shooting through her.

"Yes, for a time," Kazimir said.

"Prince Urvan said that she flaunted her lover in front of him and told him of their secret rendezvous, but worse, so much worse, he said, was that then Franziska gave to him the one thing she should have given him as her husband, something very precious, something that could only be given once in a lifetime."

"So it was true," Gavril whispered and stared over at Kazimir.

Melisande, confused, looked from face to face. "What is it? A . . . a child? Did she have a child by you, Kazimir?"

"No, there was no child," Kazimir said. He appeared as confused as the others. Only Count Gavril appeared to understand.

"That was why she had to die, he said." Magda's energy was almost depleted, and her voice was a hoarse whisper.

"I don't understand," Kazimir cried, his face twisted, his large hands clenched in fists.

"Why she had to die?" Gavril said, his voice hollow.

"It . . . it has something to do with the chalice," Magda whispered. "Because he kept saying that was why he needed the chalice now, to replace what she took from him . . . or refused to give to him . . . he was speaking my language, and he is not very good, I fear."

"Are you sure of all of this?" Gavril said. "If he was not so good at your language, then possibly . . ."

"No, I understood," she said, wearily. "He repeated it enough times. I spent many hours huddled in the cold listening to him rant."

"Urvan killed Franziska," Gavril said, his expression numb with disbelief. He shook his head, and then turned to Kazimir. "Is that true? Who killed my sister?" he asked. "You were there; if you did not do it, then you witnessed it. Who killed her . . . you or Urvan?"

"Urvan killed her. He beat her to death."

"Why did you let me think you were responsible all these years?"

"Because I *was* responsible!" Kazimir said, hitting one fist into his other hand. "I had one chance to save her, and I wasn't able. It was *my* fault. We were having an affair, and Urvan found out about it, and that was why he beat her. He beat her often, and finally . . . to death."

"I know he beat her, but only because he caught you and her together, and . . . I don't understand." Gavril's tone was hollow, pain soaked into the words. "She said you made advances and tried to rape her. She said Urvan caught you and beat her for it, and that she had to . . . had to take you as a lover and turn you."

"Turn me?" Kazimir said. "I cannot say what she told you, but our affair . . . it was her idea from the start. Oh, I was willing. She was very beautiful, and I was eager, but she *never* denied me. She was afraid of Urvan, and she had good reason to be. Urvan was even then unstable and cruel. But why would she tell you she had rejected me . . . and why that I had tried to rape her? I wanted to take her away from it all. I offered to take her away to England, or anywhere, just to remove her from Urvan's cruelty."

Charlotte, who had listened intently, said, "Count Kazimir, did she call you to her side on the night she died?"

Kazimir's gaze swiveled to Christoph's sister. "How did you know? Yes, she sent me a message, saying that she had finally decided to run away with me. I must come, she said, very precisely, at nine o'clock, and she would be waiting for me near the door in the great hall."

"And when you arrived?"

He bowed his head. "I was late . . . too late to save her. I was delayed by my regimental captain, who caught me leaving my post. He was going to have me arrested, and indeed the horse guard was called out to subdue me, but I broke away and galloped off on my horse. I was fifteen minutes or so late, and when I arrived, I heard screaming. The door was locked. I had a key and opened the door, but just as I entered . . ." He stopped, took in a deep shuddering breath, and said, "He hit her one last time."

"How did you know that she called him to her side?" Christoph asked of his sister.

"She had a cruel husband and wanted him dead. But why should she leave? Why should she suffer as an outcast, running from him? As a woman, if she left him, even for beating her, she would be the one to suffer, never able to take another husband, always suspect as a wife who left home." With a haughty tilt to her head, Charlotte drew herself up to her full height. "Instead, she would plan. She had a powerful lover. She would dismiss the servants for the night, call him to her side, then irk her husband into beating her. Her ardent lover, finding them thus, would then kill her husband, ending her marriage. Then she would get everything, would she not? He would be dead, and yet she would not be guilty of murder. Someone else would have taken care of it for her."

Gavril shuddered and slumped, his shoulders rounded, his attitude one of defeated acknowledgement. "That is why she turned him. It may be true. What other explanation is there?"

"So you were there when it happened," Melisande said to Kazimir, "but . . ."

"I tried, but I could not save her! Urvan was raving and beating her . . . I hit him, and he staggered away, wounded, but then, as she lay on the floor and I tried to lift her up, tried to bring her back to life, though she was already gone, he told me that she had taunted him with what we had done."

"So, she wished to irk him into beating her, knowing that you would come precisely at nine, and you would . . . what would you have done?" Christoph asked.

"I would have killed Urvan," Kazimir admitted. "If Franziska had not already been dead, I would have killed him to save her."

"I tried to prevent her from marrying Urvan," Gavril whispered. "I begged her. I . . . sensed something, and I feared his . . . his reasons for wishing to marry into our family." He exchanged a thoughtful look with Kazimir. "But she was determined. She would be rich, she said, for the Vasilov land is better than ours, in some senses, more vast, and with great potential. Perhaps even before they married she had planned . . . but no, I will not think it of her. It is possible that she had planned even then how things would turn out, but she is long gone, and I will not think it of her. I will remember her as misguided only."

"But I do not understand why you did not tell everyone what Urvan had done, so he could be punished," Melisande said to Kazimir, who stood in the shadows, his head bowed.

He lifted his head and stared at her. "I told my brother I was going to tell the truth and see him arrested, though beating your wife is not an offense in the eyes of the law."

"Beating her to death is!" Gavril retorted.

"Yes, but he could easily have shown a reason why he had to beat her. All he had to do was show proof that she and I had been having an affair. We were not as discreet as . . . as we should have been. Her memory would have been sullied forever. Despite that, I intended to have him arrested. I thought it worth the scandal to stop him, for what would happen if he married again? I gave him two days to get his affairs in order, and then I was going to the authorities to tell the truth."

"But he . . . he committed suicide," Gavril said. "From the bridge in Kovel."

Kazimir nodded, and said, "So we thought. There was no point after that in blackening his name. I thought he had repented and paid for his crime."

"And so you let me believe you guilty all these years," Gavril said.

"I *felt* guilty. Perhaps . . ."

Melisande sighed in exasperation. "Self-pity," she said, crisply. "I told you it would be your undoing. Where does this leave us?"

"With a clue as to where the chalice is. Think, Melisande," Kazimir said, urgently. "Magda said Mikhail told her it was in the one place in the castle he knew it would be safe. Safe. Meaning, I suppose, unfound. Where could that be? We have searched everywhere."

"I can't think!" she cried. "Please, all of you, let me tend to Magda, and I will ponder this. She has told us so much but now is exhausted and must rest."

They cleared from the room. Morning had come, and with it a misty day, the spring sunshine bathing the room in light. Melisande made sure Magda was sleeping in a healthful way and that Fanny was content to stay with the patient and administer carefully the drops of potion as she commanded.

She removed herself from the room and retreated downstairs to the breakfast room to eat a solitary meal at the oak table. What could her father have meant? They had to find the chalice that day, or it would all be too late, and they would have to concoct a secondary, riskier plan. With no chalice, they couldn't be sure Urvan wouldn't just kill Mikhail, or leave him to die in some secret, hidden spot. It no longer mattered what the legend was about the chalice and rosary, for whether one believed it or not was immaterial; Urvan did and was governed by that belief.

Kazimir entered the breakfast room and sat down by her. "Have you thought of what your father could have meant?"

"I can't imagine! What does he mean? Some place it would be safe." She shook her head.

"Come," he said, taking her hand and raising her. "We need to keep at it. Time is wasting."

They searched, occasionally coming across some of the others. Charlotte, her devious mind working still, suggested Uta's room, and she and Christoph searched there, but to no avail, nor was Nikolas's private suite of rooms the answer.

All through the day, Melisande could feel that she and Kazimir were avoiding the subject of Franziska and what had been learned that day about his relationship with her. How did he feel, she wondered, distracted only momentarily from the search. They were in the passages again, she cloaked heavily against the frigidity of the stone, while he was clad only in his normal attire and searching every crevice, every alcove.

"I confess I am lost," she said.

"I thought I had been in every part of this place," he admitted, "and yet I, too, am puzzled. Wait! I see a manner of egress into somewhere that I have not yet been!"

"How can you see in this darkness? I see nothing."

"Here," he said, moving ahead of her and taking her hand. "I will lead the way."

He tugged her behind him and found the spot, which she recognized as another, albeit better disguised, sliding panel. He pushed it aside, and they both tumbled into the room. He closed the panel behind them, and they looked around.

"Where are we?" Kazimir asked.

"Count Nikolas's private library."

"Ah, yes, I was here with Christoph . . . We had brandy by the fire." He stared at the fireplace. "That seems . . . so long ago now, though it was only days ago."

She turned and gazed at him. In this private place, the quietude surrounding them, the weight of his unhappiness haunted her. She could feel from him in waves how his guilt over the past was like a knife in his chest. She would avoid it no longer, for if she left him to brood, he would never get past it. "How long are you going to torment yourself, Kazimir?" she asked suddenly.

"What? What are you talking about?"

"Franziska . . . the past . . . the tragedy that happened. How long are you going to blame yourself for her death? She planned it all and was caught by her own design."

"Though I know it must be true, and it is the only explanation that makes sense, it is hard to understand after all of these years. Seven years." He sat wearily down in a big chair by the desk and thrust his hands through his hair.

"That is the very gesture Count Nikolas makes when he is exasperated with himself or others," she said.

"You are . . . or . . . or *were* in love with Nikolas," Kazimir said, hollowly.

He looked so forlorn when he said it that a wave of tenderness overcame her, and she ran to him and perched on his lap, holding his face in both her hands as she looked down into his dark eyes. "I thought I was," she admitted. Before she had met him, she thought, but did not add. "But I think now, looking back, that it was gratitude looking for an expression. He has been so very kind to me."

"Perfect Nikolas," Kazimir sneered.

"Do not say such a thing in so ugly a manner," she said, quietly, and he was defeated. He bowed his head. It was what he needed, she realized, a woman unafraid of him. One who would tremble at his anger or misery would only enhance those ugly traits. He needed to be challenged and forced into truthfulness.

"Only tell me you do not care for him now," he whispered. "And I will think him a very good fellow."

"I do not care for him in that way now, nor do I believe I ever really did."

She kissed him, and he put his arms around her, holding her close in his lap, luxuriating in the caress. The interrupted passion from the morning was still there, and for long, quiet moments in the chilly room—their breath steamy puffs it was so cold—they kissed and cuddled, murmuring warm words and nonsense.

"I wish I knew my father better," she finally said, glancing around. "If I did, then I would know what he would consider the safest place in this castle, but—" She stopped dead, looking around. She leaped from his lap and ran around the room, staring at the walls of books and ornaments, drawers and folio tables.

"What is wrong, Melisande?" Kazimir asked, leaping to his feet and grabbing her by the shoulders.

"This room! Oh, how could I have not known! This room! I told my father it was absolutely forbidden to everyone in the castle, even the family. This is the one safe place!"

Chapter 28

TOGETHER THEY searched, pulling books off the shelves, looking in every nook, drawer, box and jar. The room was huge, and yet there were, once they started looking, relatively few places that the chalice could be hidden.

"Do you think I'm right?"

"I'm sure of it," Kazimir said.

Melisande kept up the search, and then realized that the family Bible was, as usual, out on its lectern, which meant that . . . she raced to the spot on the shelf where a wooden cask was kept that was made to hold the tome. She pulled it out, its weight making it fall to the floor in her haste; the contents spilled out onto the floor and rolled to the middle of the soft, thick rug.

It was the Blood Amber Chalice, glowing eerily. She cried out, and Kazimir whirled, joined her, and they both stared at it.

"It is the same color as my rosary. This is it, isn't it?"

"It is."

She glanced over at him and saw a muscle working in his jaw. What did she really know of him that she trusted him so? If this relic was as dangerous as they all said . . . but she turned her attention back to it and stretched out her hand. It was warm and beckoning, and the glow from it was beautiful to look at. She picked it up and cradled it in her hands. Perhaps there was something to the legend. All she knew was that now she had it and could barter for her father's freedom. And yet in an instant, she knew that whatever they did, they must not let Urvan have it and use it during the imminent blood moon. How could she justify even for one moment purchasing her father's freedom at the cost of how many lives? It was a terrible choice that had yet to be made, how to use the chalice to barter for her father's safety, and yet ensure that the madman could never get it.

"At least we have it. Summon the others to the drawing room so we can think what to do. I have one task left, and I will meet you there."

"SHE has not yet awoken," Frau Liebner, her face gray with exhaustion, said to Melisande. "Poor Christoph; he was in earlier wishing to speak with her, but she is still unconscious."

"I just need to talk to her for a moment," Melisande said, sitting down by Uta's bed and taking her hand. She bowed her head and willed herself into the sleeping woman's mind. Uta was sitting on the woodland throne again, dressed in the same verdant green as before and looking happy, blissful.

When Melisande begged her to come, she appeared weary and sad, but she nodded.

"What do you want of me?" she gasped, awakening.

Tears streamed down Melisande's cheeks, and she squeezed her old friend's fingers, as Frau Liebner quietly wept, sitting by the window in Uta's usual place. Knowing Uta's time awake would be limited, Melisande immediately said, "I am so confused about what to do. We have found the dreaded chalice, and the blood moon is approaching. Papa is dying at the hands of that madman, but Count Urvan had promised to release him if given the chalice."

"So gif it to him."

"But if I give it to him, he is going to use it to become something awful, something terribly dangerous. What shall I do?"

Uta's breathing was labored, and her words slow. "Your dreams . . . haf you been having dem lately?"

"Not for the last few nights. You mean the dreams of wolves?"

"Yes. Think, girl, about what dose dreams mean . . . wolves . . . attacking . . . you at center of it all. You haf . . . powers you haf not harnessed. Think. Let your voice inside tell you . . . tell you what to do."

The countess sank back into her sleep state, and Mina, with a fierce expression that did not manage to conceal her grief over her mistress's worsening state, shooed Melisande out of the room.

THE drawing room was gloomy, with just a few candles and the glow of the fire to light it. Christoph was there, moodily poking at the fire, and Gavril and Kazimir were conversing, the tension between them palpable still, but with an added dimension of a seeming desire to make peace. When Melisande entered, all three men stopped what they were doing.

As she approached the disparate group, she was very aware of a new sense of power thrumming through her veins and gaining strength in her heart. She was a healer; that she had always known. But there was more to her, and tonight would test it. Her decision had come to her as she entered.

"I am going to take the chalice and go to the meeting place," she said. "It is my father's life at stake, and I will brook no interference in my plans."

Kazimir and Gavril exchanged looks.

"You don't know everything there is to know, yet, and should not make such a decision until you do," Gavril said.

"Whatever . . . power you have," Kazimir added, "and I admit you seem to have something, will not be enough to defeat Urvan, for he is determined and mad. Surely you are sensible enough to admit that whatever is the best possible chance for a positive outcome is the route we should take?"

Christoph stepped forward. "You are all forgetting you are in my home. I have the final say in this, whether you like to admit it or not."

"Being in your home does not mean you have the right to determine the course of something of which you know nothing," Gavril pointed out.

"We are all agreed on one thing, I think," Kazimir said. "Urvan must not be allowed to get his hands on the chalice, not even once, not even for one second. Am I right?"

All nodded.

"I was not suggesting I go out alone," Melisande said, anger beginning to build at the high-handed manner of the two Russians, who seemed intent on running roughshod over both her and Christoph's claim to a part in the affair. "I merely say that since it is my father who is in danger, I will have a part in this. Besides, Urvan will be put at ease, seeing me, for he will feel sure I will do nothing to jeopardize my father's well-being."

Again the two Russians exchanged a look, and Melisande tartly wondered when they had had a chance to become so friendly.

There was a clatter at the door, and Charlotte dashed in, followed by Fanny, who was pale with fear. Charlotte was out of breath but waved a piece of paper in front of her. "She's . . . she's . . . gone!"

"Who?" the others said, simultaneously.

"M-Magda," Fanny cried. "I went in to the room to give her the medicine, and she was gone, with just this note left on her pillow."

Melisande raced over to Charlotte and took the note, perusing it, irritated by Magda's disappearance and foreseeing a more complicated rescue, if she had gone back into the woods for some reason. But as she read, a dread stole into her, and when she looked up at the men, she knew her face revealed her utter horror.

"She is not only gone, but she has . . . taken the chalice with her."

"What? How?" That was Kazimir.

Gavril spoke over his compatriot. "Where was it? How would she get it?"

Melisande bowed her head and summoned strength, then held out the note. "Fool . . . I'm a fool! I hid it in my room, but she must have been awake and saw where I put it."

The others read the note, which, in Magda's semi-literate scrawl, related her own feelings of guilt, and that Mikhail, who was the kindest, gentlest man she had ever in her life met, and the first one to treat her with any kind of regard or gallantry, should not suffer for her own mistakes. Therefore she was taking the "cup" to trade it for Mikhail, so no one else would suffer.

"She doesn't know what it really is, does she?" Kazimir said, with a groan.

"No. Any discussion of the true nature of the chalice was done in a language she did not understand, or out of her hearing. She only knows Urvan wants it and has promised to set my father free if he has it. I can't believe I let this happen!"

"Hush," Kazimir said, taking her arm and squeezing her hand. "You could never have foreseen this, nor could you carry the chalice around the castle with you."

"I could have kept it in my hands. I should never have let it out of my sight!"

"Once he has the chalice," Gavril said, "Urvan will have everything, and he will not let Magda or Mikhail live any longer, I do not think. He may kill them, or he may just desert them."

Christoph glanced at the clock on the mantel. "The eclipse, according to my calculations, will begin soon. We had been counting on the urgency of the night approaching to draw Urvan out, but now . . . we must stop him. I will *not* allow Melisande's father to suffer at the hands of the madman."

Kazimir dropped Melisande's hand and stared steadily at Christoph. He said, "I know what you are. Together, we may have a chance of defeating Urvan, even if he has transformed."

"So it is true," Gavril said, gaping at Kazimir. "I was never sure from her letter, but it is true; Franziska turned you!"

"*Turned* me?" he said, his brows drawn down low over his dark eyes. "Bewitched me, you mean; enchanted me . . . cursed me!"

"You used that word before, 'turned', and I did not understand what you meant. What does it mean? What are you talking about?" Melisande cried, her gaze going back and forth between Gavril and Kazimir as Charlotte and Fanny clung to each other in fear at the awful implications of what had happened.

"She used magic . . . I felt it when it happened. Franziska was a sorceress . . . but one adept at the black arts." Kazimir shook his head. "I never asked for what she made me into," he said, turning to Gavril, "and did not know until it happened. Since that time, I have realized that it is what Urvan must have wanted from Franziska . . . He must have known about her witchcraft and courted her for it. When she gave the transformational power to me—to use against him, I see now—he went quite, quite mad."

"*Not* witchcraft! You do not understand? How can you not

know the truth?" Gavril wailed, covering his face with his bony hands.

"Tell me what you are all talking about? I don't understand any of this!" Melisande looked over to see Christoph, his face a mask of disbelief as he stared wide-eyed at Count Kazimir. "What does all of this mean?"

"I'm going with you both into the forest," Gavril said, glancing from Christoph to Kazimir.

"No, you will not," Kazimir said. "You are weak and would only die in the battle that may ensue. You are ill."

"I am not ill! I am dying . . . or rather, disappearing. I could be what Franziska made you into. It is my destiny, my *heritage*, but I chose to deny it."

"I don't understand," Kazimir said, staring at his nemesis.

"I have sworn never to use my inherited power; it is dangerous and evil," Gavril said.

"Inherited? How . . . ?" Kazimir broke off and stared at Gavril.

"Inherited!" Gavril said, staring at him. "That was what you were given, for the women of my family can give the transformation as a gift to a lover, but only once in their life. That is what overtook you, not witchcraft."

"So I am . . . what I am, for all time," Kazimir said, hollowly. "No spell to be removed, no curse to be lifted."

"You are what you are for all time."

The others stood, confused and silent, watching the two men.

"But you," Kazimir said, "knowing what you could be, knowing your potential, you choose not to transform? How does that happen? Does it not drive you mad, like some itch that needs to be scratched?"

"I will *not* transform. It repulses me! I saw my father driven mad by the power he had until he was no longer sane. It is evil, and I will have no part of it."

"Is that why you . . . weaken?"

Gavril nodded.

"You are one of the . . . the *unveraendert* in our language, the . . . the unchanged?" Christoph asked. "Uta told me about them . . . you will fade and one day disappear from sight, though always you will walk the earth."

Gavril trembled, but nodded. Fear was etched on his gaunt face, but over it was laid a layer of courage, the courage to follow his own path.

"I don't understand any of this," Melisande wept, wringing her hands together, "but we have no time!"

"She's right," Kazimir said. "Gavril, I do not understand why you choose the path of weakness, but I do know that you have no place out there, where you will only put us at more danger." He turned to Christoph. "Will you go with me? I am as you are, and we will do this together, now that hope of avoiding the worst is gone."

Christoph, his blue eyes wide with wonder and fear and courage, nodded.

"Gavril, stay here with the ladies and keep them safe." Kazimir strode to Melisande and took her shoulders in his hands. "Magda having taken the chalice changes everything, you must see that. When we had the chalice, there was still the hope of using it to bargain with Urvan, but with it likely in his hands, then you would only be a further danger to your father. If Urvan should snatch you, or . . . or if he will have already used the power of the rosary and chalice together, then you could die and doom your father, too. Please, let Christoph and I go out and do what we must."

"I don't understand," she said, gazing up into his eyes.

"Christoph and I are alike in many ways and can work together." Kazimir squeezed her shoulders and rubbed them with his big hands. "Soon, you will understand, and when you do . . . please find it in your heart to forgive me for what I am."

"I misjudged you," Gavril said to Kazimir, approaching them, his voice hollow and weak. "All this time spent hating . . ." He shook his head in sorrow. "I will stay here, for I will not endanger your safety, nor that of the boy."

"Stay here." Kazimir said, putting one hand on the thinner man's shoulder, "and protect these precious ladies."

It was only moments before Kazimir, with one long kiss, left Melisande. That the kiss was witnessed by the others did not occur to her until she saw Christoph's expression. It shocked her, the pain and jealousy, and yet the resignation on his pale face as he turned and followed the older man out. Their voices,

demanding cloaks and boots, rang out in the great hall, and then
left only echoes as the big doors slammed shut behind them.

Melisande turned to Gavril as Charlotte huddled in a chair
near the fire, weeping that her brother was gone, and without
one word of explanation to his sister. Melisande was bewildered. Had she been right to let them go? What was it all about?
"Count," she said. "What did all of that mean? You all seem to
understand each other so well, even Christoph. I want to know
what . . ."

Dizziness overtook her, and the room spun, then turned
black. As if from a great distance, she heard Count Gavril's
voice, and that of Charlotte. But the blackness receded, and she
was in the forest, mist all around, peaceful only for a moment
before wolves crashed into the clearing and began to battle, ripping at each others' throats. Then Kazimir was there, lying on
the ground, blood flowing from a wound in his throat that even
her healing skill could not correct. He was dying, and when she
turned away in horror, it was to see her father, fainted on the
snowy ground, and a huge black wolf, with yellow eyes and
fangs the length of her fingers, advancing on him. Magda was
nearby, clutching her belly and screaming.

The mist cleared, and Melisande awoke to find Charlotte
hanging over her calling her name and Gavril near the door,
calling out to the footmen for help in carrying her upstairs.

"No!" she said, scrambling to her feet. "Don't ask me how I
know this, but I must follow Christoph and Kazimir. If I don't,
one or both will die, and with them my father and Magda."

"You can't go," Gavril said, turning away from the door.

"I'm going."

"Then I go with you," Charlotte said, ringing the bell and
summoning a maid to bring them their cloaks, and to leave
word for Fanny, who had gone up to make sure Countess Uta
was still being given Melisande's potion, that they would be
back soon and to prepare rooms for Mikhail and for Magda.

"I won't let you go alone," Gavril said, his gaunt face set in
a determined expression.

"But sir, you are not well . . ."

"I am well enough for this. While I live, I am well enough
to protect those for whom I care, as I was not able to care for
my sister."

Chapter 29

"HOW DO you know about me?" Christoph asked, as he and Kazimir raced toward the edge of the woods.

"I have seen you transform back to human shape."

"And so am I to believe that you . . ."

"Wait and see," Kazimir said, grimly.

"Where are we going?"

"There is a clearing in the middle of this woods—you likely know of it—and when I have been here before, I could feel some evil soaked into the ground."

"I know where you mean. It is where Bartol Liebner murdered my mother and uncle many years ago. Nothing has ever grown over that spot."

"In searching for a cure for what I thought was my curse, I researched witchcraft and spells. I think that evil spot will draw Urvan, for it holds the power to intensify his spell, the transformation using the chalice."

The moon was rising, but it was a sickly orange color, Kazimir noted. "It is beginning. We must find Urvan!"

It took far too long. Christoph suggested they transform directly, for the loping run of a wolf was speedier than their progress as men, but Kazimir knew that Christoph was not strong enough yet to sustain his wolf embodiment and fight if they should be delayed in finding Urvan. The one thing he was grateful for was that Melisande had not insisted on coming. He did not want her to see him as he soon would be.

The sky took on a deep amber glow, and horror clutched at Kazimir. They must speed their progress, he thought, and together they began to run, Christoph now leading the way as he was so familiar with the forest and knew, now, where they were heading.

"I smell smoke!" Christoph yelped.

"Damn my brother to hell!" Kazimir growled, for he knew what the smoke meant. It meant he had begun the spell. Even over the crash of their thudding feet through the forest and the sound of his own heart pounding in his ears, he heard a weird, inhuman howling in the distance.

"Was that a wolf?"

Terror gripped Kazimir, as he pondered what they would find. "I don't know," he gasped.

The sky was turning brilliant orange, casting an odd light on their skin, but they were near the clearing. Kazimir could feel it, and sensed Christoph's anticipation. Together they broke into the open area.

"There!" Christoph said, pointing.

On the far edge was Urvan near a small fire, the flames leaping as fresh tinder caught. He was hunkered over something, while nearby a figure squirmed and cried out.

"What is it?" Christoph wailed. "What's going on?"

"There, over by the tree near him. Magda is tied to the tree, I think."

She spotted them and cried out, and Urvan whirled. He had a small wolf, and with a dagger he was draining blood from its throat into the glowing red chalice as the sky transformed above them and the orb of the moon, now deepening to a shade of scarlet, grinned, the normally benevolent face like a demon overlooking the madman's foul deed.

"Urvan," Kazimir called in Russian. "Don't do it! There is still hope for your soul." He advanced as he spoke, hoping to get into position to free Magda, at least.

"Stay where you are, " Urvan said, his voice giddy and high-pitched with emotion. "I will shoot the girl," he said, picking up his pistol and training it on Magda, kicking the dead wolf's body away with one swift motion.

"He is too far gone," Kazimir murmured to Christoph.

"What shall we do?"

"Do you feel confident in your transformation, now? Does it take you long?"

"No, not at all."

"Good. I do not wish to precipitate his transformation . . .

We are not certain, after all, that the wretched legend is correct, that it will work. It is an old story, and yet . . ."

"And yet if it is true and it works, if he becomes this most powerful werewolf, we must be prepared."

The moon began to glow red.

"Urvan, please, think of this! Once you do this thing, there is no going back. You will become . . ."

But he was lifting the red chalice to the sky and crying out some words that Kazimir could not understand. The language was Romany, he thought, so Urvan must have prepared for this moment well, learning the incantation that would hasten and seal the spell.

Then he lifted the chalice to his lips, drank the blood down, spilling it so it streamed down, staining his filthy skin and clothes with the thin red liquid. Then, with one swift motion, he tossed the chalice into the fire along with the rosary. The flames leaped up and engulfed the awful two pieces, dancing, cavorting, and throwing shadows over the forest wall. The spicy scent of incense filled the air as the two men stared in disbelief.

But the weird scene was made horrible as Urvan, standing, began to change before their eyes, becoming taller, his nose lengthening and his arms stretching, his hands crooking into paws. Magda screamed and screamed, her voice becoming hoarse, and Christoph shouted out, asking what they should do.

Kazimir knew, calmness stealing into his soul as he watched his brother disappear, to be replaced by a huge snapping, snarling wolf, with fangs as long as fingers, that there was only one thing to do.

"We must kill him, if we can."

"I hear something," Melisande cried, crashing through the brush as best as she could, fettered as she was by a heavy cloak and the mucky ground beneath her booted feet.

"I hear it, too," Charlotte said, following closely.

Gavril, sickly yellow in color from the orange light of the moon and gasping for air, leaned on a tree behind them, unable to say anything, his breath was so short. Melisande

watched him for a moment, fearful for his life. He appeared to
be almost transparent, he was so pale, as if he was fading
away before her eyes, and the red-gold light of the transforming moon only made him appear more sallow.

"It is a woman, screaming . . . Magda!" Melisande cried,
and broke into a run again, toward a clearing she could just
barely see. She approached an opening, and just as she got
there, she could see an awful change taking place, as Urvan—
or what she assumed must have been Urvan—was sprouting
hair and teeth and claws and growing, flailing, and yelping
and growling all at the same time as Magda, tied to a tree
nearby, was shrieking in hysterical fear.

On all fours, the grim, enormous black wolf of her vision
moved to Magda and, his fangs dripping with foamy saliva,
bent down over her. A shout a few feet away made her glance
over, and she saw Christoph and Kazimir shedding their
cloaks and coats; before her eyes, their bodies writhing as
they changed, they transformed into wolves, too, their clothes
splitting into rags. Without hesitation, the two leaped across
the clearing and attacked the giant beast that once was Urvan.

It was her dreams come to life, and she recognized the
shaggy dark wolf and slim silvery one; they were Kazimir and
Christoph! Deep in her soul she had known this was to take
place, and if she had only believed in herself, she could perhaps have forestalled everything.

Too late! Too late for remonstrance. Too late for anything
but action.

Magda! She turned as Charlotte, helping Gavril to the edge
of the clearing, stopped and stared as the two wolves circled
the larger one near Magda, who was whimpering and wriggling, tethered to the tree and helpless.

"I don't see Papa here! Who knows—" She broke off, her
fear overwhelming her for a moment. What if he was dead?
What if . . . No! "We must free poor Magda. The two wolves
will keep Urvan at bay . . . Urvan is the monstrous one!"

Charlotte, to her credit, though she was moaning in fear,
followed Melisande, as did Gavril, to Magda. They were
driven back, though, as the huge wolf, snapping and snarling
at the two others, backed into their path. But then the two
smaller wolves, Kazimir and Christoph, as Melisande knew

she must come to accept them, interceded and managed to turn Urvan away, keeping him occupied by snapping and snarling at his flanks.

Melisande dashed to Magda, who was struggling against her bonds. "Stay still for a moment, Magda, while I try to get these knots undone."

"Help me!" she cried, not listening and still struggling, twisting and only making the knots tighter. "Help me! Oh, Miss Melisande . . . Christoph . . . he's a wolf . . . I saw it! And the other Russian, the dark one . . . he is a wolf, too! Werewolves," she groaned. "Help me!"

"Stop! You must stop twisting!" Melisande commanded as Charlotte and Gavril joined her.

Gavril, panting with exhaustion, sank down to the ground at the base of the tree and gasped, "Concentrate, Melisande! I will keep watch and tell you if danger approaches."

The wolves had stopped circling each other. With a howl of rage, the biggest, Urvan, leaped on the other two. Yelping and growling and barking followed, and Melisande whimpered in fear, desperately trying to control it as Charlotte fumbled at the knots, too. But the ropes were tight, the knots cleverly constructed to make them impossible to loosen, and Magda's wriggling and writhing had done an even better job of tightening them.

"Do you have a knife, count, or . . . or anything?"

"No," he said, grimly. "No! Hurry, Melisande, they are—"

Flecks of bloody foam sprayed them as the battle, nearing fever pitch, raged closer. "Take Charlotte away to safety!" Melisande shouted to Gavril.

"No," Charlotte screamed.

"Then stop making my task harder," Melisande cried.

Charlotte, still whimpering with fear, backed away and twisted her hands together. Gavril spoke to her hurriedly and pointed to the two wolves fighting the big one; she cried out then, but Gavril covered her mouth before she could say the name of her beloved brother, now unrecognizable as a slim, silver wolf.

Blocking out fear, blocking out all but the knots under her fingers, Melisande, even as she worked, was visited by a vision . . . two years before, the mob of fearful and hysterical neighbors pulling and tearing at her grandmother and mother's clothes and pelting them with stones, then moving in, beating them with fists and cudgels and shovels.

How awful the vision, and yet how clear! And then her grandmother, blood flecking her wise, wrinkled visage and pain in her beautiful blue eyes, held up her arms to heaven, as one imploring it for sufferance. But not for herself. She cried out, invoking the powers above and below, the powers of good, the powers of the angels, to protect young Melisande and hide her from the awful horde. And the mob fell away, taking with it the battered bodies of Melisande's grandmother and mother to lay at the door of the church as witches and enemies of the citizenry.

Rising from her task, Melisande threw her arms up, hands pointed to heaven, and aloud said, "Help me! Help me to undo these torturous knots and so save this poor woman and her innocent child!"

Charlotte gaped and Gavril watched, his silvery eyes wide. As Melisande collapsed, the knots undid—they just fell away, and the ropes binding Magda unraveled. Melisande struggled to her feet and pulled Magda up, hustling her toward Charlotte, still gaping, and Gavril, who took Magda's arm and helped her toward the safety of the woods.

"Help her away!"

"Come with us!" Gavril begged.

But Melisande was already on her way back to the fray. She stopped for one moment and turned, though, looking at the two. "No," she said. "I have another task. Yours is to save Magda and find my papa, if you can, please! Help me thusly!"

She left them behind, trusting them to do as she bid, after what they had witnessed of her unexpected power, and she turned her force instead to the two men who had bravely set themselves to battle the unimaginable evil, the force of which suffocated her in waves, making her breathing come in short gasps.

Christoph and Kazimir, beautiful beasts with silvery and black fur and brilliant eyes, circled the awful fiend with eyes of yellow, as the blood red moon shone down, bathing them all in crimson light. This was a fight that could only end in death. The larger dark wolf, Kazimir, turned his gaze upon her, and they locked eyes; she could see the humanity, still, and the compassion and the great self-sacrifice he was willing to undergo. He would die rather than let Urvan hurt any of them, even Christoph, who though transformed was clearly not as powerful as he, nor as experienced.

Setting aside the weirdness of this all, knowing it would take its toll on her mind another day, she nodded once. Christoph and Kazimir, in tandem, leapt on the enormous monster as the red moon began to pale. Exhausted, and yet feeling a surge of power like lightning thrumming through her veins, Melisande held out her hands, cupping them, and she took into her keeping the two men's life forces, the glow burning her fingers, the power heavy like lead.

She shut out everything, all sight, all sound, and as dangerous as that was, she felt satisfied that she was doing the right thing. She joined her powerful life force with theirs and held it safe, keeping them away from harm as the terrible battle raged.

But she was weakening; she could feel huge fangs tearing at her energy, and blood dripping on her head as if it was true. The smell of blood saturated the misty air, floating like an aura around her and through the clearing, but then more of the terrible glowing color drained away, and finally silence fell.

She opened her eyes. The war was over, and the huge beast was dead, its throat ripped out, and blood soaking the trampled mud under its body.

"Where . . . ?" She looked around. There, at the edge of the clearing, were Kazimir and Christoph, men again, their clothes tattered and torn, their faces bloody, their bodies sagging with fatigue, but alive.

"Melisande!" a voice cried from the other side of the clearing. "Christoph!" It was Charlotte who raced toward them. She threw herself at her brother and hugged him, but then looked toward Melisande. "We found your father! We found your father lying some distance away, in the brush!"

Every drop of energy drained from her, Melisande saw only black and sank to the forest floor.

Chapter 30

COOL AIR blessed her cheeks, and she awoke to the feel of rain on her face, and the sensation of floating. "What . . . where . . . ?" She looked up. Kazimir's scarred, handsome face, stained with blood, bobbed above her. He was carrying her, and they were already to the edge of the forest, she recognized, coming more fully awake. "Papa!" she screamed. Was he alive? Was he dead?

"Hush," Kazimir said, gently, squeezing her to his chest. "Your father is alive and conscious. Look—Christoph is helping him, as is Charlotte."

She looked over, and there, all gathered near the edge of the forest, was the ragtag group. Magda leaned on a pale but composed Gavril, and Mikhail, weak and haggard looking, was supported on both sides by the von Wolfram siblings. He looked over and with tears in his eyes greeted her.

"Daughter! You are alive and well! That awful man told me you were dead, and I wept, thinking I had caused the death of the only one I love."

Melisande struggled and demanded to be let down. She raced to him and hugged him. "It's over . . . It is truly over," she whispered into his lank, dirty hair, grateful just to feel his thin shoulders and bony back in her arms. "Papa, it's over."

"Christoph!"

The shout came from afar, and the whole group looked toward the castle. Movement was all they could see at first, but then a figure was apparent in the silvery light of the recovered moon, a cloaked figure.

"It's Count Nikolas," Melisande gasped, watching the man stride toward them in the gloom. "What is he doing home?"

Christoph, his pale face gleaming with sweat and crusted

with dried blood from the night's exertions, helped Mikhail past the brushy edge of the forest, then broke away and stood, awaiting his uncle.

"What is going on? What the hell are all of you doing in the woods at night? And you two," he said glaring toward Kazimir and Gavril. "I suppose you are the two Russians?"

"You remember, Uncle," Christoph said, stiffly, "that I wrote to you that an old school friend of yours, Count Kazimir Vasilov, and an acquaintance of Melisande's father, Count Gavril Roschkov, were visiting?"

"Yes. Elizabeth was alarmed by the letter and demanded I return home. She had a strong sense that something was wrong, and though I thought her misled by her delicate state, it appears she was right, as I come back to find this! What is going on?" He glanced around at the disheveled party. "Is this how you look after things in my absence, nephew?"

Christoph remained silent.

Kazimir watched the interaction. The young man was intimidated by his uncle, and after that night, it was not right that he should be treated like a child, still. Not after what they had been through together. He stepped forward. "Nikolas," he said, with a bow. "It has been a long time, many years, since we have met. I think you should know how well your nephew has acquitted himself tonight, for he—"

But Christoph held up one hand. "No, not at this moment, sir. Uncle, these people are all freezing and tired and wounded. I will explain all, but the most important thing is to get them into the castle and see them taken care of. The danger that threatened us all is done, over with, and the time for healing has begun."

Kazimir noted his one long look toward Melisande when he said that. The young man had matured in just that one night, and his pale blond hair was now streaked with a duskier color.

As the group made its way up to the castle, Christoph gravely asked after his aunts Gerta and Adele and Count Maximillian, Melisande's uncle, as well as Nikolas's wife, Elizabeth, and their unborn child. All had made it safely over the Alps and to Venice, Nikolas said, where they stayed in comfort at Maximillian's sister's home.

Once inside the castle, which was alive with sleepy-eyed servants now that the master had arrived unexpectedly, all were taken care of, and Nikolas, with a long look at Christoph, said, "I think you and I have much to speak of, for it seems to me that your family heritage has been explained to you, and you have accepted the burden of it. We shall talk. Clean yourself up, change out of those tattered rags, and meet me in my library."

Kazimir felt the nervous energy of the night drain from him along with the blood he had lost. It was considerable and stained his ripped clothes terribly. He limped away, up to his room, with no need now to worry about anyone else. His world had changed, and he had to decide what to do about it.

Melisande watched Kazimir limp away, and called out, "Do you not wish to speak? Is there not much to discuss?"

He glanced at her and frowned. "I don't think there is anything, no. I will certainly see you on the morrow. Good night. Get some sleep."

Fury ripped through her. After all they had been through, all that had happened, he could just walk away like that? She took a deep breath and tried to let go of the anger. They would talk, but perhaps now was not the time.

Heinrich, Count Nikolas's personal valet, had been set the task of making her father comfortable, so when she went to his room to check on his state after such a long and awful ordeal, he was surprisingly uncomplaining. He was dressed in a snowy white nightshirt, his pale cheeks had gained some color from a shot of brandy from the count's own wine stores, and he was drowsy, with a good fire near him and food in his belly.

"Papa," Melisande said, standing by his bed and taking his hand. "You were very brave through this ordeal."

"Not nearly as brave as you, my child. I have been told by young Christoph that you . . . that you freed poor little Magda, but then would not leave the battle. I still do not understand all about the battle with that dreadful man, truly, but . . ." He yawned. "I think it will have to wait until the morrow."

He fell asleep, and restless, unable to just retire to her bed as if nothing had happened, Melisande mounted the steps up to Uta's room, where Frau Liebner and Mina were still holding their deathwatch over the countess.

"How is she?" Melisande asked, as she entered and moved toward the bed.

"Do not speak of me as if I were not present," Uta grumbled. "Sit. Tell me what happened dis night. I felt it, you know, while I was traveling in my other state. Battle. Wolves. You have accepted your power and used it to protect. My gut girl."

Melisande sat, feeling numb and unable to begin immediately. She took Uta's crabbed hand in her own, feeling how cold it was, and how distant the woman seemed from her. So much had happened, and she could not fathom how she was going to deal with it without the old woman's aid. "I am so afraid," Melisande whispered, dread shuddering through her. She put the old woman's knobby hand to her cheek. "I'm a monster, countess, a . . . a witch."

Uta squeezed her hand, some vestige of her old strength still remaining. "Not monster . . . just a woman with extraordinary powers." Her words were clipped, and she used no unnecessary ones, keeping it all for what she needed to say.

"No . . . no . . . I'm a monster like . . ."

"Like scarred one? Your handsome and commanding Russian werewolf?"

"You knew?" Melisande whispered, staring at the pale, wrinkled face.

"You haf seen Christoph . . . Nikolas also is so. It is family inheritance, and I knew from moment your Russian entered house dat another such as dey had come. I beckoned to him, and he came to me, visited me in the night. We spoke. I knew."

Melisande was silent for a long while as the candles burned down and guttered, and Mina finally retired to her bed, seeing her mistress well cared for. Frau Liebner sat in her old friend's chair by the fire and drowsed.

Finally, Melisande whispered, "I don't understand any of this. It seems that I must adjust the thinking of my whole life, that the world is a rational place, that life is ordinary and people good and bad, but not in any way extraordinary. What am I to think?"

"You are part of natural world, child. Nothing has changed." Uta paused, her breath coming in gasps.

"I should leave you alone," Melisande said, overwhelmed by sadness for her old friend, whose journey was just beginning.

"No!" Uta said, tightening her grasp on Melisande's hand. "We must talk. Let me only take my time."

And so, through the long night, with many pauses. Uta told Melisande much, relating to her all of the old tales. The von Wolfram's had discovered early their werewolfism. But not every werewolf was born so. The women of werewolf families could not transform themselves; their only ability lay in the capacity to pass it on to a man with whom they were bonded in some way.

"That is how Kazimir became a werewolf," Melisande mused. "What a shock it must have been to him! Even until last night he thought it was enchantment, and that a spell could reverse it. Now he knows the truth, that he is what he is forever."

"Harder," Uta whispered. "Much harder. For Christoph, he will have Nikolas to teach him, and I . . . I am one who told his heritage to him. But the Russian . . . he had no one."

Melisande frowned. "But . . . if Franziska Roschkov is the one who turned him, then that means that Gavril . . ."

"He is born so, but has resisted. He is fading . . . his energy leaving him. Soon . . . very soon . . . he will fade to nothing and disappear, a wraith, to walk the world unseen, never dying, but never living."

Melisande shivered, understanding, finally, all of the nonsense the men had been speaking of the night before. "How awful! Why doesn't he . . . what could . . ."

"Transforming would strengthen him. But dere are risks. For man who is werewolf, always dere is danger dat darkness will overwhelm him and he will surrender. Every choice he makes in life carries him toward gut or evil. So small, choices are, so minute, dat sometimes is not evident in which direction it will take him. If he chooses gut, den, like Nikolas, he becomes wise and powerful."

"And if not?"

"Den he truly becomes monster."

"He said his father was so, sanity deserting him, and that is why he made the decision he did, not to transform. How sad . . . he doesn't trust himself to make the right choices in life." Melisande bowed her head in the darkness and considered it all, but Count Gavril Roschkov, despite his kindness to her, was not her business. Her mind inevitably turned to her real dilemma . . . Kazimir Vasilov. There was a bond between them, but Kazimir seemed determined to keep it free of emotional attachment. What she had felt from him while he made love to her was far from unemotional, though. Whether he realized it or not, he felt things deeply.

"What is my role in Count Kazimir's life?" she asked. Then she looked up, wondering if the old woman was even still awake, but Uta's eyes were wide open and regarding her through their bleariness.

"He is very strong man, very complex, more so dan Nikolas, I think. For man like dat a weak woman would become tiresome . . . even dangerous. Man like dat . . . he needs strong woman, but also, gut woman. Like you. My . . . my angel."

Uta then faded into sleep as Mina, the dark circles around her eyes abated by a couple of hours of sleep, came in and shooed Melisande to the door. But as weary as she was herself, Melisande could not just go to her room to bed. She needed to speak to Kazimir.

She paused at his door and touched it, her fingers caressing the grained wood as she considered. But there was no turning back. They would speak now, or never. She twisted the ornate doorknob just as Christoph and Nikolas emerged from the library, both looking unutterably weary. Christoph merely glanced at her and then looked away, but Nikolas, with a shocked expression, stared.

"Melisande, is that not Count Vasilov's room? Come away from that door!"

His tone was that one would use with a child or a feeble-minded adult. She just stared at him and then entered. She was not a child any longer, though looking back at herself just months ago, and the empty one-sided infatuation she had had for Nikolas, she thought she was before Kazimir Vasilov entered her life. It was not her first sexual experience that had turned her into a woman, but her acceptance of the world for what it was, and the power within her and her ability to help one man become better than he was without her.

The room was dark, but she knew immediately that he was not asleep. She crossed to the faint square of window visible through the curtains and opened them, flooding the room with platinum light from the moon that neared the far horizon. Blessed, silvery, beautiful moonlight. She turned. He was sitting on the edge of his bed, still wearing the same tattered clothes as he had when he entered the house after the battle. His head was bowed, his shoulders slumped. One would think he had suffered a grave defeat at Urvan's hand instead of being the victor.

His brother. Just hours ago he had killed his brother!

A wave of shock hit her as she understood what none of them had taken into consideration. To all of them Urvan was the villain, evil, a beast. He had abused them, tortured them, and was a man to be reviled and hated.

Though he was all that to Kazimir, he was also the older brother he remembered from youth. Perhaps they had rough-housing to remember, and secret societies and pledges of brotherhood; maybe they had shared games that took them across the countryside in boyhood exuberance, and bedeviling the cook for cakes and walnuts. Perhaps both had begun alike, cut from the same cloth, goodhearted and full of joy.

And Kazimir had killed him, just as Franziska had originally intended. Melisande slowly crossed the floor, wondering what to say, and then decided no words were adequate, nor, perhaps, necessary. She sat beside him and took him in her arms, holding his body close to hers. He did not weep, but sighed, and the puff of air held all of his pain and despair.

"Though it is little comfort, I know," she whispered into his thick hair, inhaling the scent of smoke and forest, "you saved our lives, I am sure of it, and could not have done so had you left him alive. Christoph did his best to help, but without your courage, resourcefulness, and determination, your brother, in his madness and transformed power, would have killed us all, and who knows how many others."

He pulled away from her, got a cloth from the bowl of water that had once been hot, and began to clean his wounds.

One long gouge down his throat would leave a scar unless properly tended.

"Let me," she said, briskly, taking the cloth from him and putting it to better use. "I am a healer, after all."

"I know," he whispered, looking up at her finally. "But more . . . you are much more. I felt you, while we battled; you held Christoph's and my life within you and protected us."

Without comment, she first undressed him, swallowing hard at her first view of his whole body, thick torso, muscled legs, bulky shoulders. He was quiescent, accepting her orders, allowing her to do what she did. He sat on the edge of the bed nearly naked, and she cleaned his wounds, and then gently, after retrieving supplies from her own room, bandaged them. They were more plentiful than originally appeared. "Tell me how it happened," she said, gently, to distract him as she closed his wounds.

"What?"

"How you became as you are . . . how you have dealt with it."

He hesitated, but then began to speak . . . not of his were-wolfism, at first, but of the past. "Once, Urvan was a merry boy, smart, tough, but not evil. I'm sad that there is no one but me to remember that. The changes at first were not evident to me—I was years younger than him—though now, looking back, I can see them. He took delight in some cruel games, at first just pulling the wings off flies to watch them struggle, but then he would, when we were out hunting, delight in watching the beasts we shot die. I began to suspect he aimed not to kill them outright, but to wound them so they would die slowly." He shivered in disgust.

"He was troubled, then."

"He was going mad. He . . . began to hear voices in his head, and yet he didn't realize that the rest of us did not hear them, too. He would argue with them and quarrel, and think we—my father and I—were plaguing him by pretending not to hear them."

"I saw that in the hut, the voices. It was deeply disturbing."

Silence fell, but Melisande did not prompt him to continue. In time he did, as she pulled a blanket around him, trying to keep him warm, for his skin felt cold to the touch.

"Our parents died when I was still a youth, and Urvan became the head of the household. When he met Franziska, I was pleased, for she was beautiful and seemed . . . kind. At least to me." He lay back on the bed and stared up at the ceiling. "I was in love with her in the way a boy will be with a woman so worldly and lovely. Though I was not a boy; I was a man, though young and volatile. I thought Urvan had found someone with whom he could have a family. I thought it would heal the broken part of him. Gavril came with her, and there was a falling out between him and Urvan. I think . . . I think Gavril tried to talk Franziska out of marrying my brother. I wish she had listened."

"But she had plans of her own, it seems," she said, lying next to him, propped on her elbow and staring at his face. She pulled the blanket over his bare legs.

"I don't know if she had plans then. I would like to think that began when she learned how cruel Urvan could be." He shook his head. "There is no good way to think of this. One or the other is the worst, and I must think it of Urvan."

"But she turned to you."

He closed his eyes. "I should have seen what was happening, but I was angry at Urvan for mistreating her. She was so beautiful. Just a couple of years after they wed we began . . . we began an affair."

"At her instigation."

"I could have said no. I could have stayed away. *Should* have stayed away," he said, hammering his fist on the bed. "By then I was in the army, and yet our regiment was stationed close to my home. I visited often, and she slipped away into the village, too."

"It is painful to think of it, for me," Melisande admitted, feeling a wicked, thin spiral of jealousy . . . jealousy over a dead woman. She calmed herself, took a deep breath, and rose above it.

He nodded, accepting her comment without explanation. "She . . . bewitched me, I thought, and that was how I became as you saw me last night, a wolf."

"But it wasn't bewitchment."

"No. If only I had understood," he said.

Melisande stroked his hair off his square brow and spoke

of all that Uta had told her, of how a woman of a family with the heritage had the power to make a lover into a werewolf. As odd as it seemed, somehow she understood Kazimir and was unruffled by his wolfish side; perhaps her own burgeoning powers made her feel like him, in some way, and able to accept the part of him that was wild. "Gavril has the potential, but remains unchanged," she explained. "In German, Uta called it *unveraendert*, or untransformed. He . . . he is fading away because of that, and eventually he will become transparent and wander the earth in that form, a wraith. If he would change, he would gain strength, like you."

"Why does he not?"

"Uta says that there is great risk in the life a . . . a werewolf must lead, the choices he must make. It could become too easy to make the wrong choices and become . . . become evil."

Kazimir nodded, sadly. "And every choice takes one inevitably along a path, though the destination remains shrouded in obscurity."

"Remember Gavril spoke of his father, and how the effect of the burden of those cumulative choices was to drive him to insanity."

"I remember him saying that last night." Kazimir sighed, closed his eyes, and returned to his story. "Urvan, after Franziska turned away from him, became obsessed with finding the rosary. After he killed Franziska and knew I would turn him in, he used his supposed suicide to free himself, so letting him follow his obsession. He knew that your father had stolen it, and so hired him to steal the chalice, thinking to bargain with him for both."

"And you . . . you tried to keep them out of his hands."

"And ultimately didn't succeed. Perhaps if I had more faith, or trusted you all earlier . . ."

"You didn't know. And after all, we all live. Not one of us has suffered irreparable harm. And your brother is the one who killed Franziska, not you." She turned his face toward her and framed it with her hands. "Kazimir, you had no choice but to make sure he could harm no one else. You did the right thing . . . the only thing."

"I would kill him again . . . I would kill him a hundred

times, to protect you." He reached up and with a featherlight touch stroked her cheek as the blanket fell away from his arm. "That is the danger for me, and will always be the danger. I fear that with time I will become fierce and unrepentant." He slid his arm under her and pulled her close. "That's why, after we are married, I will take you and your father to my home, and you can live there in peace. I'll leave and go elsewhere."

"Who said I would marry you?" she asked, pulling away from him.

"But . . . it was concluded. It is what must be."

"So you say. But I don't want a husband who will leave me alone." She sat up, her back straight. "In fact, I never intended to get married. The life of a spinster does not frighten me. I would rather remain unwed the rest of my days than have a man who would leave me alone and think himself doing me a kindness."

He stared at her, his dark brows drawn down over his brown eyes. Slowly he sat up beside her on the bed. "What *do* you want, then?"

She pondered, digging deep inside of herself, beyond the fear of marriage and the close bonds it implied. "What do I want." She thought for a moment. "I want a husband who will give me children, and who will be there to help me raise them. I want a man who will love and trust me, who will rely on me, who will help me when I need help, and who will accept my help when I have it to give." She looked over at him in the fading moonlight. "I want a husband and a lover, not a self-sacrificing hero."

Kazimir looked into her dark-rimmed eyes and considered her words. In the forest, as the battle raged, he had felt her; she cradled his soul, keeping him safe. It came to him then, and he knew it to be true, that if she had not been there, either he or Christoph would be dead, or perhaps both of them. She was strong, and wise, and good. Too good for him.

"I'm not perfect," she said, as if she were privy to his private thoughts. "I can be confused and self-pitying occasionally, though I never let it last. I can be jealous and petty. My judgments are sometimes hasty. I want my own way usually and dislike bowing to others' wishes, though that has been my lot in life too often."

He smiled for the first time in a long, long time. Despite her soft and sensuous appearance, the sweet delicacy of her skin, the luscious curve of her lips, she was tough and willful, just the kind of woman who would tell him what he needed to hear. Countess Uta was right; she would ride roughshod over a young man like Christoph, a fellow of gentle and artistic temperament. The boy was toughening, now, but Melisande would have ruled him eventually with her forceful will.

She was his true match, Kazimir thought, meeting her firm gaze, one that brooked no self-pity from him, nor anything less than she knew he had to give. Like him, she was an outsider and had powers that both frightened and exhilarated her. She understood him. He had resisted for so long, but in truth, had been in love with her almost from the beginning. Though he had known that, he had thought it a doomed love. But was it? Did he have a chance? Hope trembled in his heart. Hope . . . it was a new sensation.

"Then tell me, my willful hellion," he said, touching her cheek with the back of his hand. "Will . . . will you marry me to keep me in line? Shall you manage me to within an inch of my life? Shall you harry me into being a better man than ever I would have expected?"

With a barely concealed smile, she retorted, "Despite the hitherto poor opinion I have had of marriage and the lack of examples of successful unions before my eyes, I have decided that I am capable of better things. I believe a successful marriage is possible and am of a mind to prove it. I will marry you, if only to keep you from drowning in your own worst habits."

Laughing out loud, he grasped her in his arms and kissed her hard.

Chapter 31

THEIR LAUGHTER died as they kissed, and he hastily pushed back the covers on his bed. His lips against hers, his body pushing her back on his bed, both were sensations she had learned to crave, and when he pulled at her clothes, she willingly shed them, piece by piece, touching and stroking his naked flesh, the bandages gleaming white in the fading light from the window, the only reminder of the night's torment.

The world hung still while they explored each others' bodies, Melisande feeling, for the first time, the magic in her limbs, the enchantment of his answering passion, the sorcery of loving someone so much that every other sensation was driven dormant for a time. She lay absolutely still, hands over her head, while he, tunneling under the blankets, gently kissed and tongued her navel, his big hands traveling the swell of her hips and her rib cage and her breasts, tweaking her nipples and cupping the small mounds in his hands as he kissed her belly, his breath warm and damp against her skin.

"Kazimir," she whispered, trembling with yearning. "Who would have known . . . how is it that just the touch of your lips . . ." She had no words. Just a week before she had been a virgin, unaware of this physical world except for the occasional stirrings of faint feeling, and now her body, newly minted, was tremblingly aware of every delicate whisper of his breath and his scratchy beard and his thick but gentle fingers.

And his tongue. "Oh!" Her cry echoed in the dark chamber as he moved down and playfully licked and caressed her thighs, the soft skin warmed by his breath and skillful loveplay.

"Melisande, sweetest girl," he said, in Russian, his voice gruff with yearning, "Please . . ."

"Come to me," she whispered, opening her arms.

He moved up from under the covers and hovered over her body, barely touching, and she could feel his ardent need, the proof pressing insistently against her as she spread her legs. She put her hands on his back and traced the entrancing musculature, the sinews and hewn muscles straining. He shivered at her light touch. Delighting in his control, aware of how she tantalized him, she reached down between them and touched, chuckling as he spasmed with need.

She guided him to her and pulled him down, every sensible thought lost as he delayed entry, teasing her instead with the wet, thick head of his male member. Now control was his, and he relished it, murmuring sweet Russian endearments, kissing her ear and nibbling her lobe as he pushed, slowly, relentlessly, enjoying her surrender and pleadings for release.

"Kazimir, please . . . oh, don't tease so!"

As he pushed in, his fingers tickled and caressed the nub above their joining, and she felt a swiftly rising tide of desperate craving overtaking her. Locking her feet behind his naked buttocks, she pushed up and cried out as new sensations overwhelmed her. But her actions drove him over the edge and he began the quickening thrust and push, and she clung to him, soaring to a new height and crying out her desire in her own language with words she had never had cause to use, endearments she had never thought to speak.

Her body tightened around his as he thrust again, more deeply, and his release came with hers, their damp bodies joined deeply, sweat mingling, ardor sealing them as one.

Silence, but the now dark room seemed to still echo with their desire. Her legs were still wrapped about him, and his heavy body still pushed her down into the mattress, but she didn't want him to ever leave. When he moved, she murmured, "No, please, Kazimir . . . don't leave me. I love you."

Silence. She opened her eyes and saw his face; even in the dimness just before dawn she could see the panic etched deep in the grooves of his forehead and his hard jaw. Her heart pounding, she was tempted to laugh, to make light of it, to toss her comment away with a witty afterword. But that would be too easy.

He pulled out of her and rolled over on his back.

She let it hang in the air, and finally, when the silence had drawn out too long, she said, turning and propping herself up on one elbow, "What do you fear so deeply?"

His shoulders relaxed, the tension easing. "It *is* fear," he said, in wonder. "I . . . I have never been afraid before and so did not recognize the sensation, but . . . fear . . . God help me, I'm so afraid." He met her gaze, and his dark eyes searched hers. "I . . . I fear hurting you. I fear making you sad. I fear . . . disappointing you."

She breathed out a long sigh. "Kazimir," she said, rolling over on top of him and gazing down at him, her long hair curtaining him, "You *will* hurt me. You *will* make me sad and you *will* disappoint me." She kissed the tip of his nose. "And . . . I think I shall do all of those things to you, too. But I'll always love you, and one moment of sadness, or one tiny jot of disappointment will not change that one little bit."

He pulled her down to him and found her lips, his kiss sweet and undemanding, passion replaced for the moment with tenderness. "I love you," he whispered, at last.

Long minutes passed. Uta had told her that men like Kazimir, with the wolf within them, recovered quickly from even bodily injury, and she thought after what he had suffered in the last two days, any other man would have perished. Instead she could feel the powerful life force that throbbed through him.

She straddled him, feeling everything, so sensitive that the wiry curls of his nest of hair from where his slumberous penis sprung, tickled her. Laughingly, she moved, craving every new sensation, and he groaned.

"Not yet, you vixen, not yet! I am wolf, but mortal, too!"

"I think you are more wolf than you realize," she whispered, feeling his arousal return, his rod thickening and lengthening as she teased him with her body, rubbing against him, urging him to fresh passion.

With a growl, he pulled her close and gnawed gently on her neck. "My sweet sorceress, I have never so delighted in the swift recovery being who I am has given me!"

Clasped together, naked skin meeting naked skin, they made love once more, slowly and with gentleness, the raw need between them sated by the knowledge that they would be together forever.

Sleep stole over Melisande, and a dream of a woodland glade that looked familiar somehow. It was a pleasant dream, and she walked alone, but with the knowledge that soon she would return to Kazimir. When she heard a familiar voice, she turned to find Uta, seated on a throne made of the twisted, gnarled roots of a giant tree that dominated the forest.

"Melisande, you have done so very well," the old woman said, proudly speaking German, the rich syllables of her native language rolling from her in waves. "You are stronger, even, than I knew, and I have heard that your grandmother is very proud of you."

"Have you seen her?" Melisande gasped.

"No, but I will, and soon. It is my sweet brother Willem who told me this."

"Oh."

"I have words of advice; you know how old women love to give advice, which is seldom welcome and even less frequently heeded."

"I have always listened to you, Uta," Melisande said, examining her, noting the brilliance of her clear gaze and the straightness of her posture.

"True. You are a rare one. Listen well, then, this time, too. Your man, he is strong and stubborn and willful."

Melisande smiled. "So am I. I didn't know that about myself, but I am."

"And that is good. But you . . . you have the wisdom to know when stubbornness will not do. He does not know this yet. You will need every bit of that stubbornness to deal with him in the coming years. Help him, but . . . let him help you, as well. As strong and independent as you are, to maintain this love you need, sometimes, to be soft; often what a man needs most is to help his woman, to feel that she needs him. Perhaps he will think you need him more than you truly do, but that is as it should be."

"I will remember that."

"And remember me," Uta said. "We will watch over you, your grandmother and I. I think I shall like her."

•   •   •

THE castle felt empty. In the early dawn hours, Kazimir had whispered to her that he was going to speak to Nikolas about their marriage and had crept out of bed to dress. Melisande was up and about shortly after, hungry to speak to the others now that the awfulness of the past weeks was well and truly over.

She was at peace, for unbidden some answers had come to her. She had once wondered how a kind and loving God could permit the horror and violence the world sometimes held. Now she acknowledged that free will was given them all, and there would always be sadness in life. There was no facile answer; for every person there was just a constant striving to make things better, and the hope that one would succeed.

Soon, she would go up to Uta's room to tell her about her strange dream, but first . . . the chapel. Her odd new powers troubled her. How could she reconcile what she knew of herself with her deep faith in a higher being? Perhaps it would take time before that answer would be given to her, but she would still seek it.

The castle was hushed, servants having put felt slippers over their shoes. What was going on? Melisande wondered. But steadfast in her determination, she headed through the great hall and to the chapel. When she opened the huge double doors, she paused and breathed in deeply; fresh flowers from the conservatory! The scent drifted to her, even as the light from sunrise—the octagonal tower soared above the battlements, and so though the turret was on the west side of the castle, light from both sunrise and sunset glowed through the stained glass windows—played a pattern of red and gold and green over the stone walls.

But the chapel was not deserted. Knelt before the altar was Frau Liebner, and the woman was weeping. Fear clutched Melisande's heart, and her gasp echoed up to the barrel vault of the high ceiling. She made her way down the short aisle as the older woman stood and turned, her wrinkles deeply etched. The older woman held out her arms, and Melisande ran the rest of the way.

"What is it? What is wrong?"

Frau Liebner hugged her hard, and then set her back, staring into her eyes. "Uta, my dear old friend, is gone."

The tears flowed freely; Melisande could not speak. They

clutched each other for a time, weeping together in the age-old bond that held women fast and made them stronger; tears, men opined, were a sign of womanly weakness, but in truth it was a secret strength shared among women that watered the roots of their souls, taking them past pain to acceptance. Men might never understand, and so the secret was safe, perhaps for all time. Melisande went to the altar and knelt, reaching for her rosary and remembering just in time that it had been destroyed. When something was pressed into her hand, she looked at it, and then at Frau Liebner, who knelt beside her.

"What is this?"

"It is ancient, and a family heirloom, but Uta wanted you to have it. It is left from a time before the church in Germany was reformed."

Melisande gazed down at the silver rosary in her hands, the lovely rosette beads almost like the decade beads of her lost-forever rosary.

"She told me, in the night, that . . . that you would be marrying the Russian, Count Kazimir," Frau Liebner said.

Melisande nodded.

She took Melisande's hands within her own and squeezed. "And she told me that you must not let her passing change anything." Her voice choked, the woman struggled to finish what she needed to say. "She said that she would be with you on your wedding day."

KAZIMIR had spoken to the priest in the village, giving him their natal information and asking him to read the banns. As irregular as it seemed to the old man to rush the wedding so, who would ever deny Kazimir Vasilov anything that he had set his mind to? The ways of those at the castle had always been irregular, and after all, Count Nikolas von Wolfram, his liege lord, said it was to be so. To Melisande's surprise, then, there was nothing to wait for; two days after the drama in the woods, the priest was invited up to the castle to perform the ceremony in the turret chapel, newly consecrated.

Magda had not returned to her home, at Melisande's insistence. Though she thought she was perhaps the only one who knew the girl's state, it was a secret she would not share; she had an idea who the father was, and though she had many questions, she could not bear to push Magda to answer them. It was too awful a supposition to even whisper.

There was a small anteroom near the altar, and Melisande, gowned in springtime green, was closeted there with Frau Liebner, Magda, Charlotte, and Fanny, who had helped her dress and did her hair for her. If she thought of how her life was about to change, she would break down, she feared. She and Kazimir had spoken of it often over the last couple of days, and had decided that they were returning to Russia to his neglected estate to see what could be made of the land, and her father was coming with them. Mikhail truly was ill after his ordeal, too ill to stand with his daughter and give her to her husband, so Nikolas was going to do that honor.

Charlotte, who had been uncommonly silent over the past days, fussed with an arrangement of flowers, but then turned to Magda, and, her voice unnaturally loud in the tiny room, said, "I have been unkind to you for the last couple of years, Magda Brandt. Will . . . will you forgive me in this holy place?"

Magda, weak and shaking, pale with strain, began to cry silently, tears simply rolling down her cheeks. She shook her head, unable to speak.

Swallowing hard, Charlotte said, her voice harsh with strain, "Please, Magda . . . we once were friends, in our childhood. Will you forgive me?"

Magda glanced over at Melisande, but then said, her voice quavering, "I . . . I have something to say. Once I say it, though it must be done, you may not wish to have anything more to do with me. I cannot help it, for it is merely the truth, but you may see it differently."

Frau Liebner, who had been at the door to the chapel peeking out, let the door close and turned. She gave Magda a long look, and then nodded once.

"What is going on?" Charlotte questioned, glancing back and forth between the women.

"Life has been unkind to me in many ways," Magda said, her tears drying and her voice steadying. "I blamed many . . . wrongly, it seems to me now. Wilhelm Brandt, filthy lecher that he is, began to do things with . . . no . . . no, not *with* me, *to* me when I was too young to understand, and the result, after much ill usage, is that I . . . I c-carry his child. Or . . . I think it is his child," she said, hanging her head in shame. She put one hand over her stomach as the gasps of all but Melisande and Frau Liebner whispered like echoed sighs in the tiny chamber. Charlotte was stark and shocked, Fanny weeping openly. "As awful as that is, at least Wilhelm Brandt is not my true father."

"What?" Charlotte frowned. "How can that be? He is your mother's husband . . ."

Magda looked over to Frau Liebner again, and the old woman nodded once more.

"But my mother was already with child when they wed, I have been told."

"That is right," Frau Liebner said. "Go on, Magda, tell all. Uta wanted this said, for the burden of this all has been weighty. No more secrets."

Magda took in a long breath and let it out. "She could not marry my true father, for he . . . he was already wed to another. My mother told me this once, but I did not believe it until Frau Liebner confirmed it for me. It explains much. My f . . . Wilhelm Brandt screamed it just weeks ago as he beat me for being with child . . . his child." She hung her head. "He called me . . . Wolfram's illegitimate pup."

Charlotte was staring, her blue eyes huge. Melisande looked inward, though, and it came to her in that moment why she had always felt that Magda looked so familiar. "Johannes von Wolfram?" she whispered. She glanced from Charlotte to Magda and back again, tracing the similar lines of the face. "Johannes von Wolfram."

Charlotte shook her head. "No, it cannot be! No!"

"Yes!" That was Frau Liebner, and she stepped forward, taking Magda's hand and giving her strength. "Yes, it is true. Johannes had . . . interests outside of his marriage, and Magda's mother, Bertha, was one of them. As a girl, she worked at the castle for some time, and . . . she was weak to his blandishments. He was a very handsome man, and for all of his faults, very kind. To an innocent girl such as Bertha, his kindness was her undoing."

Charlotte had sunk down on a chair and wept, her hands over her eyes. Magda pulled away from Frau Liebner's kind touch and went to Charlotte, kneeling before her. "I'm sorry," she said brokenly, then bowed her head. "I am so sorry. I wish—"

"No!" Charlotte said, trembling violently, but then she calmed herself. She put out her hands and cupped Magda's face, raising it to stare into eyes so like her own. "Look at me, Magda! As difficult as this is for me to hear, it is not your fault. I have been unfair, often, and childish, but I will stop that now. It is time to accept that things are not always as they seem, and things are not always to be as I wish. But why . . . why has no one said anything until now?" She looked at Frau Liebner. "Why was Magda made to suffer for so long in a home with that evil . . ."

"God forgive us," Frau Liebner cried out, her voice choked with emotion, "it was thought to be for the best for Magda to remain within the sphere to which she was born by virtue of her mother's status, and so a marriage was arranged with a prosperous brewer . . . Wilhelm Brandt. That was Johannes's doing, and arranged in secret to protect Anna, his wife, though I fear she knew. If we had known what a monster Brandt was, I hope and pray we would have done better."

Fanny, a silent spectator until now, went to Magda and hugged her, the tears drying on her cheeks. "I hope this truth being in the open will give you strength in the difficult time to come," she whispered, putting her small hand over Magda's slightly rounded belly.

"Magda's mother was not Johannes's only conquest," Frau Liebner said, quickly.

Melisande, seeing Fanny with Magda, both of them so blonde and pretty, gasped. She met her friend's gaze, and the woman nodded. Charlotte, quicker than Magda or Fanny, saw it too and began to cry. But this time she went to Fanny and took her in her arms, hugging her close. "Sister . . . you are my sister," she whispered. "All this time . . ."

Magda joined them in their embrace and stared at Fanny. "Is it true?"

Fanny, shaking, turned toward Frau Liebner. "Who . . . who was my mother? I have never known."

Perhaps somewhere inside she had known the truth of who fathered her, Melisande reflected, for she had accepted Johannes von Wolfram's paternity with astonishing swiftness.

"Once upon a time a young Englishwoman came to visit the castle, and . . ." The woman shrugged. "Johannes, being as he was, found such a pretty little thing irresistible. She bore a child, and was sent back in shame to live out her days in England. I have always felt that Anna Lindsay—your mother, of course, Charlotte—simply turned away from her husband and to Hans von Hoffen—poor Gerta's husband—in sadness. Lonely she must have been, and ashamed, perhaps, that her husband was so willing to go to other women's beds."

It was too much to take in, in such a short time, and Melisande, her mind racing, heard the call from the chapel that she must come, for her husband-to-be was becoming impatient to be wed. She tried to find calmness, but it was impossible.

Kazimir awaited her at the altar, and when she joined him, escorted to his side by Nikolas, and said the words that bound her to him for all time, she quailed at her future . . . until she looked up into his eyes. There was such tenderness there in their sweet brown depths, and he needed her so much. Their vows, instead of being whispered in reverence, were shouted in joy, and laughter followed. She could give him that, laughter and cheer, just as he gave her love and hope and purpose. She would drive all of the darkness from his life and give him the triumph of joyfulness. He would give her tenderness and lifelong devotion.

Uta was with her; she felt it in the dim shadows of the chapel. As their marriage was sealed, the dim, gloomy chapel was brightened by a ray of brilliant spring sunshine through the many-colored glass of the high, arched windows that circled the heights of the turret, and color exploded, a joyful array of gold and green and red, and the stained glass portraits of saints embellished the walls. Uta's spirit was at rest, for her little Melisande had found peace and security and love.

Chapter 32

HAND IN hand, with barely a moment for a kiss, they made their way upstairs to her father's chamber for his blessing. Mikhail reclined, still in bed, and Gavril sat with him in a big chair nearby; both men looked upon them kindly. After Kazimir and Melisande—he standing by the foot of the bed and she perched on the edge near her papa—had spoken of the wedding and their plans to go first to Romania to tell the church from whence the Blood Amber relics were stolen of their fate—all that was left of them was an ashy mass of black resin—Mikhail sobered and took his daughter's hand.

"When Count Urvan approached me and asked me to steal the chalice, I only did it because I had in mind to come back here with enough money for a dowry for you. I have been a pitiful father and thought I could right it all by providing you with a way of marrying well."

"Urvan came to you because he knew that you stole the Blood Amber Rosary many years before," Kazimir said. "He was sure he could get both items from you."

"I'm afraid I made it easy for him to trick me. I . . . I bragged about my little daughter's influential friends, and her life in this castle, and the protection offered to her by Count Nikolas von Wolfram. If he knew that I had stolen the rosary ten years ago, he might have reasoned that I had taken it to Melisande to keep. But . . ." He frowned. "How would he know that?"

"He saw you steal the rosary and tried to follow you, but you slipped away . . . to France, we now know, to give Melisande the rosary," Kazimir said. "He was in Constanta, trying to figure a way to steal the chalice, and he saw you hanging about, planning your next robbery . . . you did plan to steal the chalice, didn't you?"

Mikhail hung his head but finally said, "Yes. I must confess all. I thought, in my deluded mind, that if I stole one last thing, the chalice, and united it with the rosary, then . . . then the church would pay a ransom to get it back."

"So it was just for money. Did you not know of the legend?" Melisande whispered, pained by this frank discussion of her father's thievery, but knowing it must be said. She squeezed his hand to encourage him.

"No. No, I did not know . . . not then, anyway. I was drawn to the place and the chalice, and I do not know why. The rosary has always haunted me," Mikhail said, his eyes wide and his voice trembling. "After I gave it to you, I dreamt often of its companion piece, the chalice. It plagued me until I thought if I just had them both, I could then make something of them for my daughter. I thought that is what the dreams were trying to tell me."

"Magic," Gavril whispered, his gaunt face in the shadows looking haunted. "This is why I distrust it so. How can we know, even when our intentions are good, if we are using magic or . . . or if it is using us?"

"But Urvan's evil was not magic," Kazimir objected. "Mikhail never intended to use the pair for their evil intent, did you, sir?"

"No. Never. At least . . ." He sighed and shifted. He sighed again. "Truth. I must learn to tell the truth. Urvan told me tales . . . he said that owning both pieces and putting them together could make the user wealthy. I was going to do that, for Melisande's sake, you know."

"That is how Urvan thought to make you lead him to the rosary . . . He let you keep the chalice, knowing you would retrieve the rosary," Kazimir said.

"And he thought it would be easy, once I had them both, to get them from me. But once I fully understood the legend, and what it meant, I knew I could never give myself over to such evil." He shivered and Melisande patted his shoulder. He gave her a grateful look.

"Once he saw you in Constanta, Urvan planned all of it, from the beginning, I think," Kazimir said. "And used you to do his bidding. He gloated to us, in the hut, that the rosary and chalice were calling out to him."

Mikhail nodded once. "That is why, though he had access to me in the prison—I think he bribed the jailers where I was taken, and he came in and beat me, even as he let slip tiny details of the power of the chalice—he did not kill me, nor did he even push me so far as to let him have the chalice, which I would have done rather than die, you know."

Kazimir thought. "He knew something about Nikolas von Wolfram," he said finally. "Enough to know that if you sent him a message to help you, he would respond, and had the power to free you."

"I think your interference," Gavril said to Kazimir, "was the one thing he had not counted on."

"But he saw it as an opportunity to settle an old score between us."

"Your . . . affair with Franziska had long infuriated him," Gavril added.

"But mostly," Kazimir said, his teeth gritted, "because she gave to me the gift of . . . of werewolfism."

"Yes, " Mikhail said, with a fearful glance at his new son-in-law. "Urvan knew you were a werewolf, and so in Constanta he obtained wolfsbane from a witch and used it in the hut to weaken you."

"A witch?" Melisande asked.

"Yes . . . yes a gypsy witch."

Kazimir, his dark eyes wide, said, "Yes! The witch he sent to me to tell me that to reverse the . . . the curse I was under, I needed to follow the chalice."

Mikhail nodded. "He was so delighted to tell me his cleverness. It *was* diabolical . . . and worked, to a degree, though he did not foresee the final outcome. He intended to kill Kazimir, he told me when he came to me in that dreadful cave." He shivered.

"Why didn't he kill me when he had the chance?" Kazimir asked. "Why weaken me with wolfsbane and make me . . ." He exchanged looks with Melisande and changed tacks. "Why didn't he kill me while I was in his power?"

Gavril took in a long shaky breath, and the others looked over at him. "He . . . he wanted to kill you once he had transformed into that awful beast. He wanted to gain his revenge on you for Franziska having turned you instead of him, and he wanted to do it in his . . . in what he saw as his triumph over you, his more powerful werewolf form."

"He knew I would come after him once he had the chalice and rosary. He knew I would try to defeat him." Kazimir reached out his arm for Melisande, and she went to him. He held her close to his body and kissed the top of her head. "If not for my . . . beautiful wife holding Christoph and I safe with her power, he would have killed at least one of us, if not both."

Gavril said, sadly, "I warned Franziska before they married that I was afraid Urvan had some inkling of the truth, and that he might try to inveigle her to use her gift on him. He worried me; there was something about him . . . something about both of you, Kazimir, to be honest. The gift she had to give is one I wished she would not use. In our history, the men who have been given it often go mad from the strain, not being prepared by their heredity to use it wisely. She told me she had no intention of using it on Urvan. I think that was the truth; she had planned carefully how she was going to use it."

"I thought you did not want to think so about your sister?" Melisande said, staring at the ghostly man.

He simply shrugged. "Sometimes one must face unpalatable truths and accept them, just as I have accepted my eventual disappearance. It is a choice, at least. Always Franziska wished for two things: money and independence. By using her gift on Kazimir and manipulating him to kill Urvan, she would have both, as a wealthy widow."

"But Franziska was useless to Urvan after she gave the gift to you," Mikhail said, gazing at his son-in-law with awe edged with unease.

Melisande squeezed his hand and smiled at him. "Thank heaven she gave it to Kazimir and not Urvan," she said, "for in Kazimir she may not have known it, but she had a safe repository. He has never misused the gift." She stood on tiptoe and kissed his chin.

"If only I had not stolen the rosary, so long ago," Mikhail said, "or . . . or if I had resisted Urvan's offer, or . . ."

"No time for recriminations, my friend," Gavril said.

Mikhail sighed. "I suppose not. Once I figured some of it out, I tried to correct things, tried to do the right thing."

"Though you did think to use the pair at one time," the Russian gently said.

"Yes . . . to my shame. I went out to the woods to meet him one time, you know," he said, looking up at the others. "I was supposed to return to him with the rosary and chalice, but Melisande would not give me the rosary. I went out to tell him I was still working on her and would not give him the chalice until I had both pieces in my possession."

"That was the night I saw you, and you disappeared into the room on the main floor and used the passages to slip away!" Kazimir said. "It was then that I discovered the passages."

"Yes . . . yes, I remember hearing something and hastening my escape. And then, in our conversation, Urvan let slip the truth about the . . . the awesome power of the pair. He was furious . . . said the blood moon was coming, and he needed the relics before then. I obtained a book on astronomy and began to chart the progress of the moon, and I soon learned when the blood moon was to be. I misunderstood, you see, and thought, for a time, that the power the pair offered would help me to gain wealth, and . . . I was tempted, as I have already admitted," he reminded them. "But I soon felt the horror steal into my soul and saw how it would destroy not only me, but those I love." He glanced at his daughter.

"And I don't think Urvan counted on that," Kazimir said. "He would never have foreseen that you would resist the power and wish to do what was right. Even when you had decided against using the power yourself, I don't think he imagined you could ever resist his offers to buy the pair from you. He had jewels in his possession, we know that, for I have found them where he abandoned them—wealth was only ever a tool for him—and he intended to offer them all to you in exchange. He was sure you would acquiesce, in greed."

Mikhail nodded. "Yes. At first I thought I had escaped Urvan. But then I heard about someone hiding in the woods and knew it was him. I agreed to keep to our bargain and sell him the pair, though even then I wasn't sure. But in the end I could not give such a monster as he the relics . . . not even for jewels. That is when Magda came to me with the message when and where he would be waiting for me. I went out through the secret passage to tell him he must leave. I . . . I lied to him and told him I had destroyed the chalice and that the rosary was gone, but he didn't believe me. I thought I could convince him; I was an idiot, for I thought he would just go away if I told him it was destroyed. But that is when . . . he seized me and . . ." He shook his head as his voice broke, and he was unable to continue.

"Why didn't you destroy it when you had the chance?" Kazimir asked, suddenly.

Mikhail trembled and paled. "It wouldn't let me! I wanted to . . . I thought of it . . . I tried. But . . . it wouldn't let me. I hid it in different places. I would take it and look at it and try to throw it in my fire, but then instead I would hide it somewhere else. I truly thought I was going mad."

"Papa, it's over," Melisande whispered, tears in her eyes. "I think it was meant to happen. I believe deeply that the rosary and chalice were brought together at such a time as two strong men, my h-husband"—She paused and blushed at naming her new status—"and Christoph von Wolfram would be able to overcome its evil force. It is a disgrace that such relics of an earlier time were so abused, but the spirit of their first owner, poor Demetrius of Constanta, rests easier now, I feel it in my heart. Now we must go on and put this all behind us somehow."

Her father was a changed man; she felt it as much as she saw it. Physically wounded by all that had happened and days spent in a cave underground—that explained why neither Kazimir nor Christoph, even with the sharpened senses of wolves, could find them, as well as the wolfsbane that was used everywhere, on the fire in the hut and even on the bullets in the pistol—he had been wounded deeper by the close call they had all endured. It had shaken her father's lifelong faith that he knew what was right to do in every circumstance. Though it was difficult to see him so cowed and unsure, she had faith that he was on the path to deeper discovery, that he could do right and make better choices. This was confirmed in an odd way by his next words.

"Melisande, I must ask your advice."

"Yes, Papa?"

He held out his hand, and she went back to him, sitting beside him and taking his hand in hers. His gaunt face was pale, but he was steady and strong in his next words. "Poor Magda . . . she even more than I has suffered in her short life. In my darkest hour, though, when I thought you dead, when I feared for my own sanity more than for my life, she came to me in that cave and told me you were alive." He kissed her hand. "Beaten and violated as she was, she was still tender and careful of me in my misery. She kept me alive, I am certain of that. She gave me food and water and tried to warm me. I am determined now to keep to a good path, to make my way in this world as a better man. I know you and Kazimir have offered me a home, but . . . so has Count Gavril." He looked over at the pale man, who nodded to him to encourage him. "He has offered me a position in his household, and I . . . I wish to take it, and . . ." He swallowed. "Poor Magda . . . this is a point for her at which her life can become better, or very much worse. I think, if she will have me, I will marry her."

Melisande gasped, taken aback, and withdrew her hand from his.

"Listen to me before you judge," Mikhail said, hurriedly, putting out one shaking hand to touch her hair. "I will then take her to Russia with me, to Count Gavril's estate, where I will have my own apartment in the castle, he tells me. She will be away from her odious devil of a stepfather, foul beast that he is. She needs a family, and . . ." He smiled, a wistful smile that lit his pale eyes and gave color to his gray skin. "I would like to be a father again, to have another chance to be a better father than ever I was to you, poor child." He reached out. "Can you bless such a union?"

Melisande glanced over at Kazimir, who had been silent in all of this, though she needed no confirmation from him. "Papa, you do not need my permission, but . . . if this is what you want, and what Magda wishes, then . . . then of course you have my blessing."

•   •   •

THE castle had been her home for just over two years, but within its walls she had made so many discoveries, and her life had changed completely. *She* had changed completely. The day had come for her to leave with Kazimir. Since they were traveling to Romania first, though Gavril, Mikhail, and Magda were not leaving until a week or two later, due to Mikhail's healing wounds, they would likely arrive in Russia about the same time. Magda and Mikhail would wed at Wolfram Castle first. Melisande had already taken her leave of her father, Magda, and Count Gavril. Count Nikolas was going with them as far as Austria, where he was to meet his wife, Elizabeth, who traveled to Austria from Venice with Cesare, Count Nikolas's secretary. She wished to have their child at Wolfram Castle, their home.

But there were other difficult leave-takings yet. Ones Melisande needed to do alone.

"Charlotte?" she said, tapping on her friend's door.

Charlotte looked up from a skein of wool she was winding with Fanny and smiled, tremulously.

"We are leaving very early in the morning just before sunrise," Melisande said, "and I . . . I thought I would say goodbye tonight."

Fanny excused herself, hugged Melisande, and whispered a broken and tearful goodbye, then slipped out of the room.

Charlotte bent her head again to her work. "Oh, is it that time already?" she said, her tone casual, but a betraying tremor quavering it.

"Yes, Charlotte, it is that time already."

She sat by the girl and made her raise her face. It was wet with tears.

"What shall I do without you, Meli?" she said, choking back a sob and tossing aside her wool. "You were always my sensible self. You kept me levelheaded when I would be harsh. It is only because of your steadying influence that I have been able to accept all of this . . . Magda . . . Fanny. You gave me advice. You made me stronger."

Melisande shook her head. "Charlotte, you were all of those things already. I admire you. You have always been headstrong and determined; now I want you to embrace your future unafraid."

Nodding, the girl said, "We have decided, Christoph and I, to do what Uncle Nikolas wishes and go to England. He has made a match for me with some English earl or another from his dreadful list."

"Charlotte!" Melisande gasped. "Don't say you have agreed to marry—"

"No! Oh, no, all I have agreed to is that I will go to England to have a look at this fellow."

Melisande laughed, picturing such a meeting as this brash, fierce German girl would have with an Englishman. What she wouldn't give to be there! "You must write to me often to tell me of your adventures."

"My real motive is that I will take Fanny with me. We have the name of her mother now, you know, from Frau Liebner, who visited her once while in England; we are going to find her."

"Does Nikolas know of your intentions to seek out Fanny's mother?"

"Of course not!" She sighed and gave a humorous grimace. "You know my uncle . . . he would pucker up most awfully and then forbid me to go. Even Christoph does not know yet."

Melisande sighed. "And I had been thinking you sensible."

"I think it very sensible to find poor Fanny's mother," Charlotte said indignantly. "Why shouldn't she have family, too?"

Thinking about it, Melisande nodded. Perhaps her young friend was more clear thinking than any of them. "True, and now she has you! Oh, Charlotte, I will miss you." They hugged, the embrace stretching out for long, silent moments.

Finally, Charlotte asked, releasing her friend, "Have you said goodbye to Christoph yet?"

"No."

"Be . . . gentle." Charlotte looked back down at her discarded wool. "As much as he is going to be hurt when you leave, I think . . . I think you helped him, you know."

"How? Charlotte, my worst fear is that all I have done is hurt him."

Charlotte was silent for a long moment and then said, "All that happened," she whispered, referring to the horrible events of the previous months, his drugging, his illicit affair with his aunt, and then his acceptance of his werewolf heritage, "was too much for him in a way. You know how sensitive he is. He . . . broods. Not like me. I pout and stamp and yell and then I am done with it. But—" Charlotte sighed. "Loving you as he does has made him a better man, I think, for it has given him a vision of what he needs in his life."

"Oh, Charlotte!" Melisande put her hands on either side of her flaming cheeks. "So you think he truly loves me?"

"Yes . . . oh yes." Charlotte stared into her friend's eyes. "But you can't help who you fall in love with, can you? I would dearly have adored having you as my sister, but it was never meant to be."

"You have other sisters now," Melisande whispered, her voice choked with tears.

They hugged again and murmured their goodbyes. Melisande knew, as she left the room, that Charlotte would weep, as would she, but both of them were strong and would go on. Perhaps they would never meet again, but they would always be friends.

Christoph was waiting for her in the lady's library, she was told by a footman. She steeled herself for this most difficult interview. He stood at the window, gazing out at the darkness at the waning moon.

"Christoph," she said, gently.

He turned and smiled.

"Saying goodbye is difficult," she said, feeling emotion well up into her voice.

"But it is a part of life, I fear," he said, hands behind his back. He looked more like his uncle now than he did just weeks before.

"Charlotte tells me you are going to take her to England to evaluate her potential husband," she said.

"Yes. First we are staying here until Uncle Nikolas comes back with Elizabeth. We may stay until their child is born, but then . . . then we are off to England. I must thank you, Melisande, for your steadying influence on my sister. I think it bodes well for her future happiness that she has agreed to this marriage and will now settle down to becoming a good wife and mother, as a lady ought."

She choked back a spurt of laughter. If that was what he thought his time in England was going to be, she had a feeling he would be led on a merry chase by his sister, who remained as headstrong and willful as ever, if with a better heart and intentions to guide her. "Yes. Well. I . . . I hope," she said, sobering, "that you will find happiness, too. Your life has been difficult . . ."

He held up one hand. "We have all had our travails. I feel as if I am coming out of a fog, now, and life, though challenging, will be . . . interesting."

She walked the distance between them and put her hands on his shoulders. "Be careful, when you go, my friend. We each have our abilities, but we must be wise with them, for I am afraid others will not understand."

He nodded. He reached out, gave her a very brief hug, and set her away from him. "Goodbye, Melisande. I wish you a long and fruitful life." His expression was remote, but there was a glimmer in his eyes.

She let it pass unchallenged. "Goodbye, Christoph. I wish you happiness and . . . and love." She turned and ran from the room.

Epilogue

LEAVING AT dawn, Melisande, Kazimir, and Nikolas traveled all day by carriage toward Romania. They parted company with Count Nikolas, who was headed south to meet his wife at the Brenner Pass, to guide her back to Wolfram Castle, where they would welcome their child into the world later in the year. Through the long day, as they traveled, they spoke with Nikolas about Count Gavril and his determined rejection of his werewolf heritage, the inevitable result being his eventual fade into wraithdom, a fate worse than death, for he would then travel the earth in a state of invisibility, unable to be seen, and yet not dead, and so not ascending nor descending, forever.

They agreed that such an honorable man must not be allowed to live so. They would, once they all met in Russia, Melisande and Kazimir decided, enlist Mikhail and Magda in their campaign to win him back to life. As difficult as it was to balance his werewolf side with his human side, it was better by far than simply giving up, and if anyone could find that difficult balance, it would be him.

The moment Nikolas left them alone to continue on horseback to his destination, Melisande threw herself into her husband's arms, kissing and caressing him, petting him and whispering endearments into his ear. By the time they arrived at an inn for the night, both were in a state of fevered anticipation, despite their weariness and the lateness of the hour.

Making love quickly, they sated their passions, and Kazimir fell into a deep slumber. Melisande though, lay awake for a time, the excitement of the trip leaving her unable to sleep.

A shimmer in the corner drew her attention. She raised herself on one elbow.

Uta sat, enthroned as always on her woodland seat, the edges of the vision glowing and twinkling gold and emerald; the old woman laughed lustily. She winked and nodded. "A good husband you have chosen, my little friend, for he is robust and vigorous," she said. "Perhaps you and I, we are more alike than I would have thought, for such a one as he is what I would have chosen for a husband, if ever I had been able."

"Uta," she gasped, softly.

"No, no little one . . . do not look so at me; I am here but for the briefest moment. I, too, have a journey ahead. Go to sleep, my darling little child. I told you I would be looking over you, and I will. Your grandmother . . . she has been gone too long to come back as I do, and I . . . this is my last time to visit. Take care of each other. Love that man well and often, never forgetting your need for each other. And be wise . . . be wise with the power you wield, and be wise in your love."

The shimmer faded, Uta disappeared, and Melisande sighed. The last time. It was true, she felt it deep in her heart; Uta was gone forever, passed over to the world beyond sight. Melisande had never told anyone about her strange connection with the old woman and her visions of her, preferring to keep it close to her heart. Now she would never speak of it. Though it gave her much comfort to know that Uta had passed beyond safely, Melisande was lonely, and so she turned over, curling up to Kazimir, who was naked, still. She ran her hand over his warm skin, touching his chest, threading her fingers through the mat of hair and feeling his heart beat. He twisted toward her, pulling her into his embrace, kissing her, even in his sleepy stupor.

Love him well and often. That was advice she could manage, she thought, reaching down between them and caressing him, feeling his ardor rise quickly, as he sleepily murmured words of love in Russian. Advice was always pleasant when it coincided with what one would have done anyway, she thought, twining her arms around her husband and wrapping her legs around him, eager to feel him again.

"Temptress," Kazimir whispered in her ear. "Witch!"

She laughed and rolled him onto his back. "I will put a

spell on you to make love to me every night, if you are not careful."

"Bewitch me, then, fair one," he said, guiding himself to her and pulling her down onto him, ready for her. "Bewitch me well, for I would be enchanted for all time." He kissed her and moved, deepening with each thrust. "Ah," he groaned, "too late for magic spells. I am already captivated."

Turn the page to see a special preview
of Donna Lea Simpson's new novel

Awaiting the Rapture

Coming soon from Berkley Sensation!

THE EVENING had not begun nor progressed as the Earl of Wesmorlyn expected. Some odd sense of being usurped had overcome him as he watched his fiancée, Countess Charlotte von Wolfram, and his old friend, Lyulph Randell, stroll around Lady Harroway's ballroom, comfortably laughing and chatting as if it was they who were engaged. Upon first meeting, he had rather expected the young lady to be awed into silence by his rank and bearing, but instead she had appeared to appraise him and find him wanting, preferring to spend her precious time with an untitled nobody.

And now he could not find her in the crowd. Count Christoph von Wolfram, too, he could see, was covertly searching the ballroom for his sisters. He had just started toward the terrace doors when his younger half-sister, Fanny, came running up to him, whispered something in his ear, and he loped out the doors ahead of her.

Wesmorlyn followed, shocked and frightened for Countess Charlotte when he saw the brother and sister trot down the steps and head out to the garden. Had the countess fainted, or been attacked? He raced after them and circled a clump of bushes in the moonlit garden just behind the siblings; there, tightly entwined in an ardent embrace, was his fiancée and Randell. She was being thoroughly kissed, bent almost backward in the fellow's grip.

"Let her go, Randell," he shouted, elbowing past the shocked and silent Count von Wolfram.

Randell did release her, and she, her cheeks ruddy and her hair ruffled, backed away from the angry confrontation.

"What were you thinking, Charlotte?" Count von Wolfram said to his sister in a harsh and guttural tone.

"More to the point," Wesmorlyn said, strolling toward Lyulph Randell, "is what do you think *you* were doing? How dare you take my betrothed out to the garden and molest her in that insane manner?"

"He did not molest me," Charlotte protested, patting her hair back. Fanny had retreated to her side and clung to her sister.

"I promise you Wes," Randell said. "If she had protested, I would have released her immediately."

Wesmorlyn glanced around. There was no one else in sight so far, and he wished to keep it that way, for Randell's clear implication was that Countess Charlotte had invited his love-making. That could not be allowed to pass without comment and reaction. Controlling his fury as best he could, and not even looking at Charlotte, he said, "Lyulph Randell, you have trespassed on my kindness long enough and have impugned this young lady's character. As her fiancé and protector, I demand satisfaction! Tomorrow morning you shall meet me at dawn on Battersea Fields. Swords, not pistols. First blood only will suffice, sir!"

Christoph, his mouth open in surprise, stared at him.

"First blood?" Charlotte cried. "He did nothing to you! How *dare* you take this as a slight to you?"

"A duel?" Randell said, his dark brows diagonal slashes over his green eyes. "Really, Wes, are you not taking this all too far?"

"I'm not taking this as a slight to me," Wesmorlyn said to Charlotte, ignoring the other man, "but to you! Did you not hear him? He impugned your character, and yet you can defend the scoundrel?" He stared at her in puzzlement. Her pale face had two dark spots of red high on her cheeks, and she looked as if she was furious with him! She should be grateful, not angry; what was wrong with her?

"I heard no *impugning*, but just your own precious sense of outrage that he has taken something you expressed no interest in yourself!"

"Charlotte, shut up!" Christoph said, his face brick red down to his collar. His fists were balled and by his side. "You have done enough damage for one evening. I'm ashamed to call you sister! And you, Randell; if the earl had not done so,

I would have called you out for such abominable behavior toward my sister." With that he turned and stalked away, clearly struggling for self-control.

Wesmorlyn glanced back at Charlotte and his heart constricted, seeing her beautiful blue eyes fill with tears as she watched her brother stalk away. Her lips were trembling, and the tears spilled over and rolled down her smooth cheeks, dripping off her dimpled chin. Fanny put her arm over her shoulder, gave both men a look of disgust and pulled her elder sister away. Charlotte's sobs echoed.

"You have such a way with ladies, Wes," Randell said with a cynical smile, "that I'm not surprised you had to gain a wife by mail." He, too, turned and walked away.

"Tomorrow morning, Randell," Wesmorlyn called after him, balling his fists by his side. "Dawn, at Battersea Fields. I shall provide the surgeon. Choose a second and come prepared!" He whirled and stalked back toward the ballroom.

Charlotte sat on a bench in a quiet corner of the terrace and rapidly regained her composure. She smiled tremulously at Fanny in the dim flickering light from torches overhead. "I've made a mess of everything, haven't I? One day in London and I've become an example of what not to do at a ball."

Fanny sighed. "Why did you allow Mr. Randell to kiss you?"

Shrugging, Charlotte tried to untangle her emotions. "I don't know. I really don't. It sounds absurd to say, but I felt as if I was in a fog and was not really thinking about anything. I don't know if I was weary, or . . ." She shrugged again.

"Do you like him so much?"

"He's very handsome and very flattering," she admitted. "And he has the most beautiful green eyes. And Fanny, I must admit to finding it fascinating that he is a werewolf. Who would have thought we would meet another werewolf almost the moment we land in this country? But . . . I don't know why I let him kiss me. Perhaps it was in retaliation for how the earl and Christoph made me feel earlier in the ballroom, like I was some silly, horrible child who couldn't make her own decisions. How ironic that in trying to prove I am my own woman, I've just confirmed every awful fear Christoph had of my ability to behave in a ladylike manner and have truly made a fool of myself in front of the earl."

"I'm so sorry I ran to Christoph, but Mr. Randell frightens me, and I was worried."

"Don't apologize Fanny."

"But didn't being kissed frighten you? I would think it shocking."

Charlotte bit her lip. "Fanny, kissing a gentleman is really quite pleasant. It's nothing to be frightened of, certainly."

"I would be terrified. But do you really think they'll fight a duel over you?" Fanny said, her blue eyes wide. "It's so romantic!"

"It's not romantic in the slightest," Charlotte retorted, astonished by her half sister's hitherto unrevealed romanticism. "Wesmorlyn only offered the challenge because of his own injured sensibilities." She stopped and looked off into the darkness. The night had lost all of its charm, and she was back to thinking of London as dreary and dull. She faced her pain and admitted it. "I never thought Christoph would treat me the way he did tonight."

"He had no right to speak to you like that, saying such horrible things!"

Charlotte took a deep breath and let it out slowly. This was not what she had come to England for: going to balls, dancing, being kissed in the dark. She had come, in truth, solely to find her half sister's mother, and to unite the two of them so they could have a chance at a mother-daughter relationship, the chance that had been denied her by her mother's early death. And that was what they would do.

"Fanny," she said, rising and holding her hand out to help her sister rise also, "I think tomorrow we shall embark on a little adventure together, just you and I."

"What do you mean?"

"I brought you all this way to find your mother. Eleanor Dancey is out there somewhere, and I intend to find her."

"But what of the earl and Christoph?"

"If they get along so splendidly, having found a common enemy in Mr. Randell, then they can have each other and their duels at dawn and their violent ways. Men!"

"And what about the inquiry agent our uncle Nikolas hired to find my mother?"

"I have little confidence in that; he will surely draw the search out just to charge more money. Fanny, we can figure this out for ourselves. Frau Liebner told me that when she last visited Miss Eleanor Dancey, she found her living with a relative in Plymouth; the woman was happy to hear that you were a good girl and settled at Wolfram Castle. Therefore," she said, linking Fanny's arm through hers, "we shall set off for Plymouth and make our own inquiries. There's nothing wrong with two young ladies traveling together in such a manner. We'll hire a carriage and driver, and it will all be quite respectable."

"Excuse me for interrupting your conversation," a voice said out of the dimness. Mr. Lyulph Randell walked up the three steps toward them and bowed. He appeared ill at ease.

"Sir," Charlotte said, eyeing him. "I think it would be best if we are not seen talking right now."

"I agree, and I promise not to detain you. I only approached you to apologize most sincerely." He cast his gaze down at the flagging. "I am abominable. Never have I let my feelings carry me away like that, but your beauty and sweetness—" He broke off and shook his head. "I'll not meet your like again," he whispered.

Pity for his obvious discomfiture moved Charlotte to say, "Perhaps you should not have behaved so, sir, but I am equally to blame. It matters not, for I doubt that we shall meet again. I will be leaving London tomorrow."

"Where are you going? I had understood you to be settled in London for the time being?"

"My sister and I are going to seek an old acquaintance in Plymouth." The evasion came easily. She had never thought herself such a practiced liar.

"Plymouth! Why, you will be going almost all the way to my own estate in Cornwall. Who is it you seek, if I may be so bold?"

"Well . . ." She hesitated, but what did it matter really if she said something to him? "It is my half sister's mother, in fact, a Miss Dancey."

"Miss Dancey?" he said, staggering back a step. "Could it

be . . . could it possibly be a Miss *Eleanor* Dancey, formerly of Plymouth, but now . . . Oh, this is too much of a coincidence! Or is it fate?"

"Whatever do you mean?" Charlotte asked, clutching Fanny's cold hands in hers. "Do you know the woman?"

"I have just in the last few months rented one of my houses to a Miss Eleanor Dancey, once of Plymouth but now settled in Cornwall for a short while before she leaves the country forever!"

"Leaves the country?" Charlotte gasped, looking down at Fanny and clutching her icy hands in hers. "No! Oh, no!"

"Yes, for Upper Canada . . . the colonies. She came to my attention through a mutual acquaintance, and I only remember some of the letter. I wrote back that she could have Moor Cottage for as long as she wished."

"The colonies?" Fanny said, looking up at Charlotte. "Is that not a great distance away, across the ocean? And how would we follow so far?"

"That decides it," Charlotte said, brushing her skirts down with swift movements. "I will go now to Christoph and—" She stopped abruptly, remembering that she and her brother were not on terms that moment.

"What is it?" Randell said.

She chewed her lip. Would she be able to convince Christoph? And how could she tell him what Mr. Randell had said when she could not even say his name at the moment?

"I will give you the directions," Mr. Randell said, watching her, "and you ladies and your brother may set out on a little jaunt down to Cornwall. I'm sure the earl will understand once you tell him your mission."

Would he really understand a trip out of London to find her illegitimate sister's disgraced mother?

"What is it, countess?" Mr. Randell asked.

She turned back to him. "It's complicated. But after that little scene in the garden, I'm sure you understand that offering my brother your information will not be easy. It will have to wait," Charlotte said reluctantly. She turned to Fanny. "I don't see any other way. We may have to wait until I can convince Christoph. Perhaps we may get her direction and write to her," she said, turning back to Randell.

"Of course, Charlotte," Fanny said, putting one small hand on Charlotte's arm. "We shall wait. And write her a letter."

"I'm sure you're being very wise," Randell said, nodding. "If Miss Dancey should leave Cornwall this week, as she mentioned—"

"This week?" Charlotte cried.

"I believe this week or next was her projected time for sailing."

"Oh, that I could rely on Christoph to be reasonable! But he seems edgy, and the earl . . . I will not abuse him in front of an old friend, though it seems to me he has not acted like any friend, but he is so completely unreasonable that really, it matters not that I make him even angrier, for I have already made my decision."

"Your decision?"

She glanced at him, but throwing caution to the wind, she blurted out, "I'll not be marrying him."

"Then . . ." Randell paused.

"What is it, sir?"

"It seems to me that what matters most is that this young lady find her mother. I suppose you could hire a carriage driver, find the way, staying at inns along the way, and then follow my directions to Moor Cottage on the Little Honet Road near Bodmin in the Eastern District of Cornwall."

"But . . ." She glanced over at a speechless Fanny, who listened with wide eyes. "It seems such a daunting journey," she said, imagining the difficulties inherent in such an expedition. "I'm not a coward, but we don't know England at all. And with the pressure of time, I would not wish to become lost along the way."

"If it would not be too forward," he said, "it would be my great honor to give you the use of my closed carriage and driver; my man knows the way intimately, and you will have nothing to do but unite this sweet young lady with her mother."

It was becomingly said, and Charlotte clapped her hands. "Spoken like a true gentleman!" His altruistic kindness pleased her after the treatment she had received at the hands of the earl and her own brother that evening, but she paused and shook her head, reluctantly acknowledging that she could not take him up on his kind offer. "I don't think that would be wise. How would it look, sir, if we accepted your generous offer? And truly, I should stay in London long enough to consult with my brother and the earl."

He gazed at her for a moment, in the moonlight, and then said, "I must, of course, bow to your greater wisdom, but pardon me if I express my innermost fears. I'm afraid if Wesmorlyn is informed of your intentions before you go, he will stop at nothing to detain you."

"Why would he do that?"

Mr. Randell hesitated. "There may be reasons . . . reasons I cannot and will not canvass at this moment. But even beyond the reasons I cannot tell you, you saw how he was in the garden. He is just so with everything in his life; whatever he feels he possesses he jealousy guards like a dog with a bone. For example, his younger sister Hannah has a great affection for me. Our estates are very close, and I have been in the habit of giving the poor child a few happy hours of riding about the countryside in my open gig. But when Wesmorlyn heard about it, he put a stop to it. She is not allowed such treats anymore."

"How sad," Fanny said.

"How intolerably mean-spirited," Charlotte said, indignantly. She observed the man for a moment in the shadowy light from the torches. "We so appreciate your kindness, sir. My brother said something to me about you." How could she raise their shared bond, the werewolf heritage that linked them irrevocably? She had never spoken of it to anyone outside of their family, but she felt it strongly in his presence, and perhaps that was what he felt for her, too. Christoph had claimed that Lyulph Randell was aware of him as another of the wolf blood. "He told me that you are very much alike, that you both . . ." She stopped, confused about how to go on.

"Yes, well, it is not something to discuss in a ballroom setting," he said, with a smile and a hasty glance at a couple a ways down the terrace. "Let me just say," he murmured, staying back in the shadows of a small linden, "that I truly hope that the count and I can someday be as close as brothers, perhaps in more ways than one."

"You're very kind," she said, feeling her cheeks warm at his implied interest in her.

"Will you *please* take my offer of my carriage and driver?" he said, his hands clasped together in a gesture of supplication. "I would only feel secure that way, knowing that the driver will take you directly to the country home I have rented to Miss Dancey."

Charlotte glanced back into the ballroom, the swirling couples, the haughty ladies. As much as she had thought this might be entertaining, it had turned into a debacle, mostly due to her own behavior she was sure. This was not her life. She had never really cared for gowns and dancing and gossip, and she was too old to start now like some green girl in her first year. She had no intention of marrying Wesmorlyn, nor did she even intend to stay in England. She glanced over at Fanny; they had one chance, perhaps, to find Eleanor Dancey. How could she live with herself if she waited for Christoph's approval, only to find that Miss Dancey had already sailed out of Fanny's life forever?

Did she truly have the slightest idea of how to go about hiring a carriage and directing the driver to go down to Cornwall to find this cottage? If she had paid attention to her Uncle Nikolas's hasty lessons on English geography she might be able to point out Cornwall, but sadly the truth was she couldn't. She was being given the opportunity to get what she had, after all, come to England for. Making a sudden decision, Charlotte impulsively said, "Yes! Yes, Fanny and I would be delighted to accept your kind offer."

"But you must go tonight! I would not want you to be disappointed after going all that way, only to find her already gone."

"How are we to arrange it?"

"I will have my driver by your door at two o'clock in the morning, awaiting your pleasure. I shall leave a note with him telling you what inns you should stay at along the way, and where he is taking you. If I can get away after this ridiculous challenge of Wesmorlyn's, then I will meet you in Salisbury and accompany you on horseback the rest of the way. If your brother is with you, so much the better; but if he is not, then you will at least be safe."

Charlotte paused and gazed at him steadily for a long moment. "I'm not sure how to proceed if we cannot convince Christoph. To go alone in your carriage and accompanied by you—"

"Oh!" he exclaimed, hand over his heart. "It shall all be above board and completely proper, I promise you. I would not dream of traveling in a closed carriage with you, I swear."

Charlotte nodded sharply, taking Fanny's hand in her own. "We shall do it. If I don't do another thing while I am in England, it will suffice to unite my sister with her mother."

Randell bowed and disappeared back into the shadows.

Fanny and Charlotte returned to the ballroom. All she wanted was to leave. The whole trip to England ostensibly to meet the Earl of Wesmorlyn and decide if she could marry him or not had been a mistake, but perhaps she could salvage some good from it for Fanny's sake.

"Have you recovered sufficiently to behave as a lady would, for a while, at least?" Christoph muttered, as his sisters rejoined him and the earl and Lady Hannah, the earl's younger sister.

"How wretchedly you are behaving tonight," she replied, through gritted teeth. "I wish we'd never come to this miserable island."

"After tonight, I'm sure that will not be a problem."

"What do you mean?"

"Nothing!" he hissed. "Smile as if you are having a lovely time!"

She blinked, trying to hold back the tears at his continuing anger at her. She was homesick for Germany: dear, dismal Wolfram Castle, the dark forests, and even little Wolfbeck, the village. Caught up in her misery, she was unaware of anything more until Fanny tugged her sleeve. She looked up to find everyone's eyes on her.

"The earl asked you a question, Charlotte," Christoph said, impatiently.

"I'm sorry. What was it?"

"Would you do me the honor of promenading to the conservatory with me?"

Her first thought was to say no, but almost anything would

be a relief from standing in this frozen, unhappy group saying nothing. She took his arm.

Wesmorlyn had never felt such a conflict of emotions all at once in his whole steady, quiet, safe life. The fury he had felt upon witnessing Lyulph Randell kissing the countess, his betrothed bride, was an amalgam of frustration, possessiveness, jealousy, and pique. How dare this girl throw away his hand in such a bold manner! For surely kissing another man at the ball intended to introduce her to London society as his fiancée could only be considered a rejection of his hand in marriage?

He glanced down at her strolling beside him, her figure stiff, her expression unhappy. What a sight for the gossips they must be. He shuddered to think what the society column in the newspapers would hint; never before had he been fodder for them, but he feared that he was about to learn how scathing they could be, especially if word got around about his duel with Lyulph the next morning. He still wasn't sure that he had taken the right action, but the man's words had provoked his seldom roused temper.

And yet . . . he must be the bigger man. He must condescend, for though his sense of rectitude was outraged at her conduct, he would not leave her with anything of which to complain. "Countess Charlotte, I am sorry your first evening in London has been so difficult." Even though she had brought it all on herself.

"And so you should," she said, not looking up at him, but only straight forward. "I have never been so humiliated in all my life."

Staggered by her words, he restrained a quick retort, and instead managed a tolerably restrained reply. "And how would you say *my* conduct was lacking?"

Now she did look up at him, her blue eyes wide with incredulity. "You don't know? How is that even possible? You insult my poor sister—"

"I did no such thing!"

"—by insinuating to me that she is not a fit guest in this house, and then . . . and then . . ."

"And then what? I am agog to hear what else you consider my failing."

"And then you blunder into what is clearly a private moment and issue that idiotic challenge," she said, her voice cracking with fury. Her cheeks were pink, glowing with emotion, and the delicately draped curls that caressed her neck danced from her trembling.

He felt her quiver and steadied her by tightening his grip on her arm. "I had every right to issue a challenge to the man who was kissing my fiancée, and who then deepened his discreditable conduct by implying that he was only doing that which she had invited!"

"He said no such thing!"

"He may as well have. Have you no restraint? No idea of what proper conduct for a young lady is?"

She dropped his arm and stepped away from him. Her contemptuous gaze swept around the room past the knots of young men and women. "Oh, I have heard and seen enough to know what is considered fit conduct in London society," she said, her voice trembling with anger. "It is fit conduct, apparently, to insult a stranger to your shores, her mode of dress and hairstyle, even her choice of companion, as I was on my way in to meet you. It is fit conduct to be so insipid that one barely has a pulse, judging by these simpering ladies." She glared up at him. "And it is fit conduct to make a lady feel that nothing she could ever do would be good enough and that she is despoiled by the merest impromptu kiss in the garden." She whirled and began to walk away.

His temper ready to burst, a pounding headache accompanying it, he grabbed her arm and pulled her back, twisting her around to face him. "Merest impromptu kiss? You were entwined around him like the serpent in the garden. I have never *ever* seen Lyulph Randell act thus, so without some provocation on your part—"

Her hand slapping his face resounded like a clap in the ballroom, and even the orchestra did not drown out the sound of the slap. Horrified, Charlotte stared at the earl, who, thunderstruck, nursed his reddening cheek. "I'm sorry," she cried, then whirled and ran out of the ballroom.

Stumbling toward the lady's withdrawing room, Charlotte found the door and bolted to a dark corner where she huddled on a stool and sobbed. A few moments later Fanny, pale and frightened looking, slipped over to her and crouched down by her. "Charlotte, Count Christoph says if you know what is good for you, you will this minute don your cloak and accompany me outside where our carriage will be waiting. He has made his apologies to the earl for your behavior, he says, and we will sort out the rest tomorrow in a place not so public, since, he said, he c-cannot trust y-you to—"

"Enough. I've heard enough," Charlotte said, rising, her wretchedness turned to cold anger. "And did my brother even ask the earl what he said to occasion such an outburst on my part? No, he wouldn't. I don't know what's wrong with Christoph, but since the moment we landed on the shores of this dreadful nation he has not been the brother I have been able to rely on my whole life."

Fanny was silent, her blue eyes filled with tears and misery.

"There, there, Fanny," Charlotte said, patting her sister's shoulder, ignoring as best she could the curious knot of ladies who lingered nearby and rudely listened in on their conversation. "It is nothing to do with you, you know. Come, let us leave. If anything could have stayed me in my plan, it is clear now that there is not one reason to remain in this filthy city." Raising her voice, she said, with a proud look around, "German manners are to make a stranger feel comfortable and welcome, but apparently the English do not subscribe to such a code of conduct." She lifted her skirts and swept from the room.

The carriage ride back to their town house was silent; Christoph was rigid with anger and Charlotte much the same. They had not quarreled so since they were children, and she felt alone, suddenly bereft. She knew she had behaved badly, but strongly felt that each one of them had: she, Christoph, and the earl. Fanny only was innocent of any wrongdoing.

The moment they arrived she stalked upstairs, deigning to say not a word to her brother. He didn't deserve her forgiveness and wouldn't get it even if he asked. But a half hour's pacing and calm reflection cooled her somewhat. Her plans swirled in her mind, but the old habits of reliance on her brother would not allow her to abandon him without at least trying to draw him in to her scheme. She tapped on his door and in German he called out, "Come." When she entered, it was to find him at the desk in his sitting room. He was writing a letter.

"Christoph," she said.

"What is it?"

"To whom do you write?"

"To Frau Liebner, to tell her we will be going home as soon as I can arrange passage."

"What?"

He turned, his blue eyes blazing with fury. "Isn't that what you want, Charlotte? Isn't that what all of this evening's antics were about?"

"Never mind about me, what about Fanny? We are here to find her mother."

"She doesn't care about that! She never has. I asked her after you stormed upstairs to pout and she says it doesn't matter."

"Of course she would say that to you, idiot! She's *terrified* of you. And especially since you probably bellowed at the poor girl, and—"

"No, Charlotte, not another word! It has always been your scheme, not hers. The girl was completely content at Wolfram Castle until you filled her head with some idiotic idea that to feel whole she must meet her mother."

"Perhaps that was true in the beginning, but, Christoph, now we have an idea of where to find—"

"Enough, Charlotte! I've heard enough from you for one night," he said, his voice holding a harsh tone of cold fury she had never heard before. "We're going back to Wolfram Castle so I can deposit you in our uncle's care, and not a single word you can say will change my mind. I will break your engagement to the earl so he doesn't have to suffer your hideous behavior, and we will leave directly."

"Christoph, what is wrong with you?" she cried. She was the impetuous one, not he. He was always so reasonable, so thoughtful, but now he was acting as if . . . a thought occurred to her. "You don't know how to handle meeting another werewolf, is that it? Is Lyulph Randell being a werewolf behind this?"

"Don't be absurd! Shut the door on your way out, please. Good night, Charlotte." He turned away from her, hunching his shoulders and scribbling, dipping his quill rapidly and spilling blotches of dark ink over the page in front of him.

So that was it. She stared at his back for a long minute and then left, closing the door quietly behind her. She went down the hall and tapped on Fanny's door. Entering, she went to the wardrobe that the hired-in serving staff had filled with Fanny's clothes and dragged out one bag.

"What is it?" Fanny said.

Charlotte looked up. "Christoph is being completely unreasonable. He is arranging for us to go back to Wolfram Castle and will not listen to reason. So if we are to find Eleanor Dancey, we have no other choice but to take Mr. Randell up on his kind offer and meet his carriage at two. That gives us one hour to prepare."